# CLASS ACT

A BILL MURDOCH MYSTERY

# CLASS ACT

## GED
## GILLMORE

dG deGrevilo Publishing

Cataloguing in Publication details are available from the National Library of Australia www.trove.nla.gov.au

Creator: Gillmore, Ged

Title: Class Act : A Bill Murdoch Mystery / Ged Gillmore.

ISBN: 9780994178671 (paperback)
ISBN: 9780994178688 (ebook)

Subjects: Murder—Australia—Fiction.
         Detective and mystery stories, Australian.
         Suspense fiction, Australian.

Editing: Bernadette Kearns, Book Nanny Writing and Editing Services
Additional Proofreading: Ashley Casey
Typesetting: Oliver Sands
Cover design: Luke Causby @ Blue Cork

Set in Adobe Garamond Pro 10.5pt
10 9 8 7 6 5 4 3 2 1

For more information on Ged Gillmore and his books, see his website at:
www.gedgillmore.com

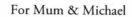

For Mum & Michael

# The Contract

'Oh, you want a detective story? A nasty crime up front, is that right? And then, let me guess, you want to spend the rest of the book working out who did it and why?'

The woman's voice was frail and tinny, trembling with the vibrations that carried it down the phone line. Murdoch wanted to correct her, but it was the first time they'd spoken; he didn't know how to do it without being rude. Besides, she was excited now, barely listening to his hesitant noises.

'A murder!' she said with a gasp. 'Some nice young girl getting brutally slaughtered. Oh yes, and you're desperate to see it solved. What you want is a book that's going to make you read late into the night, a story to make you miss your stop. You want to turn the pages breathlessly. Then, at the end, when you find out who the murderer is … you're surprised and yet it makes complete sense!'

'Well …'

'And you want to find out who did it on the very last line of the very last page of the very last chapter of the book. Am I right? Am I? Isn't that what you want?'

# The Set-Up

## 1.

When Jennifer's new housemates warned her about the rush hour traffic in Sydney, she thought they had to be exaggerating. Or, more likely, pulling her leg. No doubt they thought this country girl – newly arrived from Mudgee – didn't know how to use Google Maps and couldn't work out for herself that the drive from Cremorne to Surry Hills could only ever take half an hour, no matter the time of day. Oh, how they had underestimated her.

Jennifer liked the idea of driving herself to work. Crossing the Harbour Bridge every morning and making her way independently in the big city. She might only be a Junior Accounts Analyst for now, but – as had been stressed frequently during her interviews – her new employer was the fastest-growing PR agency in the country and the opportunities for an ambitious young graduate were limitless. As she left the house on Monday morning – the first Monday of a sweltering February – Jennifer smiled in the knowledge that she was a young woman going places. Half an hour and little more than two kilometres later, when at last she turned onto the Warringah Freeway, she saw the vehicles that had slowed her this far formed only a small part of a far greater traffic jam. Here on the freeway, dozens of cars every minute entered the throng, creeping down from suburbs further north or squeezing themselves down the irregular sliproads to join the six-lane approach to the harbour. Together they conspired to form a gridlock that spread, baking and unbroken, between her and her first day at work.

By the time she pulled up behind the offices of the Hoxton Harte Agency, Jennifer was twenty minutes late. As if that wasn't bad enough, the coffee she had drunk before leaving the house had combined with her nervousness about her new job – plus the anguish of an hour in aggressive traffic – to exert a painful pressure on her bladder. Parking badly and ignoring the sucking humidity outside the car, she sprinted around to the front of the building.

The Hoxton Harte foyer came as a shock. Jennifer's interviews had been held over the phone and in a drab airport conference room. By then, of course, she had known all about the company and its famous clients (not to mention its well-known owners); she had even seen pictures of its converted warehouse offices. But to experience them in the flesh was something else.

The end of the building inside the glass front doors had been hollowed out into a space four storeys high. Every centimetre was covered with white gloss tiles. The only visible colour was behind the reception desk, where, in acetate pinks and blues, a five-metre female face, suggestively licking a strawberry ice block, filled the wall. The space was busy – high heels clicking in all directions, dark suits moving quickly, every woman dressed in black – and Jennifer was momentarily overwhelmed. Then she took a deep breath and reminded herself she was supposed to be there: that she had a good degree and had passed the gruelling interviews. She hurried over to the long white desk, standing in line until, at last, she could speak to the receptionist.

'Could you tell me where the nearest bathroom is?'

'Do you work here?'

The woman behind the desk was as distinctive a splash of colour as the oversized image on the wall behind her. She was petite, with precisely cropped blonde hair, huge green eyes and flawless make-up. Attached to her emerald-green dress was a diamond brooch that caught the light from the glass doors to the street. As Jennifer gave her name and started to explain it was her first day at Hoxton Harte, the receptionist adjusted her telephone headset as if it, like the brooch, was a piece of expensive jewellery.

'Sorry, just one second.' The receptionist held up one perfectly manicured hand and used the other to jab at the control panel sunk into the desk before her. 'Hoxton Harte, please hold. Hoxton Harte, please hold. Hoxton Harte, can you hold? Hello, Hoxton Harte?'

*Ten minutes*, thought Jennifer. It might be ten minutes before she got to a bathroom, so her bladder would just have to wait. She wouldn't even worry about it until her watch showed eight minutes had passed. Perhaps she could even imply to the Finance Director, a rather stern woman called Emma Druitt, that the busy receptionist had been the main cause of her lateness. But two slow minutes later, her bladder threatening to burst, lateness was the least of Jennifer's concerns. Shifting her weight from foot to foot, she looked around desperately for anything that might be a bathroom. To her left was the sunlit doorway to the street, three men drinking takeaway coffees and looking at their watches. Behind her were two glass lifts and, wrapped

2

around them, the intricacies of a pale wooden staircase. To her right was a white tiled wall. The receptionist smiled at her – sorry! – and made a twirling gesture with one perfect hand, as if saying she'd just wrap up this call and then she'd be able to help. But Jennifer knew she couldn't wait that long. She returned her attention to the three men at the door. The one closest to her had sleepy blue eyes, as if he'd just woken up, pale skin and a dark mop of curly hair. He caught Jennifer looking and smiled. She smiled back, took a deep breath, and crossed the reception area towards him and his friends.

'Sorry to bother you', she said from a few metres away. 'Do you know if there are any bathrooms on this floor?'

Everything was fine. She had sounded confident; she hadn't whispered it or shouted it, hadn't said it too fast. There was nothing embarrassing about needing a bathroom.

'Through there', the good-looking man said, pointing with his coffee at the tiled wall on the other side of the foyer. 'Watch out for the step.'

Jennifer frowned and followed the direction of his arm, noticing, for the first time, a thick door-shaped line around a section of tiles in the far wall. One of the other men said 'Angus' in a warning tone, but Jennifer had already smiled her thanks and turned away, trying her best not to walk too quickly.

Close-up, the piece of wall was, in fact, a door: it even had a white door handle and this, on her second attempt, Jennifer was able to turn. The door was stiff, but, using her shoulder, Jennifer managed to push it open, wincing as its hinges protested in piercing squeals. Stepping through, she found herself in a little backyard: a dark, derelict space, damp and puddled, empty but for half a bicycle and a collapsed pile of boxes. A small patch of sky was visible high above.

'No one will mind!' yelled the man from the other side of the rush hour reception, 'but you might want to close the door behind you!'

He needn't have bothered being so loud. It wasn't like anyone hadn't noticed her standing in the dank space, blushing in her cheap black suit. Jennifer saw the man laugh, his blue eyes disappearing behind his tan as his friends grimaced into their coffees. She looked at her feet – and away from the stares of everyone else in the foyer. Stepping back inside, she pulled the door closed behind her and told herself that no matter what happened, even if she wet herself there and then, she was not going to cry.

'Angus!!!'

The receptionist's voice was like a fire alarm and several people across the lobby flinched. She was on her feet, five-foot-six in four-inch heels, headset in her right hand, one of her exquisite fingernails pointing across the tiles.

'Do you think that's funny? Do you?'

'Please', said Jennifer. 'It's fine.'

She said it quickly and quietly, with none of the confidence she'd pretended when asking for the bathroom, but everyone heard her. There was nothing else in the foyer to listen to. The receptionist made the same twirling gesture as before, pointing with her other hand this time at the pale wooden staircase that spiralled around the lifts.

'Up to the first floor,' she said. 'You'll see the sign.'

Jennifer thanked her and hurried over to the curve of stairs. As she climbed, she had a clear view of the continuing conversation in the foyer. The receptionist was still on her feet, staring at the blue-eyed man at the door.

'Which anyone with any sense of decency could have told her,' she said loudly. 'A common courtesy, you'd have thought.'

'Oh, calm down, Charlie.'

The man at the door said it a little too coolly, as though he wasn't as sure as he'd like to be that the receptionist wasn't the only one who hadn't got the joke.

'I will not calm down, Angus! That young lady there was getting her first impression of this place and I am embarrassed, *embarrassed*, yet again by your complete lack of professionalism. Why don't you pick on someone your own size for once?'

And then, in the near silence that followed, the receptionist sat down and said, as if for herself, but loud enough for everyone in the foyer to hear. 'If you can find anyone with a dick that small. Hello, Hoxton Harte, thank you for holding, how can I direct your call?'

Barely suppressed laughter rippled across the reception area, smirks and snorts echoing off the shiny white tiles. Someone coughed and someone else whooped. The man called Angus merely snapped something sharp at the men beside him before turning through the bright arch of the doorway and out into the street. Before Jennifer had reached the top of the stairs, the receptionist's voice rang out again.

'And what are the rest of you looking at?! Haven't you got overpaid jobs to go to?'

4

Jennifer's week slowly improved. As promised in her interviews, Hoxton Harte's finance department was skeletal and Jennifer worked closely with the Finance Director, Emma Druitt, herself. Emma was a small and serious woman who wore her dark hair in a tight chignon and fixed her beady brown eyes steadily on whomever she was talking to. She was friendly enough and, once they were past the awkwardness of Jennifer being late on her first day in the job, the two women got along well. Their conversation, however, rarely strayed far from the work at hand. They shared a quiet space on the third floor, separated from rows of messy desks by thick glass which, Emma explained, she had had installed to give her the quiet she needed to concentrate. The glass wall worked well, especially with its glass door closed, and, if neither woman was on the phone and they had nothing to discuss, the two of them worked in a silence that, to Jennifer, came as a welcome relief from the hustle and bustle of the world outside.

On Wednesday, Emma sent her to meet James Harte, one of the company's founders. It was unsettling to be alone with a man Jennifer recognised from the papers. She had thought famous people were shorter in real life, but James Harte was tall and broad-shouldered and, on top of that, he smelled good. He was, if anything, more handsome in the flesh than in the papers, his emerald eyes sparkling whenever he smiled. The carpet in his corner office reminded Jennifer of a bedroom and, even though she pulled herself to her full height, ignored his perfect teeth, and asked questions about the size of his balance sheet, she was utterly intimidated. Harte seemed to sense this and asked her questions about herself and how she was finding life in the big city. He calmed her, charmed her, encouraged her in her work and then gently let her go.

On Thursday morning came an invitation to lunch. Charlotte Holland's email took Jennifer by surprise and she had to consult the company directory before working out Charlotte was the receptionist who had caused the scene on her first day in the office. Jennifer wasn't sure she wanted reminding of that; every morning since then she'd arrived so early and left so late she'd found the foyer deserted. But the email was sweetly persuasive and Jennifer found herself unwilling to explain that she normally brought in sandwiches.

Besides, she told herself, it would be a good way of confirming who was who in the zoo without asking Emma Druitt to repeat herself.

The sight of The Vines at lunchtime that day made her wonder if she'd made an expensive mistake. Every table in the courtyard restaurant had a thickly-starched tablecloth, heavy cutlery and crowds of glasses that sparkled in the late summer sun. Waitresses weaved between the tables like sharks hunting in the shallows and as Jennifer crossed the restaurant – struggling to keep up with the woman leading her to her table – she wondered for the hundredth time why everyone in this city was in such a rush. As if, no matter what you were doing, you had to finish it quickly so you could do something else, presumably, just as fast. She had explained to the dark-haired waitress racing ahead of her now that she didn't even need to be led: she could see where her colleague was sitting and make her own way over. But that, apparently, was not an option.

'The manager says it's an "integral part of the customer experience",' the waitress told her, rolling her Latin eyes. 'Come on, we wouldn't want to keep madam waiting.'

As they passed tables, Jennifer recognised a few faces from the agency – presumably out with clients – and one girl who even said hello. Beyond them, either side of the courtyard, stood plate glass windows and as Jennifer crossed the crowded restaurant, her reflection seemed to join and leave the diners, like a hostess checking on her guests. She was going to have to buy a better suit.

'There you are!' Charlotte Holland stubbed out a cigarette as the waitress delivered Jennifer with an unconvincing smile. 'I was beginning to think you'd stood me up.'

'I'm so sorry, Charlotte …'

'Charlie!' The receptionist's smile was broad but firm. 'My name's Charlie.'

'Oh. Sorry. Anyway, Emma wanted to take me through the mid-year financials. We're carrying on again at one thirty. This place looks a bit fancy, I thought we were going out to a café or something.'

Charlie looked around as if trying to find something she'd describe as fancy. A few tables away were some suits from the agency and she wiggled her fingers at them. One of them smiled and raised his glass.

'They're from IT,' she said, watching Jennifer sit down. 'Don't make eye contact. How's your first week going?' She really was dazzling, more like a Hoxton Harte client than the woman who answered its phones. The intensity of her green-eyed gaze made Jennifer want to look away in shame.

'Better than it started,' Jennifer told her. 'In reception on Monday, I was convinced I was going to cry or wet myself or both. I'm so silly.'

'Oh, never you mind Angus Hoxton. He's a prize arsehole and everyone knows it.'

Jennifer's stomach shrank. 'That was Angus Hoxton?'

'Didn't you know? Oh, well, don't worry about it, darling.' The receptionist reached across the table and took Jennifer's hand. 'Seriously, don't worry. His name's above the door, but that's all. He just looks after sales. It's James Harte's business, everyone knows that. They're old school friends; that's why James even tolerates him.'

'Oh my God, I didn't think things could have gone any worse. I didn't realise I'd upset one of the directors.'

Charlie Holland's smile was unwavering. 'You didn't, darling, I did. It wasn't the first time and I doubt it'll be the last. Trust me, it'll be water off a duck's back. Angus probably won't even recognise you when he sees you again. He barely looks at anyone – except himself in the mirror.'

Jennifer forced a smile and looked around the restaurant. What if Angus Hoxton was here too and saw them having lunch together? As she studied the scene, the air grew dull and, along with everyone else in courtyard, Jennifer looked up at the sky. A grey cloud was hiding the sun, other clouds close by waiting to do the same. The forecast had said weeks of rain were on the way; this would be the last lunch anyone would be eating outdoors for a while. As the cloud moved and the sun began to reappear, Jennifer blinked and – the restaurant sparkling once more – looked across the table to find Charlie Holland examining her closely.

'I feel so silly,' Jennifer said again, just for something to say. The receptionist's gaze was unerring.

'I doubt you are.' Charlie lit a cigarette and smiled. 'Whatever else I might think about Emma Druitt, she's no fool. If she hired you, then you must be pretty switched-on. Shall we order?'

Jennifer had prepared herself for the prices on the gigantic cardboard menus, but they were still fifty-five per cent higher than she'd estimated.

She ordered a prawn salad and a glass of water, claiming a diet. Charlie ordered a glass of champagne, a starter and a main.

'Don't worry,' she said, once the waitress had shot away again. 'You're not paying for half of this. I just feel like spoiling myself, that's all. Tell me, what do you think of your new boss?'

'Emma? Oh, you know, nice enough. Very interesting the way she's structured the finance department.'

'Finance is as boring as bat shit.' Charlie underlined the statement with a plume of smoke. 'Did you know I was the first employee of the agency? After Angus and James, of course.'

'Before Emma even?'

'Oh, her. She's James Harte's sister, did you know that?'

Jennifer hadn't known that and wondered if she should have. Had she said anything inappropriate to either of them?

'And have you met James yet?' Charlie went on. 'The big boss?'

'Well, I was introduced. I'm afraid I blushed and looked at my shoes.'

It sounded convincing even to Jennifer. She felt like blushing now. The memory of James Harte's emerald eyes made it easier to believe he was the brother of the receptionist rather than of the Finance Director. Charlie checked a nail.

'He's very good-looking, isn't he?'

'Oh, well. I guess. Not really my type.' And then, because Charlie looked a little put out, Jennifer added, 'I mean, of course he is.'

Their drinks arrived and as Charlie's champagne was placed in front of her, she said loudly, 'I'm sleeping with him.'

Now Jennifer did blush; she could feel the heat working its way up her face. She waited until the waitress had smiled and left again, but still couldn't think of anything to say. James Harte was married.

'You probably disapprove.' Charlie was checking the perfect nail again.

Not at all,' said Jennifer quickly, desperate to prove herself worthy of the secret. 'What's he like in bed?'

The receptionist looked up, eyes huge in surprise, until she leaned back her head and roared with laughter. When the people at the next table looked around, Charlie put her cigarette hand over her mouth in mock shame, then leant forward to place the other conspiratorially on Jennifer's forearm.

'Fantastic!' she whispered loudly. 'He's *fantastic* in bed. Why do you think I do it?'

Jennifer leant back in her chair, more as an excuse to retract her arm than anything, and caught her reflection in the glass again. *Look at me. Only one week in Sydney and already having a gossipy lunch with a girlfriend.*

Somehow the conversation moved on to books. It was rare for Jennifer to meet someone who read as much as she did and the two of them spoke for almost half an hour about what they'd recently finished, what was short-listed for which award, who had something new coming out. Then, over food – Jennifer's thirty-dollar prawn salad proving to be little prawn and all salad – they drifted into a competition about which of them was more afraid of turning into her mother. Charlie laughed a little too loudly, and always for a little too long, but, apart from that, she was good company. Jennifer felt her shoulders drop – the first time in days – sat back and let Charlie tell her what parts of town she might want to move to. It was half an hour later, the changing sky above them more often dull than bright by now, before the conversation came back to James Harte. Charlie referred to him as her 'make-do man'.

'So, you're not madly in love or anything?'

'Oh, we are, actually. But James is far too good a man to leave his wife. No doubt you've heard how *lovely* she is. He keeps saying we should stop, not see each other again. You know, he never phones me, it's always *me* has to phone *him*. But then I get us alone together and take off my clothes and he can't resist.'

'Did you ever think it would turn into anything serious?'

Jennifer, worried she was sounding prudish, wished they were still talking about books. She watched Charlie put one china-doll hand up to her nose, fumbling with the other in her handbag until, after a few seconds, it produced a tissue. She thought for a while the receptionist had silently sneezed.

'Oh my God, Charlie, I'm so sorry. I didn't mean to upset you; are you all right?'

'I'm fine! I'm fine. I'm sorry. It's just ... I've spent the last five years waiting around for that man.'

She was talking to her tissue; it was difficult to hear. Ignoring the glances from the tables around them, Jennifer reached halfway across the table.

'I've spent a fortune,' said Charlie, breathing away the tears. 'All the perfect clothes and the perfect presents and the perfect little weekends away. Oh, but don't you worry, there's more than one way to skin a fish. I'll get what I'm owed. I know where the bodies are buried; what ASIC would like to know, and they know that I know.'

She said something else, but it was completely lost to the tissue. Jennifer reached into her handbag and supplied a fresh pack of Kleenex. In response, Charlie looked up – a badly run watercolour – smiled and excused herself.

'You eat,' she said. 'I'll be back soon.'

She was as good as her word. No more than a few minutes later she reappeared, fresh and grinning wickedly, no evidence of any blotchiness.

'So, what about you?' she said, sitting with a bump and downing the end of her champagne. 'You got a boyfriend?'

The change in the woman across the table – make-up flawless, not a hair out of place – left Jennifer momentarily lost for words. 'Um, no,' she said at last. 'I only arrived in Sydney last week.'

'No one back home? No dates lined up?'

Jennifer pretended to look for her last prawn, but she'd never been a good liar. She blushed too easily, thought too slowly.

'You have!' Charlie leant across the table, her hand on Jennifer's forearm again. 'Oh go on, share! You have to, I've told you my secret. What's he like?'

There were a thousand little lies anyone else could have used.

'Well, I know you're going to think this is weird, but I've not actually met him yet. I got to know him online. We've been chatting on WhatsApp for weeks and, when I got the job down here … well, you know. He's very funny and so kind. He works for a children's charity as an outreach worker but he really wants to join the police …'

Charlie was staring.

'What?' said Jennifer. 'What's wrong with that?'

'A social worker? Really?'

'Well, yes, I suppose. In a way, for now. So?'

'Nothing, darling! Nothing.' The receptionist cracked a smile that revealed lipstick on her teeth and went back to her starter. 'Tell me about him.'

But Jennifer regretted having said anything at all. She wasn't ready to share Michael yet; not when they hadn't even met. Not with Charlie Holland. She felt suddenly far from home. Any one of her friends would have shown a genuine interest if she'd ever told them about Michael, no matter what he did for a job. She gave nothing more to Charlie, even made up a false name, calling Michael 'Stephen' as if the whole thing had been a lie. Keen to change the subject, she asked if Charlie had always worked on reception.

'God no! I used to be James's and Emma's PA. That's how I know so much about the company. Like I said, I know where all the fucking bodies are buried. I call it my insurance policy, and, trust me, it's about to start paying up. Well, it better, or else. Anyway, they decided they needed someone to be the face of the organisation. You know, put on a good show when people walked in? So I got moved down to reception. I'm going to have some more bubbles; do you want a glass?'

It was another ten minutes before Charlie's main course arrived, a surprisingly large steak, and, as she cut into it, she caught Jennifer looking at her watch.

'Got somewhere better to be, darling?'

'Are you kidding? I could sit here all day chatting with you. Although, I think we'd both get rained on if we did – it's going to pour, by the looks of it. But, anyway, I can't; I've got that meeting with Emma at one thirty.'

'Oh, screw her. Did I tell you she's James's sister? I can't stand the woman. Only good thing about her is her husband, Oscar. Total dish and a real gentleman, I can't think how Emma bagged him. She tried to fire me once. Said I was insubordinate. She won't even give me a work phone, so I have to use Sydafone with their bloody useless coverage. And she won't give me a parking spot, the bitch!'

This time people at several tables turned to look. Worse were the others, the diners Jennifer recognised from Hoxton Harte. They simply flinched, then carried on carefully eating.

'What about you?' said Charlie. 'You got one?'

'Sorry?'

It was a quarter past one. The sky was now slate grey, but it was far too humid to walk any distance in a hurry. Jennifer tried to catch the waitress's attention, but it was as if the woman was avoiding their corner of the courtyard. She remembered Charlie had asked her a question.

'Have I got one what?'

'A parking spot,' Charlie said the words slowly through a mouthful of steak.

11

'Oh. Yes.'

'Ha! And you're just new in this week. Employee number four hundred and thirty-two you are, did you know that?' She swallowed hard and dabbed at her mouth with a napkin, leaving a spot of gravy on her otherwise perfect cheek. 'And I'm employee number three and a half. You using it?'

'My employee number?'

'Your parking spot.'

'Oh.' Jennifer found herself wincing. 'I am, I'm afraid. I drive to work, you see.'

'So, you've got a car then?'

'Yes, I brought it down with me from Mudgee.'

'Perfect. Do you reckon you could give me a lift tonight?'

The receptionist had been cutting hard into her steak again, but, at Jennifer's hesitation, she looked up, her green eyes firm as she waited for a response.

'Well,' said Jennifer, wondering why the truth sounded like a lie. 'I would, but I'm meeting that boy tonight. For the first time. It's our first date.'

Charlie appeared to have forgotten her food, her eyes still fixed on Jennifer.

'You're making that up.'

Jennifer laughed. 'No, I'm not. Why would I make that up?'

'To stop giving me a lift.'

Charlie returned to her steak and they sat without speaking for a while, silence kept at bay by the clinking of cutlery on plates, murmurs from the tables around them. The waitress walked past, but before Jennifer could attract her attention, Charlie shouted loudly.

'Oi, Annabel! We've got to head back and sharpish. You reckon you could get us a bill sometime today?' She turned back to Jennifer with a naughty little smile. 'Here's the thing. I'm out with James on his boat tonight. *Class Act,* it's called, a forty-footer; I think he named it after me. It's not exactly cruising weather, but then we're not exactly going to spend much time outside of the main bedroom, or berth, or cabin, or whatever he calls it. Anyway, we're going on a romantic little cruise – he can't get out of it. But, just in case he drops me off at Rose Bay like he sometimes does, would you come and pick me up? It's a nightmare getting a taxi that time of night, especially with my stupid phone reception.'

12

'But I'm meeting Michael tonight.'

'Michael? You said his name was Stephen.'

'I mean, Stephen. I'm meeting him tonight, we're going out for dinner in Newtown. I'll probably have something to drink.'

'Oh please, don't pretend. Besides, it's not like you don't owe me a favour after what I did for you on Monday.' Charlie's hand was on Jennifer's forearm again, its grip surprisingly strong. 'Once James has dropped me at the wharf, he's always in such a rush to get back to *Class*, especially if it's raining, and I hate standing around by myself. There's Wi-Fi on the boat and I've tried ordering Ubers, but by the time we've got into the dinghy and back to the wharf, half the time they've driven off again. Besides, it could be anyone in an Uber, couldn't it? Even someone just pretending to be an Uber. You might as well get into a random car! I'd feel much safer if there was someone there to meet me.'

'Safer?'

'Better. Come on, Jennifer, we both know you're not going on a date.'

Jennifer didn't know what to say. She scrabbled around in her handbag, praying for the waitress to come back with the bill, sure Charlie was staring at her again with those big green eyes. Finding her purse at last, she pulled out the notes needed to pay for her meal and laid them carefully on the table. Then she stood quickly, out of arm's reach, and looked down to find Charlie glaring up at her.

'I have to get back to the office,' Jennifer told her. 'I'm sorry. Thanks so much for lunch.'

'I've got your mobile number from the directory,' Charlie replied with a sudden sweet smile. 'I'll send you a WhatsApp from the boat.'

# The Prison

## 3

Murdoch walked through Bell Fair trying to work out why he hated the place. It was no dirtier than a lot of shopping malls, the lighting wasn't any worse, its piped music no more depressing. But every time he approached Bell Fair's sliding doors, he found himself recoiling, like a man catching his reflection after a particularly bad beating. After two years on the Coast, and everyone else loving the mall, he had come to the conclusion that the problem had to be with him. Finding the spot where he'd agreed to meet Suzie Bourne, he stood awkwardly looking around. He could, he realised after a minute or two, actually taste his dislike of the place: his mouth metallic and sour. He caught himself worrying about his breath. Told himself he was being ridiculous and, spotting a likely-looking woman, forced a smile and approached her.

'Suzie Bourne?'

The woman flinched, shook her head and changed direction, handbag clenched to her side and one shoulder up like it could offer protection. Watching her scuttle away across the grubby tiles, Murdoch swore quietly. He hated these little reminders that he still looked like a crook. But what was he supposed to do? Change the colour of what an old boss had called his 'disturbingly black' eyes? Join the steroid junkies and put on some weight? Spotting another older woman, he took a deep breath, tried a nice smile – like English prison dentistry hadn't ruined that idea – and tried again. He tried twice more with similar results, and was trying to breathe away his mounting anger, when he noticed a little old lady on a metal bench between two plastic palms. She was watching him closely, something like a glint in her eye. Murdoch walked over.

'Excuse me.'

'Yes,' she said, and he recognised her lilting voice from the phone. 'I'm Suzie Bourne. And you're Dr Livingstone, I presume?'

She was smaller than he'd expected and much older: the tiny remains of a woman beneath a shock of white hair. When she leant forward and held out her hand. Murdoch shook it gently and sat beside her, determined to hide his frustration.

'Nah love, I'm not the doctor. My name's Bill Murdoch; we spoke on the phone. Do you remember?'

The old lady laughed and told him that of course she did, she'd been joking. Murdoch made a note to look up the Livingstone reference later – yet another thing no one had told him about – and asked Suzie Bourne how long she'd been sitting there.

'Long enough,' she said with another little laugh. 'I was having fun watching you.'

'Really? Well, I'm glad one of us found it funny.'

The words snapped and crackled, angrier than he'd meant them to sound. Murdoch took another deep breath, decided to start again, and the old lady sat back, like she wanted to avoid what was coming next. As she did so, Murdoch spotted a walking stick, grey and ugly with heavy stoppers on three feet, leaning against the bench beside her. Shit. Maybe she'd called out and he hadn't heard her.

'Sorry,' he said. 'I just felt like a right tw—like an idiot walking up to all them people.'

She followed his gaze to the walking stick and laughed the same little laugh as before: a tinkling glass noise that was beginning to grate on him.

'That's not mine!' she said. 'It belongs to a friend. Never underestimate the forgetfulness of old women. Still, she can't have got very far, eh? But do forgive me, Mr Murdoch, I have been told I have an unkind sense of humour. That was cruel of me, but,' – that laugh again – 'it was funny.'

Murdoch's quashed frustration rose again. He resisted swearing but stood suddenly, one hand rubbing the red stubble on his scalp.

'You know what,' he said, 'maybe this was a stupid idea.'

'What?'

'Let's forget the whole thing.'

'Oh no!'

Murdoch felt a tug on his trouser leg. Looking down, he saw the old lady's liver-spotted hand was pinching at the fabric.

'Please,' she said. 'I really am sorry. I didn't mean to make you feel like a "right twat". That's the word you were going to say, isn't it? But, obviously, I'm the "right twat" for having such a stupid sense of humour. Come on, I'll buy you a cup of tea. Please?'

She started struggling to her feet and, stepping closer to give her a hand, Murdoch wondered who in the world could resist such helplessness. That alone made him feel better: the idea that these days he had to wonder. That he'd actually forgotten for a while what the scum of the earth were really like. The fact that Suzie Bourne had been lying about the walking stick – 'I can't stand sympathy' – made him feel better still. Even in the mood he was now in, he had to admit that, as a candidate, she was working out pretty well.

They took a while to get settled in the dull and functional café. The old lady moved slowly, tutting at Murdoch when he offered to help, then insisting on getting up again when they worked out they had to order at the till. It was a quarter of an hour before they were both seated again – Murdoch winning the battle about carrying the tray – with the shared pot of tea on the table between them. Murdoch offered to be mother, but Suzie Bourne told him it was a sexist expression and said, given she was paying, it was her job to pour.

'Milk?'

'Thanks.'

'Sugar?'

'Yeah, three, thanks.'

It was like a little dance; like the tea ceremonies he'd read about on Google, and something about it calmed him. They were sitting in the café's window, separated from the rest of Bell Fair – easy enough to look away from it. Apart from him and Suzie Bourne and the acned youth at the till, the café was empty. The old lady passed him his tea, the cup rattling gently in its saucer. Her eyes were keen and shiny but held only a memory of blue.

'So, Mr Murdoch …'

'Bill, please.'

'Oh.' She thought about it, her head cocked on one side. 'Yes, very good. And you must call me Suzie. So, Bill, you want me to teach you how to write a book?'

'Well,' he said, 'sort of.'

'Sort of?'

'I mean, no.'

'Oh.'

The old lady's mouth tightened. She had lifted her own cup and saucer but now put them back on the table, waiting for him to explain. There was something hard about her, he saw. Something tough under all those wrinkles.

'I don't want you to teach me how to write a book,' he said. 'I couldn't never do nothing like that. I want you to write it for me. I had a bit of an adventure last year and I thought I could tell you what happened and you could write it all down. In a story, like.'

Suzie raised her eyebrows. 'I used to teach creative writing. I never wrote much myself.'

She was a good liar, but Murdoch had evidence. 'You wrote two books in the sixties,' he said. '*Jewels in the Morning* and *The Turkish Bazaar*. I read 'em both; they was good.'

Her face relaxed and her little laugh rang out again, louder this time.

'You can't possibly have read them. No one read them even when they were in print. The internet is a marvellous thing, Bill, but you can't kid a kidder.'

She gave him a smile with her faded eyes – she didn't mind him lying, it was a compliment. Murdoch reached down into his leather tote bag, open on the floor beside the table, rifled past his magazines and found the two books. He laid them gently on the table in front of her.

'It is "marvellous",' he said, liking the word. 'You can get everything. You just find the right website and pay them enough money and they'll get you whatever you want, free delivery half the time. That one's from Canada.'

Suzie gave up on her tea again. She picked up *Jewels in the Morning*, handling it like the stolen necklace in its story, then reached for the other book, turning the pages slowly until she let out her glass laugh, a spot of pink in her cheeks.

'"… he stole through the night like a cat, the animal smell of fear on him …" Oh God, what a penny dreadful. Just because you can get everything doesn't mean you should.'

'Doesn't mean it'll make you happy neither.'

She gave him a strange look, her head cocked to the side again. She was like a little grey bird, he thought, listening to a far-off and familiar song. Then she seemed to remember the book in her hands.

'Goodness. Well, I'm touched; I really am. Maybe I should be worried? You're not a stalker, are you?' She peered down into his tote, then, looking up, caught the expression on his face. 'Joke! I was joking again; really, you are funny. But, well, I don't know. You see, writing fiction's not what I do professionally. "Did", I should say. I was a journalist for a while and, yes, then I took myself off and wrote those two books. But that was it; after that I just taught other people how to write. There are people who ghostwrite professionally, you know.'

'Yeah, but I need someone what I can trust a hundred per cent.'

'But why me ... Oh, the internet again?'

'And the library,' he said. 'The library's better for old papers, specially the local ones.'

Murdoch was reaching towards his tote bag, ready to dig for the articles he'd photocopied. But, at the mention of the papers, the old lady had flinched and was now staring into the bag like she was worried it held a weapon. Murdoch sat straight.

'You went to prison for protecting your sources,' he said gently. 'You said you was doing it not just for them but for all the other journalists too. You said if journalists started letting on about their grasses, no one would ever grass again.'

'Well,' Suzie Bourne rubbed her mottled hands together, 'those probably aren't the words I used.'

'Still though, you done it.'

The skin on the old lady's hands stayed wherever she pushed it, the noise a dry whisper, and, when she spoke again, it was to the liver-spotted skin rather to Murdoch. There was no sign of the cheeky woman who had bossed him around moments before.

'Prison was an awful experience,' she said quietly. 'If I'd had any idea, I'd have given that man's name up in seconds. Later, I swore I'd never have anything to do with that world again.' She blinked the memory away and looked up with a fragile smile. 'Besides, I'm far better qualified to teach *you* to write. It's hard work, but you can learn to do it. It's more of a skill than a talent and there are guidelines you can follow. What kind of book did you want to write – a detective story, was it?'

She reached forward for her cup again, grabbing it a little too quickly and splashing some of the tea into the saucer. Murdoch thought he heard her say 'fuck' under her breath.

'It's not a story,' he said. 'It's the truth ...'

'Ah well, it still needs telling as a story.' She was talking quickly, keen to move them on. 'First of all, we need The Crime, or even just The Set-Up, if you want to keep readers guessing what the crime actually is. And, of course, your main character – that's you – has to start in The Prison.'

'Nah, I wasn't in prison at the start.'

Suzie Bourne looked annoyed at being interrupted. 'I didn't say you were *in* prison,' she said slowly. 'I said at the beginning of a story, the main character is always in *a* prison. A prison of their own making; it's metaphorical. Either they're greedy or frightened or a snob or doing a job they hate or in a bad relationship. That's where all stories start. And then the prison gets worse and they're more trapped than ever.'

Murdoch thought back to the previous year, to his life in Sydney and what had happened to him.

'Go on.'

'Well, I won't go into it all now, but, like I said, there are guidelines to storytelling. I'm more than happy to teach you, it's really not that hard ...'

'It is.'

'No, really, it's not.'

'It *is*. I've tried it a hundred times and I can't do it. Whatever I write, it's all rubbish. I want someone else to do it!'

She looked at him in surprise and he realised he'd raised his voice. For a fleeting second, her expression seemed to change to one of intense curiosity and he thought she was about to ask him something. But then, with a tiny shake of her head, she looked away. In the sad silence that followed, Murdoch remembered where they were. He turned in his seat and looked out at the slow shoppers, everyone in the world trying to buy themselves happier.

'Another cup?'

'You what?'

'Would you like another cup of tea, Bill?'

Jesus Christ, it made him want to cry. Bad tea and piped music, nothing else happening. This was going to be the rest of his life.

'Ta.'

'Milk, wasn't it? And three sugars? You see, I'll be honest and tell you I am rather keen to get some extra income. I have friends who've invited me to join them on a long cruise and I'd dearly love to accept. But I simply have no interest in going near the underworld again.'

'Yeah, but you wouldn't have to, would you? Everyone I ever had anything to do with in this country is dead or banged up. My old gang in Sydney, the Club, they're done – otherwise I wouldn't be here to tell you about it. You wouldn't have to do nothing 'cept listening to me tell you what I did, then write it out like a good story. Them's all doing it, these ex-crooks. They publish their memories and then they get to go on chat shows and everything; hang out with real celebrities.'

The old lady smiled and shuffled forward on her chair, her turn to reach down into his open bag. Grunting with the effort, she sat up again with his copy of *Starstrike!* in her hand.

'Celebrities,' she said, opening the magazine onto the table between them. 'Like these people? Why on earth would you choose to mix with them?'

Murdoch wanted to be more annoyed. Who did this old biddy think she was, poking around in his private stuff? On the other hand, wasn't that exactly what he wanted her to do?

'Oh, this one,' she said with a sudden smile, tapping at a photograph. 'Even I recognise her. She's Australian, isn't she?'

'Yeah, she's Melissa Munday. She's in *Society*, it's my favourite thing on the telly. Actually ...' He checked his watch and looked up to find the old lady smirking. 'What?'

'Oh nothing. It's just I didn't take you for someone who would enjoy watching that kind of thing. Or reading this kind of thing, to tell the truth. Tell me, what's the appeal?'

She was like a social worker: spotting the stuff you didn't want to talk about and making you talk about nothing but that. Murdoch could have resisted, but he knew he had to give her something if she was going to help him. She was like that, he could tell: too savvy to give something for nothing. He shrugged. 'I dunno. It's how the other half lives, innit? How I'm gunna live one day. Yachts and parties and penguin suits. That's what I always wanted, not this ...' He gestured out at the mall, gave up on trying to find a word for it and pointed at the magazine instead. 'I like reading about what life could be like. You know, exciting.'

Suzie Bourne too looked out at the mall, then turned back to him with a tired look on her face.

'It gets worse as you get older,' she said. 'Everyone who's any fun dies and you're too weak to do anything interesting.' She seemed to remember something, maybe that she wasn't supposed to think this way, and forced another smile – less convincing this one – as she tapped on the magazine again. 'But I bet these people's lives aren't much better. They're probably not that exciting in reality.'

'Compared to mine they are. They all go to balls and launches and openings and stuff.'

'Yes, but that's just the bit you see, Bill. It's storytelling, like anything else. Oh dear, were you looking for your story to portray you like someone in this magazine? Or to be written like an episode of *Society*?'

'Nah, I mean, I dunno. I'd leave all that bit up to you. As long as you get the facts out, you can do it whatever way you want.'

She gave him a different look, like his proposal was more interesting than it had been, before making a small noise, a short and tidy hum, and shaking her head again. She smiled at him sadly, closed the magazine and pushed it across the table.

'We could discuss money,' he said quickly. 'Maybe that would help? I looked it all up.'

'Well ...'

'I was thinking forty grand.'

Suzie Bourne stared at him. 'Forty thousand dollars?'

'Fifty!'

'Oh!' She pressed one hand against her chest, the world smallest diamond clinging to her finger after all these years. 'My! Well, I don't know. I mean ...'

Murdoch's alarm started up on his phone, buzzing the whole table, the cups worried in their saucers. Checking his watch again, he swore under his breath and leant to pick up his bag.

'Listen,' he said, standing too quickly and bothering the table more than his phone had done. 'I've got something on, but you think about it, yeah?'

She showed him all her tiny teeth this time, a grimace as much as a smile, dentures he hadn't noticed before. When he reached over the table to shake hands goodbye, she reached up, took his hand in both of hers and shook it with the full strength of her arms. One good tug and he could have pulled them off.

## 4

Davie was in the overbright window of Deutsch & Bowler, updating the cards describing houses for sale, when he saw Bill Murdoch drive past. Immediately, he climbed backwards into the estate agency's shabby office, leaving half the cards blank and one of them hanging by a corner, and started looking around for his keys. Two minutes later he'd locked up and, without even examining the surf across the road, was hurrying in the direction of Bill's house.

It was a day to show why the white man's seasons don't work in Australia. Half spring, half winter, it was a perfect 'sprinter' day: the sky cloudless but cool, the trees and bushes full of bloom. The kind of day that usually filled Davie's head with calculations about the surf and how soon he could bunk off work to enjoy it. Today, all that concerned him was how he was going to break his news to Bill without getting shouted at.

It wasn't that Davie was afraid of his friend's foul temper – Bill Murdoch was always angry or miserable about something – more that he hated contributing to it. The trouble was, whatever Davie suggested, whatever great ideas he had about how Bill could enjoy life in Montauban, how he should try and patch things up with Natalie Conquest, they always seemed to make things worse. The Englishman seemed personally offended by the idea of joining the surf club or the bush preservation society or the coastal regeneration group. Worse than that, he had no idea how lucky he was to be invited to do so. Out of holiday season, Montauban was a sleepy place – less than half its houses occupied, barely enough business for the shops opposite the beach – and it certainly didn't welcome blow-ins. But Bill Murdoch had been an exception. The previous year, posing as a private detective – and with significant help from Davie – he had solved the case of a missing local schoolgirl, Georgie Walker. Admittedly, prior to that, Bill had been a crook – everyone in Montie knew, it had been all over the papers – but this was the Coast, no one minded that up here. Besides, everyone in Montie also knew that Bill had crossed his former gangland employers to solve the Georgie Walker case and that made him a local hero. So much so, in fact, that, when those same papers reported Bill Murdoch's death, the locals had been happy to keep up the story. In public they were supposed to call him by a different name – Davie could never remember what it was – and to tell him if anyone was asking after him. But no one ever had asked after him. Not until today.

Lost in his thoughts, Davie forgot not to lean on Bill's doorbell – you could never hear if it was working or not – and flinched in surprise when the Englishman opened the door.

'You know, mate,' said Bill, 'you only need to press the doorbell for a second and then you can take your finger off it. That's how it works.'

Wiry, shorn-headed and fizzy with energy, Bill tended to make Davie, who was floppily blond and six foot four, feel like a giant sloth.

'Yo, Bill. How you going?'

'Fine thanks. You?'

'I've got news.'

'Let me guess, Natalie said hello.'

'I wish, but no. Are you going to let me in?'

Bill checked his watch, said, 'Fifteen minutes, absolute max,' and turned back into the house.

*Jim Young*, Davie remembered as he followed Bill down the long hallway. That was the name they were supposed to use for Bill in front of anyone out of town. Davie had sold this house and its contents to a James Young, and only afterwards discovered it was really Bill. It was the best house in town. As the local estate agent, over the years Davie had been inside most of the others and not one – not even the millionaires' weekenders up on the cliffs – came close. The previous owner had been an architect with a renowned eye for art deco and deco-inspired furniture, all of which Bill had bought when he'd bought the house. The place was full of glass, brass, dark wood and curves – elegant angles that made you want to reach out and touch. Whoever said you couldn't buy taste hadn't seen this house.

Bill walked down to the kitchen, but Davie stopped halfway along the hall and pushed open the door to the living room. At this time of year, the light from the lagoon juddered shadows against the room's green walls, sparking the mirrors and the vases, an optical display even Bill had made positive noises about. Today, however, Davie found the room shut up in darkness, the only light coming from adverts playing silently on the huge television. Davie wanted to stride across to the French windows, pull

23

open the curtains and let the glorious daylight in, but that was the kind of thing Bill tended to use as an excuse for throwing him out. He called towards the kitchen.

'It's a beautiful day out there, Bill, and here's you hiding in the dark. Why don't you let the sunshine in?'

'Because I'm going to watch telly.'

'Why don't you come down the beach? I could bunk off work.'

'Because I want to watch telly?'

Davie gave up and walked into the kitchen, blinking against the brightness. Bill was at the counter, flipping through a magazine.

'Have you been out much?'

The Englishman didn't turn around. 'Yeah, a bit.'

'Nat says she saw you walking on the beach.'

'Davie, mate, I still don't want to go for a drink with her, right?'

The previous year, Bill had had a one-night stand with Davie's best friend, Natalie Conquest. Convinced the two of them still had the hots for each other, Davie had tried a little too hard to push them back together.

'So you've not been out?' he asked again, unsure how to move the conversation towards his news.

'Went to Crosley this morning, didn't I? And I see Ed Springer twice a week.'

'Oh yeah, I heard you were doing that. I heard you're getting good!'

'Course you did. I can't fart without half of Montie knowing about it, can I?'

Bill had opened a cupboard and taken out two mugs. Now he let them drop onto the counter before jabbing at the switch on the kettle. Davie grimaced and sat himself quietly at the table beneath the window. It really was a beautiful day outside. All the pot plants on Bill's patio had flowers on them, and, further down, near the lagoon, the turpentine towering over his lawn was dotted with off-white blossom. Inside, the kettle screamed itself to a boil. In the silence that followed, Davie asked how things were going with Ed Springer.

'Yeah, good.'

'And what else? Have you been out much otherwise? You should, you know. You'd get to meet some new people. You know, what about joining ...' Davie remembered he'd suggested the surf club once too often.

'… a gym again or something. Terry over at Punch in Kildare says you've not been there in months.'

'You know, Davie …'

'Or what about the idea of doing another detective job? I told you my CAPI licence came through – we'd be legal and everything.'

'Davie …'

'Or what about that woman I told you about? Suzie Bourne? You should go and see her. Didn't you say you wanted to? You said …'

'Davie!'

'Or maybe you could join Taradale Tennis Club?'

'Davie, for God's sake! Do you want me to disconnect that doorbell? Cos I will, you know. You can come round, I don't mind, but don't bleeding well tell me how to live my life. You go to the beach; you go and enjoy this bleeding little backwater and talk to all the bogans who live here, but leave me out of it, will you?'

Months before this would have counted as an argument. These days most of their conversations went this way. Davie sighed and looked out of the window again, listening to Bill make the tea. It was several minutes before he remembered his news.

'Is it possible they're still looking for you?'

'Who's that then?'

'Those people you used to work for. The Club. Is that why you're staying indoors?'

'No, you muppet. No one's looking for me. Most of them lot are dead and buried, and the ones what aren't think *I* am.'

'So why the hermit act? Have you been down the shops and spoken to Anne Lincoln?'

'Davie, there is no hermit act. I go out every day, don't I? You hear about anyone looking for me, I'll start shitting myself, if it makes you feel better. Until then, I'm—spoken to Anne Lincoln about what?'

Davie realised he was biting his lower lip, one hand combing through his hair. He stopped both and took a deep breath. It was like making yourself sick: better to get it over and done with.

'Someone is looking for you,' he said in a rush. 'Anne told me about an hour ago. There was a stranger in the general store this morning, asking where Bill Murdoch lived.'

## 5

Murdoch knew the magazines he read were rubbish and he knew the American soap he'd raced home to watch was rubbish too. At least, he remembered knowing those things, in the days before he'd moved to Montauban. Back then he'd laughed at bullshit like *Society*, couldn't have cared less about so-called celebrities. All he'd ever wanted in those days was somewhere nice to live, a decent motor to drive and to be left in peace. He had no idea why, within months of getting those things, they had stopped being enough. It was like the years of striving had infected him, turned him into someone who only knew how to strive.

After all, it wasn't like there was anything wrong with Montauban. Murdoch had loved the tiny suburb when he'd first arrived. (That's what they called small places out here: 'suburbs'; it didn't matter how isolated they were). He'd loved the way the locals all trusted each other; the way nothing ever happened. How, during the week, you could go for hours without hearing a car, just birds and the wind in the trees, the crashing of the ocean on the breeze from the beach. Then, within weeks of deciding to live there forever, Montauban had started closing in on him. The streets, once a maze, became too familiar. The plastic bins outside every house, the potholes in the streets, the drooping electric cables: everything felt like a trap. Sometimes Murdoch thought he could hear the grass growing, creaking and yawning as it pushed its way out of the dirt. Locked in the dark of his living room, *Society* was a promise of a brighter future. A vision of what one day he'd wear to parties around swimming pools; what he'd say to women in half-lit bars; how, having won a game of tennis, he'd jump over the net and shake hands fiercely with his opponent. In *Society*, people dressed up nice and had adventures, went to classy parties and had news to share. In Montauban, people looked at you funny if you wore anything but shorts and a T-shirt. In magazines, sunny weather meant champagne on yachts, birds in bikinis and high heels. In Montauban, sunshine was one less excuse to stay indoors and pretend you were somewhere else, somewhere like *Society*.

Today, though, the soap opera wasn't working. Maybe it was because, by the time Murdoch had got rid of Davie – with fervent reassurances there was nothing to worry about – he'd missed half the credits and the theme tune. Or maybe it was because, as Melissa Munday's character started seducing her boss, Murdoch found himself disturbed by lists of who might be looking for him and why. Names forgotten and half-forgotten, faces he never wanted to see again. His reassurances to Davie had been based on truth. Everyone he knew of who wanted him dead was dead themselves, or banged up long enough for it not to matter. But it wasn't what you knew that got you killed. Murdoch blinked himself back to the action on the screen – sometimes Melissa Munday took off her blouse – and within seconds found himself back with the lists. Bad men who knew what he'd done, people justified in wanting him to suffer. Again, he returned his attention to the television and again found himself back with the lists, frowning hard until, giving up, he swore loudly, jumped to his feet and, a few minutes later, slammed out of the house.

Murdoch's neighbour, Mr Minter, pulled up in his driveway as Murdoch was locking the front door. Murdoch had once liked the way he and Minter called each other 'Mister'. It was, he'd thought, like being in a black-and-white programme off the telly, one of those old series where nothing bad ever happened. He'd liked the way Minter cleaned his car every Sunday when he got home from church, the way he referred to anyone under forty as a 'young 'un', the way he was always wore a tie. Back then, those things had been a reassurance that the black-and-white world still existed, that you really could live happily ever after. Now, every little thing Minter did was a bleak reminder you couldn't.

Minter was out of his car and unloading shopping from the boot before he noticed Murdoch.

'Good morning, Mr Murdoch,' he shouted across their common front lawn. 'Isn't it a great day!'

Murdoch walked over, silent until he was close enough to lean on the other man's car. 'Actually, Mr Minter, it's probably best if you call me Mr Young. Like we agreed. Do you remember?'

Minter stood straight, a box of shopping in his hands, and looked at Murdoch with his head pulled back. 'I didn't think we had to do that any more?'

'Do you mind if we do?'

Minter thought about it. 'No, of course not'

'Thanks.' Murdoch gave him a smile. 'Want a hand with them boxes?'

Minter waved him away, frowning. 'No, no. You get on. Have a good day, Mr Young.'

Anne Lincoln's over-tanned cleavage was on such permanent display that it was as familiar to the Montauban locals as the steep hills surrounding the town. Glowering at her from the back of the general store, Murdoch found himself wondering if the skin Anne didn't reveal was as white and as pasty as his own. He pictured her naked: a Michelin man with a brown V on the chest and slightly more orange face and hands. He caught his mood, reminded himself Anne had done nothing wrong and blinked the image away to stare into the Coke fridge instead. There were two short aisles in Montauban Stores and Murdoch was at the end where they joined, as far away as you could get from the front counter but still within earshot of the endless chatter that went back and forth across it. *He said, so she said. I was like and he was like. Blah, blah, blah.* Murdoch imagined the conversations that would cross the counter if he was found dead in his house. Within hours, no one in Montauban would be talking about anything but how Bill Murdoch's past had caught up with him at last. *Ooh, I always said it would happen.* He pictured them in the street, crossing the road to share the news and— His reflection in the fridge door told him to calm down. To breathe. To wait until Anne was alone so everything could be explained.

Murdoch checked his watch and wondered how long it would be before Anne stopped nattering to John Thornton about the chemist opening next door. 'I liked it when the Blanket Bar was in there,' he heard her tell John for the fifth time. 'Such a shame it closed.' Murdoch pulled open the Coke fridge, closed his eyes and tried to focus on the noise of its motor. But Anne had a special voice for time-wasters. Somewhere between a fishwife and a dockworker, it left you waiting for foul language that never arrived.

'It's not an air con unit, you know!' she shouted down the aisle. 'You going to buy something, Bill, or are you just eavesdropping?'

'Eavesdropping.' Murdoch let the door swing shut again. 'Best way to find out anything round here, innit?'

'God love 'im!' John Thornton turned and smiled his gappy smile, his gold tooth catching the light. 'How're your ribs, mate? Must be better, cos I hear you's with Ed Springer twice a week. I hear you're getting good! Listen, Anne, I'd better be off, I've got to get the boys from school.'

Murdoch forced a smile back, pulled open the fridge again and tried to decide between the bottles of water. He'd forgotten how tiring it was to be worried. Constantly calculating the what ifs and how to respond

28

and when to tell who what. He let the fridge swing close again, no idea why he'd opened it.

A few minutes later and John Thornton really was leaving; a few minutes after that, he really had gone. Anne served two other in-and-out customers and let Murdoch hover by the magazines – a rare privilege – until they were alone. Then she beckoned him brusquely to the counter.

'I know why you're here!' She had swapped the fishwife's bray for the loudest whisper on the Coast. 'It's about that house opposite your place, isn't it?'

'Is it?'

'Oh, don't pretend to me, Bill Murdoch. I know you call me "Montie FM" behind my back, but you're straight in here when you want to find out what's going on. You want to know if it's being knocked down or not, don't you? Go on, don't you?'

'You got me.'

'Well, it is. Sorry to be the bearer of bad news. New people what bought it, they want to build up, look over you and get a view of the lagoon. Doubt if they'll get DA for it but. Not if you protest.'

Anne paused, her lips parted in anticipation. The price of information was information.

'Actually, I don't mind either way,' Murdoch said slowly. 'It's not like they'll be blocking my view, is it? Here, you going to take some money for this water or what?'

'Three dollars. What about the building noise?'

He made a non-committal face, took his change and started to leave.

'Oh Bill, did Davie tell you?'

'What?'

Eyebrows pitched dramatically, the volume right down on the whisper so he had to walk back to the counter. 'Someone was looking for you.'

'So?'

'Well, you know, it's just you said if anyone was ever looking for you, I shouldn't tell them a thing. Well, I didn't. But,' she gave a quick look round the shop like anyone had ever walked in without her knowing, 'I thought you should know.'

'Oh, yeah, right. Jesus, Anne, you're a good 'un. Probably just a journalist or a nosey-parker.'

She winced at the blasphemy but ignored it. 'Fancy journalist if she was. Lovely looking woman.'

'Oh yeah?'

'Mm, nice clothes, good manners.'

'Nice car and nice husband too?'

'Ooh, I don't know. Once people are out of here, it's not like I follow them.' Anne smoothed her V-neck like he'd questioned her reputation. 'Didn't see any sign of a bloke with her, but she was wearing a wedding ring.'

'She say much else?'

'Nothing. Just asked for you. Looked annoyed when I pretended not to catch the name. Then, when I said I'd never heard of a Bill Murdoch, she gave me a look like she didn't believe me, said thank you and left.'

And the Oscar goes to ... 'Aw well, I wouldn't worry about it, Anne. Probably an acquaintance from way back when what I'm happy not to see again. You keep telling them you never heard of me, there's a good girl. Listen, best be off, I've got to water the garden.'

The shopkeeper crossed her arms under her breasts and leant on the counter again, preparing to tell him how to do it when a group of schoolboys fell in from the street, a bundle of untucked shirts and over-packed bags far more deserving of her attention.

6.

That night Murdoch struggled to sleep. At midnight he took some Valium, not expecting them to work, and next thing he knew it was light outside and his clothes had sucked themselves onto his skin. He was tempted to change his plans for the day, to stay indoors and work out what he was supposed to do, but that would mean there was something wrong and – as he kept reminding himself – there was nothing to worry about. The Club was gone, anyone who wanted him dead was dead themselves. Everything would be fine. At ten o'clock, he forced himself out.

Murdoch generally made a point of taking the long way around to the tennis courts, along the streets that ran up from the creek that fed the lagoon, keeping his distance from the beach. The aim was to meet as few people as possible, but even on this quieter route he rarely made it all the way undisturbed. There was always someone asking after his health, his garden, his state of mind. Or just chatting about the weather, in case he hadn't noticed what another bleeding lovely day it was. Today, he crossed paths with a man he always thought of as the ugliest man in the world. The man, whose name Murdoch didn't know, seemed to spend his days doing nothing but trudging around Montie carrying heavy shopping bags. Murdoch always wondered if this explained why the man's mouth, face, ears, shoulders, everything sloped steeply down either side of his bumpy nose. Or, if it was just that living in Montauban did that to you and whether he, Murdoch, would look the same one day. Unless, of course, he already did.

'Off for your ten o'clock with Ed?' the ugly man called out as they passed. 'I hear you're getting good! Isn't it exciting about his news?'

Murdoch gave the minimum polite smile and hurried on.

Six months earlier, when Anne Lincoln had said her nephew Ed was a tennis coach looking for adult beginners, Murdoch had jumped at the chance. As he had explained to Davie, unlike anything you could learn at the surf club, tennis was swish, all them white clothes and grass lawns, club houses with fit women in pleated skirts. At the garden parties in *Society* people were always playing tennis. Murdoch reminded himself of this now as he picked his way carefully across the Minefield – a scruffy patch of green named for its popularity with dogs – and climbed through a snagging hole in the mesh that ran around the two local courts, separating them from the playground of Montauban Public School. He might not be going to garden parties yet, but when the day came he'd be ready.

Ed, of course, was late. It was ten past before he arrived, shouting his apologies from a hundred metres away. Twenty-two and young for his years, Ed Springer was at an age where sorry meant nothing, because nothing was ever his fault. Still, he was a good-enough kid, amazed by everything he was told ('Awesome!') and never asking about anything else. He had tightly curled brown hair, unpredictable skin and limbs he hadn't grown into yet.

'I've got news,' he said excitedly, climbing through the hole in the mesh. 'Kind of good and bad at the same time.'

'Bad news is you're late,' Murdoch replied. 'Good news is you're here. Everything else can wait till after we've finished.'

Because Ed always had news. He was dating a girl; he was dating another girl; he'd flunked his exams and dropped out of college; he'd applied for a job in the States. The kid had no idea what he wanted from life, only that he wanted to see the world, the way his parents had meant to. Then he'd come back to Montie and settle down happily ever after. Murdoch could never work out why Ed's plan made him jealous. Maybe, it was the belief that anyone could live happily ever after. Or maybe, today, because it didn't involve worrying if anyone ever found you in Montauban.

Tennis hadn't come easily to Murdoch but, over the previous months, with nothing else to do, he had had countless lessons with Ed. Outside of that, he had practised for up to three hours at a time. Had found walls to hit against and dragged buckets of balls to the courts so he could smack them over the net. It had been a painful process – several racquets smashed and discarded – but it had worked in the end. Today, whole rallies opened up between him and Ed, almost like they were playing a real game, and even if the kid won every point, it gave Murdoch an hour free from thinking about anything else.

'So,' said the young coach, when he'd exhausted Murdoch for five minutes more than he'd paid for, 'do you want to hear my news?'

'Thrill me.'

'Well, you know I applied for that job in California? Remember, I told you it's like impossible to get a coaching gig unless you've got coaching experience? And you said to, like, lie? Well, don't tell my dad, but I did. And guess what? I got it! I'm going to Amerikay!'

Feeling himself colour, Murdoch turned and started collecting balls. 'Right. That's good.'

'Bloody oath it is! I'm so excited. I start in May; that's spring over there.' Murdoch heard the kid hesitate. 'You don't mind, do you?'

'Me, mate? Why would I mind? You're not the only tennis coach on the Coast, you know. You should go, travel and stuff.'

Ed said nothing and Murdoch focused on the balls at his feet, trying to bounce them up with his racquet. The breeze had picked up, blowing leaves and dirty litter against the mesh between him and the rest of the world. Hearing soft footsteps, he looked up to find Ed had come around the net. The kid had taken his off sunglasses and was frowning, eyes joined to ears by untanned skin.

'You shouldn't get another coach,' he said. 'You need to play, Bill. You should join at Taradale; you're so competitive, you'd love it.'

Murdoch ran his hand over his scalp and looked around for any last balls. 'Nah, I'm not good enough. I'd look like a right twat.'

'Course you're good enough!' Ed laughed. 'You can be a complete beginner and play at Taradale. Come on, I know everyone there. I'll introduce you to a few people, get you in the right division; you'll never look back.'

Murdoch had visited Taradale Tennis Club before. A pebble-dashed building on the Coastal Highway, it was black from the exhaust of passing traffic. Sticky carpet ran between pokie machines and dirty windows to look down onto the courts.

'Nah, not me I couldn't; all them people looking. I'll just find another coach.'

There were no more balls to collect, no reason not to look at Ed's concerned young face.

'Oh OK,' said the kid, eyes all innocent like he didn't know what he was doing. 'If you're too much of a pussy, then I totally get it.'

7.

When Murdoch had been imagining, then planning, then creating his fortune, he'd always had an idea of the house he'd own. He'd torn pages from magazines and made lists of non-negotiables (a garage, a fireplace, a desk). But then the house in Montie had landed in his lap, a ready-made package, and there hadn't been much left for him to buy. The car had been a more difficult decision. He'd landed with a Merc because the girl in the dealership had smiled at him and said she'd like a ride if he ended up buying one. She said she always preferred convertibles: cream leather and all the trimmings, top down and her hair in the wind. All smiles she was as he paid in cash, pouting through her fringe as she slowly counted the notes. When she handed him his paperwork, she told him she couldn't wait for him to come and pick up the car. He never saw her again. A hairy bloke called Derek had brought the soft-top round the front and handed Murdoch the keys.

'Kylie?' he said. 'Got a job down in Sydney at Maserati. Better class of clientele, she reckoned.'

Still, he had the Merc. Ed whistled when he saw it – a blatant attempt to mend Murdoch's mood. The young coach had lobbed the word 'pussy' around twice more on the tennis court before Murdoch had sworn and shouted and then, out of excuses, agreed to fetch the car. Regretting it now, he buzzed the roof down and told Ed to get in. Then he had to answer the kid's questions about the engine and the model and the fuel efficiency until, proud of the Merc and not used to showing it off, he felt his mood slowly lift. All the same, once they had climbed the steepness of Montauban Road and turned onto the Crown Road, he declined Ed's requests to push the car to its limits. Murdoch knew the road too well for that.

The Crown Road snaked away from the coast between steep fields that fell down on one side to the lagoon behind Murdoch's house, on the other to a creek he'd never seen. The road was Montie's best feature, the only way in and the only way out, easy to see if you were being followed home. Or away from home, come to that. Murdoch caught himself checking his rear-view mirror for the fifth time in as many minutes, reminded himself he had nothing to worry about and told Ed they were going fast enough. He didn't tell him he knew from experience which of the Crown Road's curves you could play with and which were tighter than you could tell. When to pull back and when to let the car go – a tonne of metal flying down a hill. Others, he knew, weren't so wise. Deep in the night, he would hear young revheads tearing along the Crown Road, ignoring the sad flowers tied to trees, the photographs fading beneath them. He knew the revheads were young, because you had to be young to believe shit only happened to other people.

Halfway to Taradale, Ed took a call, slumping in his seat to get out of the wind. From the corner of his eye, Murdoch watched the kid listening hard, looking across at him and thinking for a second before speaking.

'Yeah,' Ed said. 'Yeah, no problem. See you in a sec.'

He hung up, sat up straight and asked Murdoch if he minded them dropping in somewhere on the way to Taradale.

'It's not far out of the way,' Ed explained. 'I've got to pick up a racquet. Do you mind?'

'Shouldn't you of asked me that before you said "Yeah, no problem" to whoever you was on the phone to?'

34

Ed laughed. Murdoch had to be joking; no way anyone could mind something like that. Murdoch sighed and rolled his eyes.

'Where is it?

'Huntingdon's. You know, the fancy sports club, sorry, *country club*, up past the private girls' school? Mate of mine strings racquets there.'

Murdoch knew the girls' school – Georgie Walker, the missing girl he'd found the year before, had been one of its students – but he'd not driven beyond it.

'Sure,' he said like he didn't care. 'No worries. Mate.'

Murdoch was constantly surprised by the Aussie definition of 'not far'. Huntingdon's Golf & Country Club was a good thirty minutes out of their way. When they found it at last, it wasn't thanks to its signage. The country club's navy-blue plaque – *'Members Only'* under a coat of arms, like they couldn't think of anything to write in Latin – was too small and too late for anyone who didn't expect it to be there. Murdoch turned the car between two sandstone pillars and he and Ed bumped along an unsealed road for over a kilometre, the tennis coach wincing an apology whenever a stone clicked off the paintwork. Murdoch barely noticed. He was sitting up straight, studying the buzz-cut lawns and the European trees planted a hundred years before.

'What'd you say this place was?'

'Huntingdon's.'

'A golf club?'

'A country club they call it, but it does have a golf course.' Ed looked at him and fidgeted himself upright. 'Members only.'

'So this is the golf course?'

'No, I think that's round the other side. This is, well, it's just the grounds, I guess.'

The club house itself was a large sandstone building with thin-pillared verandas on three sides, too many windows to count. It suited the parkland around it – even its more modern wing, stretching away in a single storey – but Murdoch was shocked to find it on the Coast. He half expected to see men riding horses between the trees, women in long dresses worried about their fans. The road turned, bringing them onto the gravel in front of the house.

'Jesus,' he said, crunching to a stop beside a row of parked cars. 'Nice place.'

'You can stay here.' Ed launched himself from the car, letting the door slam behind him. Halfway across the gravel, he turned with a strange look on his face. 'Stay here,' he said. 'I won't be long.'

Wandering along the edge of the car park, the gravel under his feet like two-dollar coins, Murdoch lit a cigarette and inspected the other parked cars closely. Like that might be enough to stop him wondering about the woman who'd asked for him in the general store. Finding it wasn't, he doubled back and climbed the sandstone steps that ran up to the veranda around the club house. Ignoring the house's huge front door, he cupped his hands to peer through its windows instead. Inside were high-ceilinged rooms full of old-fashioned furniture: sofas on carved wooden feet, towering bookcases with glass in the frames. Wandering further around the veranda, he found steps down to a pathway that led through a brick arch to a lawn and the view.

Huntingdon House had been built on the top of a rise. Behind it, ten or more grass tennis courts, half of them empty, terraced down the hill. Beyond them was the golf course, a patchwork of greens and distant bunkers. Past that, woodland; in the distance, the ocean. The fact there were places so close to home that he'd never heard of was strangely reassuring – a reminder you wouldn't have to run far if someone really was after you. Murdoch drew slowly on his cigarette and stared at it all rolling away from him under the broad blue sky. The breeze, gentler this far from the coast, carried his smoke away and replaced it with the sound of tennis balls pocking politely back and forth, then laughter from players running behind the sponsored gauze. Closer, there was birdsong from within the flowering shrubs, the phut-phut of sprinklers hidden somewhere. Murdoch looked at it all for another thirty seconds, killed his cigarette on the bottom of his shoe and put the stub carefully in the pocket of his shorts.

He was halfway back across the gravel when a little red Honda pulled up in a spray of stones that barely missed him. Two women climbed out, continuing a conversation, and walked past him towards the courts. Like that's what they did all day – climbed out of sports cars, ignored the peasants and walked past fancy buildings. They were both blonde, in the way some women will always stay blonde; one of them older than the other – skin tighter on her jaw, slacker on her legs – but both in good shape. Like him, they were both dressed for tennis. The difference was that their whites – bouncing pleats, thin white T-shirts, even the sweatbands on their wrists – were matching outfits: Nike for one, Lacoste for the other. Murdoch felt grubby in comparison, but, still, he couldn't resist.

'Scuse me ladies?'

They were hardly past him, the older one showing her friend something on her racquet, but at Murdoch's voice, they stopped and turned abruptly, surprised to find they weren't alone. Their smiles lasted as long as the time it took them to look him up and down.

'Yes?' said the younger one.

There was something about her attitude that stopped her from being hot: a nasty little curl to her lip. Murdoch ignored it.

'Yeah, first time here for me,' he said. 'I was just wondering if you knew where the gents is?'

'Are you a member?'

She was on the point of saying something else, something a bit hoity you could tell, but her friend interrupted her.

'You'd better ask at reception,' she said with a tight little smile, nodding up to the veranda. 'Come on, Lara, we'll be late.'

She took the younger woman's elbow, whispered something into her ear and guided her away towards the courts. As Murdoch reached the steps up to the veranda again, he heard the two of them laughing.

The reception area was dark after the sun-drenched gravel and it took Murdoch's eyes a while to adjust. He had expected a tiled floor and a sweeping staircase, vases of lilies and angels on the ceiling. Instead, he found a beige carpet running to a modern desk, narrow stairs that climbed a wall before turning out of view. Either side of him a doorway opened onto the high-ceilinged rooms he'd seen from outside: bright compared to the space he found himself in. He blinked and realised there was woman standing in the dull corner behind the desk. She was taut and tanned; the first thing he'd seen since he'd left the main road that looked like she belonged on the Coast: a woman who'd been on her feet half her life. Her warm brown eyes were surrounded by wrinkles from smoking too young; her jaw was firm with determination, her hair pulled back so tight it had to hurt. She was wearing a crisp, white shirt, smart black trousers and a badge that called her Irene.

37

'Hello, Irene.'

'Hello?' She gave Murdoch a smile that was part of the job, obviously struggling to place him. 'You must be Mr Branson; how was your game with … Oh!'

She was looking down past his knees at the carpet behind him. Turning, Murdoch saw a footprint and a half of dog shit had followed him into the hallway. Immediately, he smelled its foul stench.

'Aw shit!' he said. 'I mean …'

But Irene was already around the counter and squatting beside him with a roll of Chux and a bottle of spray.

'I'm really sorry, love. I'll take my tennis shoes off.'

'It's fine,' said Irene, rubbing hard at the carpet and not looking up. 'Really, don't worry. It's the local dogs …'

He took his trainers off anyway, just to show he was helping, then stood with them in his hands, feeling like a fool in his tennis socks but not knowing what else to do. Apologising again, he carried the stinking trainers outside, wiping the dirty one on the grass at the bottom of the steps and then, as an afterthought, hobbling in his socks across the gravel and opening the boot of his car. He threw the shoes onto a newspaper he'd left lying there, the sight of it reminding him of Davie's news – the stranger looking for him – then of Ed's news, his own life getting smaller still. He slammed the boot shut on both of them.

By the time he was back at reception, there was a broad wet stain on the carpet and Irene was behind the desk again. She'd washed her hands somewhere and was drying them on a small towel, 'HGCC' embroidered on one corner.

'I'm really sorry, darlin'.'

Irene smiled her professional smile. 'Really, Mr Branson, it's not your fault. Now, I understand you're thinking of becoming a member? Mr Hughes is going to show you around.'

'Well, I might be interested in being a member but …'

His phone started vibrating and, remembering not to swear, Murdoch struggled it out of his pocket. It was Davie: perfect timing as ever. Murdoch killed the call and looked up to find Irene with a phone in her hand.

'I'll just give him a call. Bear with me … oh, here he is. Mr Hughes. Mr Hughes!'

A stocky little man with an old-fashioned moustache was crossing the reception area from one side of the room to another. When he turned and raised his bushy little eyebrows, Murdoch was reminded of a talking teddy bear he'd seen once in a film.

'I heard you the first time, thank you, Irene,' said the man called Hughes, in a prim English accent. 'Do you know who owns that Mercedes out there? It's not on the register.'

'That'd be me' said Murdoch.

'Oh. And you are?'

'This is Mr Branson,' said Irene. 'Your eleven o'clock.'

The west end of the house held the indoor pool, where an old man was swimming laps, stroking so gently back and forth that Murdoch wondered if he'd been doing it for years and everyone had forgotten he was there. On the other side of the pool, bifold doors concertinaed onto the terrace that held the larger outdoor pool: a rippling square of blue surrounded by neat rows of sun loungers under yellow-and-white striped cushions. Only three of the loungers were occupied. On one, a woman in towels and giant sunglasses was reading a thick book, glancing occasionally at three children playing in the water. On two others, sat an elderly couple, slow with newspapers and murmuring chat. Beyond the terrace, the land dropped away – you'd get a good view of the tennis courts – but from where he and Mr Hughes stood, Murdoch could only see treetops and sky.

'It's quiet,' he said.

'Yes, well, it is midweek. Come here at the weekend, or during the school holidays, and I'm afraid it's a *very* different story. All children must remain supervised, of course. And as a tennis player, you'll find there's no end of people looking for a game, day or night. I've known people drive up from Sydney for one. I don't play myself, but it appears to be quite addictive.'

Hughes ended every sentence with a little lift in his voice, like he needed confirmation it was OK to talk. Supervised, of course? Quite addictive?

'No, I mean, it's silent,' said Murdoch. 'Them kids in the pool, they're even playing quietly.'

Hughes raised his bushy eyebrows again and gave a weak and uncertain smile.

The new building that bordered the gravel car park, Hughes admitted, was for administrative and support services. Racquet stringing, equipment hire, overflow changing rooms. He explained it in a hurried and quiet voice, like he was talking about armpits and anuses: things you needed, but no one wanted to hear about. He was prouder of the main building in which they stood – the 'old house' as he called it. The eastern end ('we can hardly call it a wing') held the drawing room, the television lounge and the dining room. Each of them with double-height windows and a view to the coast. They held fat porcelain lamps on marble-topped tables, heavy wooden armchairs and sofas you could go to sea on. Gilt-framed portraits hung high on the walls. But it was the last room on the ground floor that made Murdoch whistle. When the cantilevered door closed behind them, he and Hughes were surrounded by three solid walls of books. Ceiling to floor of thickly bound hardbacks – whole series in deep greens or faded blues. The fourth wall was two more windows and that view again. Murdoch remembered he wasn't wearing shoes and wondered if it was too late to explain why.

'This is the library,' said Hughes

'No shit.'

Hughes blinked uncertainly. 'Ah, yes, indeed. And that's a straight line out there to the ocean beyond Taradale, although, thankfully, you can't see the dreadful place.'

Murdoch's phone was vibrating against his thigh again, the fourth time since his tour had started. He let it ring out. It would only be Davie wanting to talk about the woman who'd been asking for him and what it could mean and asking *how do you feel*. How he felt, right now, was good for once and he didn't want Davie spoiling it. He joined Hughes in squinting at the horizon.

'It's due east.' Hughes told him. 'On Midsummer's Day, some of the keener members have a little gathering on the veranda to see the sun pop up.'

'Nice.'

Murdoch had used the word repeatedly over the previous minutes, but it was nice; the nicest place he'd been in years and he decided there and then to join, no matter what it cost. His phone vibrated again and he remembered the word 'charming'; he should tell Hughes the room was charming. But it was too late, Hughes was beckoning him back to the hallway and upstairs, keen to show him the one- and two-bedroom suites available for members at an extra fee depending on notice and availability. He was talking faster now, they'd obviously run over time, walking on so Murdoch had to follow rather than stop and look around him. He was explaining the laundry service when Murdoch asked how much it was to join.

'Well, I can give you a schedule of fees,' said Hughes quietly, money on the same list as racquet stringing and overflow changing rooms. 'But, naturally, we'll have to go through the approval process first. Now I understand John and Gina Carrington are proposing you as a member—'

'Oh, no. Irene got it wrong, I meant to say. My name's Bill Murdoch. I don't actually know anyone here.'

Hughes blinked again. 'You're not Mr Branson?'

'No, I meant to—'

'And you're not the friend of a member?'

Murdoch's phone was buzzing in his pocket again.

'Not yet,' he said. 'But I can get along with anyone me, no problem.'

They were standing in a corridor that ran along the back of the house's second storey. The windows were smaller than downstairs, but Murdoch could see the sea clearly now, the distant roofs of the Taradale shops. He checked his phone quickly – seven missed calls from Davie – then looked up to find Hughes had changed shape. Shoulders back, he was standing to attention.

'I'm sure you knew I was under the impression you were someone else.'

'Someone else what wants to join.'

'Well, really.'

'But what's the problem. I can join, can't I?'

'To become a member of Huntingdon's Golf and Country Club you must be the friend of a member who proposes you.'

'Well, how do I become a friend of a member if you don't let me in? That doesn't make sense.'

'Maybe not to you.' Hughes turned and walked away so Murdoch had to follow him along the corridor. 'I'm very sorry, Mr ... but I'm a busy man, so I'm afraid I'll have to let you get on now.'

'Look, Hughes, you've met me. Can't you propose my membership?'

'Goodness, no. That wouldn't do at all.' The little man was almost running now, Murdoch struggling to keep up. 'As the manager here, I'm also the Membership Secretary. I couldn't possibly propose someone I've barely met.'

41

They reached a set of narrow stairs and Hughes scurried down them, afraid to be seen with this person he didn't know. Then the stairs turned and they were above the reception area, looking down on the stained carpet, where two red-faced men in tennis whites stood complaining loudly to Irene. Over Hughes' shoulder, Murdoch saw the receptionist glance up at the noise on the stairs above her. He couldn't tell if she was struggling to hold back tears or to control her temper.

'This gentleman says he's Mr Branson,' she said tight-mouthed to Hughes.

'And this is a Mr Murdoch, who is just leaving.'

Hughes reached the bottom of the stairs, turned with one hand hovering and seemed to struggle with the decision before deciding not to offer it to Murdoch to shake. Instead, he turned again and held his hand out to the real Mr Branson.

'You said you were Mr Branson,' said Irene to Murdoch sadly, as if unable to believe he had let her down. The two red-faced men turned their glares on him.

'No,' said Murdoch. 'I meant to tell you but—'

Ed Springer's silhouette appeared in the brightness of the front door. 'Bill! I've been looking for you everywhere. I thought you were going to stay in the car? What are you doing in here?'

Everyone was looking at Murdoch and for a second none of them said a thing. Then Irene coughed.

'I think you should go,' she said quietly. Like it was a nice try, but he'd failed.


Ed's nervous chatter – people at Huntingdon's were, like, totally uptight – ran out before he and Murdoch cleared the country club's grounds. They drove the remaining forty minutes in a stony silence until Murdoch, white-knuckled at the wheel, nearly missed the entrance to Taradale Tennis Club. He made the turn at the last minute, swearing brutally, making the Merc's tyres sing and answering another car's horns with a single finger and several single syllables. In the sudden stillness of the car park, neither he nor Ed seemed to know what to say. Looking past the tennis coach, through the thick concrete legs that held up the club house, Murdoch could see the

42

asphalt courts. He knew he should take a deep breath, force himself out and join everyone else Running Around and Having Fun.

'You go in,' he said. 'I don't feel like it no more. You all right to get home?'

'Yeah, sure.' Ed looked like he was struggling to hide his relief. 'You deffo don't want to give it a go?'

'No.'

'Well then, I'll see you when I get back, I guess.'

'Yep.'

'Good luck.'

Murdoch found a smile from somewhere. 'You too, mate. Keep out of trouble.'

An awkward grin and a slam of the door, white socks running up the dirty steps and the kid was gone forever. Murdoch stared into space for a few seconds – he could still change his mind – then swore out loud and put the car into gear. He was looking for a chance to pull into the sun-steeped traffic when he remembered the missed calls from Davie. He reversed back into the shade, litter exploding under his tyres, and dialled up his voicemail.

'I just saw Hattie in the chip shop.' Davie was trying to sound calm. 'The woman that was looking for you. She was back here this morning, asking after you by name again.'

8.

The Montauban chip shop was the kind of place you stepped into for a minute and stank of for the rest of the day. Murdoch wouldn't have felt guilty wearing his soiled tennis shoes in there. In the event – despite all his attempts to look like he couldn't care less – he forgot he was still in his socks until after the conversation with Hattie was done.

Every time Murdoch saw Hattie, he remembered she was a mother of five. She had a constantly harried look about her, dark hair frizzing in all directions and darkness under her eyes. Her vague smile was only ever there for a second before she remembered something else she was supposed to be doing. Every time he talked to her – let alone, her husband John – Murdoch wondered how her five kids had made it through alive.

43

'Ooh,' she said when saw him in the chip shop doorway. 'You been playing tennis?'

'What gave it away?'

'The tennis clothes you're wearing. And it's Tuesday. You always play tennis on a Tuesday and a Thursday. That's how I knew, see? That's what gave it away! Now, how are your ribs?'

There were days when Murdoch was tempted to get beaten up a different way, just so Hattie and John Thornton would ask after something else. Over a year now since he had been hurt and all they ever asked about was his bleeding ribs. He mumbled some nonsense about still not wanting to laugh too much and watched Hattie not get it as he approached the counter. She asked him if he was after some chips.

'Seems like the best place to get them,' he said.

This was a blatant lie. How Hattie Thornton's cooking oil could pollute clothes remotely when it was incapable of cooking chips all the way through was a famous local mystery. Hattie turned to the cold vat behind her and flicked it on before shaking a basket of potatoes that looked like they'd been chopped days before.

'So,' said Murdoch. 'What's new?'

Hattie was more than happy to tell him all the gossip he couldn't care less about. Planning approvals, updates on her children, a new chemist in town. Almost all of it was a repetition of what Murdoch had heard her husband discussing with Anne Lincoln the day before. Even after she'd handed over his chips, Hattie failed to remember she had any news for him.

'Here,' he said, 'I heard there was a woman asking after me. Is that right?'

'Oh. Yes.'

'Today was it?'

'Oh yes.'

'Say what she wanted at all?'

Hattie smiled at him and shrugged. Murdoch tried again.

'What did she look like?'

'Aw, you know. Normal.'

'Tall, short? Fat, thin? Old, young?'

'Just normal.'

'Good-looking?'

Hattie shrugged again. 'I told her that Bill Murdoch had never been here. Never lived here and not even ever visited.'

'Not that you'd never heard of me?'

'Same thing, isn't it? I'll tell you one thing for nothing, though, she did have a lovely fancy car. Very flat and curvy with a soft roof – a real sports car. John said it was top of the range. It was an Aldi, I think.'

'You mean an Audi?'

Hattie shrugged again, smiled again. She was as ditzy as – that's what all the locals said – but you couldn't help but love her. Murdoch thought he could manage it. Still, he resisted sighing or rolling his eyes and, instead, turned away to the door again. But then Hattie called after him to tell him he'd forgotten his chips *and* forgotten to pay, wasn't he a galah! So he had to turn back and hand over cash for all her precious information.

## 9.

That night he slept at Davie's on the strict instructions he *Didn't Want to Talk About It*. It was the mention of the fancy car that had shaken him. His old nemesis at the Club, Harris, had driven an Audi, not that that meant anything. It was a common enough car. But any fancy car was a worry. There were a few people who might innocently want to talk to him – the organised crime squad, the New South Wales witness protection programme – but it was unlikely any of them would ask for him by his real name. Even less likely that they'd drive an expensive car.

Murdoch had forgotten how Davie's tiny shack rattled with every breeze, and what a bleeding mess Davie lived in, but for once he was grateful to be there. Video games and violent movies and not punching Davie in the face were good distractions from his other thoughts. All the same, it was still early when he claimed a headache and said it was time for bed. No, he still didn't want to talk about it. Except he did, of course. Trouble was, Davie would interrupt and misunderstand, ask for irrelevant details and miss the point. Or he'd smile as pathetically as Hattie Thornton and say exactly the wrong thing so that they'd argue, leaving Murdoch feeling guilty and more alone than ever. So he said goodnight, took Valium for the second night in a row, and lay in what had once been his room, listening to the drip of the tap through the bathroom wall and ignoring the noises from outside.

The next day he was saved from time alone by a phone call from Suzie Bourne. The old lady informed him politely that she had thought about his proposal and believed they might be able to work together after all. Back home, it took him half an hour to convince himself no one had tampered with his car, then forty-five minutes of looping strange routes to believe he wasn't being followed. Somehow, he still arrived at the old lady's early.

Crosley, the closest 'city' – Australian word for big town – to Montauban, stood at the end of a huge ocean inlet called Broadwater, surrounded on three sides by dense bushland. Years before, the city had been malled to death by the opening of Bell Fair a few kilometres away. Now, its streets were lined with shops that either stood empty or were too low-end to pay the mall's rents. As a result, during the week Crosley was either deserted or occupied by scratchy types looking disappointed the meth clinic hadn't moved up to Bell Fair too.

Painful experience had taught Murdoch to be careful leaving a car in Crosley. But that had been down on the flat ground near the shore, in the mess of roads that curved round the three-sided football stadium, built – like everything else in town – to give a view of the water. Brionie Street, once he found it, felt like a different town. Tree-lined and quiet, it climbed the hillside north of the inlet, too steep, apparently, for the smackheads who roamed the town centre. All the same, when Murdoch found number thirty-four, he turned the Merc and parked it on the other side of the road. If Suzie Bourne's unit was at the front of the building, he could keep an eye on it from her window.

The unit block was made of pink bricks: some architect's attempt at softening the blow of its brutal shape, perhaps, or, who knew, maybe just a joke. Murdoch rang the right bell, then waited so long that his finger was hovering again when, without a voice from the intercom, the smoked-glass door into the block clicked discreetly open.

'Hello?' he said to the metal grille.

Nothing.

On the sixth floor, he found a featureless blue corridor stretching away in dim light. Halfway down it, the door with Suzie Bourne's apartment number on it was open. Inside was a hallway with a grey carpet, no pictures on the walls between the doors.

'Hello? Suzie? Miss Bourne?'

Murdoch called again louder in case any neighbours were listening. He knew how it looked: a bloke like him in a nice part of a nasty town, creeping into an old lady's place. Besides, there was something disturbing about the silence.

'Suzie?'

Her head popped out of doorway halfway along the hall.

'Oh, hi. Come on in. And don't leave the door open like that or we'll catch our deaths.'

Murdoch did as he was told and found her in her spartan kitchen preparing a tray: teapot, sugar bowl, milk jug, everything matching. Apart from the kettle, the only other thing on the work surface was a fruit bowl, empty but for one apple and one banana. Murdoch leant in the doorway.

'You shouldn't leave the door open like that,' he said. 'It's not safe. Someone'll come in here and do you over.'

Suzie didn't look up, just tutted as she clipped her heels across the lino, back and forth between the fridge and the milk jug, the pantry and the sugar bowl, the cutlery drawer and the tray.

'You sound like my daughter. But I won't have my home made into a prison. Crosley wasn't always a dump, you know; there are still some good people here and we won't be locked away.'

'Better a prison than a hospital,' said Murdoch. 'I've known blokes what wouldn't think twice about knocking you down for your cash. Imagine being stuck in bed with broken bones.'

'How intriguing. Did you ever do that?'

Now the old lady looked up, her pale blue eyes glinting above a sharp smile. Murdoch felt himself colour and coughed, stood up properly and offered to help with the tray. Suzie waved him away smirking and told him to go on through, she'd only be a minute.

The living room surprised him. Only the carpet – like something from a pub but nicer – and a dark wooden clock looked like they'd been chosen by a little old lady. Everything else was brightly modern. A cream sofa and two cream armchairs, a metal desk in the curve of the window, a moulded resin coffee table. On the far wall, steel shelves held books and photographs, an empty vase and the heavily ticking clock. Murdoch walked to the window, meaning to press his head against the glass and check on his car, but the view over Broadwater distracted him. The inlet stretched away to merge with the horizon; you'd think it was open ocean, if it wasn't so flat. He stared out at it, at the jet skis drawing fine lines on its surface, the boats bobbing around, the cars speeding around its edges. All those people with normal lives. He couldn't believe it was only days ago he'd been bored by the safety of Montauban. If this thing got sorted, if the woman looking for him turned out to be harmless, he'd take Davie up on all his stupid offers.

'Is it still there?'

The old lady seemed tinier than ever, struggling under the tray, but she shooed him away when he tried to help. Murdoch saw her notice a well-thumbed cruise brochure she'd left lying on the coffee table, then watched her place the tray carefully to hide it. That done, she sat with a sigh in one of the armchairs and looked up at him, still waiting for an answer.

'Is what still there, love?'

'Your fancy car. Not many places in Crosley you'd want to leave that standing around.'

He pictured her at the window where he was now, one hand on the glass as she watched him arrive. Wondered if anyone else had been watching and blinked the stupid idea away.

'Yeah, tell me about it,' he said with a sigh. 'Should be all right there, though, don't you reckon?'

Suzie shrugged her shoulders, like he'd asked if it was going to rain, and started pouring the tea. Her wrists were tiny and he wondered what it was like to be so vulnerable, then remembered that maybe he knew.

'Milk?'

'Ta.'

'Sugar?'

'Three, thanks.'

The same little dance as before.

'So, Bill. It seems we're going to write your story.'

He didn't want to talk about that yet. It felt safe in here; he wanted to sit and enjoy it. Wanted to talk about the weather, listen to the dull ticking of the clock, not talk about the dirty past that maybe he hadn't left behind.

Suzie Bourne was wearing a tweed skirt, like Miss Marple on the telly, and he could be the vicar, visiting with news. It occurred to him, the first time in years, he might never know what it was like to be old. The old lady asked him to sit down and he chose the sofa, sinking more deeply than he'd expected, staring at his knees and asked himself why the hell he was there. There had to be better things he should be doing: security, surveillance on his house, disappearing into the bush.

'Now,' said Suzie, passing him his tea, 'I thought we should sign a contract. You have, after all, offered me fifty thousand dollars to write your story. That's quite a commitment on both sides. It only makes sense to formalise it.'

She pulled herself to her feet and crossed to the desk, a hand on each piece of furniture on the way. There she found some stapled pages which, after slow progress back to her seat again, she handed over. Murdoch flipped through them, unable to focus.

'Bill?'

'Yeah, fine. Sorry, what?'

'You seem distracted.'

'No. No, this looks fine, really. Just got a bit on my mind, that's all.'

She looked genuinely concerned at that, frowning sympathetically. She was like a relic from an earlier age, he thought: a time when you could let strangers into your home and give them tea. He found himself staring at her, then looked down at his hands instead. When Suzie spoke again, he could hear she was cajoling him.

'You still want to do this. Trust me, you do.'

He could imagine her coaxing her sources, getting them to tell her stuff that was going to get them into trouble. But he didn't need convincing, not today. If anything ever happened to him, this story was all he had to leave behind, the only clue he'd ever been on the bleeding planet. He asked for a pen and, under the old lady's eager eyes, scribbled his signature under each of hers on the two copies of the contract, initialling, at her request, next to the payment amounts and dates. That done, he drank his tea as she hauled herself up and across to her desk again, swapping her copy of the contract for a lined notebook and pencil.

'So,' she said, back in her seat. 'We're here to write a story.'

'Nah, it's not a story, it's real.'

'Aha, yes. But we must write it as a story or it won't be interesting, it'll just be a boring list of events. Now, I suggest we start with your desire line. Tell me, what were you yearning for last year?'

Murdoch stared at her. 'You what?'

'Your desire line? What did you want above everything else?'

'I thought we was going to write about how I found that missing girl.'

'Yes, we will, we will. But unless the reader knows what you really wanted, it won't be very interesting, will it?' There was a grit to her, he remembered, a stubbornness he liked. If it wasn't for the money he'd offered, he wouldn't be here at all. Suzie smiled and started talking again. 'A story, after all, is only ever about what someone wants and whether they get it or not. So, during The Prison, we also need to establish your true desire. Something idiosyncratic would be good. Then along comes your sidekick and we see the tension between him and the detective – that's you. Oh, you do have a sidekick, don't you?'

'Yeah, no. Well, maybe ...'

'And then, of course, comes The Turnaround, which is normally the same as The Client. Someone mysterious and vaguely suspicious turns up.'

'Yeah, but it didn't happen like that.'

'Well, we must make it happen like that. That's how detective stories work—'

'Why can't you just write what happened?!'

He'd raised his voice at her again. Brought the dirty worries of his life into this lovely room, just like he'd walked the dog shit into Huntingdon's. Was there nowhere he couldn't ruin? He studied his fingernails and the black beneath them, then swore, apologised, put his cup and saucer back on the table and got up to check on his car again. It was still there, alone. He apologised again, not wanting to turn around, to see the look on her face that meant he had to leave. Suzie's voice was even gentler than before.

'More tea?'

'You what?'

'Would you like more tea? And a biscuit, perhaps?'

People really lived like this. Tea trays and tiny gold watches and any unpleasantness brushed away with kindness. Or maybe she was just smarter than him. He crossed the room, gave himself to the sofa again and reached forward to pass her his cup.

'You see,' she said, performing the little ritual of tea and milk and a gingernut on the saucer, 'stories are like music. You can compose what you want, but there are still rules that need to be followed. Once you learn the rules, you can play around with them, do whatever you want, but you have to learn them first. You're not convinced?'

Murdoch realised he was scowling, but not because he disagreed with her. Still now – years after getting out of prison – he hated discovering all the things that no one had bothered to tell him about. Each one was a little sting, a pain he never got used to.

'I've read loads of stories,' he said, taking his cup and trying not to sound annoyed. 'No one told me about no rules.'

'Well, most people don't know about them. It's the same with music. Most people, the vast majority, in fact, listen to music without knowing how it works and, of course, that's absolutely fine. But imagine how much more you'd enjoy music if you did know how it works! And the same is true with stories. Imagine if you could see all the building blocks that are in every story and appreciate how they're being played around with every time you read. It's not just books, it's films, advertisements, nature documentaries, the television news. There's an art to telling everything as if it's a story.'

There was an edge to her eagerness. A desperate need for him to understand – or maybe just a fear he'd change his mind. Their contract, he knew, wasn't worth a thing without witnesses for the signatures. But it wasn't just that. He thought she really did want him to understand. And wasn't that what he wanted too? To know stuff so that next time he wouldn't feel so stupid.

'Listen,' he said, 'I'll be honest, I don't really get it. But I trust you, right? So you tell me how it works and what you want to hear about, and I'll try and tell you. Answer your questions, like what you want.'

'Great,' she said, with obvious relief. 'Let's go. Now, why don't we start with The Turnaround? That might be easiest. Tell me about the event that kicked this whole story off.'

Murdoch took a deep breath, closed his eyes and started telling her about the events of the previous year. Hearing her pencil scratching at her notepad, he opened his eyes and saw she was drawing strange lines, nothing like writing, her fingers showing a nimbleness that mocked her legs.

'Shorthand,' she said, seeing him stare. 'Such an underrated skill.'

And once again he felt the sting. Yet another thing no one had told him about.

# The Turnaround

Halfway back to Montauban, Davie phoned. Murdoch was already talked out for the day, but he took the call. Relating the events of the previous year had calmed him, reassured him of everything he'd already survived. And, much as he hated to admit it, it had reminded him how much he owed Davie.

'Davie, whassup?'

'Bill, where have you been? Are you all right?' Davie sounded excited. Someone had probably recognised him.

'I'm fine, mate. You?'

'You're not driving, are you, Bill?'

'Why?'

'I just want to make sure you've pulled over before I go on. Can you pull over?'

Murdoch rolled his eyes and told Davie he was parked and having a fag. As if to help the lie, he leant forward and pushed the cigarette lighter in. 'So, mate, what's happening?'

'Well, I just got back from Kildare about ten minutes ago and I bumped into Orange. You know, the stoner? Anyway, guess what? He said a woman had been asking after you, he heard it from his boys. Apparently, she was asking the local kids if they knew a Bill Murdoch. Now Orange knows from Anne Lincoln we're supposed to say we've never heard of you, but his kids don't know that, or maybe they've forgotten, I don't know. Anyway, one of them told her about you. When Orange told me, I acted cool, didn't make anything of it, just asked what she was like. Tall and pretty, apparently. Female, early thirties, Caucasian—'

'Jesus, Davie, it's not a fucking cop show. What else?'

'I don't know. You said I should call you—'

'What else, Davie? Tell me everything.'

Murdoch accelerated as the traffic lights ahead of him turned amber. He knew from experience that if he put his foot down, he'd get through the next set too.

'Well now, Bill, don't get upset, he's only a kid. But Orange's little boy, Max or Ty, I always get them mixed up, the younger one. Anyway, he's little, right? It's not his fault.'

'What's not his bleeding fault?'

'He told her where you live.'

Murdoch took a deep breath. 'When was this?'

'Well, they told me about ten minutes ago, and they said it was not long before that. Anyway, I just drove past. Subtly, don't worry. She's still there, outside your house. Leaning against her car, but I didn't see her face. The car's black, but I couldn't see what type.'

The cigarette lighter popped out and Murdoch flinched in his seat. He accelerated again as, just ahead of him, the next set of lights turned red.

'Thanks,' he said.

'That's it?'

'Yeah, thanks. Don't drive by again.'

'Are you sure you're not driving?'

Murdoch hung up and swung right too fast onto the Crown Road. Took four deep breaths, told himself to slow down and drove home like he was trying to kill himself.

She wasn't there. An Audi TT was parked in his driveway with its roof down, its sleek black curves ready to pounce, but when Murdoch rolled slowly past, squinting hard at his mirrors rather than directly at the driveway, he could see there was no one near it. Fifty metres further on, around the curve and out of sight of his place, he parked, got out and listened carefully. Nothing. No footsteps, no engine starting up, no carefully shouted orders. Just the gum trees rustling overhead and, in the distance, a dog somewhere. He walked back to the first house of the five on the lagoon, four doors along from his own. The guy who lived here, Dick or Dennis or Desmond, would be at work, so Murdoch walked confidently up the path and, once out of sight of his own house again, kicked the front door to mimic the sound of it closing. He waited a minute – still nothing – then found the path that ran along the side of the house and down the slope towards the water's edge. All five houses on this side of the street backed onto the water, their gardens running into each other: 'gardens' being Murdoch's English word for half-cleared bush gone wild again. His own plot was the only one ever cared for – the previous owner had been a keen gardener – and now Murdoch was able to approach it hidden by undergrowth.

Progress was noisy, at least to his ears. Every step tore a twig or rustled leaves, crackled brittle grasses or snapped needles from the scrappy casuarinas. He forced himself on and, sooner than he'd expected, found himself looking up at his home, staring at the windows for a good three minutes until he realised there was no way of telling if someone was in there or not. An insect landed on his mouth and he bit hard and spat it out, sickened to be looking at his own house like this, crouched and sweating in the undergrowth. Maybe there was an innocent explanation. Why shouldn't a stranger ask around for a man who most people thought was dead? Refuse to take no for an answer; ask kids because kids always forget to lie? Two lorikeets whooping low through the trees made him jump and swear silently to himself, crouching even closer to the ground. Then he took another step forward and saw her.

She was standing on his patio smoking. A tall woman or maybe that was just the angle – the ground was steep at this point and she was five metres above him. Wearing pale green, a skirt and a matching jacket, huge sunglasses that hid half her face. The other half wasn't bad at all. Full lips, cheekbones, a dainty little nose, all of it framed by hair someone had spent time and money on. He looked past her, trying to see if his back doors were broken, if this was the boss on a break while the heavies rummaged through the house, but it was impossible to know. All he could see was the woman as she turned and walked a few steps away from him. He stood and leaned himself along the back of a tree, a wide and delicate web obscuring his view. Reaching out and ripping it down, he watched the woman turn back, then turn away again, pacing back and forth until, suddenly, she seemed to make a decision. She walked over to his ironwork patio set, stubbed her cigarette hard into the ashtray on the table, pulled a tissue from her pocket and took off her jacket to hang it on the back of a chair. Then she walked down the steps to the lower half of the garden until she was level with him, no more than ten metres away, her pale silk top catching the light. If she had a weapon she'd left it up near the house. Murdoch watched the woman carefully as she looked in each direction, pulled up her skirt, pulled down her knickers and squatted close to his retaining wall. There were no lorikeets overhead now and even the breeze held its breath so the only sound he heard was the patter of her urine hitting his lawn.

He'd wanted to say something cool like, 'Make yourself at home,' or 'Don't mind me,' and take advantage of her embarrassment, but the woman heard him coming through the trees and screamed, falling to one side in a mess of underwear and shoes. He hadn't figured on a scream but, without time to think, ran up to the patio all the same. There was no gun in her jacket or on the table, the back doors to his house were all secure. No one else in sight and no sign of anyone out of sight either. Within a minute, he was back beside her on the lawn. Enough time for her to have pulled up her underwear and sorted out the hem of her skirt, but no more than that. She was still struggling to her feet and gave another half-yell, a loud 'Oh!' when she saw him. But when she pulled off her sunglasses, there was no fear in her big brown eyes.

'What the hell do you think you're doing?' she said. 'You disgusting—'

'What the hell are you doing pissing in my garden?'

'Your garden? Oh. Oh no!'

Now she was embarrassed. She crumpled: a flower dying in fast-forward. She really was tall, especially in those shoes, but shame bent and curved her, cringed her into elbows and wrists: a beggar in designer heels. She blushed and garbled apologies, explained in three different ways how long she'd been waiting, then slipped in the wet puddle at her feet, caught herself on the low wall and started all over again. Apology, explanation, apology again; half her face hidden by her repositioned sunglasses, the rest by fallen hair.

'You've cut yourself,' he said.

The nasty scratch from the wall was the last straw. She could stand everything but the moist red line running down her arm. Through sudden tears she apologised for crying, wiping her face with the back of her wrists – he could see her conscious she hadn't washed her hands – and then, suddenly, falling silent, gathering herself together again with a slow deep breath.

'I'm going to say this for the last time,' her arm held out so the blood didn't drip on her expensive skirt. 'I'm very sorry. And very embarrassed.'

'That's all right, love. The lawn needed a water anyway.' He would have smiled but he knew women liked him better straight-faced. 'So, then. Who the hell are you?'

## 11

He didn't want her in the house. He'd made up his mind she wasn't a pro, at least not the kind the Club would use, but there was something not right about her, something familiar. He left her on the patio at the ironwork table, returning a minute later with his first aid kit, scissors removed. He started an apology for frightening her, but she refused to have it – it was all her fault – and his unfinished words drifted off with the breeze. She gave him a smile and complimented him on his garden, ignoring the scrappy red robin and saying how she liked the way the lawn ran into the lake. He didn't tell her it was a lagoon. Instead, he let her talk, observing her closely, the breeze raising goosebumps on her pale arms, her skirt whispering silkily whenever she moved. He knew now he'd seen her before, but knew equally he couldn't have forgotten her. Her skin alone was like ... he didn't know what. Something perfect. He remembered her scratch and pushed the first aid kit towards her, watching her struggle for a while before sliding it back across the table.

'It's too close to my wrist,' she said. 'Sorry.'

So it was him who had to clean the wound, choose and unwrap the plasters. It occurred to him that he hadn't touched a woman's skin since that night with Natalie Conquest over a year earlier. Could that really be true? He moved the ashtray out of the woman's reach like it was in his way. She'd told him her name, nothing else, but even that bothered him.

'Amanda Hoxton,' he said, close over her arm with another Band-Aid. 'And what does Amanda Hoxton in her fancy black Audi TT want with me?'

He looked up to find her smiling. A tiny scar interrupted the outline of her full top lip.

'The car is a tax dodge,' she said. 'Don't be fooled by appearances.'

When he didn't respond to that, she smiled again, showing him her beautiful teeth this time.

'You're an intriguing man. Do you know that?'

He pressed the sticking plaster against her soft flesh and felt himself grinning.

'You're the second woman today what's told me that. What is it, d'you reckon, what makes me so intriguing?'

'Oh a few things. My husband was in our place up here early last year when you first arrived. Talk of the town you were, and this is a little town that likes to talk. The cavalry had arrived; a private detective named Bill Murdoch. You were going to find that poor girl. And now, here I am, not much more than a year later, and here are *you* are living in that poor girl's house.'

Relief settled on him like a warm blanket. He shrugged it off, sat up and looked at her carefully.

'Bought it off her family, didn't I? What's so intriguing about that?'

'Oh, that's not the intriguing part. The intriguing part is why it was so difficult for my sister-in-law and me to find you. The lady who runs the general store said she'd never heard of you, she was quite adamant about it, although in my experience she knows everything that happens in Montauban. The woman in the chip shop clearly knew your name but said you'd never been near here. The lady who runs the café virtually ran away at the mention of you.'

'But you kept on asking.'

'Most people are terrible liars. There's something reassuring in that, don't you think? Listen, I don't mean to be rude, but you wouldn't give a girl a glass of water, would you?'

Like she'd popped round for a cup of tea and he'd forgotten to put the kettle on. He thought of Suzie Bourne and her tray of nice things and wished he had one the same: something impressive for an unexpected guest. All he had were badly chipped mugs: the house had come with furniture but little more than that. He offered tea all the same, but Amanda Hoxton just smiled and said water was fine, thank you.

Pretending to let the tap run, he stared at her from the kitchen window as she struggled into her jacket and rearranged herself nicely on the ironwork chair. No way he'd ever met a woman as classy as that. He remembered there was a bottle of champagne in the fridge and imagined putting it in an ice bucket and taking out his best glasses. He could sit on his patio with this fancy woman and her thick brown hair and watch the sun go down. Except something didn't add up.

'I recognise you,' he told her from the doorway. 'I've seen you before.'

'You say that like it's a bad thing.'

'Mostly is, in my experience. You was gonna to tell me why you're here.'

She pulled a pack of Cartier's from her jacket pocket and held them up. 'Don't mind, do you?'

'Be my guest.'

He put the glass of water in front of her, sat opposite and let her work out where to begin.

'My husband's name is James Harte,' she said, after a few pulls on her slim cigarette, a few breaths of smoke into the air between them. 'You may have heard of him? We have a publicity agency down in Sydney. Last year …'

She raised her perfect eyebrows and stared at him with round eyes. Murdoch realised he'd held up a hand.

'Sorry,' he said. 'Go on, love.'

'Last year—'

'You're Amanda Hoxton Harte.'

She grimaced and blew a plume of smoke towards the lawn, taking a moment to watch it disappear.

'Actually, I'm Amanda Hoxton and my husband is James Harte. The only Hoxton Harte is the agency. You obviously read the gossip magazines. Says a lot, don't you think, that they can't even get my name right?'

She reassembled her smile and gave it up to him. If she was a little annoyed, it wasn't his fault.

'You was at the Formula 1 down in Melbourne,' he said. 'Your brother is Angus Hoxton, that Bachelor of the Year bloke.'

She laughed aloud and held his eye again, happily back in control. 'Oh my God, he'd love you for knowing that. Tell me, what else do you know about us?'

'You're a Pom, like me.'

'Now you're guessing because of my accent. Actually, my parents are British, but I grew up here. What about my husband?'

Her smile encouraged him to give it another go. It was like a quiz show, except you didn't have to wait for the repeats before you knew the answers.

'He's in prison,' he said slowly.

'Very good. Why?'

'Fraud?'

'You're guessing again.' She looked relieved. 'You obviously weren't reading the press nine months ago.'

Nor was she or she'd have thought Bill Murdoch was dead.

'Carry on,' he said. 'Tell me all about the Hoxtons and the Hartes.'

Something shifted in the temperature between them then. She crossed her silky legs and sat back in her chair. Watched him light up his cigarette and, only then, once she had his full attention, started to tell her story. As she spoke, the day died around them, the lagoon changing from blue to red, then to a glistening and oily black.

# The Plan

*'It's very important the reader understands what the main character is planning to do,' Suzie told Murdoch that day in her living room. 'And we need to understand it on every level. Only then can we understand why the character – that's you, Bill – might be less than completely frank with the people around him. And, far more importantly, that way we can enjoy watching the plan go horribly wrong every single step of the way.'*

## 12.

Murdoch slept better than he had all week, the innocent explanation far more innocent than he could have hoped for. The relief he had resisted on the patio dragged him down beyond dreams and gave him long hours of uninterrupted rest. The next morning, he felt like he did after an illness: so good it was almost worth having been ill in the first place. He got up early and rushed out to share the good news.

Halfway up Montauban Road, the hill that ran out of town, were turnings to the left and right. The one on the left was La Mer Street, a row of mismatched houses that looked out over the houses behind the shops to stare at the beach and the ocean. Murdoch walked up, enjoying the late spring air, listening to the raucous birds and counting off the trees whose names he knew. Squiggly gum, stringy bark, iron bark. The front door to number twenty-five was open so he curled his magazine into a roll, walked past the *'Open for Viewing'* sign and padded quietly inside. Beyond the short hallway, he found a large empty room, a huge blue view filling the window in the opposite wall, tankers tiny on the horizon. To his left there was a kitchen, bare and white but for some glossy brochures on the counter; to his right, carpeted stairs ran down to the bedrooms further down the hill. Murdoch stood and waited, the magazine tight in his hand, and after thirty seconds he heard footsteps below. Then he waited some more and heard them start up the stairs. Stepping backwards into the kitchen, he stood out of sight in the hole left for a fridge, let Davie get halfway across the carpet, then jumped out and said 'Boo!', tapping Davie lightly on the head with the rolled magazine. Davie yelled and threw glass cleaner, cloth and newspapers into the air between them.

'Oh, very funny, Bill. Ha, ha. Hilarious.'

Murdoch laughed and watched Davie squat down to gather the terrified newspapers back together. Then he remembered why he was there.

'Oh mate,' he said. 'That was stupid. I'm sorry … here, let me get that.'

He joined Davie down on the carpet just as Davie finished tidying up. They stood at the same time, awkwardly avoiding each other. Davie's tie was flipped backwards over his shoulder.

'You apologised,' he said, still red in the face and scowling.

'You what?'

'I've never heard you apologise before.'

'Bollocks.'

'First time for everything, I suppose. What do you want?'

Noticing his tie, Davie sighed and pulled it forwards, pushing past Murdoch to hide the cleaning things in a cupboard in the empty kitchen. Then he touched the brochures on the counter softly, like that might improve their fan across the Caesarstone.

'Who says I want anything?'

'I do.' Davie scowled at him again. 'Last time I heard from you properly, you were on your way to see who that woman was. Remember? The woman *I* told you about? Then it's radio silence apart from a text to say stop calling you. And now you're here, so you obviously want something. And you apologised, so you definitely want something. By the way, I'm expecting some interested parties, so if you could make it quick.'

Murdoch turned to hide his smile, walked across to the huge window and told Davie the property had a nice view. He wasn't lying. Below him, reds and oranges were scattered through the trees that hid the shops. There were soft flowers on the gums and cockatoos flashed white between them. The beach was tiny and yellow, the surf rearing up and dumping out of sync with its noise. Beyond, the ocean was endless. Davie fussed around the kitchen, then up and down the empty hall, quiet minutes before he joined Murdoch at the window.

'It's only a nice view if there's someone to look at it,' he said bitterly. 'Six parties said they'd be here, which normally means three. I've been here an hour and all I get is you.'

'You been marketing it much?'

'Well, I was supposed to, but … you know, so boring.'

'Sorry I made you jump.'

'Crikey, Bill, that's the second apology in five minutes. You really do want something.'

'Nah, I wanna tell you something. About that woman what was looking for me. It's exciting.'

He watched Davie try to resist. Watched him straighten his tie again, run his hands through his hair, sigh deeply and look out the window. It lasted less than a minute.

'So who is she then?'

'Well, it's good news. Turns out she's nothing to do with my old life. In fact, she wants to hire us. As detectives I mean.'

Davie's head swung round, a huge grin lighting his face, all thoughts of shitting his pants and no-shows forgotten. He had, Murdoch hated to admit, been instrumental in helping solve the case of Georgie Walker. There had been a time shortly afterwards when Davie had entertained thoughts of *Murdoch & Simms, Detection Services*. He probably still had the business cards.

'No way!' he said now. 'You're kidding? How did she hear about us?'

'Her and her old man've got a place up here. They heard about me – I mean, us – looking for Georgie. Then they had their own mess to deal with, so they didn't hear how I ended up.'

'What's her name?'

Murdoch snorted and shook his head. 'Bleeding typical, that, innit? Anywhere else it'd be "What's the case?" Around here it's, "What's her name?" Cos you probably went to school with her and you can tell me what happened already.'

'So what is her name?'

Murdoch unrolled the old copy of *Starstrike!* and showed Davie photographs from the Formula 1. A red carpet struggling against the curl of the paper, smiles flashed over full-length dresses.

'Which one?'

'Which one?! You got many beautiful celebrities with places up here?'

Davie squinted at the pages again. 'These aren't celebrities, Bill, they're just people who've got themselves in front of a camera. Oh, look! This woman here, I know her. I was at school with her husband. And her brother too, I think? Good-looking girl, I can never remember her name. Amanda something.'

Murdoch snatched back the magazine, muttering obscenities as he rolled it tight again, wishing he'd hit Davie with it harder.

They put the *'Open for Viewing'* signs into the boot of Davie's horrible little car and locked themselves inside the house, the balcony doors open so Murdoch could smoke while they sat on the sunlit carpet, backs to the bare walls. Davie was beside himself.

'So the woman outside your house was Amanda Hoxton! She was always gorgeous, I remember. And, that's right, she married James Harte, the dil. He was in the same year as me at Knox. And her brother, Andrew.'

'Angus.'

'Angus, that's right. Funny, I could never work them out as mates. James was really smart, one of those guys who was always going to make a million before he was thirty. Obsessed with money, like pretty much everyone else at Knox.'

'Apart from you.'

'Yes, apart from me. Money's not important, I keep telling you, Bill. You know it's been proven to have no relationship whatsoever to happiness?'

'You was talking about Angus Hoxton.'

'Oh yeah. Well, Angus was all right, but he wasn't really on James's level. Girls loved him though. Jeez. I think the two guys went into business together. Advertising or consultancy or something.'

'Public relations.'

'PR! What a load of rubbish, typical of that whole crowd, I reckon. They always were up their own backsides. Never once spoke to me at school if they could help it.'

Murdoch managed not to comment on that. Instead he leant to one side and dug a crumpled page from his pocket, unfolding it and then tilting it into the sunlight.

'You finished? Right, listen to this. Last year the Hoxton Harte Agency was doing well, doubling revenues every six months, four-hundred-odd employees and lots of fancy clients. Trouble is, James Harte is banging his secretary—'

'Yes, I read about it! Pretty girl, I remember her name. Don't tell me, don't tell me—'

'Charlie Holland, thirty-three years old, from Ballarat. Nice girl, or a bit of a gold-digger, depending on who you talk to. That's what Amanda says. Anyway, Ms Holland joined Hoxton Harte six years ago when it first started up. Started doing overtime on James Harte soon after that. Then, in February, she and the boss are having a romantic little cruise around the harbour – on his forty-foot yacht, no less – during a rainstorm. Which is a bit weird, if you ask me. Anyway, accounts vary as to what happened next. The accused states he dropped Ms Holland off at Rose Bay wharf, like he normally did. The police contest he took her back to his mooring at Vaucluse Bay, where he caused her injuries leading to her death. Either way, the remains of the deceased are found four days later floating within sight of Harte's vessel. What?'

Davie had a stupid grin on his face.

'You sound like a policeman' he said. 'Like you're in court.'

'You want a smack in the mouth? Where was I? Oh yeah, so Charlie Holland's body, what's left of it, is found bumping against the rocks off ...' Murdoch squinted at the paper '... Bottle and Glass Point. Only a few hundred metres from where Harte moors his yacht. Charlie's body's a mess, so much so they struggle to identify her at first. Sharks have taken her legs off. Don't know why they didn't go for the rest—'

'Sharks don't like human flesh.'

'You what?'

'They don't like the taste of it. Once they've ripped a bit off, they generally spit it out again.'

'Really? That must be very reassuring when you're bobbing around out there with your legs in the water. Anyway, listen, will you? Sharks have taken Charlie's legs off and the fishies have had a good nibble at everything else, but it's clear her head's been smashed in and it's that what's killed her. Dead before she hit the water – they can tell apparently. Her personal belongings, phone etcetera, never recovered. According to a colleague of Charlie's ...' Murdoch squinted at the paper again, struggling with his own handwriting. '... a Jennifer Bailey, Charlie was blackmailing Harte, so the police figure he's got motive for wanting her dead. They reckon he lured Charlie out on his boat, screwed her, knocked her on the head and chucked her overboard.'

'Bastard.'

'Client.'

'What?!'

'James Harte is our client, Davie. Right now, he's sitting in the clink waiting for his trial to come up. He'd probably be out on bail – God knows, he can afford it – 'cept years back, him and his business partner, Angus Hoxton, got into a blue with some lads at a twenty-first birthday party. Next thing, they're both up on an ABH charge, and the court gives them bail. Trouble is, young guns that they was, they couldn't resist going on a little holiday overseas. Skiing in Japan or something. They was lucky not to get thrown inside as soon as they got back. Not so lucky for Harte now, though, cos the judge reckons he's a flight risk and ...' Murdoch checked the paper again, '... made some comment about suspecting Harte might try and influence witnesses too. Don't know where he got that from. Anyway, the upshot is Harte's stuck inside, can't come along himself, so he sends his wife to find us instead. Which, good girl, she does. "A marriage takes what a marriage takes," she says. That's what she talks like – dead posh.'

'Still a looker?'

'Yeah, gorgeous – and dead classy to boot. Anyway, she tells me her old man admits the affair but denies the blackmail and the murder. Trouble is, it's not a good look, is it? Harte was the last one what saw Charlie Holland alive, having just rogered her and, next thing, the half of her they can find is bobbing up and down within sight of his boat in Vaucluse Bay. Best odds his lawyers can give him is fifty-fifty and, when they make noises about him pleading guilty to get ten per cent off the sentence, he sacks 'em. What means, there Harte is now – new lawyers but no new evidence; the cops, no doubt, running around to strengthen the DPP's case; bail refused and him with a snowflake's chance in hell of getting off. Desperate times and Harte wants a private detective to find out something new sharpish. Trial's coming up in February, so we've got about three months.'

Davie stared at him open-mouthed: a kid on his way to Disneyland. 'Crikey, this is really happening, isn't it? We're like, real private detectives. Where do we even start?'

'Easy. See, Harte reckons he's been framed by someone what knows him well enough to be sure him and Charlie was out on the yacht that night. So he wants us to hang out with his close mates, get to know them and stuff.'

Sniff around till we find something he can use. Who knows, we might even get to prove who done it? None of them'll know we're on the case; no one but his wife.'

'Unbelievable.' Davie readjusted himself on the carpet, pulling his legs out of the sun. 'I mean, where do these guys find them? Politicians and businessmen, they do all this dirty stuff and their wives just stick up for them, I never get it.'

'Yeah, except in this case, the wife don't think he did it.'

'Amanda doesn't think Harte was rooting Cheryl Holland?'

'She knows he was screwing *Charlie* Holland, Davie, but she's dead set he didn't kill her. All the evidence against him is circumstantial. There's no forensics on the boat to suggest he did her in there. Mind you, if you ask me, if Harte had knocked Charlie down anywhere what wasn't under cover, three days of Sydney rain would have cleared evidence of that away better than he could have done. But the point is, Amanda don't reckon he done it and she don't want him spending the rest of his life in prison for it neither. So ... what now?'

Davie was looking at him sideways, blue eyes narrowed in suspicion. 'Why are you interested, Bill?'

'Why shouldn't I be interested?'

'Because last time we spoke about doing any more detective work, you said you'd rather stick pins in your eyes. "Never again," you said.'

'It doesn't matter what I said, you muppet. Just shut up and listen, will you. I'm trying to ask you something.'

'Oh well, that makes perfect sense, doesn't it?' Davie struggled with his tie until it came off in his hand. 'I said it when you came in, I knew you wanted something. Come on, out with it.'

Murdoch examined his knuckles and listened to a car making its way up the hill out of town. Change of tack.

'What I want to ask you is, will you help me? Like before, when I ... when *we* was looking for Georgie Walker. Will you take on the case with me?'

'Oh. Oh, well ...' Davie seemed to have forgotten he'd already agreed and pretended to think it over. 'So we have to infiltrate that crowd?'

'One of us does. Best if the other one remains hidden, gives us more options. One of us hangs out with Amanda and all Harte's friends, the other one does all the exciting bits.'

Davie grimaced and sucked air through his teeth. 'Oofee, I'm not sure. I remember James and Angus and their friends at school. They're all so competitive. I think James's sister was the only person who ever beat him at anything. And they were all absolute snobs. You know Hoxton Harte has a corporate account over at that hideous Huntingdon's place? It's that kind of crowd.'

'Yeah, Amanda mentioned that.'

'It's all fancy clothes and who's got the biggest car and all that rubbish.'

Murdoch nodded thoughtfully. 'Well,' he said, 'how would it be if I did that bit? If there's any infiltering needed, I'll do it. I'll hang out with the nobs and you can handle the research and, you know, the other stuff.'

Davie looked at him again with narrow eyes.

'How does that make sense? Surely it should be the other way round? I was the one at school with James Harte. I should probably be the one to hang out with his friends.'

'Really? And why's that, then? After you just said you don't wanna do it? Why shouldn't I go to the fancy parties and pretend to be an old mate of his?' They both knew the answer to that one, but Davie obviously wasn't feeling brave. Murdoch went on. 'Amanda Hoxton seems all right with me doing that and you doing the rest. She remembers you, by the way, and says her hubby will do too. And besides, you're not exactly free during the day, are you? So I hobnob with them lot and you do the other stuff. It'll fit in better with your day job, won't it?'

Davie looked despondently around the room, like he was only now remembering he was still an estate agent.

'Besides,' said Murdoch, 'there might be some extra expenses involved what we can't charge back. New clothes and shit. I don't mind covering them if I'm the one what gets to go to the parties. To investigate, I mean.'

'Well, if you think you can pull it off.' Davie looked relieved and Murdoch remembered Ed, desperate to get out of the car at Taradale Tennis Club. 'I certainly don't want to do it, Bill.'

'And I do. So, deal?'

'Yeah, OK. Deal.'

Davie put out his hand and Murdoch leaned over and shook it. So it was too late when Davie thought to ask, 'What do you mean, the other stuff?'

# The Client

## 13.

A southerly came up overnight and the temperature dropped five degrees. The following days brought rain and wind with a cruel sense of humour. Trees were down, roads were flooded, warnings were of worse to come. Davie, whistling tunelessly and jabbing between stations to avoid the news, told himself the foul weather was a good thing. On any other day it would have kept him indoors, bored and lonely and deprived of his chances to forget that. And if the sun had been shining, the sky blue and the beach beckoning, he'd have been sour at this long drive south, the traffic clogging and clotting all the way, the surf only glimpsed in the distance.

Yeah, right. This journey was the most exciting thing that had happened to him in months. Not that he minded his day job, not in theory. He knew he had things sweet: enough houses in Montie selling themselves to keep his area manager from visiting too often. He managed to surf most days there was surf to be out on, opening the office late and leaving it early, chucking an easy sickie on days like today. Still, the fact he had to work at all annoyed him. What he didn't understand was why it didn't annoy everyone else. How come the rest of the world was happy going to work five days a week? How come they had already had enough fresh air to last them forever, didn't mind spending the best years of their lives shut indoors? Sometimes he wondered if he had a clarity no one else shared, like the sighted man in the story who struggled in the kingdom of the blind. He couldn't imagine how much money he'd ever have to earn to make it worth going to work in the dark and then leaving in the dark again, seeing each unique day pass unexplored beyond a pane of glass. He touched the rabbit's foot hanging from his rear-view mirror and thanked his lucky stars.

It was raining upwards by the time he arrived at Longreach and, by the time he'd found the right car park and then the right entrance to the right building, he was soaked. 'Terrible weather!' he said cheerily to the uniforms who greeted him and sent him down one corridor after another. None of them responded.

The waiting room he was looking for stank of disinfectant, its floor still sticky from a recent clean. The room was low-ceilinged and about ten metres long, rows of blue plastic chairs attached back-to-back, the only light from fluorescents so yellow they made the dozen or so people waiting there look jaundiced. Or maybe the people were all jaundiced; it wouldn't have surprised him, none of them looked particularly well. Most of the people waiting were overweight or painfully thin, a white woman sitting nearest him clearly anorexic, an unshaven man further away at least five times her weight. Everyone looked up and stared at him when he pushed through the swing doors into the room. Not in a good way; not because they recognised him, or thought they recognised him but couldn't remember why. Just because he was there.

Years before, Davie had spent a few months on the dole, turning up once a fortnight to sign his name and scurry away again as quickly as he could. He'd thought that was bad – an office that defined you like no job ever could – but this place was much, much worse. Whatever unemployment might threaten to do to you, here it had already happened. He smiled at the room at large, pushed his wet hair out of his face and loped up to the desk that filled the far wall; heavy-duty plastic under heavier-duty glass, everything metal-sealed at the edges. Someone had written *'One at a "Time"'* in angry biro on lined paper and taped it to the counter.

'Morning,' said Davie.

'Name?'

The man behind the glass was barrel-chested and bearded, in glasses so thick and dirty Davie could barely see his eyes. The sleeves of his grey jumper were rolled up to reveal hair, tattoos and a surprisingly delicate watch.

'Oh. Yeah, hi. My name's Davie Simms and—'

'ID?'

At the other end of the desk, a metal chute opened with a clunk that made Davie jump and he thought he heard someone snicker behind him. He turned around to check, but there was only a small Aboriginal woman who'd followed him up to the counter. Everyone else in the room was immersed in their phones, those wearing headphones nodding to different rhythms. Davie walked over and dropped his driving licence into the chute.

'You're not in till eleven thirty,' said the man behind the glass. 'We'll call you once. You miss that call, you're not going in. You want to talk on your phone, you take it out to the corridor. Next.'

'What about my driving licence?'

'You get it at the end, moron,' said the Aboriginal woman, pushing past him. Then to the guard she said, 'Gaskell, Elizabeth.'

It wasn't the kind of waiting room to have magazines. There was a badly folded newspaper on one of the seats, but, on closer inspection, Davie decided not to touch it. He didn't want to sit down either, his wet trousers sticking to his thighs. Instead he walked slowly to the noticeboard and pretended to read the leaflets from support groups and counselling services, ignoring the smell of disinfectant from the floor. After a while, the leaflets were strangely comforting. Davie might be grateful for having avoided salary slavery, but he spent so much time dealing with people buying houses he could never afford, he'd got used to the idea he was at the bottom of a ladder. But just now, for the first time in years, he'd not had the worst car in the car park. And reading the suicide prevention literature and the homelessness education brochures made him remember he wasn't anywhere near the bottom.

Above the noticeboard, out of reach of anyone wanting to tamper with its tock-tock-tock, was a clock that had once been modern, black hands behind dirty glass. Twenty past eleven. Ten more minutes and he'd never need to come here again. Then his phone rang, the theme from *Star Wars* on full volume so that everyone in the waiting room looked up at him again. Halfway out to the corridor he stopped too soon to answer the call and the swinging waiting room doors smacked him on the back and shoulders, so that the end of 'Hello Hannah' came out as an exclamation.

'Hello? Davie is that you? What are you doing?'

'Nothing, sorry. How are you, Hannah? What's wrong?'

'What do you mean "what's wrong?"'

'What do you mean, what do I mean? I mean "what's wrong?"'

And there they were again, seconds into a conversation and already arguing. Davie sighed and let his chin sink to his chest. Whoever had cleaned the floors had swept a pile of dirt and dead cockroaches into the alcove that held the doors. He apologised and asked Hannah again how she was, then listened to her start over too. He could imagine her pale eyelashes fluttering with the effort of being polite. She was probably checking her watch to ensure she hadn't given him more than the allocated time. Through the wired glass in the swinging doors, the waiting room clock said eleven twenty-two. Davie asked after Tom, Hannah's nephew, and listened to her explain how he was growing up fast, enjoying school.

'Listen,' she said suddenly. 'You're probably wondering why I'm phoning.'

*Which is why I asked what's wrong,* thought Davie, but he said nothing. With Hannah it was easier if you let her talk.

'It's about the house, Davie. Tom and I need a bigger place in Sydney so I need to release some cash and the obvious place to start is with that place; so I'm going to sell it. I've thought about it and it seems reasonable to offer it to you first and that way I'll save fees. I've organised for two agencies to come and value it and, of course, you can do your own valuation. I'm expecting to get about six hundred and fifty thousand for it. What do you think?'

'Sorry.' Davie stepped to one side so a large redhead and her body odour could enter the waiting room. 'What house are we talking about?'

'Pay attention, Davie. Your house, of course. Or my house, I should say. I need to sell it. I want to be reasonable but I can't throw money away.'

Her house. Davie heard so rarely from his ex-wife that he sometimes forgot the house he lived in actually belonged to her. Her parents had bought it when they moved out of Montauban, a bolt hole to come back to whenever they visited. Davie and Hannah had moved in when they'd first married; he'd never moved out. Hannah's parents died after she'd divorced him; he knew he had no legal hold over it.

'But where will I live?'

It was out before he realised how pathetic it sounded, the way Hannah always made him sound pathetic.

'Oh, come on, Davie, you're an estate agent, for God's sake. You've got a job, so get a home loan; that's what everyone else does. If you'd done this when I first suggested it, you'd have a chunk of it paid off by now.'

He didn't rise to that. The thought he might still, after ten years, be married to Hannah was like reading suicide prevention brochures.

'Davie Simms!'

His name crackled the air both sides of the swing doors and he could see people in the waiting room looking around to see who would stand up.

'Someone's calling you,' said Hannah.

'Yes, thank you, Hannah, I'm aware.'

'So, you'll think about it?'

'Yes, Hannah.'

'Let me know by the end of the month?'

'Yes, Hannah.'

'Bye then.'

'Yes, Hannah. I mean—'

But she was gone.


## 14.

James Harte was still a good-looking man, somewhere in there, under the tired pale skin and the permafrown. He was tall and broad-shouldered, his features well-arranged beneath the hair he should have cut months before, his jawline strong. But Davie had seen him as a teenager at school, seen pictures more recent than that, and he knew the man who limped into the echoing room was a ghost of his former self. If Davie had passed him in the street in normal clothes and if he'd recognised him – a bigger 'if' that – he would have known Harte had fallen on hard times. Drugs, mental illness, gambling, booze. But prison? Crikey, who'd have thought.

The smell of disinfectant was no less powerful in the strange hall where they met than in the waiting room three corridors away, but here it mingled with other, more human smells. Six sessions a day of eight visitors and eight prisoners overseen by sixteen guards. No windows and, as far as Davie could tell, no air conditioning either. Just a series of well-sealed doors so the smells of thirty-two people at a time had nowhere to go.

Harte, like the seven other prisoners who shuffled in before and after him, was wearing white overalls over his prison greens, the word *'Visiting'* emblazoned across the chest in orange, in case anyone might forget why they were there. When Harte pulled his chair back from the table, the harsh scrape it gave made Davie flinch. He'd thought they'd be talking through glass, one on one. The realisation that a meagre row of tables was the only thing between him and hardened criminals was unnerving. Around him, at the other tables, visitors and prisoners leant in close to each other. Then Harte leant forward too, pale forearms on the table, and Davie found he wanted to do the same. Like he was focused on nothing but the man opposite him, not thinking about his conversation with Hannah at all.

'Davie Simms.' Harte's smile was weak but determined. 'Weren't you a big pop star last thing I heard?'

No matter how often people said it, it was like being slapped: as much shame and humiliation as actual hurt. Davie pulled on his c'est-la-vie face. 'And now look at the two of us.'

That made Harte smile properly, white teeth out of place in the gloom. If they were to compete on anything, it would be on who had had the greatest downfall.

'So now you're a private detective,' he said. 'How did that happen?'

Davie wasn't sure he had the strength to compose a response. Had Hannah given him a deadline? He'd have to phone her back, ask her to repeat the conversation and put up with her sarcastic remarks. If he had a few months, maybe he could do something. Or had she said weeks? He frowned himself back into the room and followed Murdoch's instructions.

'It's a long story,' he said, nodding at the clock at the end of the room. 'But we don't have time for it now. Once we get you out of this, I'll tell you all about it over a cold beer. But for now, you need to talk, not me. Tell me what happened and keep an eye on the clock.'

Harte looked at Davie differently then, like the lanky kid from the back of class, the pop star from the radio, really might have something valuable to add. He gave a little cough, but it made his voice no less croaky than before.

'First thing you need to understand is this: I didn't kill her. You got that? Good. Secondly, yeah, I was banging her out on the boat that night. Charlie and me ... well, she was always there, you know? Always up for it, always suggesting stuff you didn't want to turn down. She was hot. She was ... Anyway, we were out on *Class* that night. That's my boat, *Class Act*. I picked Charlie up from Rose Bay and dropped her back there, using the tender to get between *Class* and the wharf, just like I normally did. Then I motored back to our mooring in Vaucluse Bay.'

'Why?'

Harte sighed at being interrupted and Davie remembered him properly, what he'd been like at school: a man-boy who liked to speak rather than be spoken to. He remembered classrooms ruled by Harte rather than the teacher, the young student something between a bully and a leader. There was something about him, an intimidating energy that made you want to listen. Or maybe just prove yourself worthy.

'Why what?'

'Why did you normally drop Charlie in Rose Bay?'

'Oh. Because Amanda and I moored *Class* in view of our place in Vaucluse. I didn't want Charlie to be seen getting off the boat, for obvious reasons. She lived over in Bondi somewhere, easy enough to get home from Rose Bay. At a push, she could have walked it.'

'Did she?'

Harte narrowed his eyes at the question. 'Did she what?'

'Did she ever walk home to Bondi? It's not that close.'

'I doubt it. Especially not that night, it was pouring. I gave her a huge golf umbrella, but Charlie was a princess: she'd moan about walking to the fridge. Meanwhile, I got soaked getting back to the boat.'

'So why didn't she phone for a taxi to pick her up from the boat?'

'She had a shitty phone, couldn't ever get any reception. Ubers were no better, apparently. Charlie always said it was impossible to get them to hang around long enough, something like that.'

'Why?'

Harte sat upright, both hands helping his questions. 'You're fucking with me, right? What the fuck do I know about what Ubers do or don't like doing?'

He'd raised his voice and the nearest guard, a metre to his left, made a vague movement, a shuffle from foot to foot, a scratch of his beard. It was the subtlest of warnings, but enough to make Davie give the guard an apology as if he'd been the one at fault. Maybe he had. He'd been over-compensating, trying to show he was listening, not thinking about Hannah selling his house. Six hundred and fifty thousand dollars, she'd said; that wouldn't be a guess. He apologised once more – to Harte this time, eye contact and sincerity – and told Harte to go on. Harte sat forward again and pushed his hands through the dark tangle of his hair.

'You know, the lawyers asked me all these fucking questions which the police had already asked me and I answered them again and again and ... look where it's got me.'

Davie told him to carry on with the story.

'I'm sure you know the story, Davie. My wife told your partner everything I told her. It was all true. Charlie and I got it on, we had a drink and motored back to Rose Bay. I took her back to shore in the dinghy, went back to the boat, motored home. Monday morning she's not at work;

then they find her body and I'm the only suspect, despite a complete lack of evidence and no discernible motive.'

'Except Charlie was found in Vaucluse Bay.'

'No, Charlie was found just outside the bay, on the rocks of the Point. You ask anyone who's ever sailed in the harbour. The tide through the heads goes up and down the western shore there – it could have easily taken her that far. If she'd died in Vaucluse Bay, it would have dragged up towards Watsons Bay or even out through the heads. Those lawyers I fired, they laid it all out. Get Amanda to show you the documents.'

'Could Amanda have murdered Charlie?'

Harte glared at him, his mouth twisted in a snarl. Then, catching himself, he forced it into a smile: torturous but immediately convincing. All those teeth.

'I should thank you for asking that. If you hadn't, I wouldn't have trusted you, not in an hour or so. I'd have thought … well, anyway. Yes, after me, she's the prime suspect, I give you that. She's certainly got the motive. But she didn't do it. For one thing she wasn't in the country at the time. And for another, I checked. Had someone check.'

'A private detective?'

'The police actually. They looked at her email accounts, phone records, everything. If she had someone do this, and God knows how she'd have done that, then she didn't have any contact with them for two years beforehand. Same with my sister, same with Angus.'

'But you don't trust her?'

*Not trusting your wife, imagine that. What's she going to do, sell your home from under you?*

'For God's sake,' said Harte. 'I'm in prison for a crime I didn't commit, I shouldn't trust anyone. But, for the record, yes, I do trust her, actually. Made me feel like shit pointing the police in that direction, particularly when she's never questioned me once. She's a good woman, better than me. Trust me, it wasn't her.'

'So why did you want to brief us yourself?'

Harte appraised Davie again. Looked him up and down, held his eye as if they both knew the secret now. His next smile was more honest, sad and tired.

'You're good at this, you know.'

76

Davie didn't reply. The last question had been Murdoch's too. 'Don't ask that and you may as well not bother going.' *Not bovver gaan.* He watched Harte wipe his hands over his face and found himself wishing they could swap places. At least Harte knew where he was going to be living in six months' time. Davie caught the stupid thought and squashed it, pushed everything about Hannah away for later. Then Harte looked at him again and Davie saw something else he remembered from school. A fierce little spark in the man's green eyes, a hint of the fire raging away in there.

'Someone who knows me really well has done this, Davie. Someone who knew I was on the boat with Charlie, someone who knew she'd get off at Rose Bay. I trust Amanda ninety-nine point nine per cent. Same way as I trust Emma and Angus. You're here for the rest, including the zero per cent I trust my friends.'

A fat woman with yellow hair three tables along burst into laughter, the raucous noise a shock amongst the dull echoes of the room. All the prisoners and their visitors turned to look at her, looked at each other looking, then returned to their conversations. Two of the guards close to the woman shifted closer still, one of them dropping a comment Davie couldn't hear.

'What about the blackmail?' he said. 'One of your employees said Charlie was blackmailing you.'

'There was no blackmail,' Harte snapped back. 'This woman at the agency—'

'Jennifer Bailey?'

'Yeah, I met her once. I've no idea what she's talking about. Charlie wasn't blackmailing me. Maybe she meant to, who knows.'

'Would she have had something to blackmail you about? Apart from your … affair?'

Again, that appraising look.

'Who knows? Maybe. I'm not sure she was that smart, but, yeah, everyone's got secrets and I guess I've made a few enemies.'

'One of whom put you in here.'

'You're not listening. A friend has put me in here. It has to be someone who knows me really well, you understand? I didn't exactly broadcast the fact I was banging Charlie and I'm sure she didn't either.'

Davie found himself nodding sincerely. 'If we take the case.'

'What's the issue?' said Harte. 'Money?'

'Well, we should discuss terms.' Davie hated this, hated it at work too, would rather give a house away than quibble over money. Any house apart from his own. 'It's five hundred a day. Billable in half-days, payable monthly.'

Harte tapped a finger on the table between them. 'Listen to me, Davie Simms, money is not an issue. You get me out of here and I'll give you a million dollars cash. You got that?'

Davie stared at him. 'Are you serious?'

Harte chuckled again, something sour behind his white teeth. 'Oh, now I've got your attention. Yes, I'm serious. A million dollars if I walk free. So, you'll take the case.' No question mark there. 'You'll go in amongst those bastards and find out whatever you can?'

'My partner will be doing that.' Davie had practised this. 'I'm tied up with other matters at the moment. Besides, if anyone chose to do any research on me, they'd find I have a PI licence. So it makes sense if he's the one to go in amongst your friends.'

'Do I get to meet him, at least? Amanda told me you and he are a double act, but I thought he'd be the one visiting me today.'

'No, you only ever liaise with me. It's better that way, in case someone gets curious and follows him here. Too risky.'

Too risky for Murdoch that meant. Too risky someone who needed to think him dead might recognise him as very much alive. Davie watched Harte think it through.

'And your partner, he's, you know, like us?' Harte asked after a while. 'Good school and stuff, knows how to behave?'

'Oh, yeah,' said Davie, with his best smile yet. 'No worries. He'll be fine.'

# The Warning Sign

*'Of course,' said Suzie, 'it wouldn't be fair to introduce any danger without giving the main character – and the reader – plenty of warning of what's at stake. For the main character, you see, it's a chance to receive good advice about what he mustn't do. And, for the reader, it's a chance to watch the main character ignore every word.'*

## 15.

Sunday lunchtime and the surf club was full. The weather had kept the weekenders away, but all the locals were there, each wondering what the others were up to; like any of them were ever up to anything. Murdoch took a deep breath and made his way up the stairs. He was stopped three times before he got to the top. The barman, whose name he always forgot, needed a hand bringing up some chairs; don't mind, do you? On his second attempt, John Thornton cornered him, asking about his ribs. Then, near the top, the ugliest man in the world, bags in hand, wanted to know about his garden. Had it survived the storm all right? And how was the new red robin coming along? Murdoch was telling the ugly man about his viburnum when, over the bannister, he saw Anne Lincoln coming in from the car park. He mumbled a hurried apology and pushed on into the function room.

As he entered, hands were raised at various tables across the room. Hi there. Hello, how you doing? Hi. Murdoch nodded and forced a smile, put his head down and walked to the bar. The surf club carpet smelled bad at the best of times, but the week's wet weather had added something new, like a body had started rotting under there. A crowd of kids were running around barefoot, one of them yelling as she chased the others. Murdoch took a menu – like he didn't know it off by heart – and made his way to one of the last free tables. Before he got there, Davie appeared in the doorway, spotted him and raced to reach the table first.

'You're still late, Davie.'

'You just got here yourself, I saw you.'

'The deal is, you're never late.'

'You're not even sitting down yet. That doesn't count. Hey, you want to hear about Harte?'

'Without a beer?'

Murdoch sat with his back to the wall and watched Davie get halfway to the bar before being stopped for a chat by a group of locals. It was ten minutes before he returned with two schooners.

'Kitchen's closed till one,' Davie said, slopping the beers down between them. 'Jen's sick again. We all reckon she's pregnant.'

'Fascinating.'

'You want to hear about Harte then?'

'Can't wait.'

As Davie explained what had happened at Longreach – interrupting the story of his interview with Harte to relay in detail his phone call with Hannah – Murdoch rubbed his hands and hunched against the cold. The furious wind kept bothering the balcony door half-open and his ankles were frozen. When he reached down to rub them warmer, he saw Davie notice his white linen trousers and sat straight up again.

'Why are you wearing those?' said Davie. 'It's freezing.'

'Just trying them out.'

'Trying them out? What for?'

'Nothing. It was a joke. What was you saying about Hannah?'

Davie's impression of his ex-wife was surprisingly good: the blinky eyes and the words she'd use, but his face became his own when he explained how he might lose his home. Murdoch realised slowly that he'd never seen Davie angry before, not for more than a few seconds. It was like watching an actor in a different programme from normal: one he wasn't so good in. Davie's face was spotted with pink, his eye contact all over the place, hands in his hair even more than usual. Hannah knew the shack was his home, he was saying; she had no right, not morally; she hated the place. He'd tried saving, but it was impossible; he wanted to live there forever. He stopped mid-ramble to take a sip of beer and Murdoch knew this was the point where someone else might offer to lend Davie the money, give it to him even.

'Sorry to hear that, mate,' he said. 'Really, I am.'

'Yeah, well, you know what that place means to me.'

'You don't treat it like it means much to you. House is a bleeding pigsty.'

One of the kids, the raggedy-haired girl who'd been chasing her friends, pulled open the door to the balcony and damp air swept into the room again.

Paper napkins and beermats lifted and everyone turned to look. One of the men by the bar ruffled the girl's hair with one hand and pushed the door shut with the other.

'Anyway,' said Murdoch, 'you was going to tell me about Harte.'

'He says he knew nothing about the blackmail.'

'Yeah, right.'

'I believe him. Like you said, he reckons he's been framed by one of his mates, or at least someone who knows him really well. But not Amanda; he seems pretty certain she's not involved at all.'

'Yeah, well, I could have told you that.'

Davie raised his blond eyebrows over another sip of beer.

'You didn't meet her,' said Murdoch. 'She's nice, a real lady. Soft, like. You can tell.'

'You fancy her.'

'What else did Harte say?'

Davie sighed. 'He doesn't think Angus Hoxton did it either. Oh, and he offered us a million dollars if we get him out of prison.'

Murdoch laughed. 'Don't give up the day job.'

'Seriously, Bill, a million dollars. My half of that's pretty much my house, you realise that don't you?'

'Davie, you reckon we're going to jump a bloke from prison just by hanging out with his mates? Get real. We haven't a chance.'

Davie looked like someone had told him Santa wasn't coming. 'So what are you saying? We're not taking the case?'

'Did I say that? You hearing voices or something?'

'So why do you want to take the case if there's no chance of getting Harte out? What's the point in that?'

'What do you mean? It's a case, isn't it? And besides, I get to go undercover with all them nobs, hang out on yachts and shit, wear fancy clothes and drink fancy cocktails. Why d'you think I wouldn't do that?'

'But what about if someone recognises you? Someone from the old days?'

'Jesus, Davie, how many times do I have to tell you? Anyone who wants me dead is either banged up or dead themselves.'

'But you said …' Davie caught the look on Murdoch's face. 'What about the million dollars?'

'Mate, this is what I think of the chances of that. We get that million dollars, you can have the whole lot.'

'Shake on that.'

Davie stuck out a hand like he did too often, knowing it was a contract Murdoch couldn't break. Promise you'll be nice to Natalie. Promise you'll come to the surf club every Sunday for lunch. Promise I can have a million dollars. But it was like owning a puppy – if you let it annoy you, you'd probably end up killing it – so Murdoch reached over and they shook hands for the second time that week until Davie winced and pulled away.

'But you have to try,' he said flexing his fingers. 'You can't just go to parties and do nothing. This is important to me, you know, and I remember what you were like with the Walker case last year.'

'The case I solved.'

'The case *we* solved, Bill. Why do you always …' It was suddenly freezing again and they turned to look at the raggedy little girl swinging on the door to the balcony. 'Skye! Get away from that bloody door!'

It was Davie who shouted, embarrassed as soon as he'd done it, hiding his blushes in his beer. The guy who'd closed the door the previous time reached over and grabbed the girl by the arm, gave her a slap on the back of the legs and sent her sniffing down the stairs.

'Jesus, Davie. You all right, mate?'

'I'm fine. Don't worry about it.'

They drank in silence until Davie spoke again.

'It's the house. I'm worried I'm going to lose it. Hannah said I had to make up my mind by the end of the month. I reckon that means I can say yes then and put her off for another few months while I get the money together. But at best that means two and a half months to find six hundred and fifty grand.' He pushed his hands through his floppy hair and tried a smile that didn't reach his eyes. 'So we'd better solve this case. And you better do your bit. You will, won't you, Bill? You promise?'

'Course I will.' Murdoch pulled his phone from his pocket, found a text that had come in earlier that morning from Amanda Hoxton and held it up for Davie to read. 'Starting Saturday lunchtime, in fact. Look at that. Yours truly is going to a barbeque. In Palm Beach! Jesus, Davie, don't look so impressed.'

'I'm not impressed. You wouldn't catch me going to that kind of thing in a million years. I can just imagine the crowd you'll meet there. Rich people are rich for a reason, Bill, remember that.'

'Yeah, because they've got more money.'

'Ask yourself how they got it. You hang out with them all you like, but don't forget what they did to Harte. I know that crowd; they were third-generation arseholes at school and they won't be any different now.'

'Relax.'

'I'm serious! Watch your back.'

'Davie, I'll be fine. Me and a load of toffs, what could go wrong?'

# The Suspects

'We have to introduce lots of people who could have committed the crime. The client, for example, that's always a good place to start.'

'But the client had nothing to do with it.'

'So what? It's a whodunit, not a theydunit.' Suzie smiled again, a reassurance they weren't arguing. 'Think of it this way, Bill; a detective story is mostly anti-communication. The writer knows upfront who did it and spends hundreds of pages telling the reader everything but that. Do you see?'

Murdoch shook his head. Maybe this was why he'd never got an education. He gave up too easily, was more interested in another biscuit.

'Try this,' Suzie said gently. 'Looking back now, you know who did it. But, at the time, I'm sure everyone seemed suspicious. You must have wondered about all of them. So now we need to raise those same questions in the reader's mind. No questions, you see, no turning of the pages! And, after all, someone did do it, and it has to be someone you mention early on or otherwise it's just not fair.'

16.

Saturday was the last day of November, officially the last day of spring. It arrived wrapped in blue, the weather of the week before a damp and distant memory. It was warmer than before the storm – only the calendar still resisting summer – and Murdoch found himself forced to interact with the ticket officer, the wharf man, even the driver of the ferry who shouted through the open cabin window. Yes, yes, yes, wasn't he lucky to be dressed up nice and carrying champagne on a beautiful day like today! Ha, ha, ha, fuck off.

He'd wanted to arrive at Palm Beach with a firm hand on the railing at the front of the boat, the wind ruffling his white linen suit, the man from Del Monte on his private yacht. But the ferry from Ettalong turned out to be a squat and ugly boat, something like a flattened bus, all the seats on the inside and the door so small and awkward that he banged his forehead on the way out. Still, Amanda Hoxton got to see him walk along the jetty to the shore, one hand in his pocket, the other around the neck of the Veuve.

'A white suit?' she said. 'How ... summery.'

'Don't you like it?'

'No, it's fine. You look very dapper.'

'You don't look so bad yourself.'

He said it out of embarrassment as much as anything else – there had been something ironic in her tone – but his compliment was sincere enough. Her cream-coloured dress was a single piece of smooth material tied with a belt of the same fabric. Murdoch suspected one good tug would pull it open again. He held out his hand and she shook it briefly, her smile tight beneath her sunglasses.

'How polite.'

'Well, I'm supposed to be an old friend of James's, innit? Got to get my manners up.'

'Yes, about that. Let's talk in the car.'

Her black TT was parked illegally across the road. Maybe that explained her coolness, maybe she needed to rush them along before she got a ticket. Or maybe she didn't like the beard. After two minutes of silent driving, she still hadn't relaxed.

'You all right, love?'

'Fine, thank you. You?'

'Don't you like my suit?'

Amanda looked over like she hadn't noticed it until now. 'It's fine.'

That got them around the road from the ferry station and into the trees, the road climbing steadily up the escarpment over Pittwater. The car in front of them was crawling. It was a family of tourists enjoying the view as they vaguely searched for a parking spot, only a small child in the back aware of the traffic behind. Murdoch heard Amanda swear under her breath, the butt of her hand hovering over the horn.

'What's up, then?' he said.

'Nothing. I told you, I'm fine.'

She turned to him with a forced smile, then looked back at the road just in time to see the car in front had stopped. She braked suddenly, the jolt jarring them both against their seatbelts, and this time she did use the horn. When the other car still failed to move, Amanda swung the steering wheel and sped past, hitting the horn twice more for good measure. A minute later she spotted a parking spot and pulled into it. Took off her sunglasses and rubbed her eyes.

'You all right, sweetheart?'

'I'm fine.'

'Like fuck you are.'

She swung around, like he'd called her a name or accused her of something nasty. At the vicious look in her eyes, the set of her chin, Murdoch pulled back, thinking she was going to slap him. Amanda closed her eyes and turned away.

'Sorry,' she said.

'Sorry for what?'

She didn't respond and, not knowing what else to say, Murdoch sat silently too. He watched a stretch of traffic roll past them up the hill, at its end, the family of tourists still looking for a parking spot.

'You got their park,' he said, thinking the Australianism might impress her.

Amanda opened her eyes and followed his gaze to the car with the family, the small child in the back waving in recognition.

'Serves them right,' she said, trying to smile. 'Sorry.'

'You're all right, darling. What's up?'

'It's nothing, really. It's just, well, I never normally go to these things.'

'Barbeques?'

'Barbies, parties, functions, any of it. Not since James went away.'

'You miss him?'

'God, no!' He could tell she'd said it more vehemently than she'd meant to. She shifted in her seat, the fabric of her dress rustling around her as she turned to look out at the water, one arm of her sunglasses at her mouth. 'No, it's not that. James always used to disappear as soon as we got there anyway, off on the prowl. I don't miss that, hunting through the crowd for him, knowing he'd be off with some tart somewhere.'

She put her glasses back on and turned further still, staring out at nothing. 'Listen, you may as well know. Our marriage was a bit of a sham really. We'd started talking about divorce. Just idly, the way other couples plan their holidays, I'm sure. Maybe next year, maybe when things are less busy with the agency. Then things would be fine for a while and I'd hunt for little signs we were back on track. A weekend away, a thoughtful present, romantically insisting I change everything into my married name. But then he'd go and do something to remind me what a prick he is.' She sighed and he could see her hands itching for a cigarette. 'Divorce. I don't know why I didn't push for it more. I just kept noticing another month had passed and we were still married.'

'So why are you still helping him?'

Amanda took a deep breath and turned back to him – again the rustle of the dress – with a sad and tired smile. 'Because, as I said in your garden, a marriage takes what a marriage takes, even when it's on the rocks. And because James is not a murderer. He's a philanderer and an arrogant prick and a world-class arsehole, but he's still my husband. What kind of a woman would leave her husband rotting in jail for a crime he didn't commit?'

She started up the engine, looked over her shoulder and pulled out into the first gap in the traffic.

'Plenty,' Murdoch told her. 'Happens all the time. Half the time, it's the wives what put them there. Did the crime just to frame the husband. Oh, shit, I don't mean—'

There were seconds of horrible silence until Amanda grinned.

'That's funny.'

'Seriously. I didn't mean that, darlin'; I'm not saying you did that.'

'Don't worry. Sometimes, I wish I'd thought of it. Although I'd have done something far more fitting. A class action paternity suit or something. Or maybe I should have just cut his dick off.'

She gave him another smile, easier this one, then concentrated on her driving, looking for the right turning. As she leant forward to peer at street names, he caught a glimpse of the cream lace of her bra, and was conscious of the champagne clutched between his thighs. Then there was a gap in the traffic coming down the hill and she swung them across the other lane and into a shaded side street, even steeper than the road they'd left.

'So why are you stressed about this party, then? What's the problem?'

'This is going to be my first outing,' she said, growling the car slowly up the hill. 'Since James went away, I mean. And these people – eugh. I never understood why James enjoyed hanging out with them; it's not as if he liked them. Trust me, they'll all be gloating through their smiles, dropping little hints and pretending they care. It's going to be hideous. But I've told my brother, Angus, to come. He likes these things, fits in better than I do.'

'So why didn't you get him to bring me?'

Amanda gave him a quick glance. 'Oh Angus,' she said, like that was explanation enough. 'Besides, James's sister Emma and her husband, Oscar, will be there too, so I'll have some moral support. They don't know about you, of course, so we stick to a story.'

'An old friend from England. From when he worked there.'

'Well, about that …'

As they had climbed the hill, the trees overhanging the winding road had been replaced by high stone walls. Now the wall on the right suddenly ended and a broad curve of gravel cut back from the road. A dozen or so cars, half with their roofs down, stood across it.

'This is the back door,' said Amanda, parking deftly between a pair of BMWs. 'The front door's down the hill on the main road, but Benny likes to show off the view. Now, about your cover story.'

Murdoch was halfway out of the car already. At the other end of the gravel, a tall wooden gate stood open and he could hear voices and live music, glasses and laughter.

'Bill, wait! I need to talk to you about your story. I don't think the "old friend from England" thing is going to work.'

Here we go. Murdoch sat heavily back into the seat and braced himself for the things Davie hadn't been brave enough to say.

'Oh yeah,' he said. 'Why's that then?'

'Well, there will be lots of people here who knew James in those days. It'll be strange that none of them ever met you. I was wondering, do you think you could pretend you know James from Longreach? No one will know him from there, of course. We could tell people you've just come out, that you were kind to him in there, that you have useful business contacts and he wants me to look after you. Do you think you could pretend to have been in prison?'

She took her sunglasses off for the last question, lending it her innocent brown eyes. No hint he wasn't the kind of bloke James Harte would be seen with in a million years – not out in the real world.

'Course,' he said. 'No problem. If anyone asks.'

She put her hand on his forearm, squeezed it gently and smiled.

'Oh, they'll ask,' she said. 'These people are vipers.'

The invitation had said 'barbeque', but Davie, on hearing the address, had told Murdoch not to take sausages. Amanda went one step further, insisting he leave the bottle of Veuve in the boot of her Audi, her little gift was more than enough. Whatever it was, in its intricate wrapping and recognisable bag, she gave it to the security man who met them inside the gate. Then, putting her arm through Murdoch's, she led him through the crowd that filled the bright terrace.

'This is Bill,' she told people after she'd kissed cheeks and accepted compliments. 'A good friend of James. I promised I'd look after him.'

Murdoch shook hands, said hello and smiled. He wanted to be annoyed at the change in story, but he couldn't stop grinning at where he was. At a smart party on a high terrace with a pool, in the sky above the rest of the world. As Amanda was pulled into conversation by a silver-haired couple – like something from an airline advert – a pretty girl introduced herself as Penny and asked Murdoch if he'd like a drink. He wanted a beer, or maybe a water, but everyone else was holding a glass of champagne, so he said he'd have one of those instead. Penny grabbed one from a nearby waiter and passed it to him with her easy smile. Murdoch asked her how she knew their hosts, Benny and Phoebe Robbins.

'I don't,' she said, trying not to laugh, 'I just work for the catering company.'

Amanda turned to him – he wasn't sure if she'd heard – and put a hand on his forearm.

'Let's go and find Phoebe,' she said.

Progress across the terrace was slow, Amanda introducing him to a dozen people she hadn't seen in *ages*. Murdoch was normally good with names, better still with faces, but today he struggled to concentrate. The men with their blue shirts and beige shorts, the women with their bright dresses and floating hair, they were parts of a bigger picture he needed to take in before he could focus on the details. He let Amanda do the talking and listened with half an ear as he stared around at the view. It wasn't just the people. Across the empty azure pool, separated from the terrace by frameless glass, was the massive mouth of the Hawkesbury, the Coast green and hazy in the distance. Below the terrace, the rest of the house fell down the hillside in sharp angles of stone, metal and glass. Thickly planted gardens – bushes garish in bloom and giant succulents reaching for the sun – pushed against windows and walls.

'So how you do know Harte then?'

Murdoch turned to find a fat man Amanda had introduced a minute earlier was staring down his nose at him. Barry or Harry or Gary, tall and confidently overweight, a polo shirt stretched across his important stomach. Amanda was talking to the fat man's wife and Murdoch saw her flinch at the question.

'Business,' said Murdoch.

'Ha, business with Harte. Bet you didn't make that mistake twice!'

'You in PR too?'

No, the fat man was in telecoms and very happy to talk about it, given how fascinating the smartphone retail market was just now. Murdoch let his sunglasses look interested and wondered what everyone else was talking about. He could hear laughter from across the pool and tried to see who was standing there. He wanted to go and laugh beside a pool too. Over the fat man's shoulder, he saw Amanda despatch the man's wife with a smile and turn towards them. Before she could interrupt his monologue, however, a small woman with dark hair and unruly eyebrows appeared at her side. The smaller woman put one hand on Amanda's arm, nodded briefly at her greeting and stood on tiptoe to whisper into her ear. As the fat man moved onto the subject of NFC and smart watches, Amanda's face hardened. Then she turned and followed the other woman away through the crowd.

'You see,' the fat man was saying, 'the whole industry is still developing at a rapid pace. Take your phone out, let me show you what I mean.'

'You what?'

'Give me your phone. I'll show you.'

Murdoch didn't know how to say no. He wanted to follow Amanda, but it was too late now, he wouldn't find her if he tried. He fished in his pocket and handed over his phone.

'Access code?'

Murdoch hesitated, then gave in under the other man's stare.

'See,' said the fat man, swiping his finger across the screen, 'you have hundreds of photographs in here, but how many do you really ever look at? Goodness, nice car, is that yours?'

'Er, yeah.'

'What was it you said you and Harte worked on together?'

Murdoch was struggling to remember what other photos were in there. Anywhere else he'd have snatched his phone back and told the man to mind his own bleeding business. 'Let's take a picture now,' he said, reaching out his hand and letting it hover there, until the fat man looked up from the photographs.

'Why did you take a picture of that?' the man asked, holding up a photograph of the red robin hedge struggling in Murdoch's garden.

'Let's take a picture now.' Murdoch repeated, determined not to lose his temper. 'Then you can show me what you mean.'

'Oh. OK.'

The fat man beamed but still didn't hand over the phone. Instead he barked at a group of men near the pool, telling a man called Jez to come and take their picture. He put a hairy arm around Murdoch's shoulder, his champagne breath in his face.

'Take a picture of me and Phil,' he said, handing the phone to the man called Jez. 'Cheese.'

Murdoch turned uncomfortably under the weight of the other man's arm and, spilling some champagne on the cuff of his shirt, grimaced at the lens. He had to endure several more minutes of the fat man's monologue before he got his phone back.

The party wasn't contained to the terrace. The tumbling gardens below the pool were empty, but the house – large rooms joined by broad shallow steps – held countless groups of white people. Catering staff moved smoothly between them, offering trays or clearing glasses, signalling to each other with nods and whispers. Murdoch asked for directions to the bathroom as an excuse to look for Amanda. He'd tell her there were too many people for him to choose between, he needed her guidance, her arm looped through his as she showed him around. A waiter directed him to a bright hallway where he found a group of women chatting outside a locked door. They looked up as he approached, gave him momentarily curious glances, then returned to their conversation: deer unafraid in a field. Only one – the small dark-haired woman who'd whispered in Amanda's ear – acknowledged him. She smiled timidly and, nodding towards the stairs, told him the bedrooms had en-suites if he didn't want to wait.

'Half this lot are only standing here for the gossip,' she said, loud enough for the other women to laugh in agreement. 'Trust me, it won't be the fastest-moving queue.'

Murdoch wanted to ask where Amanda was, but in front of this group of confident women he thought he'd sound like a lost little boy asking for his mummy. Instead, he climbed the polished concrete stairs.

There was still so much about the world that Murdoch didn't understand. Like how the people who knew how get their hands on serious money legally managed to keep the secret, so that everyone else didn't do the same. Or like who decided what was tasteful and classy and who decided what was common. He'd never have chosen half the stuff in the house he lived in, but he knew from magazines it was nicer than what he'd have bought. At the top of the stairs he found a similarly tasteful space: a cream-carpeted corridor, mirroring the one downstairs, but this one rich with light. It ran along the side of the hill, windows overlooking the terrace, and he stood for a moment at the glass, staring down at the crowd: the bigger picture he'd wanted to see before. He saw some faces he'd been introduced to and tried to remember their names, knew he should get down there and talk to them, do what Amanda called 'mingling'. Hadn't he promised Davie he'd try? He decided instead to find a toilet – he genuinely needed to go now, it was the champagne and the excitement – and then he'd give it a go.

Between its evenly spaced doors, the corridor reflected the sunlight in irregular patches, the glass of framed photographs catching it at strange angles and twisting it further. Forgetting the toilet for a second, Murdoch studied the people behind the glass. Their smiles at parties, on mountainsides, in boats and on beaches. As he walked further, the colours in the frames faded and became black and white, then sepia brown. There were hunting parties, combed hair and strange trousers. He remembered the photograph on his phone and pulled it out, grinning at himself in a summer suit on a terrace. He texted it to Davie along with a smiley face, laughed out loud at nothing and opened the next door he found.

If he'd examined the room on his way to the en-suite, he'd have easily guessed it was the master bedroom. But studying rooms like that, working out how much time they were worth, was something he was proud not to do any more. He was allowed to be here, was *supposed* to be here, he was doing nothing wrong. So he crossed the room without looking and used the bathroom without worrying. Took his time washing his hands, smelled the soaps, examined the tiny hand towel. But at the sound of the bedroom door opening, he flinched like he was young again, hands turned into fists, eyes darting around for a weapon. He caught his reflection in the bathroom mirror and rolled his eyes. Was on the point of calling out to excuse himself – he hadn't shut the en-suite door properly – when he heard the name 'Amanda' followed by a naughty laugh.

'That's too funny,' said a woman's voice. 'I wouldn't put it past her.'

'She's got some balls, I'll give her that.'

The second voice was older: a woman with a slightly nasal twang. Murdoch heard a door slide, wooden hangers bumping softly, a rustle of cellophane and cloth.

'Frankly,' continued the older woman, 'I always thought she and James deserved each other.'

'Don't!' There was a smile in her younger friend's voice. 'Imagine someone heard; you know her bloody temper. Look, it's this one, what do you think? It's shorter than it looks.'

'Oh God, I don't know; try it on. You don't mind, do you? These shoes are killing me.'

Murdoch heard the bed crunch, then a silence undone by a zip and the slide of one fabric against another.

'What about this latest piece of rough, then?' It was the older woman speaking. 'I can't believe she brought him along with her. Did you know she was going to do that?'

'Oh, sort of. She mentioned a friend of James's and I thought, "Oh yes, I bet". Lucky cow, I wish someone would bang Benny up so I could run around and have some fun. By the way, did you see my darling husband looking at her? I thought we might have to clear up the drool.'

'Oh Phoebe, don't be ridiculous, you're imagining things. It's been ten years since they were engaged …'

'Twelve, actually.'

'Well, exactly, twelve years then. And, after all, you're the one he chose … Oh, that's lovely!'

'Do you think so? I was thinking of wearing it with this.'

'Oh. Well …'

Murdoch listened to his hostess and her older friend talk about skirt length and shoes and wondered if he could brazen it out. Flush the toilet and come out looking surprised. The older woman coughed slightly.

'You've still got that tickle, I am worried.' The younger woman – he had no doubt now she was Phoebe Robbins – was approaching the en-suite door. 'Do you want a glass of water?'

'Maybe. Oh, what's this?'

'Ha!'

The bark of the hostess's laugh was close to the door and Murdoch's skin tightened. He could see a strip of her through the crack between the hinges. She was much younger than he'd imagined, platinum-haired in a silvery skirt and a well-filled bra. He opened his mouth to breathe more quietly and prepared his surprised face.

'That,' she said, moving out of sight, 'goes with this.'

A drawer was opened with creak and both women laughed.

'Put it on now,' demanded the older woman. 'Go on, you have to!'

'A costume change?'

'It *is* your party.'

They laughed again and Murdoch heard another zip, another rustle of fabric, the creak of the bed again as the older woman stood. Then, after a giggled confirmation of what fun it would be, the bedroom door opened and closed and the room fell silent. Murdoch looked at his reflection again and gave it a James Bond wink.

A few minutes later he was back on the terrace; twenty minutes after that, he was still alone. He was looking out at the view, telling himself not to be angry with Amanda, realising slowly he was angry with himself. Davie had once told him you should never mind being alone in a crowd because if you looked carefully, there would always be others alone too. But Murdoch had looked long and hard and, as far as he could tell, everyone on the terrace knew at least two other people there. Hands were shaken and cheeks kissed, friendly smiles given out like gifts to everyone but him. He managed to start a few conversations, but people tended to drift away when he said he was a friend of Harte's, one woman refusing point blank to talk to anyone who could call himself such a thing. Murdoch gave up after that. He stood apart, feeling like a tool in his white linen suit and his four-hundred-dollar loafers. The view was more welcoming.

'Are you looking for Montauban?'

The woman who'd taken Amanda away and given him directions to the bathroom had appeared beside him, a huge glass of red wine in each hand.

'You can't see it from here,' she said. 'That furthest point you can see out there, that's two headlands to the south of it.'

He hadn't been looking for Montie. He lived there, why would he want to see it from a distance?

'Right,' he said. 'Thanks.'

'I'm Emma Druitt.' She put out a little finger for him to shake. 'James Harte's sister. You're Bill Murdoch. You're ... Well, you've been kind to my brother in Longreach, I hear. I can't imagine what that means, but thank you.'

She was out of place on this terrace of bright and beautiful people: a mouse who'd crept into the aviary. Her navy-blue dress was practical and plain, her dark hair a neat bob. She was small and made herself smaller by stooping slightly, like she was afraid someone might notice she was there. Murdoch asked her where Amanda was.

'She's had to leave, I'm so sorry. She asked me to pass on her heartfelt apologies. Oh, I suppose I've just done that. Anyway, there's been a problem with a client and she's had to go and sort it out. But all is not lost. She thought you might like a game of pool?'

'In the pool?'

He'd not misheard. He was buying time, trying to understand why he was so disappointed.

'Come with me,' Emma Druitt said and turned so he had no choice.

She took him to the hallway where he'd last seen her, then to the right and down some stairs, to a part of the house he'd not seen before.

'Sorry, love, did you say we're going to play pool?'

'Oh, not me!' She didn't turn around, but he could hear her smiling. 'You are. Well, if you want to, that is.'

'I don't understand why Amanda had to go and sort out a client. I thought her brother, Angus, was in charge of sales.'

At this Emma Druitt slowed, turning over her shoulder and smiling again, less kindly than on the terrace.

'Yes, well. You would have thought it was his job, wouldn't you? But things generally work better if Angus is kept out of them and I'm sure you'll agree how charming Amanda can be. Now then, here we are.'

They entered a room open on two sides, the views towards the Hawkesbury limited only by a ceiling and a floor, white polished concrete rippling in blue-green light. Only a track for sliding doors, bifolded out of sight, confirmed this was really part of the house. In the middle of the room stood a pool table set ready for a game. The only other feature was on their left: a long bar, white marble on top and front, the glass wall behind it looking into the swimming pool and then, through more glass, to the gardens beyond. Leaning over the bar and looking up through the water, Murdoch could make out the blurred and bobbing heads of people on the terrace.

'I found him!'

Emma Druitt called to two men who were sitting on the floor beyond the pool table, their legs dangling over the edge of the view. They turned and, one after the other, pulled themselves to their feet. The first to reach Murdoch was tall and lean, smooth-faced with sleepy blue eyes under a mop of curly dark hair. He gave Murdoch a smile and reached out his hand.

'Hello, mate, I'm Angus. Nice to meet you.'

He was a good-looking boy, even Murdoch could see that. Like something off an Aussie soap opera.

'Beer?' he said, wandering behind the bar. 'Or something stronger? I'm having a whisky chaser, although I'll need to be quick before someone tells me I can't.'

Angus made a comedy scowl at Emma who tutted and stood her two glasses of wine on the bar.

'And this is my husband, Oscar,' she said. 'Oscar, I got you a Pinot.'

Oscar Druitt was wearing a pink polo shirt, like that was a thing grown men wore. He was thick all over, obviously strong, the kind of man who didn't look tall until you were standing next to him. He had dark Mediterranean skin, thick black hairs curling on his arms and from the V of his polo. He raised his eyebrows as he shook Murdoch's hand.

'You're a friend of James?' he said. 'I don't think we've met?'

Angus laughed behind the bar. 'Oscar, you idiot, this is Bill Murdoch, the guy Amanda was telling us about. From Longreach. He was watching out for James in there – no doubt he needed it – and now we have to be nice to him. Which Amanda does by dragging him to a party to make useful connections and then abandoning him.'

If either of them was fazed to be dealing with an ex-con, they didn't show it. Oscar apologised profusely, while Angus pushed the red wines to one side and replaced them with beers drawn from a golden tap.

Once Emma had made her excuses and left, the men talked about the house, the view, some of the people at the party. Murdoch was waiting for questions about Longreach, about James and how he was, but they never came. Instead, after twenty minutes or so – the traffic up from Sydney, cars, travel, another beer – Angus suggested a game of pool.

'You go for it,' said Oscar. 'I'm useless.'

'I'd of thought it'd be snooker in a house like this,' said Murdoch examining the table.

Angus smirked. 'You've obviously not met our host.'

He leant over the table and was about to break when they heard voices approaching from the hallway. Murdoch saw Angus and Oscar exchange a glance, then watched Angus break so rapidly he almost missed the triangle of multi-coloured balls.

'Your go,' he said quickly.

Murdoch picked a cue from the rack, but, before he'd had time to choose a shot, the voices brought two men into the room. They were older than the group already there, greying at the temples, thicker-skinned. The shorter of them, the first to enter, had the same Mediterranean colouring as Druitt, but this was not a man who'd ever worn pink. He was five-foot cubed, waddling with muscle, in a black shirt and heavy jewellery. The man behind him was only slightly taller, but the muscle on him was sharper, more recently toned. He too was dark, but only because of the tan he looked like he'd been wearing since the eighties. Murdoch recognised them immediately – recognised their type at least. He turned to his drink at the bar, watching them carefully in the reflective poolside until he was sure he didn't know them better than that. The shorter man was telling Angus they'd been looking for a game.

'You gonna be long?'

'We've not even sunk a ball yet,' said Murdoch. 'You take the table.'

The man turned and looked at him for the first time. 'And you are?'

'Benny,' said Angus, 'this is Bill. Friend of James's. He's come as Amanda's plus one. Bill, this is our host, Benny Robbins.'

'Nice house,' said Murdoch as they shook hands. 'Very impressive.'

Robbins squeezed his hand hard and held his eye, checking it was clear who was in charge. But Murdoch had expected this, had a deferential smile ready and waiting, insisted again the host have the use of his own table. He ignored the heat of the taller man's stare.

'No worries,' Robbins told him in a thick Westie accent. 'You's already playing. Finish the game, while I mix us a drink. You might be a friend of that thief Harte; doesn't mean you're not welcome here.'

In Murdoch's experience there were two kinds of pool. The chatty kind: blokes in a pub wobbly with beer, excusing yourself past people, shouting over music, gold coins on the table. And then there was the proper game: pool halls and minimum-security prisons, skinny kids who didn't see enough daylight, air you smoked. This was the game he preferred. It was where you learnt how good you were, learnt from watching other blokes, learnt that practise was the only way to get good at anything. But he'd always made more money in the pubs. By the age of sixteen, he could sidle up to a table and pretend he was as pissed as the blokes already playing there, make them suggest a game for money so that he was the one to be persuaded. It was a risky business: you had to act surprised when you took the cash, insist on buying a round, but that was what made it fun.

It was stupid to hustle now, but there was something about Robbins, the way he spoke to Angus, the way Oscar retreated to a corner as soon as the man appeared. Murdoch only let himself win when both he and Angus were on the black, playing like he wasn't sure of the angles. He'd just sunk the last ball, surprised how much Angus cared about losing, when they were all diverted by a silent explosion behind the bar. A lithe young woman in a black string bikini had dived into the pool. Her legs and arms stroked slowly through the blue-green water, untanned skin revealed where her bikini had slipped on her buttocks and was rippling away from her breasts. Murdoch smiled, then caught Oscar's eye. A tiny shake of a head.

'Gemma!' said Angus before adding quickly, 'Benny, I didn't know the girls were here.'

Robbins swore under his breath and his tall friend, a man who still hadn't been introduced, walked quickly from the room. Angus squatted down, hunting in the table for the sunken balls. Oscar found something in his glass.

'Table's yours,' said Murdoch, looking carefully at Robbins and not at the half-naked girl swimming behind him.

'King of the table, actually,' Robbins said. 'I know a good player when I see one – no offence, Angus – and I do quite like a challenge. You up for it, Bill?'

Again, the tiniest eye contact between Angus and Oscar, faster this time, more frightened. Behind Benny, the girl went up for air and a minute later disappeared from the pool.

Robbins broke open the game – no toss or consultation – and walked quickly around the table, sinking ball after ball until he missed a table-long shot, swore viciously, and kicked his cue. Angus and Oscar were at the end of the bar, neither of them watching, but both of them tensing at the outburst. Murdoch sank three balls and then deliberately missed the fourth. Never overplay the reaction: that was the trick. Best not to react at all; just blink and stand and smile at your opponent. He listened to Angus and Oscar talking about the rugby, dragging the conversation through lists of names and quibbling over scores neither of them cared about. Meanwhile his opponent sank another three balls. It was only when Robbins slammed the black with unnecessary force into a middle pocket that he heard their voices relax.

'We should be sociable,' Oscar told the room at large. 'I'd better go and find Emma.'

There was a sound of wet feet on the floor near the door and they all turned to see the girl from the pool. Up close, the bikini was made of spider's webs and paper clips, her nipples fighting the wet fabric.

'Daddy, why can't I swim—'

'Not now, Gemma!'

She recognised the look, or the tone, and blushed, smiled at each of the other men in turn and stomped her perfect bottom back out of the room.

'Another game,' said Robbins. 'You want another game, Bill?'

Murdoch could have resisted Robbins' swagger, but he didn't like how the man had behaved to his daughter, let alone to Angus and Oscar. Not when they'd been so nice to him.

'Yeah,' he said. 'Not sure how interesting it'll be for you, though.'

'We could make it interesting.'

A tiny second of silence surrounded them, like when something precious has been broken. Then, after a polite cough, Oscar spoke. 'Now, Benny,' but Robbins had held up a hand, his eyes still on Murdoch.

'You want to make it interesting, Bill?'

'Well,' said Murdoch. 'I don't normally gamble.'

'You not good for it? Struggle to get the money on the table?'

'I'm good for it. What we talking? Ten grand?'

'Ten grand!' Robbins laughed. 'Well, you don't do things by half, do you, Bill?'

'Oh, sorry, mate.' Murdoch scratched the back of his neck, so innocent. 'I mean, I thought that's what you meant. We don't have to.'

'Oh, but we do now, don't we, Bill? OK, ten grand, is it? I suppose we should shake on it in front of friends, then neither of us can pretend we didn't mean it.'

Murdoch smiled, like he was shy about it, stuck out one hand for the shake and with his other took the good cue from Robbins' grasp.

'My turn to break,' he said.


## 17.


Davie sold two houses that day. He'd been optimistic about the deals all week and the previous night, when viewing the surf forecast, had promised himself if they both came off, he'd spend some serious time in the water. All day long he caught glimpses – from the office, from his car, from the auctions – of his friends making good use of the waves. His plan was to be out there by four and surf till it was properly dark. But after the second sale, when he raced back to the office to change, he found three large boxes on the pavement outside the agency door. He knew what they were and, for a second, he hesitated. But no, he was going for this surf if it killed him. Dragging one box after another into the office, he hurried into the little room at the back where he kept his wetsuit and his board. Changing, lost in commissions and the weekly tide table, he forgot about the boxes and tripped over them on his way back out, smashing his surfboard against the sales board and dislodging an early autumn of Post-it notes. He left them where they lay, locked the office door behind him and, three minutes later, was in the salt water, washing off his work.

But he'd remembered the table wrong. The tide turned sooner than he'd thought and he caught no more than three or four spillers before he found himself bobbing up and down on water too full to stand up on. It shouldn't have mattered. He'd surfed Montie all his life: he knew well enough what to do. Ten minutes of hard paddling would get him out to the point; he could see others on their way there now, the spray haloing their silhouettes in early

100

evening gold. Davie sat up on his board and watched them. He took a good five minutes to make up his mind, knowing with each second he could be closer to the point, squeezing more enjoyment from the daylight. Instead, he sighed, lay down slowly and paddled back to shore.

It was another hour before he opened the first box. The beach shower and changing took only twenty minutes, but, on the paddle in, he'd promised himself he was going to do this thing properly. If he lost his house, so be it, but it wouldn't be for lack of trying. Once he'd changed, his wetsuit stewing in the tiny office sink, he found a blank pad, created a new folder on his computer and rearranged his desk. Amanda Hoxton had had three large boxes of Hoxton Harte financial and commercial information and one box showing the logo of Ghan & Bavin Legal couriered over. He was going to read every page, understand everything, be strict with himself. How long could it take? Davie ripped into the first Hoxton Harte box with a pair of scissors and sat back, aghast, as he discovered smaller boxes inside, each one full of USB keys: an endless Russian doll of reading.

It was only at the sound of knuckles on the window that he pulled himself back into the world. He was surprised to find the office in darkness, layers of shadows behind the lamp that lit the HHA stationery. He had no memory of turning on the lamp. His monitor had darkened and he hit a key to bring it back to life, a white page of Word hurting his eyes. He typed quickly, keen to make a note about Angus Hoxton's surprisingly small salary – not much more than Davie himself earned in a year and far less than any of the other Hoxton Harte directors – but whoever was outside must have seen the computer come alive, seen his illuminated face as he squinted at the screen. They rapped again, harder this time, shaking the glass in its frame. Then he heard a familiar voice call his name and remembered he'd told Natalie she should pop in on the way home. He had thought he'd be nearly finished by then.

'Jesus, Davie,' said Natalie, when he let her into the office at last. 'Are you going deaf or something?'

'What? I mean, no. How you going, Nat?'

Detective Constable Natalie Conquest, his oldest friend in the world. As fit as an athlete, with jet black hair and deep green eyes, Davie had always thought she was gorgeous. Friends he'd tried to set her up with thought differently. She was too hard-faced, they said, unable to hide her cynical attitude or the various chips on her shoulder. Others said that, given she was always such a tomboy, you had to wonder which way she swung. Murdoch, Davie thought, had been the perfect fit, but their brief liaison hadn't ended well. Natalie found a chair and rolled it closer to his desk, the white light of his monitor sharpening her features.

'Who's Angus Hoxton?'

Davie grabbed her by the shoulders and rolled her away from the computer, ignoring her complaints as she tried a late grasp but missed the desk in the darkness. He regretted telling her to drop by, resented the intrusion when he had just now, at last, found something interesting.

'I'm kind of in the middle of something,' he said. 'Something important.'

'Really? Hoxton Harte, what's that then? You doing commercial property too now?'

This time he gave her chair a tug and, when she told him it was bad for his eyes to work in the dark, stood between her and the desk and told her the light switches were by the door. Maybe if she could see the look on his face, she'd get the message at last.

'When did you start working so hard, anyway?' she said, feeling her way back to the door. 'What's got into you?'

'What do you mean? Nothing's got into me. I've always worked hard.'

'Always worked hard! In all the time you've ever worked for D&B, I've never seen you here after lunchtime on a Saturday. And I've never seen you in here after dark.'

As if to prove the point, she flicked the switch and they both stood blinking under lights he'd never seen on before. Davie nearly told her to go away then – she wouldn't have to see him this time either. Instead, he fetched two beers from the office fridge. Back behind the desk, his monitor turned so Natalie couldn't see it, he asked about her job, then had to listen to a long list of frustrations as she paced around the office. The main problem, apparently, was her boss, who refused to believe she had the experience to go for Sergeant.

'Even after everything that happened last year—'

Natalie stopped abruptly. Everything that had happened last year had brought Murdoch to the Coast and they'd agreed never to talk about that.

'Anyway, how are you?' she asked quickly, plonking herself back down in the seat and gesturing at the monitor. 'What's all that about?'

'Oh, you know, work.'

'Yeah, right. And when did you ever stay in the office until nine o'clock working?'

Davie checked his watch, shocked by the time. He'd barely scratched the surface of all the reading he had to do, didn't have time to sit here defending himself.

'Whenever it's required,' he said curtly. 'I do know how to work hard, you know.'

Natalie made a sucking noise with her mouth and took a swig of beer. Davie sighed loudly.

'You know, Nat, ever since I was sixteen years old people have been telling me I should be working harder. And you know what? It's rubbish. Look at all the people you know who work hard, really hard. What do they get out of it? And look at the people who've made it big and lounge around all day. I don't think it was hard work that got them there. In fact, the most success I ever had was when I was taking it easy.'

'Oh, Davie, that was a fluke and you know it. And how long did it last? Eighteen months?'

'Three years, actually.'

'At a stretch! Either way, fame spoiled you. That's the only word for it, Davie. You're spoiled. You don't know the meaning of hard work; you just want everything handed to you on a plate.'

She held his eye, challenging him to contradict her. He was determined not to lose his temper.

'That's not true.'

'It's completely true, Davie. You've no idea how good you've got it. Did it ever occur to you that some people would give their right arm for what you've got? Cushy job, surfing whenever you feel like it? I'm sorry, but I'm glad to hear you're working hard at last, maybe it will make you appreciate what you've got. Or maybe it'll get you out of that hovel you live in and grow up at last.'

Had Charlie Holland spoken this way to James Harte on the boat? Maybe there was a blunt weapon near to hand and he'd lost his self-control.

'Get out,' he said.

'What?'

He wasn't aware of standing up or moving around the desk, just as he hadn't been aware of turning on the lamp on as the room had grown dark.

But now he found himself towering over Natalie and yelling into her face, telling her over and over again to get out, get out, *get out*.

'Davie, for God's sake, calm down. What the hell's wrong with you?'

He staggered backwards, the desk scraping on the floor as he leant against it. Putting his hands over his face, he felt to his shame there were tears there.

'Oh my God, Davie, what is it?'

He told her to get out again, his hands still over his eyes. Listened to her get up from her chair, walk towards the door, then back across the room to him. Felt her put both arms around him and pull him into her. After a while, when he opened his eyes, he found she'd turned off the lights.

'It's all right,' she said.

They'd been like this as kids: when she'd failed an exam, or he'd got mugged, or when life was too hard for either of them. Ten years earlier, when his stardom had come to a surprisingly sudden end, her sympathy had been the only one he trusted. He wanted to stay silent in the dark, his head bowed down on hers, but Natalie was too much the detective for that. He ended up telling her everything: about Hannah and the impending loss of his home, about the case being his only hope.

'Jesus, Davie, you love that place. I'm sorry I called it a hovel. I mean, it *is* a hovel, but it's *your* hovel. If there's anything I can do to help …'

His outburst had been genuine; he was embarrassed about it now, but still he saw his opportunity.

'Actually,' he said sniffing in the darkness more than he needed to, 'there is something you could do to help.'

And so, a new argument began.

18.

Murdoch's phone was never a good passenger. On Monday afternoon it started ringing as soon as he hit the freeway. Murdoch winced when he saw Amanda's name flashing across its screen and told himself, for once, he'd be good and not answer while driving. Then, when he pulled into his driveway after four missed calls, he told himself he should be sitting down when he spoke to her. A beer in the garden and a fag lit up, calm enough so he wouldn't react to whatever she might say. Trouble was, when he lifted his shopping bags out of the boot, he found he couldn't resist trying on his new stuff. He ran up to his dressing room, rummaged through the bags and put everything on. Which meant that, when she phoned for the fifth time, he was looking like the dog's bollocks in a suit and a tie and nice firm shoes. Murdoch gave the wardrobe mirrors a little nod of Bond before picking up the phone from the bed.

'Amanda, I was about to call you.'

'I should bloody well think so too. Did you get my voicemails?'

'I was driving.'

'So what do you have to say for yourself?'

There was something not right in her voice, something borrowed for the occasion. He was going to make a joke, but, not wanting to risk it, forced himself to apologise instead, sitting on the bed as he spoke.

'I don't know how it happened.'

'Oh, don't you, Bill? Well, why don't I tell you how it happened? It happened because you bet him ten thousand dollars for one game of pool. It happened because you did this in front of people so he couldn't get out of it. It happened because you very obviously pretended to be a worse player than you actually are. And it happened because you did it in *his* house at *his* party despite, I'm sure, being perfectly able to guess the kind of man he is.'

'I didn't mean to make a scene. We left straight after. I even gave him the money back.'

'That's not what I heard.'

'No, honestly. Angus made me give him the cash so he could take it back in to Benny.'

'You gave it to Angus? Are you mad?'

Nothing borrowed about that tone of voice.

'Well, like Angus said, I couldn't exactly go back in and give it him myself, could I?'

There was silence on the line. Murdoch felt behind him and pulled an uncomfortable lump from under the bedspread. A long-lost tennis shirt.

'I don't know if this is going to work.' Amanda sounded exhausted. 'Maybe this whole thing was a mistake.'

'Nah, don't say that. Listen, I fucked up, I admit it. I didn't know he was going to react like that, did I? Did anyone else notice?'

'Oh no. No, I'm sure no one batted an eyelid as four security men escorted you and my brother through the crowded terrace and out of the party. And I'm sure him screaming at everyone else to get out too went completely unnoticed. For God's sake, Bill, you were supposed to mingle, get to know people, find things out. I'm not paying you to amuse my brother; he does enough of that for himself.'

It was true Angus Hoxton had enjoyed it. So much so, he'd insisted on taking Murdoch out in Sydney to celebrate. The rest of the afternoon had blurred into a long night of drink and powder, Angus insisting they get rooms at The Langham, call some girls he knew. Murdoch had passed out on his bed sometime after four in the morning – no idea if the girls had turned up or not.

'I did find something out,' he said to Amanda, telling her, in as little detail as possible, what he'd learnt about her and Benny Robbins. How they'd once being engaged, how Benny Robbins still held a flame for her, how jealous Phoebe Robbins was.

'How on earth did you learn all that?'

'I mingled, I got to know people, I found things out. I think there might be something there, love. Seriously, I'm beginning to think this might work. These people, they all talk, you know.'

He looked at himself in the mirror again and listened to her think about it, but it was too hot to be in a suit in this tiny room where the windows sucked in the sun. He loosened the tie, stood and wrestled himself out of the jacket, passing the phone between his hands as he pressed it to his ear. Maybe it was the added heat of undressing, maybe it was the idea of talking to her naked, but he didn't stop when he got to his socks and underwear. When, at last, she spoke again, he could hear her attempt at anger was failing and he imagined Angus making her laugh with his version of the story. He imagined her admiring him, Bill Murdoch, for standing up to Benny Robbins, although maybe that part was a bit less likely.

'I hear Oscar took you to his tailor,' she said. 'Did you get anything good?'

Murdoch turned and looked at his reflection.

'Oh yeah,' he said, 'I wish you could see it.'

## 19

Summer crept in over the following weeks, the temperature rising so slowly it was difficult to say when it really began. Murdoch remembered how much he enjoyed his own company and how far he lived from Sydney. There had been a time when the hour and a half drive had felt dangerously short: too easy for a group of henchmen to drag their knuckles up the freeway and find him, intentionally or otherwise. Now the danger was he'd fall asleep at the wheel on what had become a near daily commute. Angus and some friends were meeting in a restaurant in the Cross, did Murdoch want to come along? Oscar and the guys from the agency were heading out for drinks in Surry Hills, any interest? Some clients had organised a reception. There was a book launch, a showcase, a 'pop-up happening'. Murdoch learnt how to mingle, how to nod at people he'd met before and let them chat, how to stop gawping at the fancy bars and competing flower arrangements and drinks laid out for free. To tell himself this was where he belonged and, whenever he was feeling conscientious, how to make the conversation drift back to Harte and what a bastard he was. But he learned nothing useful and, having spent the previous months mostly home alone, the effort exhausted him. So many names and reasons to concentrate reminded him of the tricks the cops used. Faces leaning into your space, then out again; seats less comfortable than they looked; unnatural light and endless repetitive questions. How are you, who are you, what do you do?

He preferred it when he could stand and watch, or deal with people like Oscar and Angus, who asked less and spoke more. One of the two was always out – normally, both of them. Angus was a fun guy, generous with his cash, aware of how lucky he'd been and keen to share the party. Most nights, Murdoch would make his excuses and leave early, his one beer policy stranding him sober in the wake of the roaring crowd. Each time Angus would look at him aghast, telling him the night was young, the fun hadn't even started. Didn't he want to go here or there and see what it was like?

Oscar was more sensible. He would intervene and tell Angus to leave Bill alone. Didn't he know some people needed more than four hours sleep a night? No matter where they were, no matter what time of day, Oscar was always immaculate. Tanned and relaxed, not a hair out of place, wearing clothes that looked like they'd never been worn before. His manners were perfect too. Murdoch was particularly impressed by the way Oscar spoke the same way to everyone. It could be an important client or a junior colleague or a barman or a total stranger, Oscar was always polite but never too polite. Like he was in charge and could choose not to talk to you at all if he fancied it, but weren't you lucky because he was interested and wanted to know what you had to say. Oscar laughed a lot and tipped well and half the places they went, he received more attention than anyone else in the room. Soon Murdoch found himself copying Oscar when he wasn't there, talking to people more than he needed to, joking with them about their answers. He didn't always get it right, but half the time he did, amazed by how everyone in the world responded to a bit of charm, even when it was obviously fake. Everyone but Oscar's wife. No matter what Murdoch said to Emma Druitt, she would look at him, blink and find an excuse to walk away. He saw her so rarely he didn't mind. At client functions she'd make a showing, blink at everyone and then disappear again – back to the office according to Oscar – working until late in the night.

Murdoch saw Amanda Hoxton least of all. If she went to events, she would arrive late and leave early, checking everyone was having fun before she left them to it. Each time, Murdoch found himself impatient for her to be there, disappointed when she'd gone. As soon as he saw her – in a bar or a gallery or an echoing foyer – he would find an excuse to abandon whatever conversation he was involved in and talk to Amanda instead. It was customer relations, he told himself. Keeping the client happy. A pure coincidence that Amanda was the best-looking woman in the room. And nothing to do with the fact that, occasionally, when they brushed shoulders, or Amanda laid a hand on his forearm, he felt an almost electric charge, teasing his muscles and thrilling his skin.

It was a Wednesday morning, and Murdoch was in the garden when Davie came around for their meeting. That's what he'd called it the night before: a 'meeting', shouting the word down the phone line so Murdoch could hear over the hubbub of a gallery opening. Davie was excited: he'd made progress on the case, they needed to compare notes. Murdoch had rolled his eyes, knowing it would be nothing and wondering what he himself could come up with to keep Davie happy, but he had agreed to meet. He wanted to tell

Davie about the events he'd been to, relive them through the telling, share the exciting news of his most recent invitation. Ten sharp. No, he wouldn't forget. Promise.

That morning he got up late and wandered around barefoot, studying his lawn. He watered the red robin the way the ugliest man in the world had recommended in what felt like a hundred years before. The hedge was spindly and slow-growing, the individual plants not yet touching each other, the soil between them a scar on the garden. A pair of kookaburras started cackling in the trees and Murdoch found himself smiling, remembering how, until recently, he'd always hated the noise. But then Oscar had said, 'Kookies are only laughing at you when you think they are,' and now Murdoch could believe it too. His phone vibrated in his pocket and he let it buzz its way towards voicemail. He was in his garden, he was busy. It would only be …

'You forgot, didn't you?' Davie, impatient outside the front door, was wearing the serious face that always made Murdoch want to laugh.

'No, mate, I didn't.' He was out of breath from the run up from the garden. 'I just didn't realise what time it was. I'm barely out of bed. You coming in or what?'

They sat across from each other at the kitchen table, paper and folders from Davie's office laid out neatly between them. He'd even brought two pencils and Murdoch had to cover a smile with a yawn because that really was too funny. Like two kids on the telly doing their homework together.

'You want a coffee, mate?'

'No thanks'

'Toast?'

'I'm fine, Bill. Let's get on with this, I've got a viewing at twelve and I can't be late.'

'Twelve! Are you joking? Almost two hours of this? What did you want to show me? Who killed Charlie Holland and why? Here, guess where I'm off to tomorrow?'

Davie frowned at him, then noticed the crumbs of Murdoch's breakfast on the table between them. He lifted his paper and dusted them onto the floor.

'Bill, we've got to compare notes. I'll tell you what I've found out about Harte's associates and you tell me if you've met them.'

'Associates?'

'It's the word they use in the police file.'

Murdoch stood and fetched the dustpan and brush. He was squatting down on the floor before he heard the silence. Above him, Davie was smirking.

'What?'

'I said, it's the word the detectives from the murder squad use in the police file. Where they note the whereabouts of Harte's close associates at the time of Charlie Holland's murder.'

'And where was they?'

'According to the *police file*, you mean?'

'Yeah.'

Murdoch watched Davie turn a familiar shade of pink, then turned back to the crumbs.

'Did they mention anyone called Benny Robbins?' he said.

'Who?'

'The police.'

'What? You mean in the *confidential police file*, Bill, which only police officers can look at because it's *confidential?*'

'Yeah.'

Davie sighed and pushed his hands through his floppy hair. 'Who's Benny Robbins?'

'Owns a few haulage companies, apparently; although he looks more like a crook to me. Never done much business with Harte and says he can't stand the bloke. They do have something in common, though.'

Murdoch told him what he'd overheard in the bedroom at the Palm Beach party, about the host having been engaged to Amanda, about his reaction to the pool game. 'Maybe you could find out something about him?' he said. 'You know, dig up if he's got any previous or something?'

'Oh sure, I'll just hack into the government's security mainframe and download his police records. Shouldn't take more than a couple of minutes.'

'That'd be good. But you know, Davie, I was going to say to you, I don't want you getting your hopes up about this case. You know, the chances of us finding anything useful, they're zilch. If you want to keep your house – and I know that you love that place, mate, even though you treat it like a pigsty – well, this case isn't the most likely way to do it.'

Davie sat tight-lipped, shuffling through his papers like a schoolteacher while Murdoch carried the crumbs to the bin and put the dustpan and brush away.

'Charlie Holland's phone was never recovered,' Davie said at last, 'but her phone records show no unusual activity in the days preceding her death. None of the belongings she had with her that night – handbag, wallet, ID – were recovered either. There was no forensic evidence of her being murdered on the boat but, if the murder happened on the outside deck, that's just about possible, given it was raining so hard and if James had cleaned it. There were traces of a recent clean, but James says that was before the rains came and there's no way of proving it either way. Anyway, based on his testimony, the police made the wharf at Rose Bay a crime scene too, but it was more than a week after Charlie had last been seen and the wharf's a public place with lots of people going up and down it every day, not to mention the heavy rain.' He flicked further through his notes without taking a breath. 'It's funny, you can see them thinking at first that James was unlucky with the weather, then that maybe he'd been waiting for a downpour and planned it that way. It's the same with the tide charts. Apparently, it's completely possible Charlie got off the boat in Rose Bay, like Harte says, got killed there and that her body was dragged up to the mouth of Vaucluse Bay. And that it could have happened at any time, given how, here it is: "estimation of post-mortem interval in water is unreliable". But the police think that's a bit of coincidence and it's just as likely she was killed close to where she was found.'

'Typical. Cops'll think anything as long it gets them a bleeding conviction.'

Davie looked up from his notes, shook his head and, before Murdoch had a chance to say anything else, carried on in his newsreader voice. 'The Hoxton Harte Agency is a family affair. There's Amanda Hoxton, James Harte's wife and fellow board member. She was in New Zealand, Auckland to be precise, on the night Harte was out on the boat with Charlie, verified by passport control and the airline. Then there's Angus Hoxton, Amanda's brother, also on the board and Sales Director, although as far as I can tell, they don't pay him much.'

He looked up again and, this time, Murdoch got in first.

'Really?' he said. 'That surprises me. We've been out loads of times and he's always cashed up. Either way, he's a top bloke, a right laugh.

Here, Davie, why don't I just tell you about everything I've done and who I've met?'

'Angus was also in New Zealand on the night of the murder, also verified. He'd arrived there three days earlier and, on day two, Amanda was asked to fly out and help him out with something.'

'What's weird, innit? I mean, the bloke's in charge of sales but keeps on calling her to sort stuff out. Generous to a fault, maybe that's his problem? He took me out the night after the barbeque, insisted on paying for everything. I couldn't put my hand in my pocket.'

'And the last board member, apart from Harte himself, is his sister, Emma Druitt, Finance Director. Running the company in Harte's absence. At home on the night of the murder with her husband, who also works at the firm. Not quite clear what he does; a bit of everything I think, guy called ...' Davie squinted at the papers, trying to read his own writing.

'Oscar Druitt,' said Murdoch. 'A real gent. Listen, why don't I just tell you all about what I've been up to? There's something on every night, even midweek. Guess where I'm going tomorrow?'

'Just tell me what the Druitts are like first.'

'Nothing. Normal. She's quiet, bit miserable; he's a nice bloke.'

'Really? The police didn't like him. The interviewing officer said he was defensive, gave them the impression he had something to hide. But his alibi stacked up and they had no reason to suspect him. Still though ...'

Davie started making notes again and Murdoch, bored at looking at the top of his head, sat down in his chair and sighed.

'Davie.'

'What?'

'Did you hear what I said about your chances of getting that million dollars?'

'Yes.'

'And?'

Davie flipped pages as he spoke. 'And if I don't manage it, Bill, then it won't be for lack of trying. I know you just want to dress up and go to parties and we both know you can afford this to come to nothing. But I can't. And maybe it won't work, but I'd rather bust my arse and fail, than just sit on my arse and think "what if". There's plenty to do, after all. The police file mentions an expert witness, I'm going to contact him. And ...'

He'd obviously forgotten the rest of his list. 'And … if nothing else, doing this thing properly might stop people telling me how lazy and spoiled I am.'

This time, Murdoch couldn't help but laugh. 'Right. And how is lovely little DC Conquest?'

Davie scowled at him. 'I got a look at the bloody police file, Bill. The NSW Homicide Squad is based in Parramatta, do you know that? It wasn't like Nat just had it in her top drawer.'

'I'm impressed. Really, I am. That's great, mate. Now will you do me a favour? That lawyer friend of yours, what's his name?'

'Guy Hawthorne?'

'Yeah, that's the one. Will you get him to draw up a contract that Harte can't get out of? And will you take it to the prison and get him to sign it and get someone official to witness it? Because if I've learnt nothing else, it's that Harte's one sneaky bastard when it comes to business. Half the people what I've met think he deserves to be behind bars. Not for murder, maybe, but definitely for some other stuff what he's done. It'd of been easier finding suspects if it had been him what got himself killed. So get it in writing, Davie, and get it good. You got me?'

Davie looked up and they sat for a second in silence: chess players without a board.

'And will you help me on the case?'

'Course.'

'No, I mean it, Bill. You need to do more than just hang out with these people and have fun. You need to sniff around and find stuff out.'

'I just told you a load of stuff, didn't I? Look at all them notes you took. And I'm seeing half that crowd again at the races this weekend, so it's all good. Plus, guess where Angus's taking me tomorrow.'

'And you'll help? You promise?'

'I said so, didn't I? Go on, guess where we're going.'

'I don't care. I want to take you through the notes I made from the police file.'

'Yeah, well, we'll do that in a minute. But go on. I bet you can't guess.'

'Oh, I don't know,' said Davie and guessed on the first go, so it was Murdoch's turn to grow pink with frustration.

## 20

The address Angus had given him was at the top of the hill, overlooking the rest of Paddington. Hearing the name of the suburb, Murdoch had expected a five-storey house, filigree ironwork on the balconies, steps running up to a heavy front door. What he found was a modern block on Oxford Street; it was fancy enough, but not as fancy as any of the buildings he'd passed. He leant on the bell four times with no answer. Angus couldn't have forgotten – the invitation had been repeated the previous night via a badly spelled text – but Murdoch found himself cursing all the same. Trust him to open his gob and show off to Davie; now it would never happen. Then, on his fifth go at the bell, the intercom crackled and Angus's voice croaked out asking who the fuck he was and what the fuck he wanted.

The building's only lift opened directly into Angus's apartment, the mirrored doors parting to reveal a plushly-carpeted hallway. Angus was at the end of it, pyjamas skew-whiff below his hairless abs, hair sticking up at strange angles.

'What time is it?' he said, scratching and blinking uncertainly. 'And why are you here?'

'It's a quarter past nine ...'

But Angus had turned away muttering. Murdoch caught up with him in the huge living room where, beneath tall windows with views down to the harbour, the white carpet matched the low furniture. There was bright modern art on the walls.

'Bleeding hell,' said Murdoch. 'Nice place.'

'Yeah,' said Angus, looking around vaguely. 'Listen, I'll make some coffee. Why don't you wait outside?'

The terrace was bigger than the living room, tiled and quiet, with manicured hedges and flowering bushes bristling in the breeze. Murdoch raised his eyebrows and whistled. He hadn't known you could have sofas outside, not with cushions and stuff. He tried both of them for size – a regular little Goldilocks – then several of the seats around the dining table, before deciding on a swinging egg chair. As he sat, the Manly ferry came into view down on the harbour, slow and silent in the distance, dragging the millions on their way to work. Murdoch thought of Davie, desperate to make some money, and promised himself he'd try and find out something useful today.

'So why are you here?'

Angus had shuffled out, wincing in the sunlight and plonking a coffee for Murdoch onto a small side table.

'We texted,' Murdoch told him. 'You said ...'

'Oh yeah. That's today, is it? Listen, I'm going to have a shower, so do us a favour and make yourself at home. Read the paper or something. Some mates will be here in a bit, can you let them in? I'll be fine soon enough.'

An hour later, Murdoch was still alone. He didn't mind too much, not on a nice balcony in the sunshine with a fresh pack of fags and a view. Angus had said to make himself at home, so he made more coffee in the black marble kitchen, found a newspaper in the hall and carried them both back to the sunshine. He sat there happily smoking and sipping and scanning the stories while the day slowly remembered it wasn't spring any more. Then he walked to the hedge and stood on tiptoe to look across to the next terrace, empty but for some leaves in a corner. He imagined buying the place, sitting on his own terrace with a newspaper and a coffee, shouting over to Angus to ask what spiffing new adventure they were going to have today. His thoughts were interrupted by the doorbell.

'Zachary Henderson,' said the first man out of the lift. He was thickset and blond, like a German in a black-and-white war movie. He stuck out a hand but looked down towards the living room as Murdoch shook it. 'Where's Hoxie?'

'In the bathroom, getting himself pretty.'

'Smithy,' said the man who came next, big smile and frighteningly blue eye contact. 'Don't mind Zach, he's an ignorant bastard, always has been. What's your name?'

'In the bathroom, my arse,' said Henderson, striding down the hallway. 'Hoxie, you lazy bastard, get out of bed!'

Smithy smiled at Murdoch as they listened to Henderson slamming open doors until he found the room with Angus in it. Then Smithy laughed at Angus's loud croaks of complaint, so Murdoch laughed too. He didn't want to look like he'd believed Angus was in the bathroom.

'I'm a friend of James Harte's,' he managed eventually. 'Anyone else coming?'

'Shouldn't think so.' Smithy lowered his voice. 'We couldn't get tickets. Zach was supposed to get freebies in the members' stand, but they fell through.'

They watched Henderson cross the living room, pushing Angus in front of him, out from one doorway and in through another, a brief whiteness of bathroom before they were lost to view again. The door remained slightly open behind them, its handle and the wood around it smashed, and Angus's complaints grew louder as the shower started running and they heard Henderson bullying him into it.

'We've got Buckley's of seeing the first ball,' said Smithy. 'I'm not going to let Zach forget this. Any idea how the TV works?'

Before Murdoch could reply, Henderson's head appeared around the bathroom door, steam thick behind him.

'For God's sake, Smithy! Mix him a drink.'

But Smithy was concentrating on the remote control, discovered under the coffee table. It was the size of a small keyboard, so well designed you could hardly see the buttons. Murdoch said he'd mix the drinks.

Forty minutes later they were crossing Oxford Street and walking down towards the Sydney Cricket Ground. Yes, said Angus, he had the passes. And cash, he had loads of cash – he pulled out an impressive pile of hundreds and started waving it around. But what about drugs, how the hell could they get some drugs? Henderson told him to shut up and put his money away and Smithy told them both to hurry for maths. Murdoch, unsure how to behave, smiled and said little. The other three men had been at school together. The insults they traded were half vulgar, half ancient code, at first spoken so loudly Murdoch wondered if it was a competition to see who was the most confident. But then, as they got closer to the SCG and the pavements around them grew crowded, the three calmed into good behaviour. Murdoch noticed it was the presence of older people and women that affected them most. Like there was a different code about how to act around them, a different language from when it was just the men alone.

'You been here before?' Angus asked when they reached the gates, fans of all ages pressing around them. Murdoch admitted he hadn't.

'You should go into the main stand,' said Smithy. 'Soak up the atmosphere. Angus, give him his ticket and he can meet us up there.'

Angus turned, furious. 'Later, you idiot. Once we're inside the box.'

Smithy shrank back in a blush while Henderson, stepping out of Angus's line of sight, rolled his eyes and mouthed an obscenity.

'You guys go up,' said Angus quietly. 'You too, Bill, stick close with them. I'll see you up there.'

Then he turned and disappeared into the crowd.

Murdoch followed Henderson and Smith upstairs, behind sections of seating, through doorways, trying to work out which signs they were following. The three of them passed through numerous security checks, middle-aged men in fluoros glancing at their tickets and waving them on until, after several minutes and two more sets of stairs, they reached a quiet carpeted space: a pastel curving corridor with glimpses through tinted windows of the crowd below.

'Here we go,' muttered Henderson as he led them towards a grey door holding a laminated Hoxton Harte logo. 'Smile, ladies.'

In front of the door stood the first security man they'd met who looked like he could provide security. Bald and pale-eyed with thick lips under a squashed nose, he was broad around the shoulders and stomach. Henderson and Smithy flashed their passes, not a smile between them, and Murdoch dutifully did the same. But then, before the security guard could open the door, Henderson stopped suddenly, like he'd forgotten something.

'Excuse me,' he said to the security guard. 'I think a friend of mine is in one of the other boxes, but I can't remember the name of it. Mind if I have a look?'

'Sorry, sir,' said the bald man, 'I can't really let you—'

'Why don't you come with me? That way, if I find the right one, you can go in and ask. Check I'm not doing anything wrong. Come on!'

The guard had no choice but to follow as Henderson strode down the corridor squinting at the logos on the other doors, none of which had security.

'Go in,' said Smithy, shoving Murdoch toward the Hoxton Harte door. 'Back in a bit.'

'What the—'

'Go in!'

The Hoxton Harte SCG Corporate Hospitality Suite was a medium-sized room that stepped down twice to floor-to-ceiling glass overlooking the pitch. In front of the wide green view was a loose row of bar stools, the only furniture in the suite. Closer to the door, at the back of the room, was a small, well-stocked kitchen, snacks on the counters and a short-skirted girl

117

beside them smiling hello. The girl was young and freckled, gingerish hair and an eager smile; maybe still a teenager, maybe a bit older than that. As Murdoch walked in, she picked up a tray of drinks, her brow creasing in concentration.

'Welcome to the Sydney Cricket Ground,' she said. 'My name's Ursula, can I offer you a beer?'

Before Murdoch could answer, the door behind him flew open and Angus and Smithy pushed through laughing, shutting the door quickly behind them. Murdoch knew each of the men had a valid pass for the suite, he'd seen the tickets himself. So why the need to divert the guard?

'Welcome to the Sydney Cricket Ground,' said the young hostess again. 'Are you gentlemen together?'

'Oh no,' said Angus, still laughing as he lunged forward to swipe a Crownie. 'We're all yours, darling.'

Then Henderson arrived and they were off.

Murdoch had never had much time for cricket. He'd known blokes who'd listen to it on the radio for hours; blokes what told him that watching a game with a beer was the closest thing to heaven on earth. Murdoch had never believed them. A game that lasted five days? Some people didn't know how to kill time. Still, in the previous week he'd read the rules four times and, once done with that, learned the names of all the players in both teams. He still didn't get why this series of games was such a big deal, or what to say if someone got caught short or whatever it was, but he thought he'd got the basics. He needn't have bothered. Even Smithy, so keen to see every ball of the day, seemed only half-interested in the action on the pitch. Angus and Henderson barely mentioned it, staring disinterestedly at the players as they talked about everything and nothing, drinking beer like it was water in the desert and making less than subtle references to Ursula's youthful figure. The hostess did a good job of ignoring them, but when Murdoch tried to give her a comforting smile, she ignored that too, keeping her distance behind the snacks.

As Murdoch listened to the other men's conversation, waiting for an opportunity to mention James Harte, he squinted down at the pitch and tried to remember what to look for. It was a good enough view – the best in the ground he guessed – but each time the crowd roared outside he felt like he was missing something. Like he was inside the telly instead of watching

118

it; at a famous battle or a riot or something, standing where he couldn't see what was happening. He stared and stared at the men in white, running and throwing and catching, but he only saw the ball once or twice, the rest of the time it was too fast or too far away or both. At the back of the room – or the box, as he learned to call it – in the corner above the kitchen units was a telly and there he could see the action perfectly. Whenever something interesting happened (he could tell by the crowd's reaction), all he had to do was turn and he could see it repeated in slow motion, while below him the real players were standing around or rubbing their hands or waving at each other silently. He'd have been just as well off at home, he thought, but perhaps he was missing the point.

The crowd was more interesting. Half of them had dressed up for the occasion: groups of ten or more in matching T-shirts or stupid big hats, even a gang in fake mediaeval armour waving shields with the England flag. He could see them all laughing and yelling, shouting at the players on the pitch, swaying in one motion as they sang together. He watched them throw up their arms and scream with joy or pain or just for the fun of being in a Mexican wave.

'The bottom's dropped out of reinsurance,' Henderson said to Angus about two hours in. They had sent Ursula off to find more beer.

'No margins,' said Smithy.

'That's right, the margins aren't in it any more. Quantified risk, my arse. It's a mug's game. Wished I'd gone into advertising like you, Hoxie.'

'And James,' said Murdoch, deciding the conversation wasn't going to go that way by itself. 'Do you know Angus's business partner, James Harte?'

'It's PR,' slurred Angus. 'I've told you, Henderson, every time I've seen you for the last five years. P fucking R. When's that tart coming back with the beer?'

Murdoch flinched at that, but as he turned from the glass to say something, he saw Henderson catch Smithy's eye. Smithy nodded, a tiny movement, then slid off his stool and patted himself down, checking every pocket.

'Just going for a pee,' he said.

'Here,' said Angus, leaning heavily on Murdoch's shoulder. 'You and my sister, what's that all about then?'

Murdoch felt himself colour. Henderson had heard the question and was waiting for an answer too. 'What do you mean?'

119

'What do I mean!' Angus turned to Henderson. 'You should see the two of them, little lovebirds. Perving at each other like there's no one else in the room. And when Mands isn't there, Murdoch looks like a lost puppy.' He caught the look on Murdoch's face. 'Don't worry! No harm in it. When the cat's away and all that. Here, look at them!'

Angus had spotted the men in armour. He insisted everyone look at them, stupid Pommie cunts, why didn't the Aussies in the crowd turn on them? Then Ursula arrived back with more beer and Henderson crossed quickly to take two from her before Angus could get off his stool.

'You're a Pom,' he said to Murdoch, holding out a bottle like Murdoch hadn't refused the previous four offered. 'You don't want to take that kind of shit from Hoxie.'

Murdoch laughed. 'You're just stirring, mate. You don't even know what side I'm supporting. It's like I once said to James—'

'You are a Pom, though,' snapped Angus, swiping the bottle from Henderson and pointing with it accusingly. Murdoch held his eye.

'Yeah, but I'm Aussie too, aren't I? Got two passports, thanks very much.'

'You can use that to avoid paying tax,' Henderson told them. 'Tell the tax man you're out of the country, show him your Aussie passport records, sneak back in on the other one.'

Murdoch thought that sounded like bullshit, but before he could respond Angus was proposing a toast. 'Screwing the taxman, let's drink to that!' He took a long swig from his beer, then seemed to remember what they'd been talking about. 'So, Bill, where are you from? Are you a cockney?'

Murdoch explained what a cockney was and how you had to know where you'd been born. Then he answered Angus's slurred questions about why he had come to Australia, did he like it, and who was he actually supporting? More questions than Angus had ever asked until Murdoch realised he'd never seen him this drunk before. Neither of them noticed Henderson leave.

'Here, look at that,' said Angus from nowhere. He'd lost interest in Murdoch's answers and was looking past him, to where the window onto the pitch turned a corner and looked into the adjacent box. Turning on his stool, Murdoch saw the back of a woman leaning against the glass. She was a slim redhead in a tight black skirt and red-soled high heels, long legs and a thigh gap. Her hair wobbled as she talked to someone out of sight.

'Ursula,' shouted Angus. 'Beer!'

'Please,' said Murdoch when he saw the expression on the hostess's face. She'd picked up two beers but was hesitant to leave the safety of the kitchen. Murdoch walked over and took one of them from her.

'Thanks,' he said quietly. 'Don't worry, love, he doesn't bite.'

'He does grope, though,' she said and he realised she was close to tears. 'And I don't like it.'

Murdoch was surprised. He hadn't seen anything like that, but then he hadn't really been looking. Now that he thought about it, Ursula had been hiding behind that counter for over an hour.

'I'll keep him away from you,' he said, quietly. 'You'll be all right.'

'What are you two whispering about!' yelled Angus from the window, still staring at the redhead in the adjacent box. 'And where's my fucking beer? Hey, look at this.'

He checked they were both looking, then stood unsteadily, unzipped himself and pressed his floppy cock against the window, dry-humping the glass between him and the back of the redhead. His realistic sound effects were interrupted by a sob from Ursula before she turned and ran out of the room.

'Angus, mate. Come on, put it away, no one wants to see that.'

'Oh dear.' Angus turned and looked up with a surprised smile. 'Oops!'

Ursula had let the door slam behind her, but now it flew open and a huge half-untucked man appeared, tie loose around his neck, his face red and flushed. He smelled like he'd had as much beer as Angus but he moved a lot more steadily: an ex-footballer or something. Pushing past Murdoch, he took the steps down to the window in one go and pinned Angus against the glass.

'What the hell are you playing at, you dog? That's my wife!'

'Take it easy,' said Murdoch.

'That's my wife, my fucking wife, you arsehole.'

The big man let go of Angus with one hand so he could stick a fat finger in his face.

'Who the hell do you think—'

The end of his sentence was lost to a strangled yell as Angus put his full mouth around the finger, bit down hard with his molars and tore at it like a dog determined to win a tug-of-war. The crowd outside the window roared to life, twenty thousand people cheering or wincing, the noise a surprise even through the thickness of glass. Murdoch was caught off guard. He took a second to realise the crowd was reacting to a different fight and was still trying to work out how to get Angus off the other man's finger when the bald security guard arrived with an even wider friend. They piled into the low space near the window and Murdoch decided to let them sort it out. He noticed Ursula in the blue-carpeted corridor outside, her face blotchy with tears.

'You're animals,' she said to him. 'You're disgusting.'

The dark-skinned man who sorted things out introduced himself as Vincent. Murdoch was impressed. Not by Vincent's Italian suit or his frightening physique or even the complete calm with which he handled things. No, it was Vincent's manners that Murdoch noticed. He shook Murdoch's hand, firmly but not too firmly, called him 'sir' and asked him his relationship to Mr Hoxton. Even the way he said 'Mr Hoxton' was perfect, like it was a medical condition, the polite way of saying something embarrassing, something you didn't want to talk about. Vincent helped Angus back into his trousers and then sat him in a corner with Murdoch, the bald security guard watching over them awkwardly. Then Vincent sent the other wider security guard off with the injured husband, his now fully untucked shirt missing a few buttons and a thick white towel around his hand slowly turning pink. When Vincent spotted the fat quarter finger Angus had spat out onto the green carpet, he picked it up, like a gardener plucking a caterpillar from his precious lawn, bundled it with ice into another towel and told the bald guard to run after his colleague. No, he didn't know if it could be sewn back on. Then Vincent had to calm the redhead wife. He'd managed to keep everyone else out of the box, telling Ursula to help next door, asking Murdoch to sit with his back against the side window so no one could see in that way. But the wife pushed her way in from the corridor and stood screaming at Vincent at the kitchen counter, one hand on the door so none of them could leave, every second word emphasised with the jab of an expensive nail towards Angus and Murdoch. The words 'psychos' and 'madmen' and 'scum' punctuated her rage.

'Jesus,' murmured Angus. 'If I'd seen the front of her, none of this would have happened.'

The crowd outside the glass roared as another wicket fell and Murdoch instinctively looked up at the telly to watch it fall slowly again. Someone out there was having the day of his life.

'Yes, madam,' he heard Vincent say, 'you are, of course, more than welcome to call the police. But, I think you might find it more financially rewarding to settle with Mr Hoxton separately. He tends to pay well in such situations, although it's up to you, of course.'

That took the wind out of her sails. She wanted witnesses' names, she'd taken photographs, everyone had seen what had happened. But she'd also seen the logo on the door, recognised the sound of money in the name and ranted for only another few minutes before she told Angus he was going to pay till it hurt. Then she turned on her red-soled heels and left. Only then was it Vincent's turn to lose his cool. Angus and Murdoch heard him in the corridor giving it to the bald security guard, back from his little delivery.

'How the hell did that idiot get in here? What did I tell you? What was the number one thing I said to you about this suite? Your job title has the words "security" and "guard" in it; tell me which bit of that is unclear?'

Murdoch sat thinking about his survival instincts, how quickly he'd lost them over the previous weeks, living the fat and lazy life. He should have known something was on the way as soon as Smithy and Henderson left. He looked over at Angus, his pretty-boy face smirking at the heated lecture outside. Then Angus wobbled on his stool and, righting himself, glanced up and caught the expression on Murdoch's face.

'Everyone loves Angus!' he said.

'Can you blame them?'

'No, I suppose not. I'm not charming like James or clever like Emma and I don't get away with stuff like Amanda. Why would anyone love me?'

They both looked up at the sound of the door opening. Vincent appeared, so calm that Murdoch wondered if it had really been him shouting at the guard.

'Look, mate,' said Murdoch. 'I'm really sorry about this.'

'Take him home, please, sir, and don't bring him back here again. We don't want the publicity, so we're happy to divert people from pressing charges, but it won't always work. And we really don't want him here.' He gave Angus a last look and shook his head. 'He's like one of those chihuahuas. Always going for the biggest fight he can find and expecting everyone else to protect him.'

# Clues and Obstacles

*'Like I said before,' said Suzie, 'a story is nothing more than a demonstration of how someone gets what they want. Or, perhaps, how they don't. But whether they get what they want or not, if the outcome is too easy, then there really is no story. "Once upon a time there was a man called Bill and he wanted to solve a murder. Then he solved the murder. The End." What kind of a story would that be?'*

*'A short story?' tried Murdoch, keen to pretend he was keeping up.*

*'Yes, but even then, not a very interesting one! Because, if you think about it, Bill, the vast majority of any story is made up of the obstacles that get between the characters and what they want. You think of any book you've ever read, any film you've ever seen, any interesting documentary – eighty or ninety per cent of it is made up of obstacles between the main character and his or her goal. Now, in your case, because we're going to write a murder mystery, we need obstacles that look like clues, and, of course, important clues that look like nothing but obstacles.'*

## 21.

For almost its entire length, Pierre Street formed the northern border of Montauban Public School. It ran parallel to the minefield, past the tennis courts and alongside the tiny playground where Davie, as a child, had often sat and cried. Then, at some point, it became La Mer Street. In Montauban it was difficult to tell where any street ended and another began, few houses bothering to display street numbers. Being the estate agent in this suburb, thought Davie, pulling up outside number fifty-four, required a specialised knowledge, one shared only by Bob, the postie.

'Fifty-four Pierre?' old Bob had said to him, hearing the house was up for lease again. 'Old Faithless on the curve there? She'll keep you in business forever, Davo. Place must be haunted, no one ever wants to stay.'

Bob was right about that. Half the houses in Montie were weekenders for Sydneysiders and a good part of the rest were owner-occupied. Permanent rentals like Old Faithless were famously hard to come by, but the house at 54 Pierre Street struggled to keep anyone for more than a year. Bob was wrong about the reason, though, unless by 'haunted' he meant 'so damp you have to wear shoes inside to stop your feet from getting wet'. Davie had shown the house yet again earlier in the week, embarrassed by the rent demanded, but knowing the couple who had sneered at every room would soon come back and sign. After that, Davie would have to listen to them complaining for a year until they moved out again. He'd have his annual conversation with the landlord about making improvements to the place; he'd watch the landlord ignore him and put up the rent; then he'd start doing viewings again. God, he hated his job.

On his visit earlier in the week, Davie had remembered the house's 'third bedroom' was a windowless box halfway down the dingy hallway. The two brothers who had just vacated the place had apparently used it as a study, leaving a desk in there that looked like it had been found on the street and, clamped to its front, an ancient anglepoise lamp that actually worked. *Perfect,* Davie had thought, looking at it in the gloom. *Just perfect.*

Living alone with a view only marginally better than the one from the office, Davie had, until recently, never understood the point of working from home. His shack could be lonely; whereas, from his desk in Deutsch & Bowler, he could see whoever was passing by and decide whether or not to pop out for a chat. More importantly, he only needed to stroll across the road to tell if the surf was worth nipping out for. But recent weeks had revealed to him the flip side of these advantages. Anyone walking past Deutsch & Bowler could also peer through the window and see him at his desk and, if they felt like it, pop in for a chat. And, no matter how much he needed to concentrate on the reams of Hoxton Harte financial data he had still to get through, there was no way he could concentrate when the surf was pumping less than a hundred metres away. He had thought he'd prefer not to hear the ocean to know it was rolling without him. Or – and the truth of this bit him, although he'd never admit it to Bill – knowing it was a perfect day for going to the cricket, the first day of the most exciting tour in years. And as for working in the shack? Forget it. How could he concentrate in the home he was about to lose?

So, hiding in the study at 54 Pierre Street had seemed like the perfect solution. Now, though, a closer inspection of the dank and windowless room made him question his wisdom. He hesitated in the doorway, smelling the mould in the air and trying to shake the idea that all too soon this was the kind of house he'd be shown around himself, desperate for the opportunity to live there. He forced the idea away, clapped his hands and rubbed them together, forcing the smile he gave when showing others a better property. Before he could change his mind, he turned and strode out to the car to fetch his laptop, a camp chair, four blankets and the remaining boxes of HHA company information. Back in the windowless study, he turned off his phone, found where he'd last left off and threw himself into the work.

Often, in bed at night waiting for sleep, Davie would pretend he was somewhere else. In a cave during a blizzard, on a sleigh racing across the Russian steppes, in a spaceship withstanding a meteor storm. Always somewhere cosy surrounded by harsh elements. Wrapped in warm blankets in a damp house, it was easy to play the same game. To enjoy his little pool of lamplight, making notes against the tiny numbers until they made some kind of sense. Whoever at Hoxton Harte had sent across the information hadn't held back. There were copies of invoices, receipts, telephone bills, itemised accounts, surprisingly large restaurant bills, payslips, tax returns, share certificates, bank statements, payroll ledgers. Davie learned that Angus Hoxton's salary had been small from the start and never increased, not even in recent years when payments to the other directors had grown exponentially. The financial reports went back to the very beginning of the agency and, time and again, Davie found the signatures of the other directors – and, in the early days, that of Charlie Holland – but never anything signed by Angus.

Davie went through every piece of paper, every line in every spreadsheet, remembering his promise to himself to be diligent. He had grown up helping his father do his books, but otherwise his finance skills were self-taught, honed largely on massaging his monthly sales and leasing results until they looked like something close to his targets. Maybe this explained why the P&L results from the early days of Hoxton Harte didn't make sense to him now. They looked, if anything, like the opposite of what they had to be. Deciding to search for a confirmation of his limited understanding online, but with no Wi-Fi in the empty house, he decided to tether off his phone. He had barely turned the thing on, flicking through 'Settings' to remember how things worked, when it started vibrating in his hand. 'She Who Must Be Avoided' in white letters above an invitation to 'Answer,

*Message or Remind Me Later'.* Where, wondered Davie, was the option to *'Reject Forever?'* He took a deep breath.

'Deutsch and Bowler, this is Davie Simms; how can I help you?'

'Davie, where on earth are you? You're bunking off work again, aren't you?'

'Hello, Hannah.'

'Are you at the beach?'

'Did it occur to you I might be at work?'

'Well, it did until you answered the phone like that. You only ever answer that way when you're not at work and feeling guilty about it. Are you still in bed?'

'No. Funnily enough, I'm in the office and a bit busy right now. How can I help you?'

She paused and he pictured her choosing her words, her pale eyelashes fluttering. 'You were going to call me on the thirtieth to let me know what you'd decided about the house. That was over a week ago, so now I'm phoning you.'

'Sorry, I'd assumed you'd call me on the thirtieth. At nine a.m.'

'Don't be sarcastic, Davie, it doesn't suit you. I need to know if you're going to buy it or not. If not, I think it's only fair—'

'I'm going to buy it.' Davie was surprised to hear the words come out of his mouth. They felt as borrowed as the house around him. Then again, it was probably the house around him that was motivating him to say them.

'What did you say?'

'I said I'm going to buy it, Hannah. You said six hundred and fifty thousand and I think that's fair, despite the state of the roof and the steps out the front. So let's do it. But you'll need to wait a couple of months. I won't have the money before then.'

'A couple of months! That's at least two, which means ... February? That's crazy. It's already been two weeks since I first mentioned it to you.'

'Are you in a hurry, Hannah? Have you already found the new place you want to buy?'

'Well, no, but—'

'But you are happy to throw me out of my home of over ten years just so you can release funds. Well, you know what, you're going to have to wait two months.'

127

He gained a few seconds of silence from that: an impressive achievement on any scale. Surprised by the success, he shifted nervously in the camp chair, its creaks echoing in the dark. It was strange that Hannah had thought he might be at the beach: it must still be light outside.

'The first of February,' Hannah said at last. 'You have that money to me in full by the first of February or I'm selling that house from under you.'

'Fine. It's a deal. Anything else?'

But Hannah didn't reply and Davie realised, with a strange mix of horror and delight, that she had hung up on him. He relished that for a minute or two, then remembered why he'd turned on his phone. Within minutes he was lost again, comparing numbers and names in his little cocoon of lamplight and screen light and blankets.


## 22.


The weekend arrived on an arid orange wind that salted the air and spread fire bans. It flattened the ocean and somewhere – you could smell it – pushed flames through the forest. Saturday morning found Murdoch on the freeway again, on yet another drive to Sydney. The incident with Angus at the SCG had done nothing to dampen his enthusiasm for his new-found social life. So Angus Hoxton could be a twat when drunk – he wasn't on his own there. Half the blokes Murdoch had ever been banged up with were inside for something they'd done under the influence. Drink, drugs, gambling, jealousy, lust, greed. Some fuels were illegal, but most of them weren't.

Friday night, Murdoch had phoned Davie to tell him what had happened at the cricket. Not because he honestly thought Angus Hoxton could have killed anyone, not intentionally. More because he was pissed off with the man. Suggesting Angus might have framed his best mate – talking to Davie about the possibilities – felt like a fair enough little revenge for a ruined day down in Sydney. Except Davie, of course, had almost wet himself with excitement, explaining how the others seemed to keep Angus away from money. How maybe that was a motive. Then Davie had reminded Murdoch time was running out: it was only a few months until Harte's trial. He was spending every spare minute reading through the documents the agency had sent over, but they needed to narrow their focus.

Murdoch reminded Davie not to get his hopes up. It could still have been anyone, he said, but sure, he'd keep his eye on Angus for now.

'And everyone else too,' said Davie. 'Find out whatever you can about any of them. When are you seeing Oscar Druitt next?'

There was a catch to Davie's voice that Murdoch had never heard before and he wondered what that was about. If Hannah had called him again. 'I'm on the way to see him now,' he said. 'Why?'

'I found a transaction from years ago. An F Druitt & Co deposited three hundred thousand dollars into the HHA trading account. It seems to have been repaid two years later over several instalments. Could you ask about it?'

Murdoch promised he would, no idea how that was going to come up in conversation.

'And keep an ear open for anything else,' said Davie, that strange catch in his voice again. 'Anything could help.'

Murdoch found himself promising, yet again, to do whatever he could. He didn't admit he thought that was probably nothing.

He was thinking about this conversation now, on his drive to Sydney, when, lucky in the fastest lane on the climb from the Hawkesbury, he passed a convoy of tall black coaches. His reflection was clear in their panelling and he took a good look at himself, driving along with the top down, sunglasses keeping the world at bay above a well-cut khaki suit. Recently, it seemed, life had taken a turn for the better. Two kilometres later, realising he was burning, he indicated across two lanes then pulled into the hard shoulder to stop and put up the roof. Hearing horns behind him, he looked in his rear-view mirror and saw a white hatchback had made two thirds of the same move, crossing the middle lane to pull into slower traffic. The car it had cut up beeped again and Murdoch watched the two of them pass. The white car – a Corolla – had an insignia on its door: a yellow logo with *'No Birds'* in black. It was a hire car, you saw lots of them about. *'No Birds'* was a joke that Davie had explained, but he couldn't remember what it meant.

He passed the Corolla a few kilometres later. It was crawling downhill in the slow lane, ignoring a sixteen-wheeler tailgating behind. Murdoch noticed the first three letters of its number plate – BUG – and thought, 'Yeah, that makes sense'. Which would have been that – la de da, next random thought on the drive to Sydney. Except ten minutes later he left the fast lane again to let through a trio of bikies. They left fifty metres of clear road in their wake, until a white Corolla pulled out from the middle lane. Murdoch watched it approach, blinking to be certain. Then, as it glided past, he made a note of the number – BUG 159 S – and made himself think nothing of it. Same hire car company, different car. Thousands of them about. I wonder what Amanda will be wearing? He refused to keep an eye out, just picked lanes instead, sticking mostly to the right as he caught up with and sped through thick groups of traffic. But as he started the final descent towards the Wahroonga exit, there it was again, mirroring his manoeuvre from the right-hand lane. He moved left again and let it pass – BUG 159 S, a large man driving. No reason for it to mean a thing.

Leaving the freeway to become part of the groaning Pacific Highway traffic, he deliberately chose the wrong lane, then did it again: the opposite of the game he normally played. Stay left at Boundary Street instead of merging right. Stay right at Roseville cinema instead of moving to the middle. Then, the normal game. On the left at Ashley Street for a faster go at the lights, in the middle at Lane Cove because there was always a bus turning right. And always there, faster or slower than the rest of the traffic, eight or ten cars behind – BUG 159 S. *No Birds*.

When he had stopped to put up the roof, Murdoch had also taken off his jacket and laid it on the passenger seat. Now, he reached across, fumbling inside it, while he kept one eye on the traffic behind him. He had put today's invitation in the jacket's inside pocket, bending it to avoid creasing either the embossed cardboard or the jacket's silk lining. Now he wanted the invitation back, to get the exact address into his phone so he could find a quieter route there and take a better look at the guy in the Corolla. But the jacket didn't want to let the invitation go. The Corolla appeared behind him again and Murdoch swore, both at it and at the khaki jacket twisting and creasing on the seat beside him. As the Corolla disappeared from view, he gave a final tug and the invitation came away in his hand, the jacket crumpling in defeat onto the floor in front of the passenger seat. Murdoch scowled at it, swore again and looked back at the road ahead of him, noticing too late a bus indicating slowly into his lane. During the second it took him to realise the bus wouldn't stop, he thought of Amanda doing something similar in Palm Beach, stopping suddenly and beeping her horn at a car full of tourists. But he was too late to stop without hitting the bus so he accelerated and curved left around it instead, wincing as it hissed and screeched, its dirty reflection filling his mirrors as it juddered to a stop and missed him. Twenty metres back, in his rear-view mirror, the Corolla caused more horns as it forced its way into the right-hand lane that was pouring past the bus.

At the next set of lights, as the traffic slowed and stopped around him, Murdoch had his idea too late, or acted on it too early, maybe. Either way, by the time he'd undone his seatbelt and was out of the car, the lights up ahead were already changing. And by the time he'd reached the Corolla, the cars behind his empty Merc were leaning on their horns. Not that he gave a shit about that, but the lane to his left was moving now. When the driver of the Corolla saw him approaching, he swung into it – more complaints from horns and tyres – and accelerated out of sight. Murdoch saw him clearly through the windscreen: a thick-necked man, dark, with dark eyes, pockmarked skin and a grey T-shirt, staring straight ahead and ignoring Murdoch like he hadn't even seen him.

'What are you doing, you moron?!'

A blond man in a Volvo with two children in the back, stuck in the traffic behind Murdoch's Merc, had wound down his window and was yelling at him. Murdoch walked up close, held two fingers to the man's face like a gun and slowly pulled the trigger.

23.

It took him forty minutes in a side street to breathe away his anger. Murdoch knew the dangerous depths of his own temper, knew the man in the Volvo had been lucky he'd had no real gun. Rage: that was another fuel to power you to prison. But not today. No one was going to steal this day from him, not when Amanda had promised she'd be there. If her sudden appearance in his life had taught him anything, it was that he had no need to be paranoid. He'd worried so much about her when she'd first appeared in Montauban, and look how well things had worked out. The man following him, it would be something to do with the case – at least now he'd have something real to tell Davie about. The blond man in the Volvo, he'd not done nothing wrong. Murdoch spoke to himself this way until he was bored of the arguments. After that, he forced himself to stop thinking about anything at all, just to listen to his breath instead, to the sounds of the street around him, the dry and barely moving air. Forty minutes.

Back on the Pacific Highway, there was no sign of the Corolla, ahead or behind him. The thick traffic wanted to ruin Murdoch's mood again, but he resisted with more breathing exercises until, in Randwick, the process of parking made things properly better again. One glance at his ticket by a grey and crumpled security guard was enough to direct him to the VIP car park, tucked behind the main grandstand. There, a closer examination of the thick cardboard – both sides – was cross-checked against a list by a smartly dressed West African in a tiny shed. The man sighed and frowned and then produced a huge white smile, pressing a button beside him and pointing across the car park. There, in the wall of the grandstand itself, a barrier was rising in jerks, a red-brick courtyard visible in the shade beyond. As Murdoch rolled the Merc slowly inside, one eye in the rear-view mirror, a tall brunette appeared beside the car. She was wearing a chauffeur's uniform, or some designer's idea of what a female chauffeur would wear: military green with a peaked cap at an angle on her lustrous hair. She watched the barrier close behind him, motioned for him to lower his window, then leant in and offered to park his car.

'Complimentary service for our pavilion guests, sir. May I?'

It was hot outside, but Murdoch remembered to take his jacket from the floor of the car, dusting it lightly until the brunette took it from him and held it open for his arms.

'Nice suit.'

'Thanks. It's new.'

'The entrance is through there.'

She smiled again, no invitation to more conversation, got into his car and drove it into the shadows.

Murdoch had been to the races once as a kid. He'd have been thirteen or fourteen, so it must have been when he was on a day release, or maybe a summer between institutions. A mate of his, Tommy Sterling – dead a few years later from an overdose – had had an uncle who was a bookie. The uncle had told them where to climb the fence and they'd done pockets all day – just cash, wallets thrown to the ground like they'd fallen there. It had been fun until they'd got drunk, then they'd started gambling themselves.

Tommy's uncle was a small Irishman; Murdoch could picture him like it was yesterday: a pale bloke with fast and furtive hands and a vicious mouth that barely moved, even when he spoke.

'Keep dur money dine. You want me to lose me feckin' licence?'

He told the two boys of a horse that couldn't lose and they had rolled up everything they'd got that day – over seven hundred quid – and put it into his briefly open hand. It was the best thing that could have happened to him, Murdoch knew that now – he'd never gambled on chance again – but it had stung like a punch at the time.

He walked out of the shadows of the grandstand and told himself to relax. No way someone could have followed him through here. Whoever the man in the white Corolla was, he could wait. There was nothing he could do now. He might as well have fun in the meantime. Blah, blah, blah, until again he was bored of his own voice in his head. He took some more deep breaths, followed a high-fenced corral into the sunshine and spotted the tent he was looking for. Not that they called it a tent, of course. It was a 'pavilion', because you could charge double for anything in French. One of four white structures in a row, it stretched forty metres towards the track. The area around it and the other pavilions – the *enclosure* – was relatively quiet, sealed off from the rest of the racecourse by wire fencing, goons in suits checking invitations at the openings. Beyond the fence was the main crowd, packed in tight in their fancy clothes. It reminded Murdoch of the cricket, except here he was glad to be removed from it all. Behind the wire, cross currents carried people untidily through the ocean of suits and dresses. Everyone was shouting over everyone's shouts while phones rang and were yelled into and tiny hats wobbled with laughter. Drinks were held high, hands were waved with impossible optimism while stragglers just laughed at the madness of it all. Murdoch found himself looking for the pockmarked man from the Corolla and blinked the idea away.

On his side of the fence things were calmer. Murdoch found a tissue and pretended to blow his nose so he could follow the progress of three catwalk models towards the furthest pavilion. They moved slowly, like they were testing the grass beneath their spiky heels before fully trusting their weight. Legs and arse, legs and arse, they looked more related to the horses than to the rest of the crowd. He passed a real horse, a fake jockey on its back handing out flyers, the man at its muzzle in a top hat and tails on the hottest day of the summer so far. The man smiled at Murdoch and Murdoch remembered he was allowed to be there. William Murdoch, Esquire hadn't climbed the fence; he'd been sent an invitation with his name on it. But then, at the entrance to the Champagne Pavilion, stood two huge Islanders, strong features offset by collars and ties.

'Good morning, sir. Your invitation, please?'

Murdoch told himself it wasn't the Islanders' fault. They hadn't looked at him in a way you could punch someone for; hadn't said it like they were surprised he'd even got that far. But still, here they were between him and where he wanted to go. He'd left the invitation on the Merc's passenger seat, distracted by the brunette who'd helped him into his jacket. A hint of his earlier mood reappeared – a fleck of soot on a washing day – and he turned before he could see the Islanders smirk.

'Back in a sec. I left it in the car.'

Please let them challenge him on that. Please let them accompany him back to the courtyard and the brunette and his beautiful car, just so he could see their faces when he held up the thickly embossed cardboard with his name on it.

'ID will do.'

Murdoch turned back and looked the two men up and down.

'Sorry?'

'Have you got any photo ID on you, sir?' The bigger of the two Islanders, a man with a long-before broken nose, gave him a warm smile. 'Your driver's licence, for example? We can look you up on the list; shouldn't be an issue.'

Murdoch flipped open his wallet and handed over the plastic with his face on it.

'Nice suit, sir, if you don't mind me saying. Mr Murdoch, here you are, sir. This way please.'

Murdoch resisted the open arm and turned instead to look across the enclosure at the crowd beyond the wire fence. There was no one there he recognised. All the same, conscious of the Islanders watching him, he raised a hand and gave a wave. Like he wanted to say goodbye.

Inside the pavilion it was easier not to think about what had happened on the drive down. The smell was the same as in any other tent – broken grass, trapped air, canvas – and the light was the same too, softened and thickened as it came through the fabric, floating above the crowd like all their chatter had produced a harmless gas. But there, all comparisons with any other tent Murdoch had known stopped. The enclosed space stretched across panels of wooden flooring towards its open end where two dozen people were facing the track. Behind them, halfway towards him, was a large square bar where slim women in the same green uniform as the brunette who had parked his car were pouring drinks for punters on all four sides. Oversized arrangements of green and white flowers sat on the bar's corners, drooping over ice buckets full of green bottles. The pavilion was full, but the crowd moved differently from the heaving throng he'd seen beyond the fence. It was the same dance but in slow motion and whispers – excuse me, thank you, that's very kind – no one in a hurry at all. It was loud though – the enclosed space, the happy chatter, the jazz trio in the corner – and when a green-uniformed girl approached him with a smile, Murdoch struggled to understand what she wanted.

'Right,' he said. He forgot every time. 'Just a beer, thanks.'

He did a full circle of the bar before he found anyone he knew but he was more than happy to take his time. To smile and wait for the crowd to part, to step sidewards and let another beautiful woman through. On the side of the bar nearest the track he recognised someone from the telly. Andy something. It was a daytime fashion programme; Murdoch hadn't often watched it. The TV presenter was fat, less fat in real life than on the screen, but fat all the same. On the telly he was always laughing and he was laughing now, that was why Murdoch noticed him. The loud throaty cackle he'd heard before. Andy was sitting between two skinny men with leather faces and stiff hair, all three of them on high bar chairs, the TV presenter's arse hiding the sides of his, so he looked like a man on four stilts. As Murdoch watched, Andy put back his head to laugh again. Then the man to his right leant forward and whispered something and, again, the presenter laughed, the camp throatiness breaking for a second to catch a breath before starting up again. Murdoch watched Andy put his hand over his mouth, pretending to be embarrassed as he looked around, then take it away and laugh some more. It was more than enough for Murdoch, but he had to press past the three men to get around the bar. As he did so, the small crowd behind him burst into cheers, like it was competing with Andy Arthur – that was his name: 'AA' they called him – by screaming horses' names. It reminded

135

Murdoch of the cricket again: Angus tearing at the angry man's finger. He blinked the image away, turned and stood on tiptoe and watched as the horses burst into view. They were surprisingly close, their hooves vibrating the ground beneath him, their sweat and meat and speed filling the gap at the end of the tent with life and colour and then – just as suddenly – gone. A scattering of people cheered while the rest groaned or looked feverishly at the papers in their hands. Murdoch pushed on around the bar.

He spotted Oscar Druitt first, taller than anyone around him, his dark suit making him look powerful, his white shirt emphasising his tan. Murdoch allowed the group nearest him to push him into Druitt's line of sight and heard his name barked across their heads.

'Bill! Come and join us! Was wondering where you were.'

Oscar reached out a long arm to shake Murdoch's hand, then used his grip to pull him closer.

'You been betting on the horses? Or did you get stuck in that dreadful traffic?'

'The traffic,' Murdoch told him. 'Worth the wait, though. This place is all right, isn't it?'

Oscar looked across the heads of the crowd: a millionaire at an auction. 'Same people, different venue,' he said. 'Have you noticed how all the women at these things look younger than the men they're with? I can't work out if that's because they're not the original wives, or those aren't their original faces. Mind you, pretty girls in uniform serving alcohol, never a bad thing, eh?'

A small woman nearby turned at this and Murdoch saw it was Oscar's wife, Emma. She was wearing brown, head to toe, a hat drooping like a bad joke.

'I heard that, Oscar. Oh, you didn't tell me Bill was going to be here.'

She said it with a smile, but there was an edge to her voice: someone really should have told her.

'Just found out two seconds ago, my love' said Oscar. Then, with an almost imperceptible wink for Murdoch, 'Now, where's Amanda got to?'

'Getting Angus back on the leash, I suspect,' said Emma curtly. 'Stay there, I'm going to get another drink. Oscar, I'll get you a Shiraz.'

She gave Murdoch a sharp look, then disappeared into the crowd.

'Twelve years I've been married to that woman,' said Oscar, 'and she's still pushing red wine on me. Can't stand the stuff, but can't bring myself to tell her I've been lying about it for the last twelve years. Now, what do you think of that then?' He gestured subtly with his champagne flute. 'Even better than on the small screen, eh?'

Murdoch followed the direction of Oscar's glass and saw, two metres to his right, a young woman pouting at the screen of her phone, oblivious to the people stepping around her. She was tiny: a petite woman made smaller by big blonde hair and an oversized hat. She was wearing a white lace dress with, at first glance, no underwear beneath it. At second glance too, although no nipples showed through the holes in the lace. Murdoch took a third look, all the way up to find her huge eyes staring into his. It was Melissa Munday from *Society*.

'Seen enough?' she said.

'I ... er ...'

'He's a big fan,' said Oscar. 'Watches your show every week without fail. Don't you, Bill?'

He nudged Murdoch in the back. 'Don't you?'

'I didn't mean to stare,' said Murdoch. 'I do like your film. I mean, programme. On the telly, I mean.'

Melissa Munday rolled her eyes, shifted her weight from one hip to the other and returned to the screen in her hand.

'What are you two naughty boys up to?'

It was Amanda, looking like she too had been transported from the television. One of those women who make you wonder where they are and why you never meet them. She was head to toe in canary yellow, soft fabric cut in a way that made Murdoch want to stare.

'Melissa,' she said. 'Have you met my friend, Bill Murdoch? I know you know Oscar.'

'I'm a friend of James Harte ...' said Murdoch. It had become his catch phrase, an opener when he didn't know what else to say.

'Aw, shit.' Melissa Munday bit her lip and looked up, waiting to be asked what was wrong. Oscar did the honours. 'It's the paps. Fucking cameras everywhere. I better go and make myself look respectable. Any of yous know where the dunnies are?'

Amanda pointed her towards a gap in the canvas, then frowned at Oscar as he made a full appraisal of the actress's departing rear. Murdoch turned to try and see as another thundering finish passed the open end of

137

the marquee and the crowd there roared again, but they were too far back now, the bar in their way, and he saw only the tops of the jockeys' heads flashing above the crowd.

'How are you, Bill?'

Amanda's hand was on his forearm – the same electric charge he'd happily get used to – and she reached in to kiss his cheek. Murdoch froze, kissing the air too late as she pulled back and gave him a warm smile. 'I was beginning to think you weren't coming.'

'I reckon he was at the TAB,' said Oscar with a grin. 'Throwing his money away without coming to me for tips.'

'Not me,' said Murdoch, 'I'm not a gambling man.'

'That's not how I bloody well remember it!'

Benny Robbins had pushed through the crowd, a tall, platinum-haired woman in a jumpsuit holding onto his arm and struggling with the difference in their heights.

'Benny,' said Amanda. Another lean in, another kissed cheek, pinching Murdoch with jealousy. 'How are you? Now, I hope you're not going to be unpleasant?'

'Have you met me, darl? I wouldn't know how. All's fair and that.'

Benny Robbins acknowledged Oscar with a stiff little nod but stuck out a podgy hand for Murdoch, shaking it like a competition as he introduced his wife.

'Don't think you've met my Fee?'

Murdoch slowly recognised Phoebe Robbins from the crack in the bathroom door. She was prettier than he remembered, or maybe he hadn't noticed her face that time. Now, the eyes she gave him over their lingering handshake made him wonder what would have happened if she'd found him in her bathroom.

'We should have a little bet on the next race,' said Robbins. 'Just you and me.'

An icy silence descended around them and Murdoch saw Oscar looking for an escape route. Amanda started to say something, but Phoebe Robbins got there first.

'Benny-boy, please! You just want to win back that money which, I hear, Bill won fair and square. In a game of skill, I might add.'

'It's all right,' said Murdoch. 'I gave him that money back. Seemed a bit rude to go into someone's house, use their pool table, drink their booze and charge them for the privilege. We was joking about; making a scene, wasn't we? Benny?'

At the sight of Robbins' face, Murdoch last questions came out less certain than he'd planned.

'What you talking about?' said Robbins.

'The ten grand. I handed it to Angus to give back to you, before we even left. He took it back in.'

Again, a silence: longer this one, and, again, Amanda started to speak. This time she was interrupted by a hacking burst of laughter from Robbins. The little man turned red and coughed. Let his wife hit him on the back, her breasts struggling in the tight jumpsuit, then bent double and laughed some more.

'What's so funny?'

Oscar had disappeared into the crowd, but Amanda took Murdoch's arm and said, 'Don't worry about it, Bill. Let's go and find a drink.'

He could hardly resist without pulling her off her heels. She dragged him away through the crowd, past the bar and to the other side of the tent. Eventually, he raised his voice, pulled on her arm to stop, but, when she turned to him, her smile was the same as the one he'd seen in Palm Beach: all relaxation gone. He couldn't bear to be the cause of that, so he told her not to worry and followed her on through the crowd. Then she spotted the TAB queue along a canvas wall and asked if he wouldn't mind waiting with her until she placed a bet. They joined the line and chatted painfully, Amanda asking about his day, how the journey down had been, looking in all directions as he trotted out his answers.

'Who you looking for?' he said. 'What's wrong?'

'No one. Nothing'

'You looking for Angus?'

That got her attention. She grabbed his arm again and he realised it was a habit: something to do with her hand when not smoking. Not that he'd ever mind.

'Why? Have you seen him? Where is he?'

She saw his wry smile, heard herself, withdrew the hand and tried to find a smile in turn.

'Sorry. Once a big sister, always a big sister, I suppose.'

'What's the problem?'

Like he didn't know. He had an image of Angus getting beaten up somewhere, was sure Amanda was thinking the same thing. She frowned and said nothing.

'It's all right,' he said, 'you can tell me. I sort of know already. Wouldn't be much of a detective if I didn't, would I?'

There were more empty seconds until at last she sighed and frowned and spoke to the wooden flooring between them.

'Angus doesn't have a stop button. The rest of us, you know, you drink too much or drive too fast or stay up too late, eventually you just stop. But Angus, he doesn't know how to stop; he just keeps going, more and more until … He can be so lovely, but, well … we keep him on a tight leash. Keep him away from money. You know, if he doesn't have any cash, he's fine.'

Murdoch didn't comment on that. Blokes like Angus could find trouble in the Sahara.

'No one who knows him will lend him anything,' Amanda went on, 'so he can't normally afford to drink too much or take too much of whatever there is around. But, ever since … well, since all the business with James and Charlie Holland, he's been out of control. I think it's because he's upset. He's throwing himself into booze and drugs and partying more than ever. God knows where he keeps getting the cash.'

'He certainly wasn't short of it when we went out after Benny's party.' Murdoch decided there was no need to mention the cricket. 'He must have spent thousands.'

'Mm. Ten thousand, maybe? Ten thousand in cash? No wonder Benny was laughing.'

Murdoch swore. He wanted to spit on the ground.

'Don't be angry, Bill. Please.'

'Jesus. I feel like an idiot. Angus must think I'm a right sucker.'

'Not at all. He won't even remember it. Trust me, he never does after a big night. And the way he is, it's like an illness; he can't help it. Everyone else already hates him, so please, Bill, try and be different. And, please, let me go and find him before he gets into trouble again.'

Oscar was good company. Not a fraction as good as Amanda, but better than no company at all. He made jokes about half the people there, sharing what gossip he knew and telling funny little stories. Murdoch tried a few times to bring the conversation around to James Harte – he and Oscar had barely spoken about him – and who might have a grievance against him, but there were limits to what he could do subtly. He had almost given up, when Oscar started talking about women.

'Melissa Munday, I wouldn't mind. "Deux fois", as they say, "dans le visage". And what about Phoebe Robbins, eh? Hot or what?'

'Yeah,' said Murdoch. 'Makes you wonder what is she sees in her millionaire husband.'

Oscar liked that. 'Well, she's not in it for the sex. She gets plenty of that elsewhere. I saw the way she looked at you, you lucky dog. You're just her type.'

'Scrawny and ginger?'

'Short or tall, she likes a bad boy.' He was looking over the heads of the crowd again. 'That's why she was always so hot for James.'

'Harte?'

'God, yes, the two of them were at it for years. I'd love to see the fireworks if you-know-who ever finds out.'

'Robbins, you mean?'

Oscar laughed. 'I meant Amanda, actually. There's only so much a woman can take. You wouldn't think it, but she has an incredible temper on her. Mind you, so does Benny – and he's the kind that would stay angry. I certainly wouldn't like to be in James's shoes if Benny found out about him and Phoebe.'

'Maybe he already did?'

Oscar stopped smiling and looked at him. 'God, what a thought. Well, if that's the case then prison's probably the safest place James could be.'

The conversation moved on: more women for Oscar to comment on, a few acquaintances met. It was almost half an hour before Murdoch managed to raise the subject of Harte again. They were talking about charisma.

'Not enough, though, is it?' said Murdoch, remembering his conversations with Davie. 'James has got loads of that, he could charm the birds off the trees. Seems like a great bloke, but half the people I've

141

met can't stand him. No idea why. You ever do any business with him? Outside of working for the agency, I mean?'

Oscar was looking through crowd again, as if seeing who he could spot, and at first Murdoch thought he was going to get nothing in return. But then, after a glance behind him, Oscar leant in close and Murdoch realised he wasn't quite sober.

'I did, actually, and a word to the wise, Bill, don't you do the same. I'm not supposed to talk about this but, years ago, I persuaded my father to lend Harte a significant amount of money. This was back in the early days of the agency. Not that I exactly had a choice in the ... Anyway, the point is, even with my darling wife doing the books, it was a struggle to get that money back. If it hadn't been for Emma, I doubt we'd have ever seen a penny of it.'

'What do you mean?'

It was Murdoch's standard response to any talk about Harte. A request for more detail few could resist. But he could see Oscar was already regretting having shared so much. He gave a tiny shake of his head, stood straight again, and raised his glass at someone across the room, apparently, although Murdoch couldn't see anyone raise a glass back. A minute later and he had pushed through the crowd, leaving Murdoch alone.

Even now, after all these parties, Murdoch felt uncomfortable starting conversations with strangers. Today, he tried a few times, thinking of his promise to Davie, and maybe if it had got him anywhere, he'd have tried a few times more. But feeling like a dick, joining a group who had been laughing and chatting until he got there, what was the point? Alone, sober and refusing to gamble, his afternoon began to drag. This wasn't exactly the party with friends he'd needed to make up for the cricket. He realised he was jealous of a person he couldn't see: whoever was talking to Amanda.

It was close to three when Oscar reappeared, flushed and angry. He'd been warned by 'those idiots at security'; about what, he refused to say. 'Bugger them,' he said suddenly. 'No one has any sense of fun any more, have you noticed that? Sometimes I think Angus is the only sane person I know. I'm out of here.'

He pushed past Murdoch and stumbled towards the exit. There, Murdoch saw, he also pushed past the Islanders minding the door, saying something sharp to the smaller one before disappearing out of the tent.

Emma Druitt appeared at Murdoch's side, her mouse-like eyes glancing around like she was scared a cat had got in.

'Have you seen Oscar anywhere?'

'I think he just left.'

'When exactly? And why?'

'I don't know, love, sorry.'

'But if you think he just left, then you must know more or less when he left? Did someone tell you he left, or did you see him leave yourself?'

Emma Druitt's little brown hat wobbled on every question and Murdoch found it difficult not to smile. Seeing this, she gave up on him suddenly, pushing away furiously through the crowd.

Over the following hour or so, as the crowd around him grew drunker and louder, Murdoch had the sense that he was in the wrong place. His suit, his shoes, the stupid shirt and tie: it all felt fake. Like he'd tried something but had failed. Inevitably, with nothing else to think about – the beauties around him less beautiful by the minute – he found himself wondering about the man who'd followed him down the Pacific Highway. Whether he really should be worried about him. Whether the man had, after all, stolen his, Murdoch's, beautiful day.

Eventually he admitted to himself he wanted to leave. He'd given up on Amanda coming back and there was no one else there he knew, not unless he felt like talking to Emma Druitt. Halfway to the exit, the crowd thinner now, but still bubbling and loud, he noticed a queue of people on a makeshift ramp climbing up to a patch of red carpet. Eight or nine couples were standing there, waiting to have their picture taken in front of the champagne sponsor's huge plastic logo. What the hell, thought Murdoch; he wouldn't mind a souvenir. And maybe Amanda would turn up before he'd reached the top and she could be in the picture too. He'd just taken his place at the end of the queue when he spotted Phoebe Robbins through the crowd. Benny wasn't with her and Murdoch was tempted to go and say hello. While he was deciding whether to or not, one of the two Islanders appeared and asked him if he was waiting for the photographer.

'Is that a problem?'

'Not at all, sir. But you'll have to be the last. We start clearing the pavilion soon and we can't have any obstructions. I'll just set these up behind you.'

He was carrying two heavy-based brass posts joined by a velvet rope.

'Sorry,' he said to a couple as they approached. 'This gentleman's the last one.' He turned to Murdoch and apologised. 'You'll get sick of hearing me say that.'

Murdoch told him not to worry about it. He never got sick of being called a gentleman.

The last race finished in a cheer fuelled by alcohol alone and people started drifting away, discarded programmes and bookies' chits visible on the wooden floor. As Murdoch progressed up the ramp, his view across the tent became clearer, but there was no sign of Amanda's yellow hat. Andy Arthur was still at the bar, laughing less regularly now but still loudly enough that the space around him was clearer than anywhere else in the pavilion.

'No, madam, I'm sorry. As I said, no more.'

The Islander's tone made Murdoch turn. It sounded like something from the real world, like the spell of politeness and refinement was running out of magic. He'd reached the top of the ramp by now and had a clear view across the tent, but whoever the Islander was talking to was hidden by his huge frame. Then she stepped to one side and pointed up at Murdoch. It was Melissa Munday.

'But I'm with him,' she said. 'We're supposed to be in the photo together!'

The Islander turned and looked up at Murdoch.

'She with you?'

Murdoch hesitated. He suspected Melissa Munday wanted the podium for herself, he'd not get his picture taken at all.

'Sure,' he said and watched as the actress tottered up the ramp towards him, grabbing at his arm for the last steep metre.

'Having fun?' he said.

It didn't feel like he was really there with her. It didn't feel like anything at all.

'How do I look? How are my teeth?'

She bared them at him, her breath sour with champagne, and he said fine and looked away over the thinning crowd. If he saw Amanda now, maybe he could still beckon her over. As he searched the dwindling crowd for her, he noticed a commotion near the bar. A man had shouted and now, as Murdoch watched, a woman in a pale blue dress stepped back too quickly, making a second woman stumble and spill her drink.

'Come on,' said Melissa Munday. 'We're up.'

Murdoch let her drag him onto the flat of red carpet, but he wanted to see what was happening at the bar. He stood on tiptoes and saw the crowd move again, then suddenly part, as Andy Arthur struggled to turn on his stool. The TV presenter was bright red and clutching at his throat, coughing or choking it wasn't clear, the men with stiff hair standing either side of him, one hitting him on the back, the other rubbing his knee. Then, as Murdoch watched, Andy the Dandy from *Everyday Style* vomited a mass of white liquid onto the ground in front of his stool. It fizzed and flowed and disappeared into the joins in the wooden flooring. The people nearest it recoiled and the effect pushed like a wave through those left in the tent, until others further away pushed back. Then people moved again and the scene was lost to view.

'Smile,' said the photographer.

'Smile!' Melissa Munday tugged on Murdoch's arm, pulling herself taller.

The flash was blinding, like a punch in the nose, and by the time Murdoch had blinked it away he was alone, only the Islander looking up at him from the bottom of the ramp, his expression tired and pleading. Couldn't they all just go home?

The walk to the car was a journey past a battlefield. Beyond the wire fence, the ground was full of litter: plastic glasses and paper cups discarded like used artillery. The less drunk propped up the walking wounded, while others lay where they'd fallen, friends wobbling around them and wondering what to do. Murdoch looked away. The photographer in the tent had disappeared as quickly as Melissa Munday and he hadn't been able to buy a copy of the photo. What a waste of bleeding time; no one would ever believe him. Worse, now every time he saw her on the telly, he'd think of her breath and Andy Arthur vomiting champagne and peanuts.

The brunette in the car park saw him coming and his car was ready by the time he reached her. She passed him his keys, trying not to look bored, then hovered until he realised she was expecting a tip. He was looking for a small enough note when he heard heels on the bricks behind him.

'Bill! You're not going without saying goodbye?'

He forced himself not to turn. Instead, he gave up searching and gave the girl in the uniform a twenty, took his keys and thanked her. Watched her walk away towards the other low cars and, only then, turned to Amanda.

'Paying off girls in uniform?' she said with a smile. 'I wouldn't have thought she was your type?'

'Is that a fact? And what would you of thought was my type?'

Amanda gave him a smile happier than he'd ever seen on her before. She looked relaxed for once and he wondered how it was possible that it made her look more attractive than ever. She took a step forward and started straightening his tie. Murdoch could smell her perfume and a tiny hint of sweat. He looked at the sky, but that wasn't enough to push away the thought of how easy it would be to lean forward and kiss her. He forced himself to think of anything: onion sandwiches, rotten eggs, old people naked. He remembered Suzie Bourne and realised with amazement that Amanda would be as old as her one day, everything faded but the eyes and the jewellery. Why couldn't Suzie Bourne write this down, rather than the story of the previous year? His day at the races, the sexiest woman in the world fixing his tie.

'You looked very smart today, Bill.'

'Thanks.'

'Good choice of suit.'

'So people keep saying.' He looked at her at last. 'Don't look so bad yourself.'

She looked down at her yellow dress, like she'd forgotten what she was wearing, then looked up and smiled. 'You said that once before.'

'What?'

'When I picked you up from the ferry in Palm Beach. I said you looked nice and you said, "Not so bad yourself".'

He didn't know what to say to that, couldn't believe he was so happy she'd remembered. *Now*, he thought, *kiss her now. No, no – take her hand. Anything.* He asked if she'd managed to find Angus.

'Eventually. And then I found some friends who dragged him home, so that's all fine. But it took a while, so sorry about that.'

He nodded and they remained where they were, looking at each other, until a movement behind her caught his attention.

'Here's Emma,' he said.

Amanda rolled her eyes and winked just for him. Then she prepared her face, turned and said, 'Look who I found!'

There was a second of hope on Emma Druitt's face. She quickened her step, her little brown hat bobbing along optimistically. Then she peered past her sister-in-law and saw Murdoch in the shadowy courtyard.

'Oh,' she said sadly. 'It's you. Where's that bloody girl with the car?'


## 24.

The map function in Murdoch's phone gave directions in a firm female voice that Murdoch had once liked to think belonged to a woman called Scarlett. Scarlett was bent naked over her maps somewhere, squinting at the street names so conscientiously you didn't mind her pronouncing things wrong. Bondi was 'Bondy', Clovelly, 'Cloverly'. Murdoch was barely out of the racecourse car park before he needed her help. There had been a disturbingly familiar sight in his rear-view mirror. He pulled over and started swiping at his phone, studying the map for a good ten minutes before choosing a street for Scarlett to take him to. But when the firm female voice gave its first instruction, he almost forgot the car behind him. Was it his imagination, or was the vaguely English accent similar to Amanda's? He imagined her sitting in the car beside him, calm and knowing just what to do. Why was it always in these moments of pressure, that his mind focused on anything but the matter at hand?

'Turn left,' said Scarlett, who was now Amanda.

Murdoch would have thought right, but he knew better than to second-guess the phone. Then Amanda said right and right again, so soon it made sense. As he followed her directions further east then north, Murdoch swore aloud and made himself think about what he was going to do.

He was halfway to Watsons Bay, the roof down to keep him conspicuous and the traffic loud around him, before he spotted the white Corolla again. The guy was good and Murdoch realised that if it hadn't been for his sudden lane change on the freeway, he might never have spotted him. On single-lane roads, he struggled to spot him now. But Carrington Road and then Old South Head Road were two lanes wide with no parked cars in the way. By repeatedly lane-hopping – like he was trying to beat the flow – Murdoch could check the mirror and see down the lines of traffic behind him. He did it again and again, to be sure. Any flow of traffic would have a white Toyota Corolla in it at some point. But, after a final check, it was him all right – BUG 159 S.

'At the roundabout, take the second exit to continue straight,' the imaginary Amanda said.

'In two hundred metres, continue straight.'

'In four hundred metres stay on Old South Head Road.'

'Continue straight.'

On and on, always the same road to the very edge of the continent. The traffic thinned after Vaucluse, like everyone was only out for a gawp at Australia's richest suburb. Then the road climbed again and there was nothing but houses on the left, greenery on the right with gaps to the ocean beyond. Murdoch passed a cemetery and then, straight from a postcard, a white lighthouse reared up, stark against the blue of the sky. He didn't slow to look at it, just followed Amanda's instructions into the harbour's lower jaw, wishing it really was her, sitting there beside him and knowing what to do.

It was only around the last corner, when the sentry box and gates appeared, that Murdoch realised his mistake. The spot he'd chosen on the map was a deliberate dead end, the only one he'd found long enough to tempt another driver into. He'd seen green shading around it and thought it was a national park or a lookout point or some kind of undeveloped land on the narrow headland. Now he grabbed the phone and zoomed in, in and in until at last it said 'HMAS Watson'. A naval base behind metal gates and sentry posts. Murdoch swore and threw the phone onto the seat beside him, ignoring the firm female voice – it was no longer Amanda, not the mood he was in now – as it told him to continue straight for two hundred metres to find his destination on the right. He swung a hard left instead, the only other option, and found himself in a tight street of houses, huddling in the shade between the ocean and the harbour. He had no choice but to follow the one-way signs, right and right again, the phone struggling to keep up, the road one block from the water in almost every direction, the headland tight around him. 'Turn right,' said the phone, determined to get him back to the military gates. Instead he braked, pure luck there was no one behind him, and let the phone slide to the floor.

'Turn right,' it said again.

Murdoch reversed quickly into a small car park where he had seen a dozen or so people loading cars at the gritty end of a day at the beach. Open car boots, children in towels, parents laden down with bags and buckets and folding chairs. Murdoch looked at them jealously and spotted an old Holden reversing. He indicated, made eye contact with the driver and raised a hand in thanks. Just to remind himself he was part of society now: a man who knew how to behave.

At one end of the car park was a tarmac path. Murdoch followed it twenty metres or so until it opened onto a tiny harbour beach, the skyscrapers of the CBD clear across the water. To his left, half a dozen villas backed onto the sand, preferring heavy walls at the bottom of their gardens to a beach shared with strangers. He stood for a few seconds, uncertain what to do. A sign said *'Camp Cove'* and another pointed along a path towards *'Lady Bay Beach'*. Skirting the sand, self-consciously smart amongst the shorts and swimsuits, Murdoch followed the path north along the shore. It climbed in wooden steps and steep tarmac through dry scrub and soon he was sweating. It was too hot a day to be walking in a suit and, as he climbed the path, he wrenched off his tie and shoved it into a trouser pocket. Then the scrub around him thinned and the highpoint of the headland came into view, weekenders ambling across it. Murdoch put his head down and stomped on until everything around him was sky and sea and wind but for another lighthouse: squatter this one, painted in red and white stripes like a helter-skelter: a scene from a boiling nightmare. He was surrounded by water, everything to the left, the harbour; everything to the right, the ocean; no shortage of cliffs. He was suddenly scared, no idea why, and – not caring how crazy he looked – hit himself hard twice on the head until he remembered he was the hunter now. He left the path, intending to stride across the grass, but then climbed onto the rocks behind the lighthouse instead, the wind tearing at his jacket and pants, his shadow tiny by his feet. Far below, the ocean smashed white as it hit the shore. He turned and jumped back down to the grass, frightening a crowd of seagulls who opened their wings to soar effortlessly into the air, mocking him with their smackhead cries. He scowled at them and, just like that, his fear really did disappear: it too blown away on the wind. All he felt was pure, white rage.

It was twenty minutes before the driver of the Corolla appeared. Murdoch had planned on waiting in the scratchy scrub beyond the lawns, but the lighthouse provided a better solution. There was an open doorway in its hollow base, a rectangle of black in the overbright day. Stepping through, he found himself in a dank and sandy space littered with condoms and half-smoked cigarettes, so dark it took a few minutes to see what he was standing in. He went out and tested it again, the light painful at first, the wind noisy again. There was no way anyone on the path could see inside. But the 'anyone' was a problem. Murdoch might not have heard of this part of the city, but plenty of others had. Back in the darkness of his tower, he watched young couples with strollers, tourists of varying shades, people holding hands on awkward dates. Still, it was easy enough to recognise the driver of the Corolla when he appeared. Not just the pockmarked skin and the grey T-shirt, more the type of man that filled it. He looked like a pro, thick-necked but fluid, something Neanderthal about his jaw. He had a tattoo on his neck, a scrawl of writing that began with a 'D'. Murdoch swore as he found himself trying to read it, spat between his feet and told himself to concentrate. He watched the other man hesitate and look around, his expression hidden behind thick Ray-Bans. Murdoch let him come all the way, studying his size and how he moved. Then the man turned and looked back the way he'd come and Murdoch, seeing his advantage, stepped into the light and let his eyes adjust.

'Oi, sunshine,' he said. 'You looking for me?'

## 25.

Davie was looking for the right chocolate milk when Mrs Dunnevirk spotted him. The milk was his supermarket treat: a bribe for his inner child, something sweet to tempt him down to the shops. Seeing Mrs D, Davie put on his a great-to-see-you grin and remembered why Bill preferred to do his grocery shopping online. It was impossible to come to Coles in Kildare without bumping into half of Montauban. He asked Mrs Dunnevirk about her hip.

'I saw you born, little Davie.'

She said it every time she saw him and he knew it was true, although he could never remember the story. Had she been a midwife, a good friend of his mother? Maybe a fairy godmother because today, apparently, it gave Mrs Dunnevirk a licence to inspect the contents of his trolley.

'How's your hip, Mrs D?' he tried again, fishing out his phone and turning on the function that five minutes later would make it ring as if he had a call coming in.

'It's nice to get to talk to you properly,' said the old lady. 'You're normally flat out like a lizard drinking. That's good, of course, you need to make money while you can. You know that chocolate milk is full of sugar, don't you, darl?'

Davie gave up on the hip and talked to Mrs Dunnevirk about her sons instead – both in prison – until his phone rang and he smiled apologetically, throwing the wrong chocolate milk into his trolley and wheeling the faux call down to the cheese section. He had made it through seven more enquiries after his health and as far as the checkout queue before his phone rang again. He was loading his shopping onto the conveyor belt and listening to Fred Pearson, a friend of his father, complain about Indian immigrants.

'They used to be poor,' Fred was saying. 'You could hire them for nothing. Now they've all got degrees, know their rights, want paying more than I earn.' This was unlikely. Fred, a gnarled and knotted man with bright eyes and nostrils full of hair, had a chain of carwashes and limitless tricks to avoid paying minimum wage. No local ever worked for him twice. 'By the way, your English friend with the fancy car was in last week. Doesn't say much does he?'

'Bill?'

'He's a bit rough, he is. He went past again yesterday, had to stop at the lights out the front. Should have seen the state of him! Black and blue he was. You want to be careful, hanging around with people who get into fights.'

Davie had been struggling with a bunch of grapes, the fruit choosing certain death on the supermarket floor over a future at home with him. Now he stood upright and looked at Fred Pearson.

'What do you mean? Is he all right?'

But this was when his phone rang again, this time indicating a genuine call.

'Take it,' said the old man, pushing Davie on past the checkout. 'I'll finish these for you. Do you good to do some work for once, you might even sell a house.'

Davie took the call, a number he didn't recognise, and stood watching Pearson load the rest of his shopping onto the conveyor belt, shaking his head at the chocolate milk. The old man started reading out the ingredients to the checkout girl, a mother of five called Denise, whom Davie had known since kindy.

'Mr Simms,' said a stern female voice, 'I'm calling from Professor Barker's office. We have received your letter and your payment. I'm calling to arrange the appointment to discuss the matter you mentioned. I was wondering if you could let me know the details?'

Davie turned away from Fred and Denise and took a few steps towards the next checkout. It was empty, the conveyor belt wet from a recent clean.

'It's about a murder victim called Charlie Holland,' he said quietly. 'Professor Barker provided a report as an expert witness.'

'And what is the nature of your enquiry, Mr Simms?'

'Well, as I said in the letter, it's confidential.'

'In what way?'

'In a confidential way. Maybe you'd get Professor Barker to call me back if you're not able to make the appointment on his behalf?'

Another silence, shorter than the one Davie had achieved from Hannah earlier in the week but, he suspected, no less of a victory.

'I don't know,' said Professor Barker's secretary sniffily. At least, Davie presumed she was the professor's secretary, she hadn't introduced herself. 'He's very busy. He could maybe see you on Thursday. At eleven o'clock?'

He could hear her picking the time he'd be least likely to make.

'Perfect.'

And then, because he was clearly on a roll of victories – and because the only way to cope with bullies was to bully them back – he gave the woman his email address and asked for a confirmation of the appointment.

'Confidential?' said Pearson as Davie walked back and gave his credit card to Denise. 'That sounds interesting.'

'Yes, Fred. Very confidential.'

'Ooh,' said Denise, awake for the first time in days. 'Tell us all about it then, Davie.'

Davie phoned Bill from the supermarket car park. An hour earlier he'd left bright sunshine outside. Now the sky was grey and featureless above him and further west, in his rear-view mirror, it hung low and black. Bill answered on the first ring.

'Bill, it's Davie. You want to cook me lunch?'

'No.'

'Go on. I bought you a chocolate milk.'

'No, I mean I'm not at home. I'm out. So, no good, I'm afraid.'

'When are you back? I've got some news about the case. Good news.'

A tiny spark in the mirror caught Davie's eye: lightning in the clouds behind him.

'Not today.'

'What about tomorrow?'

'Not tomorrow neither. Why don't you tell me 'bout it over the phone?'

'Then I won't be able to give you the chocolate milk.' He heard Bill sigh, heard the theme tune to *Antiques Roadshow* suddenly muted. 'Is it because you don't want me to see your black eye?'

Davie had thought this might earn him a third little silence on the end of the line, but Bill swore so loudly he had to pull the phone from his ear. When he put it back, the Englishman was still shouting.

'What is it with this bleeding place? How do you all know every single fucking thing that happens to anyone? Do you have hidden cameras what only the locals know about? I drove home the back way, Davie; no one in Montie saw me, I know that for a fact. What the fuck is this?'

'Put the kettle on,' said Davie. 'I'm coming round now.'

He gasped when Bill opened the front door. The Englishman's right eye was shut, the skin around it the colour of an eggplant, shiny with something he'd applied. The swelling turned red and then orange as it continued down his cheek and across his nose, his upper lip fat and split.

'Don't say anything,' Bill told him, the words blunted by his swollen lip. 'Don't say a fucking thing.'

'Oh my God, you look awful.'

He reached out a hand and the Englishman swatted it away.

'Like that, for example. Don't say that. And don't ask if I've been to a doctor or if I need anything and, for fuck's sake, don't ask if I've been to the police. Any of that; just don't say it.'

Davie held out the chocolate milk and Bill snatched it before turning down the hallway, apparently indifferent as to whether Davie followed or not. In the kitchen, he turned again and asked if Davie had brought a straw.

'What?'

'Davie, I drink out of this I'll end up wearing half of it. Look at my bleeding mouth, you moron. You get a straw or what?'

'No, I ...'

Even if Davie had got his hands up in time he'd have struggled to catch the plastic bottle. Instead, it hit his chest and cracked along its length, the brown liquid pouring into his best work shirt.

'For God's sake, Bill!'

Davie ran across the tiles, carrying the broken bottle like a wounded animal, liquid dripping through his fingers. He dropped it into one of the sinks, pulled off his shirt and threw that in the other, running the taps and rinsing the fabric furiously. Ten minutes or more he went at it, filling the sink and emptying, soaking the shirt even when it was clear the stains were there to stay. Ten minutes until he heard Bill behind him.

'Sorry, Davie. It's not your fault.'

'You don't say.'

'I'm not used to people helping me.'

'No wonder.'

'I'm not used to being like this. Look at me.'

Davie didn't look. He carried on kneading water into the fabric, listening as Bill walked away, dragged a chair and sat in it, elbows heavy on the kitchen table. Davie had started ringing out the ruined shirt before Bill spoke again.

'I've always been tidy in a fight, know what I mean? No one's got the better of me since I was a kid. You let this happen to you on the inside, just once, and it's a slippery slope, see? Next thing you know it's happening every day. My reflexes are shot; it was like I was walking in treacle.'

Davie turned off the taps and heard the rain had arrived, huge drops slamming into the patio beyond the window. Then the world outside was brighter than the kitchen and, a second later, loud with thunder. He turned and saw Bill had his head in his hands. Walked over and put a hand on the Englishman's back, then stood awkwardly for a second, searching for an excuse to remove it.

'Does it hurt?'

'Of course it bleeding well hurts.'

'What happened?'

Normally there was no point in asking, but today, for once, Bill was willing to share. Or maybe, judging by his voice, he was still working it out himself. Davie took his hand back and sat in the chair on the other side of the table.

'Big bloke in a hire car follows me down the freeway; it was only by luck I spotted him. I was sure I'd lost him on the Pacific Highway but, coming out of the races, he's behind me again. So I takes him up Watsons Bay, tease him out of the car, then ask him what his game is – what the fuck he wants. Next thing, he hits me and I'm down on the ground.'

'My God, those injuries are from just one punch?'

'Course not. He ran off after he smacked me, so I chased him, didn't I? Got him down and then … well, he got the better of me. Right mess; nice people out for a stroll and us two rolling around between them.'

Davie didn't know what to say. He had so little knowledge of physical violence, he had no idea what questions were appropriate.

'Was he bigger than you?' he tried after a while.

'They're always bigger than me, Davie, always was. That's got nothing to do with it. I'm out of shape, that's all. I've got lazy and, worse than that, I've got stupid.'

'Don't blame yourself …'

'I do bleeding well blame me self. I always swore I'd never get like this. First you get lazy, then you get fat, then whoever fancies it can come do what they want, can't they?'

'And what did he want?'

Bill took his head from his hands and looked up, his injuries a surprise even on second viewing. He frowned and rubbed his hand across his close-cropped hair, as if searching for a part of him that wasn't injured.

'Do you know what?' he said slowly. 'I haven't the foggiest.'

Murdoch fetched Davie a T-shirt and, when they discovered his trousers were ruined too, found him the bottom half of a tracksuit. Then he grabbed a cloth and squatted down to clean the kitchen floor.

'I'll get you a new one,' he said, not looking up from the tiles.

'Don't worry, they're full of sugar anyway.'

'No, you muppet, a new suit. I'll buy you a new suit and a new shirt.'

155

Davie didn't respond to that, just shifted about in his seat, his feet and legs the only bit of him Murdoch could see. Then, of course, he started on about the case, about how he had some exciting news. Murdoch sighed. Every part of his face hurt, and bending down like this was making it throb. He was so tired he wondered if he was going to be able to stand up again.

'Oh yeah,' he said. 'What exciting news is that then?'

'I've got us an appointment with the expert witness who wrote a report for the Director of Public Prosecutions on Charlie Holland. It was mentioned in the police file. This dude, Professor Barker's his name, he lectures at Sydney Uni. He teaches those doctors who can tell you why someone died.'

'Forensic pathologists.'

'What?'

'Doctors what write about how someone got done in, they're called "forensic pathologists".'

'Crikey, Bill, all things you don't know and then you know that. Anyway, Professor Barker's going to talk to us – for a fee, of course. We can ask him if there was anything unusual, you know. See if there's anything no one else noticed.'

Finished with the floor, Murdoch stood, avoiding looking at Davie, walked to the sink and threw the cloth in next to the twisted shirt.

'Wouldn't he of put that in his report?'

'Well, maybe, but there wasn't a copy in the police file. And you know, perhaps if we speak to him, he can tell us something useful. We're seeing him next week. On Thursday.'

Murdoch held onto the edge of the sink. 'We?'

'Of course.'

'We? We ain't going nowhere.' He turned, even that small movement causing him pain. 'Look at me, Davie. I'm not going down to see some police expert looking like this, am I? You go. I'm over this bleeding case as it is. Not exactly a pretty party outfit, a face like this, is it?'

'Bill, you promised. You know you're better at asking questions than me. You always notice things ...'

'Not gonna happen, Davie.'

'Go on ...'

'I said no!'

They stared at each other and then away, neither of them knowing what to do with the fresh outburst. After a few minutes Davie stood and told Murdoch he'd get the T-shirt and tracky daks back to him the next day. Murdoch told him to sit down, have something to eat. Wait for the rain to stop. Davie put his hands in his hair.

'You know, Bill, the advantage of hanging out with someone with no social skills, is that when they offer you food they generally mean it.'

'I do mean it.'

'Oh. Good. What've you got?'

'Whatever I've got, you're bleeding well eating it.'

So they ate. As the mood mellowed between them, Murdoch told Davie what he'd learned from Oscar Druitt, about how his family had lent the agency money in the early days. The olive branch was accepted and they drifted into the normal round of speculation. Who could have done what and why. Endless pointless talk, back and forth, round and round. But, in the end, they were both grateful because, just before he left, Davie said, 'Isn't it weird about that guy following you from the races?'

Murdoch, chewing painfully on bread, gave him a look that meant he was listening.

'Well, you said you thought you lost him when you were driving down to Sydney. And you know about following people, so you're probably good at spotting when someone's following you? So if you think you lost him, you probably did. But then when you left the races, there he was again, behind you.'

Murdoch forgot his mouth was full. 'So?'

'So if you lost him, how did he know you were at races? It's almost like ...'

'Someone went off and told him.' Murdoch sat up, swallowed and rubbed his hand across his hair. 'Jesus, Davie, you're right. Shit, that's frightening.'

'Why?'

'Mate, if you're noticing stuff before me, then I really am getting slow.'

## 26

Murdoch washed and dried all the bed linen he owned, folded it into piles and carried it up to the small bedroom at the very top of the house. It was an awkward space of sharp angles, the only window a skylight that whistled in the wind. He poured bleach into a bucket of water and wiped down the metal of the bed, then the window sill and the skirting boards. Back in the kitchen he found a metal tray and carried up cough mixture, a thermometer and an old metal cup for water. He tucked the sheets in as tightly as he could and added extra blankets. Climbed in and slept deeply, five senses persuaded he was somewhere safe.

He'd disconnected his doorbell so he had no way of knowing if Davie visited again but, after two days of sleep interrupted only by food, the bathroom and slow reading, he gave in to temptation and checked his phone. Four missed calls: three of them from Amanda; the six from Davie didn't count. Murdoch dialled Amanda's number and she answered immediately, her voice noticeably colder than when they'd said goodbye at the races. He apologised for not being in touch, told her he'd been unwell.

'Oh. So not working on the case then?'

'Not these last few days, no.'

'It's just I got an invoice from your partner, Davie Simms.'

'Well, we have both been working on it, darlin', you know that. Just not in the last few days.'

He pulled himself upright, wincing at the pain and swearing under his breath. Above the rain-blurred skylight a tree moved with the wind.

'You know,' said Amanda, 'I was thinking we'd have seen some progress by now. I'm keen not to throw good money after bad.'

'Yeah, well, everything's always a good idea until you have to pay for it.'

He was still groggy from sleep and his face was hurting; it came out harsher than he'd meant it to. Amanda's sigh floated down the phone to him.

'Well, if that's your attitude, Bill, maybe I should stop paying completely? Maybe we should call the whole thing off?'

'No! I mean, no, don't do that, love. Trust me, I'm not exactly enjoying the case either.'

'What's not to enjoy? Parties, races, I see you're making lots of new friends. Angus thinks you're a gem; hardly a glowing recommendation.'

'You sound angry.'

'I'm not angry. Believe me, if I was angry you'd know it. I'm just frustrated with the apparent lack of progress. I'm frustrated I've got someone asking me for money and I don't quite know what for.'

'There has been progress.'

'Really. What?'

Murdoch hesitated, knowing he had to give her something. He told her to hang up, took a photograph of himself and texted it to her. Thirty seconds and the phone rang again.

'Oh my God, Bill, are you all right? What happened to you?'

Which almost made it all worthwhile. He told her he was fine, it looked worse than it was. Let her contradict him, let her make him promise to be more careful, let her apologise: she had such a short fuse when it came to money. She asked him if there was anything he needed. What he needed was her on the bed beside him, mopping his brow with that little frown on her face. He told her about the Corolla, asked her if she knew why he was being followed.

'Of course not. Do you think it means someone's getting nervous? That would be a good thing, don't you think? I mean, maybe this means you're actually getting somewhere?'

'Making progress, you could call it.'

He thought that might get another apology and swung his legs out of bed so he could sit up and enjoy it. He'd hidden a half pack of fags under the mattress.

'Absolutely,' she said. 'So how do we capitalise on that?'

'Capitalise?'

'I mean how do we take advantage of it. Move forward. What's next?'

The cigarettes had fallen to the floor, too far back for him to reach. He stood up and gasped at the throbbing behind his eye.

'Bill?'

'Here.'

'So what's the next step?'

'The next step.' He looked up at the skylight like the answer might be written there. Rubbed his hand across his head, looked for alternatives, gave up and told her in detail what the next step involved. Anything to make her think good of him.

159

The following week brought the sunshine back, this time with real heat and the holidays. The foot traffic in front of Murdoch's house was constant. Rush hour in Montauban: girls giggling towards the beach with little brothers trailing behind, corporate surfers on their annual escape, families bickering in both directions. Murdoch's wounds flattened, the purple giving way to yellow, the red dulling to a smarting pink. He got up early, gritted his teeth and walked down to the shops.

'I heard you'd had a fall!' Anne Lincoln's curiosity was barely restrained by the counter. 'But then I also heard you'd got beaten up by a jealous husband, mugged on the way home, and back in the ring. Which one is it, then?'

'Flat white, thanks. To go.'

A man with long hair sloped in, naked but for board shorts and a good layer of beach, every soft step adding sand to the floor. Anne sold him some board wax, nodded goodbye and let him go without telling him how to apply it. Then she looked over at some tourists hovering in the doorway.

'Thongs are on special,' she shouted. 'T-shirts, full price.'

The tourists smiled weakly and retreated, leaving Anne to cross her arms and lean forward on the counter. Her roots were coming through: more grey than brown under the blonde these days.

'Looks nasty,' she said. 'You put a steak on it?'

'Frozen peas.'

'Mm. Anyway, go on, what happened?'

He looked at his shoes. 'It's embarrassing.'

'Aw go on, you can tell me. Nothing's embarrassing between friends.'

'It's my own stupid fault ...'

'Did you get beaten up?' Anne was wide-eyed, her mouth slightly open. Murdoch imagined her at home with the news, waiting for the footage of random violence. 'Part of your detecting work was it, Bill?'

'Nothing so exciting. As I said, it's embarrassing. I was down in Sydney last weekend, went to the races don't you know. Anyway, went out that night, drank a bit too much, fell down some bleeding steps on the way home. Spent half the night telling the police I was fine, other half trying to find a hotel what would let me in.'

She looked at him through narrowed eyes.

'Flat white.'

160

'Please.'

She turned away to the coffee machine, unscrewed the filter and banged it violently on the side of the bin. 'You off to Sydney now then?'

'No, I'm off to see a man about a dog.'

'It's just I saw Davie this morning and he was on his way to Sydney and he said he was going to see you down there.' Just to be clear about who was in charge of the information flow here.

Murdoch forced a smile and rubbed his nose. 'Yeah, that's right. I'm seeing him down there later. But first I've got something else to do.'

'What are you—'

'Here, what's going on with that house over the road from me? Building company gone bust or something?'

For a while the only response was the hissing and gurgling of the coffee machine. Then, when Anne finally produced his flat white, she plonked it so heavily onto the counter that some of the coffee spumed through the hole in the lid.

'Lies,' she said. 'Lies and obvious distractions.'

'Sorry?'

'Story they're telling everyone is the building company's got problems. But it's lies! It's them what's got the problems. They's getting divorced. But you didn't hear it from me, right?'

'Oh, right,' he said. 'Of course.'


The fourth missed call had been from Suzie Bourne. She'd left a voicemail to say she needed to see him, making it clear when he phoned back that, no, it couldn't wait. There was something she had to show him in person. Murdoch tried to be angry – why was the world determined to drag him into daylight? – but if all of Montauban was going to hear he'd had a fall, Suzie Bourne could hear it too.

He followed another man into the lift and up to the sixth floor of her unit block. Halfway up the other man smiled and made a comment about the weather. Murdoch nodded and smiled back, told him at least they didn't have to climb the stairs. Meaningless, harmless words, anything would do: the guy just wanted confirmation this bruised-up bogan wasn't going to mug him. He and Murdoch exchanged smiles again when they found themselves waiting outside doors two units apart. The other man was about to say something about it when his door was opened by an old lady: white hair, yellow cardigan, half the size of her visitor who said, 'Hello, Mum', bent down and kissed her cheek. When he stood straight again, he gave Murdoch a last smile, a 'know what I mean?' like they were comrades-in-arms. Murdoch wanted to put him right but, before he could find the words, the man had followed his mother into her unit. Then Murdoch saw Suzie Bourne standing in front of him, an excited smile crinkling her face. He bent down and kissed her on the cheek.

'Oh, my goodness,' she said. 'What on earth's that for? And what happened to your face?' Then, as she turned to lead him down the corridor, 'By the way, is it possible you're being followed? By a man in a white car?'

Murdoch normally thought well on his feet, but what he did next was stupid. He should have followed Suzie to the living room and peered down at the car from her vantage point. Instead, he left her wondering what she'd said and ran down six flights of stairs two steps at a time. He tore through the street door at such speed that the thug in the white car – same guy, different car, an Astra this time, still *No Birds* – couldn't help but notice. He started the car immediately and put it into reverse, whining down the hill and into the next street before doing a U-turn. By the time Murdoch reached the corner, the Astra was out of sight.

'I don't want to talk about it,' he told Suzie, back at her front door.

'Oh, go on, it sounds so exciting.'

'I said I don't want to talk about it. And don't ask about my face neither, I fell down some steps.'

'Oh, yes, of course you did.'

Suzie looked up at him gleefully, but he sidestepped her, stomping down her hallway to the living room. She was smart enough to leave him there, calming himself as he listened to her heels clip back and forth across the kitchen floor, to the clock ticking slowly on the shelf. After a minute or two, he stood and tilted the armchair he'd been sitting in onto its two back legs, examining the impression its front feet had left in the carpet. He crossed to the curtain, pulled it back and found the walking stick still leaning beside the desk. On the shelves, each of the photographs were where he'd last seen them.

'What are you doing?'

162

He'd forgotten to listen for her footsteps. He walked over and took the tray from her.

'Your place is really nice.'

'Yes, you said that last time you were here. What were you doing?'

Murdoch smiled and looked away to the window

'Checking nothing's changed,' he said. 'Everything's in exactly the same place. All that other shit that goes on out there doesn't matter, does it? Because in here, it's always the same.'

She made a 'humph' noise, sat in the chair he'd looked underneath and nodded him towards the sofa. 'You make it sound very boring.'

'Nah, not at all. I mean, it's the opposite. It's, like, I dunno.'

'Reassuring?'

'Yeah, that's it.'

'No, trust me, it's boring, albeit a little less boring than it usually is. I must confess, I'm rather enjoying writing up your story. It reminds me of the *excitement* of that world without, well ...' She looked down at her engagement ring. 'I have to admit, it feels like some kind of vicarious crusade. Like it's me bringing those bastards down at last. I never told you. When I went to prison, it was all for nothing. The man who gave me that information ended up dead. Nothing was ever done about it.'

Murdoch recognised the bitterness, the unresolved anger. At herself as much as anything, if he had to put money on it. But there was something else too: an 'excitement' like she'd said, and he realised, for the first time, just how well-matched they were. Suzie was a good person, he reckoned, but, even now, there was something in her that enjoyed badness. She looked up at him, raised her eyebrows and told him the tea wouldn't pour itself. Waited until he was mid-flow before saying, 'Those injuries aren't from a fall.'

But Murdoch had been expecting this. He used the tea tray to his advantage, looking at the cups and not meeting her eye. 'You said on the phone you wanted to show me something?' he said as prepared the tea slowly, milk and three sugars, no milk and none, until the old lady gave up, stood again and walked out of the corner of his eye. When he looked up at last, cup in hand, she was holding a pile of papers towards him. He swapped them for the cup, dozens of tightly typed sheets.

'What's this?'

'It's the start of the book. Your book. Well, our book, I suppose.'

'Nice one. I'll look forward to reading that.'

'Oh no, you have to read it now! I won't sleep until I know I'm on the right track. I'll convince myself you hate it and I won't be able to write another word.'

She stood there, her free hand fluttering like a butterfly, her smile less in charge than he'd seen it before.

'Thing is, Suzie, I've got to be in Sydney before long. I thought we'd just chat for a bit. I'll tell you what happened next and then I'll be off.'

'Yes, well, we can do that too. But I'm very keen for you to read it.'

'I'm sure it's fine.'

'Please?'

He looked down at the first page, twenty-five lines of type. Flipped through the other pages, all of them thick with words.

'The thing is ...'

'Oh my God, I'm so sorry.' Suzie put the butterfly hand up to her reddening face. 'I mean. It didn't occur to me, that maybe, well ...'

'I can read.'

'Oh. Of course you can. I wasn't implying otherwise.'

He watched her sit and smile at him hard, until he looked down and started to push along the lines with his finger, whispering around longer words until they made a recognisable sound. When he turned the first page, he checked his watch and saw ten minutes had passed.

'I like it,' he said. 'It's like a proper book. But you should of emailed me; it's going to take me ages to get through all this. I thought we was going to talk about what happened next? After all the clues and obstacles and stuff.'

'You're absolutely right,' she said quickly. 'It was silly of me. Why don't you take it away with you and let me know what you think when you've got through it all?'

She was embarrassed and Murdoch let her take the pages back from him. Watched her cross to the desk, bump them back into neatness and slip them into a large yellow envelope. By the time she was opposite him again, she was smiling properly, the awkwardness left with the envelope on the desk.

'So, what did happen next?' she said cheerily. 'We need a subplot, you know.'

'A subplot?'

'Oh yes. You know, a single story is rarely enough to keep a book interesting for long. Especially in crime. We need something else to be happening too. It fills in the gaps nicely, you see, keeps things toddling along. Just when you resolve something in your main storyline, oops! Up pops the subplot and puts in you in a pickle again.'

Murdoch felt the wounds in his face starting to itch. He scratched his scalp instead of them, took a sip or two of tea. More than anything in the world he wanted to curl up on Suzie's sofa and fall asleep.

'A subplot?'

'Yes, that's right.'

'OK. So "sub" means "under", I know that. Like in submarine or a subway; it's, you know, Greek.'

'Latin.'

'Whatever. So you mean there should be this main thing I was doing, and then there was something else I was doing at the same time, like a different plot going on underneath it?'

'Exactly!'

'Like on CSI.'

Suzie grimaced, like she needed convincing.

'Yeah, you know,' he said, 'there's the serious bit about who killed the bloke at the beginning. The perp. Then there's the bit about whether the two coppers are going to get it on.'

Suzie laughed. 'Well, exactly. A romantic subplot is always good, it colours out the character, you see. Let's us see their more fragile side, which helps us associate with them more.'

He thought of Natalie, his scabbed lip creaking in protest as he smiled. 'Not happening.'

'Well, it doesn't *have* to be romantic. It could be something from the past, some skeleton in the closet out to get you. There's all sort of subplots. Why did you have to leave Sydney in such a hurry for example?'

He stared at her and she stared back, eyes innocent at first and then smiling with victory.

'Lucky guess,' she said. 'Want to tell me about it?'

So he did. All about the Club and the business they were in. How he'd grassed them up and brought them down, faked his own death before returning to Montauban. There was something reassuring about hearing the story out loud, something real after all the parties and the high-life. Suzie liked the violence the most, he could tell: her pupils dilating as she scribbled furiously every time somebody got it. The badness again.

'Oh, I could listen to you all day,' she said. 'But I think we've got more than enough for now. Weren't you supposed to leave at eleven?'

He looked his watch and swore, jumped up and banged his shins against the coffee table, the tea tray tittering at his clumsiness. He hovered there awkwardly, wondering if his cheek kiss on the way in meant he owed her one on the way out too. He gave up on the idea and walked to the desk instead.

'Oh no,' she said. 'You can leave those.'

'But you said …'

'A momentary weakness! They don't even make sense now. I've got to go right back to the beginning and drop in a new opening. Otherwise this subplot's going to appear from nowhere. Please, leave them.'

She said it sharply, trying to hide the effort it cost her to pull herself up from her chair.

'Sorry for swearing,' he said.

'Oh lord. Frankly my dear, I don't give a damn! Now, come here, give me a kiss and run along with you.'

# The Subplot

## 27.

Murdoch had always thought he was clever. One of his earliest memories, in fact, was sitting in a new school and realising he was more advanced than the kid he was talking to. It was a primary school, he'd have been six or seven at most. He and the other kid had been barefoot: little Billy Murdoch in awe of his friend's scarred and twisted toes. It must have been one of those days when he had no trainers for PE. Why the other kid had been barefoot, he had no idea.

'My brother ran over my foot with a lawnmower,' the kid had told him proudly. Then, when Billy Murdoch had looked suitably impressed, he had gone on. 'You should try it. Have you got a brother?'

In those days Murdoch hadn't known the word 'irrelevant', but he'd got the concept all right. He'd also understood – and this part of his memory was crystal clear – there would have been no point in explaining to his new friend that the lawnmower, not the brother, was the ingredient he needed.

Throughout his life he'd experienced similar events, catching onto things quicker than the people around him. Sure, he'd made some stupid decisions – the bank job shortly after his eighteenth birthday: the mother of them all – but in day-to-day life, he knew he was cleverer than most. 'You're so sharp, you wanna watch you don't cut yourself,' a prison boss had once threatened him. After that, he'd learnt to hide it, especially around people who liked to think they were the smartest guy in the room. It was a hard habit to break and he didn't feel too bad for letting Suzie Bourne think he could hardly read. What did she think he'd done in prison for all those years, pick his toenails? The trouble was, in recent weeks, Murdoch had started to think maybe he wasn't so smart after all. Not after everything that had happened: the scene with Angus; Benny Robbins' cash; the guy in the white Corolla. Like he'd said to Davie, he'd got lazy and stupid. But it wasn't just that. Hanging around with James Harte's successful friends and acquaintances, he'd begun to wonder if maybe the only people he was more intelligent than were the crooks he'd known in prison. Crooks stupid enough to have got caught; what kind of a yardstick was that?

Thursday morning, waiting in the hallway of the University of Sydney, it was difficult not to think maybe he wasn't clever at all. People half his age sat reading books whose titles he didn't understand. Noticeboards held posters that might as well have been in a foreign language. Signs pointed to faculties that taught things he'd never heard of. Murdoch reminded himself that not knowing things was ignorance – a lack of education – nothing to do with a lack of smarts. It didn't make him feel any better. Not getting an education, how fucking smart was that? Other blokes inside had managed it. He noticed a group of passing students who'd seen his bruises and were unconsciously slowing to stare. He stared back and snarled until they looked away and hurried off in whispers.

'How d'you do it?' he snapped, when Davie strolled up at last. 'Do you work out what time I'm going to be here and add on thirty minutes?'

'Sorry. Traffic.'

Davie was at his least convincing. He had a satchel slung over one shoulder and, despite his shirt and tie, looked the same age as the students meandering past. Murdoch gave him a flat-eyed stare.

'What time d'you leave Montie?'

'Ten-ish?'

'So it wasn't the traffic.'

Davie bumped down into the seat beside him. 'What's happening?'

'You wasn't here and the appointment's in your name so we got bumped to quarter to twelve.'

Davie checked his watch. 'Oh, that's good, we've got loads of time, then.' It was probably a joke, but when he caught the look on Murdoch's face, he let it fall flat between them. 'Professor Barker suggested we meet him over the road, after his meeting at the Coroners' Court, but I thought you'd feel more comfortable here.'

'Why's that?'

'Well, you know, because it's not a court building?'

'Really? And tell me, Davie, why wouldn't I feel comfortable in a court building?'

'Well, you know. You and your ... er, history.'

'Me and my ... er, history are fine, thanks very much. I've not got nothing against the law.'

'Excuse me?'

168

'Trust me, mate, most of the blokes banged up inside deserve to be there. The world's better off without them running around.'

Davie crinkled every part of his face. 'What? But you're always saying there's as many crooks on the street as there are innocent men in prison.'

'Yeah, but that's not many. The law's just like anything else. If you're smart, you can beat it, if you're dumb, it'll beat you. For most people, it just works.'

'Really?' Davie hesitated. 'And for you?'

Murdoch's scowl must have been worse this time, because Davie blushed and started examining the strap of his satchel. Murdoch leant forward with his elbows on his knees, talking quietly like he was sharing a secret.

'I did a bad thing or two, I can't deny it. But I did my time and now I'm a good boy. So no, a court building wouldn't bother me too much at all. This fucking place bothers me more. At least I understand what goes on in a court.'

'Mr Simms, I presume!'

A tall man in a suit as grey and dishevelled as his hair was approaching them from the reception desk. Half the red wine he'd drunk the night before – or maybe at lunchtime by the smell of him – was stretched across his nose in tiny veins. He shook their hands vigorously, looking curiously at Murdoch's wounds but deciding not to comment, and took them to his office on the first floor.

'Excuse the mess,' he said, although the small room – two sash windows overlooking the quad – was perfectly tidy. 'They keep telling me I can't keep my office, so I never really make myself at home. Then the new term comes around and there's my name on the list again.'

'Professor Barker lectures in pathology at the university,' explained Davie, helpfully. 'When he's not consulting as an expert witness.'

'No shit.'

Davie winced, but Barker caught Murdoch's eye and laughed. Then he gestured them into chairs dating from the seventies and insisted on making tea, telling them how exciting it must be to be private detectives. It was almost ten minutes before he was sitting behind his leather-topped desk. He pulled open a drawer and produced a thick manila file, opening it onto the surface between them.

'Ah, Charlotte Holland.' He looked up at them, tapping his nose with a forefinger. 'Plenty in here, that's good to see. Like they say, it's not what you know it's who you know.' He gave Murdoch a knowing wink, like they both

169

knew who he was talking about. Murdoch didn't have a clue, but he was pretty sure it was someone in authority who didn't mind doing whatever it took to put people away. He took a deep breath and reminded himself he wasn't angry at Professor Barker, or at anyone really. He was just in an unfamiliar environment surrounded by people who knew how the respectable world worked.

Beside him, Davie started making simpering noises about how grateful they were – like no money had changed hands – and how it was all for the greater good and how much they appreciated it, until even he realised no one was listening. Professor Barker was going through the file: a mixture of typed pages, handwritten notes and oversized photographs.

'So how come the police got you involved?' Murdoch asked him. 'I'd of thought they'd rely on the forensic pathologist's report.'

Barker didn't look up from his papers. 'Mm, well, the pathologist's report deals mostly with the cause and not the manner of death. The police asked me to look at the autopsy evidence in conjunction with the other evidence and to give them my opinion on whether it all fitted with the findings of their investigation. Normally it's the defence who get me involved but here – I don't know – maybe the DPP weren't too sure how their case was stacking up? Now, I have to be honest, I don't really remember this one. Read about too many corpses in my life to remember any but the headless ones, ha, ha. Unless ...' Barker squinted at some notes. 'Oh yes. This was actually a legless one, wasn't it? It was in the papers, I seem to remember. Let's have a look.' He pushed through some shiny photographs and held one up to the light. Put it down and returned to the typed pages. 'No, I do remember it now. Millionaire boyfriend on his boat or something? Knocked her on the head and chucked her overboard.'

From the corner of his eye, Murdoch saw Davie sit straight and turn away from the images now strewn across Barker's desk. Murdoch himself leant forward and, by changing his angle, was able to study the shots.

'Not much left of her face,' he said.

Barker caught his eye, then pushed the photographs towards him. Davie stood and stepped away. 'Does this open?' he said, tugging weakly at one of the sash windows.

Murdoch snorted quietly and studied the photographs. 'How can you tell she died from a knock on the head?'

'Because the autopsy report stated blunt force trauma to the skull and consequent brain injury as the cause of death.'

'But that doesn't mean someone hit her, does it? Maybe she fell over, bumped her head and rolled into the water?'

'No, that's not possible. Firstly, she would most likely have shown signs of drowning, which she didn't. No frothy foam in her airways, no inflammation or signs of pre-death waterlogging of the lungs, no rib imprints on the tissue protecting the lungs – the list goes on and on. Secondly, the force required for this level of skull damage and immediate cerebral contusion – sorry, that's traumatic brain injury to you and me. Well, to you at least, ha, ha. No, the force required to create such an injury couldn't be caused by simply tripping over. It would need a fall from a height head first onto a hard surface.'

'How high?'

'Higher than would be possible on the yacht she was supposedly on when she met her death. Besides, for the force needed to cause an injury like this, it's not just about height, it's also about velocity. It's the kind of injury you sometimes see with pedestrian injuries. When someone is run over, it's their head hitting the road that often kills them.'

Davie stopped struggling with the sash window. 'So she could have been run over? That's possible? Really?'

At Davie's tone, Murdoch turned. 'Why you asking that?'

'Something in the, you know, in the file—'

Davie was staring at the photograph in Murdoch's hand. He went pale, the veins in his temples protruding slightly, and returned to his battle with the window. Murdoch turned back to the professor.

'Could she of been run down?'

Barker smirked. 'Well, theoretically, but it's obviously not the case given she was in the middle of the harbour. No, in the circumstances, the most likely manner of death was a deliberate blow to the head struck with force.'

'Mind if I look at the report you did for the DPP?'

Barker shrugged, passed over the report to Murdoch and went to help Davie with the window. Between them they opened it all the way, the photographs on the desk lifting before resting in place again while Murdoch read in silence, scratching his scalp slowly. Professor Barker told Davie to take deep breaths and, for a while the, room was silent but for the traffic noise wafting in from the Parramatta Road. Then Murdoch said, 'Here,

Professor, I can't find where you say it was like she might of been run over by a car. Is there a special way of saying that in Latin or something?'

'No word for car in Latin, dude,' said Davie, whose own head and torso were now fully outside the window.

Barker laughed at that. 'I didn't say she might have been run over, Bill. What I said is that the level of force required for such a head injury was similar to a pedestrian who had been run over at speed.'

'Right. So where do you say that?'

'Well, I probably didn't. As I said, it seems very unlikely on a boat. I know, I know, you're going to say she could have been hit by a car and the force could have thrown her into the water. Let's have a look.' Barker returned to his desk and started rifling through the papers lying there. 'No. There were no lacerations or tyre imprints on the torso, no evidence of secondary impact at all.'

'Secondary impact?'

'Yes. When someone's run over by a car, the primary impact is the bumper and bonnet hitting the legs and pelvis. Then the person hit generally turns, their head or upper torso hitting the upper bonnet or windscreen of the car – that's the secondary impact. Then they hit the ground – tertiary impact – which is normally the bit that kills them. Makes you think twice about crossing the road in a hurry, eh?'

'Right. So Charlie Holland couldn't of been run over then?'

'Well, actually, theoretically she could have been. The legs are gone, of course, so no evidence there, but if a vehicle is still accelerating at the point of impact, the victim can be thrown straight into the air, somersaulting and landing—'

'From a height head first onto a hard surface.'

'Indeed. Except then there is inevitably road matter, and often glass from the windscreen too, in the damaged facial tissue.'

Murdoch pushed through the photographs again. 'Yeah, but half of Charlie Holland's face was eaten away and I'm guessing the fish would go for the smacked-in bits first, wouldn't they, cos it'd be easier to nibble on?'

Barker hesitated, looked Murdoch up and down and smiled softly: a father coping with a naive little boy. 'I imagine there are papers outlining the feeding habits of marine creatures on submerged cadavers, but I can't quote from them offhand.'

'But why didn't you mention that it's possible Charlie Holland was run over?'

'For the same reason I didn't mention the victim could have thrown herself out of a window, or that she could have been used like a battering ram to knock down a heavy door, or any one of the many different things that could have happened to her but which, in the middle of Sydney harbour, seem unlikely.'

'Yeah, but the way you've written it here, it's like it's definite she was hit on the head by someone. "Consistent with being hit with deliberate force by a heavy implement." That's what you wrote. But it might not be true, had it? Charlie Holland might have fallen out of a window or been run over and then chucked in the water.'

'Amongst many other possible scenarios.'

'None of which you mention.'

'Bill, that's not my job. As a professional witness, my job is to give an opinion – based on my years of experience, I might add – as to the likely cause or manner of death based upon the body of evidence presented to me.'

'But you miss other bits out if it could jeapordise a conviction?'

'Jeopardise,' said Davie from outside the window.

'Bill, try to understand. The service I provide has clients like any other business, and my client in this case is the Director of Public Prosecutions.'

'And you're more likely to get more work if you give your client what they wants.'

'Well, yes. I mean, no.' Barker sat forward, hands on his desk. His soft smile had gone and the red from his nose was invading the rest of his face. 'I hardly think you're in a position to question my work.'

'Well, someone ought to.'

'Yes – a barrister. And they often do.'

'You should be ashamed of yourself.'

'What?'

'It's people like you what put innocent ...' Murdoch realised he was about to contradict his earlier comments to Davie. It didn't help his mood. 'You're a professional liar.'

'How dare you! I didn't even have to see you two, you know. I certainly didn't expect you to come in here and insult me.'

'Well, I certainly didn't expect to come in here and find you writing stuff what's used to put people in prison written according to what the police want to hear.'

'Well, really. How dare you!'

Murdoch wanted to tell Professor Barker exactly how he dared, but found he was talking to the back of Davie's legs.

'Thank you so much, Professor Barker.' Davie was reaching forward over the desk to shake the pathologist's hand.

'This is ridiculous.' Barker, half hidden by Davie, had raised his voice. 'Who do you think you are?'

Looking down at the pain in his knuckles, Murdoch found he was gripping the arms of his chair. He told himself to breathe.

'Off we go then!' Davie had turned to face him and Murdoch let himself be pulled to his feet and guided to the door.

'Who the hell do you think you are?' Barker demanded again behind them, then shouted something else that was lost as the door to his office closed.

They were back in the Merc, Davie driving, before Murdoch spoke again.

'Well,' he said, buzzing down the window and lighting a cigarette, 'that was interesting.'

'Yep.' Davie stared at the road head. 'Stoked you decided to come after all.'

28.

Crosley Police Station was the neighbour left behind when everyone else moved to the mall. Wedged between two deserted shops on what had once been the main street, it was no cleaner than the sad buildings either side of it – tagging the cop shop was a rite of passage – but stood out because of the lack of wire caging protecting its dirty windows. The day after their visit to Professor Barker, Murdoch was leaning against the building, scowling at his watch and wondering how he'd been persuaded to turn up there, when Davie ran up out of breath.

'You been in yet, Bill?'

His hair was wet, he'd obviously got as far as the shower or the ocean before remembering where he was supposed to be.

'After you, mate,' said Murdoch. 'This was your idea.'

The police station was dull after the brightness of the day, fluorescent lighting somehow adding to the gloom. The desk inside the heavy front doors was unmanned, but through a smoked glass screen behind it, they could see two blurred figures: a couple of uniforms chatting, one of them relaying parts of the conversation down the phone. Murdoch looked around uncomfortably, caught Davie watching him do it, and wandered over to the noticeboard. He read the neighbourhood watch notices and the underage drinking posters, a cartoon warning of the dangers of leaving valuables in your car. Someone had pinned up a forlorn piece of tinsel, like they were trying to give the crime warnings some festive cheer.

'What time's she expecting us then?'

When Davie didn't reply, Murdoch turned to find him frowning at his phone, mumbling under his breath.

'She stood us up or something?'

'What?' Davie's mind was somewhere else. 'Oh, no. Just had a sale fall through. Nice couple from Sydney; I really thought they were going to go for it.'

'Right. So, what time's the appointment?'

'Well, they were going to come for a final viewing this arvo, but I guess they won't do that now.'

'No, you muppet, what time's our appointment here?'

Davie looked up from his phone, blue eyes wide, like he'd been asked a maths question no one could be expected to answer.

'Oh! No, we don't have an appointment. I figured we'd just drop in. I mean, I know Nat's at work today, Anne Lincoln saw her on the way in.'

They stood in silence for another ten seconds, Murdoch drumming his fingers against his thighs until he suddenly said, 'Sod this. Natalie's not expecting us. No one's here, let's go.'

'What's the rush?'

'Who's in a rush? I just think she's not likely to see us without an appointment. And I don't feel like hanging around an empty nick in my spare time.'

'Someone will be out in a minute or two.'

'Yeah, well, I'm out of here now.'

175

Murdoch was halfway to the door when one of the uniforms, a round-faced Aboriginal girl with a ponytail, appeared from the behind the smoked glass screen.

'Can I help you, sir?'

She was talking to Murdoch, like people were only interesting when they were trying to get away. Davie told her they were looking for DC Natalie Conquest.

'And you are, sir?' She was still only talking to Murdoch.

'My name's Davie Simms. She knows me.'

'And who's this gentleman?'

'He's with me.'

'Name?'

Murdoch turned and approached the desk, ignoring the squeak of the heavy door behind him.

'What's your bleeding problem?' he said. 'This guy wants to see Nat Conquest, he's given you his name, I'm just leaving. What you want to know my name for? It's not a crime, is it, hanging around waiting for you lot to get your arses in gear?'

'There's no need for that attitude, sir. I was just asking your name.'

'His name's Bill Murdoch and he's a fucking moron.'

Murdoch and Davie turned as one. Natalie Conquest had entered the reception area and was standing, arms crossed, dressed in her normal uniform: jeans, white T-shirt and a foul look on her face.

'I suppose you've come to apologise,' she said once she'd calmed the Senior Constable at the desk and led them to a bleak interview room. 'Well, if you have, you can save it. It's too bloody late. I've had my Inspector giving me grief all bloody morning because of you and your idiotic behaviour.'

She scraped a chair and sat on it heavily like it was threatening to resist arrest. Davie sat opposite her, but Murdoch stayed on his feet.

'What idiotic behaviour?' he said. 'What you on about? And, anyway, why do we have to talk in here? Why don't we go and grab a cuppa or something?'

Natalie scowled at him. 'Oh, suck it up, princess. What's the matter, aren't you comfortable these days unless you've got a glass of champagne in your hand? Maybe you'd like me to ring for room service? And what the hell's happened to your face, someone managed to get to you before I could?'

Murdoch held her eye but took the chair next to Davie. The table was too small for the three of them and he had to twist to avoid his knees brushing against hers. Someone, he noticed, had carved *'PIGS'* into the wooden tabletop in aggressive angular letters.

'Go on then,' said Natalie, chair rocking back, hands in her pockets. 'Let me at least hear the words come out of your mouth.'

Like the round-faced Senior Constable at the desk, she was only talking to Murdoch.

''Scuse me?'

'You've come to say sorry, so say it. I want you to know how pathetic it sounds.'

'We've come here to ask you a favour,' said Davie. 'What are you so angry about?'

'You going to tell him, or shall I?' Natalie was still only looking at Murdoch. She always looked best when she was pissed off: it took the weakness out of her mouth. He remembered how much he'd fancied her the first time they'd met. Before he knew she was a copper.

'Sorry, Nat,' he said, honestly for once. 'I don't know what you're talking about, love.'

'The photograph? Back when you were pretty.'

'What photograph?'

She frowned her little frown, coloured slightly then seemed almost to grin. Yep, thought Murdoch, definitely best when angry. He watched her stand, chair harsh against the lino, then walk past him and Davie and out of the interview room. The door slammed ominously behind her.

'What's she on about?'

'Beats me.'

Within a minute she was back, a glossy magazine rolled in one hand. She stood opposite them, flipping the pages until she found the right one, then laid it firmly on the table, turning it the right way for them. Someone had ripped open a perfume advert and the sickly-sweet smell filled the air. Davie leant forward like he was supposed to, but Murdoch was too familiar with interview room games. He stayed upright, staring at Natalie as she sat down.

'Oh crikey,' said Davie. 'Oh, Bill!'

Natalie smiled and nodded towards the magazine until Murdoch gave up. What the hell, he'd done nothing wrong. It was *Starstrike!* magazine: the society section. Thumbnails of couples smiling for the camera, larger shots for minor celebrities, a quarter page for him and Melissa Munday grinning for their lives at the races.

'What the ...'

'Yeah,' said Natalie, her voice sounding far away. 'That's kind of what I thought. Kind of what my Inspector thought too. Kind of what the Specials said when they phoned me and asked if I had any clue how much it actually cost to get you a brand-new identity?'

It was him all right: it even looked like him. There in the glossy pages of *Starstrike!*, Melissa Munday on his arm. *'Melissa Munday and Friend'*, it said, like he was one of them playboys what went to fancy parties with international soap stars on their arm. The scab on his top lip was hurting and he realised he was grinning. He put his face in his hands, like a man shocked and tired, then drew them slowly down.

'I didn't know,' he said.

'Oh, really?'

'Really. It's not my fault. No one asked me if they could put my face all over the place. Cheeky bastards.'

The last two words fell as fake as they felt. Natalie let him have it again, told him how much grief she was getting, the cost, her career, laughing stock. Murdoch was only half listening. *Him. Him and Melissa Munday in a celebrity mag!* The only shame was seeing it like this, here in an interview room, like it was something he was supposed to deny. He looked up at Natalie, frowning as best he could.

'Sorry.'

'Whatever.'

'No, really, Nat,' said Davie. 'He is sorry. He wouldn't have done it on purpose. Only a few weeks ago, he was paranoid when we thought someone was looking for him.'

Murdoch resisted the truth of this, annoyed they were spoiling his moment, taking away the magic of him in a magazine with Melissa Munday on his arm. At the races.

'Seriously, Nat,' Davie was saying, 'if we'd have known about it we'd have warned you. Phoned to let you know or something. We know how much you did for Bill last year. Don't we, Bill?'

'Hang on.' Natalie narrowed her eyes. 'Why are you here, then?'

'Well!' Davie, triumphant. 'Like I said, we were going to ask a ... I mean, we need—'

'There's been progress on the case,' Murdoch told her, closing the magazine so he could focus. 'It looks like there might be something the police missed.'

'Which is perfectly understandable,' said Davie quickly. 'It's just, I remember seeing in the file that someone said they saw Charlie Holland being run down by a car. And the expert witness the DPP are planning to use? Well, he said that was possible, so I was just thinking if I could have another look at the file, then we could follow up that witness ...'

His excitement withered under the heat of Natalie's glare. She had sat herself bolt upright and was holding onto the edge of the table. When she spoke her jaw barely moved.

'Not here.'

She stood, motioned for them to do the same, led them out of the interview room and silently down the corridor. At the front desk, the ponytailed Senior Constable was flipping through pages on a clipboard.

'Back in a bit,' said Natalie when the other woman looked up. 'Want a coffee?'

'Just had one, thanks.'

'Right. Back in a sec.'

They were a hundred metres down Macquarie Road, still blinking in the brightness of the afternoon, before she spoke again. Murdoch steeled himself but, this time, it was Davie's turn.

'If you ever, ever, ever mention ever again that you looked in that file, I will rip your nuts off and make you eat them. Do you understand?'

Davie looked like he was going to cry. He stared at his shoes and nodded. Murdoch wanted to punch him.

'And you,' Natalie turned on him. 'I never want to see you ever again, you understand? Not in the flesh, and certainly not in a fucking magazine. Otherwise, I'll be the one calling whoever it is who'd like to see you dead and I'll be the one telling them where you live. You got it?'

'An innocent man's in prison,' he said. 'And a murderer has gone free.'

'Oh, lick me.'

Watching Natalie stomp away, Murdoch realised he was still holding the magazine.

'Guess I can keep this then, eh?'

'Don't, Bill,' said Davie. 'It's not funny. There's no way she'll help us now.'

'Oh, you wait, she'll come around. She's too much of a do-gooder not to help us out. She just needs to calm down a bit.'

He unrolled the magazine and found the page again, holding it at arm's distance for a new appreciation. Davie sighed again.

'What I don't understand,' he said, 'is how come you're so relaxed about it? A few weeks ago, you were all jumpy because someone was asking for you, now you're cool with your face being in the national press.'

'Yeah.' Murdoch frowned. 'Doesn't make sense, does it? But then again, that person looking for me turned out to be a new client, so we're all good. And, besides, I can't hide away me whole life, can I?' Murdoch rolled up the magazine again and used it to poke Davie in the stomach. 'You know your trouble, mate? You worry too much. It'll be fine, you'll see. It'll be absolutely fine.'

29.

It was Wednesday before he and Davie spoke again. Murdoch was just back from having his car cleaned – he took it to a place in Kildare where nobody knew his business – and was trying to work out what looked best. Top down or top up. Sports bag out of sight in the boot or on the passenger seat next to him with the handle of the racquet sticking out. In the adverts, sports cars always had a leather overnight bag on the passenger seat and Murdoch was concerned his sports bag looked a bit scruffy. He was putting it back in the boot when his phone rang.

'Davie, perfect timing.'

'Hi, Bill, listen, I was just wondering if you'd heard anything from Natalie?'

'Me? Are you joking?'

'Well, it was long shot, it's just I haven't either. I thought she might have, you know, got curious or something? If she doesn't get in touch, do you think I should call her?'

Murdoch looked at his car again, studying it from a new angle before remembering to reply. 'Nah, Davie, not on your nelly. Let her come to you. She will in the end.'

'Crikey, I hope so. I've got a bit more Hoxton Harte reading to do, but then I'm at a dead end. What about you?'

'What about me?'

'Have you managed to find anything else out? Are you seeing that crowd again soon?'

'Oh. Yeah, right. Actually, I'm about to go off for a game of tennis with Oscar Druitt. Thought I'd, you know, dig around and find things out. Listen, if you were going to play tennis up at Huntingdon's, would you arrive in your tennis gear or would you wear your normal clothes and get changed there?'

'Oh, I don't know. Depends what you're doing afterwards. You two having lunch?'

Murdoch hadn't thought of that. He swore and checked his watch. Now he'd have to get changed again.

'Listen, Davie, I've got to go. I'll let you know if I find anything out.'

'Great. And Bill ...'

Murdoch waited, listening to Davie choose his words. He could picture him, sitting at his desk in the estate agents, about to forget what he wanted to say.

'What is it, Davie?'

'It's just that, well, you probably don't, but it's just that I wondered what you were doing for Chrissy? Day, I mean. I'm going to my parents' place and I thought, you know, you don't want to be alone. Not on Christmas.'

'Who says I don't?'

'Well, I was just thinking maybe you didn't. I mean, you know.'

Murdoch spotted a smudge on back of the car. He stretched forwards and rubbed the edge of his T-shirt against it.

'You're all right, mate,' he said. 'I don't do Christmas, too bleeding depressing. Every time someone says "Happy Christmas" to me, I pretend they're saying "I want to lick your hole." And when I say "Happy Christmas" back, I'm really saying "Give us two quid and you can." Makes me smile and gets me through.'

'But don't you miss it?'

'Miss what, Christmas? You know what, Davie, one of the best things about living in Australia is, I don't miss it at all. It's lovely and hot, big blue sky, everyone's on the beach. If you don't watch the ads on the telly and you don't go to the shops and you avoid people, you wouldn't even think it was Christmas at all.'

'Well, if you change your mind, let me know.'

Murdoch smiled. It was nice to think someone was looking out for him when they didn't really want to. But when he ran upstairs to get changed, the house seemed strangely empty. He considered calling Davie back, taking him up on his offer, but he knew that would be worse: sitting around with people he didn't know and watching them all love each other. Noticing the time, he pulled on a white shirt, a pair of jeans and his smartest black shoes, told his reflection he was the dog's bollocks and ran back down to the car.

Murdoch was relieved to find Oscar Druitt waiting for him in Huntingdon's car park. He was keen to avoid a repeat of the scene with Mr Hughes. Not that Oscar would care, he'd wave it off or bark Hughes back into his corner. Still, though, he wanted to make a good impression.

'Don't forget, I'm just a learner,' he said as he and Oscar shook hands on the rich gravel.

Oscar's white smile broke his tan. 'Me too. It'll be a competition of who's the least worst. Or lesser worse, I suppose. Seriously, don't worry. If we're that ill-matched, we can just practise serving at each other. You know, if you want to play a lot, you should think about joining this place. It's got the best courts this side of Sydney.'

Murdoch looked around like he was considering the idea. 'You reckon it's worth the money?'

'Well, probably not. Not just for the tennis. I mean, you can have a good bash over a net anywhere, can't you? But then I suppose you're paying to know you're not just anywhere. It's like flying business class. Wouldn't be worth a cent if you couldn't see all the mugs back in economy.'

Murdoch nodded slowly. He hadn't flown often and never in business class. 'D'you reckon they'd have me, though? There's probably some nomination process or something, inn't there?'

'Oh God, I wouldn't worry about that. I'm on the membership committee. I could nominate you, get one of the chaps to second you and have you all signed up in one meeting.'

Murdoch wanted to sound bored by the idea: the way Oscar always sounded faintly bored. He picked up his racquet and started examining the strings. 'Well, in that case ...'

'Hello, Druitt!'

An ageing, fair-haired man was walking towards them in tennis whites. He was a fifty-something schoolboy: parted hair, legs too long for his shorts. Oscar introduced him to Murdoch as Peter Christensen.

'Was just saying to Bill here, he should join. Listen, if I nominate him at the next membership meeting, would you second him?'

'Mm, don't know about that.' Christensen looked Murdoch up and down. 'Looks a bit rough and we're very picky.'

He and Oscar laughed, Murdoch joining in a second later. Haw, haw, haw – weren't they all friends? Oscar suggested the two men swap numbers.

'Pete's so-called mates are always blowing him out. That's how it works around here, anyway; always someone looking for a game.'

He and Christensen looked at Murdoch until, realising they meant it, he scrabbled in his bag for his phone. *Jesus*, he thought as he typed in Christensen's name and number, *I'm in*.

Ed Springer had taught Murdoch that a standard knock-up consisted of a few minutes of balls across the court, then a few minutes down the line, then some serves. But Oscar started by peppering the court at random, slowly at first, then turning up the power on every hit. Murdoch managed to return almost every ball, some of them with winning shots, but he had little chance to celebrate before the next one came plummeting over the net.

'I think that'll do, don't you?' said Oscar after a minute or two.

Murdoch hesitated to check he wasn't joking. 'You what? What about a serve or two? I haven't been on a court in weeks.'

Oscar sighed. 'Well, if you must.'

He stood there, watching as Murdoch put two balls long, two into the net and then two into the service box. Then he said, 'Shall we?', picked up the six balls and walked to the other end of the court.

As things turned out, they were evenly matched. At least, they were once Murdoch stopped worrying about what Oscar thought of him and started focusing on the game. By that time, he was one set down, although Oscar made encouraging noises when they stopped for a swig of water.

'This is fun,' he said. 'We should do it more often.'

Encouraged, Murdoch surprised himself by winning the first two games of the second set and then, after a tussle around deuce, found himself three–love up. It was on the next game things started to change.

'Out!' shouted Oscar on what Murdoch had thought was a good shot down the line. Then, two rallies later, he did it again.

'Are you sure, Oscar, mate? It looked all right to me.'

'No doubt at all. It was right in front of me and it was definitely out.'

Murdoch played more cautiously after that, placing the ball further inside the court. Oscar took advantage and powered every return so that within fifteen minutes the score was three all. Again, Murdoch pulled ahead, and, again, Oscar responded by calling two shots out, resulting in a score of five–four in the second set.

When they next changed ends, stopping at the net for more water, Oscar was as friendly as ever, making chatty small talk about what a tough game it was. Murdoch, not knowing what else to say, asked how many sets they were playing. Like he didn't care either way.

'It'll have to be best of three,' said Oscar. 'I've got to run off to lunch. It's a work thing. Some of us do have to work for a living, you know.'

Murdoch had been taking a swig from his water bottle. Now he lowered it slowly.

'Not that I'm complaining,' said Oscar with a smile. 'Apart from when Emma makes me her bloody delivery boy. But this isn't a bad way to spend a Wednesday morning. I'm having fun, are you?'

'You get to pick your own hours, then?'

'Well, not entirely, but pretty much. Trust me, one overly ambitious workaholic in the family is more than enough. Actually, that's not fair. Poor Emma has her work cut out for her, trying to get the agency in good shape; I've never seen her so determined. Her brother might be a genius at making money, but he's a bloody fool when he comes to spending it. Amanda's more level-headed; at least, when it comes to business.'

He looked at Murdoch as he said this last sentence, like it needed a reply. When Murdoch said nothing, Oscar softened his voice and carried on.

'You like her, don't you?'

'Who's that?'

'Don't be coy, Bill. You like Amanda. I've seen the way you look at her. I can't blame you, but a word to the wise – be careful about fishing in that pool.'

'What do you mean?'

'Just, be careful. James is no angel.'

Murdoch dropped down to retie a lace. This much he owed to Davie.

'None of us are angels, mate.'

'No,' said Oscar. 'But not many of us are devils either. Don't get me wrong, it's not that I think James killed poor beautiful Charlie, but ...'

'Did you know her?'

'Charlie? Of course! You couldn't spend much time with James without knowing her. She was always turning up. Anyway, as I say, I don't think James killed her, but he's not a good man, no matter what he might have told you.'

'You talking about struggling to get that money back off him?'

Oscar looked embarrassed and Murdoch realised he'd forgotten their conversation at the races.

'No,' he said quickly. 'More that ... well, James is the type of person who will use anything he knows to get his way. Trust me, no one's going to say it's a travesty of justice him being locked up in prison.'

'So why should I be careful?' Murdoch moved onto the other shoe. 'Oscar?'

But, just as at the races, Oscar seemed to be regretting his indiscretion. He stood silently until Murdoch was done, then put his hands out for the six balls.

'So, here's me serving for the match,' he said, like nothing else had passed between them. Murdoch managed a smile, like he couldn't care less who won, but, as he handed over the balls, a movement behind Oscar flattened it again. A white car with a yellow logo was crunching the gravel up by the main building. As Murdoch watched, it stopped and a familiar man got out, wandering his thick frame over to the top of the slope to stand looking down at the courts. There was no point in running up there: the bloke would see him a hundred yards away. So let him look: let him study a man who's got it going on. Murdoch in his whites, playing tennis at Huntingdon's during the week: living the dream. Murdoch turned and walked to his end of the court. He'd barely turned back before Oscar's serve had come flying over the net, the ball past him before he could properly respond.

'And that,' Oscar shouted, 'is what I think they call an ace!'


30.


Murdoch arrived home so angry that, at first, he didn't recognise the man waiting for him there. The heavy in the *No Birds* car had, of course, disappeared by the time he and Druitt had finished their game. Murdoch had driven home with one eye on the mirror. This time he hoped he was being followed: he was desperate for a second go at the heavy, pretending that man alone was to blame for the foul mood he, Murdoch, now found himself in. Because why would it matter if Oscar Druitt was a *cheat*? He spat the word aloud along the Crown Road, congratulating himself for not saying it to Oscar's face, trying to believe it had been the right thing to do.

The worst of it all was how obvious Oscar had been, like he'd been testing him, seeing what Murdoch would do. Full eye contact and a strong handshake when he'd won the final point, virtually goading him into a reaction. *Go on, have a go, show us what you're really like.* Murdoch hadn't seen that kind of behaviour since he'd escaped from the animals. He spat properly, his phlegm a line in the wind, and called Oscar a cheat aloud again. He should have told the man to his face. No, he was better than that. He was still arguing with himself when he pulled into his driveway, turned off the engine and noticed a small blue Suzuki in the shadows across the road, a wide man in the driver's seat.

Pretending he'd seen nothing, Murdoch buzzed up the Merc's roof, then its windows one by one as he squinted into his mirrors. The man in the Suzuki – a man too huge for the tiny car, one fat arm hanging out of the window – wasn't pretending to do anything but stare. When Murdoch got out of his car at last and turned to stare back, the fat man smiled and suddenly Murdoch realised who he was. The Suzuki was fifteen metres away and he was a good thirty kilos heavier, but there was no doubt it was him.

Murdoch's first instinct was to run. To get inside his house as quickly as possible and lock all the doors. Instead, he took a deep breath and walked towards the Suzuki.

'Ibrahim Hussein,' he said. 'You look like you've eaten yourself.'

Hussein pulled his arm in and started the awkward process of getting out of the tiny car. Murdoch beat him to it, the violent kick he gave the Suzuki's door clicking it shut again.

'Hey,' Hussein said in a whine. 'Mind the car. I've got to get my bond back on this thing!'

He wasn't the man he'd been when Murdoch had last seen him. It wasn't just the shocking weight gain. The gangster's confidence had gone along with the sharp suits and the hard-man build. And he obviously wasn't armed. Hussein had been the kind of guy who liked you to know if he was carrying; liked to wave a weapon in your face and threaten you with it, like he'd been doing the last time Murdoch had seen him. That had been until the police arrived – late, of course – and put a hole in Hussein's shoulder. Murdoch took a step closer to the Suzuki and threw a punch through the open window. Hussein saw it coming and recoiled, but he was a big man in a small car and the blow caught him on a flabby cheek. There was a scrabbling of arms between them until Murdoch stepped out of reach.

'Leave it out, Murdoch, for fuck's sake.'

'What do you want?'

'What's your problem? Can't an old workmate have a friendly chat?'

'We was never mates. What do you want?'

Hussein tried to get out of the car again, but Murdoch leant on the door, pushing the button lock down and threatening another punch.

'You don't get to threaten me.' Hussein had found his tough boy voice at last. 'You don't get to do that, you understand? Nice little set-up you got going on here. Nice car, nice house, nice flash lifestyle with hot girls on the red carpet. Or did you forget that there's people out there who want you dead?'

'How did you find me?'

Hussein gave up trying to get out of the car. He leant back and put on his fat smile again, ignoring the sun in his eyes. A nearly empty can of Coke was dripping stains on the passenger seat beside him.

'Wasn't exactly difficult, I've still got connections, y'know. Mate of mine works at the track and he has a mate in marketing. Easy enough to get the names and addresses of all the people invited to that fancy champagne thing. You remember, the one you went to with Melissa Munday? Wouldn't have thought you were her type, tell the truth. And imagine my surprise when I look at the sponsor's guest list and see you haven't even changed your name. So I visit the place the invite was sent to and here you are, living the dream, you ugly bastard.'

'So who's your friend in the white *No Birds* car?'

Hussein's piggy little eyes squinted in confusion and Murdoch realised he'd missed the mark. The two men had nothing to do with each other. He heard footsteps and looked around to see Mr Minter walking up from the shops, nodded at him and looked away. Waited until Minter had gone up his driveway, the front door closing loud behind him, then turned back to Hussein.

'Oh dear,' said the fat man. 'Don't we want to upset the neighbours? Don't they know what you really are?'

'Listen to me, you arsewipe, you think I can't do maths? You went down for ten years with a minimum of eight on the bottom. And here you are on the street again less than two years later. You must have done a deal yourself. You open your fucking mouth and you're dead before I am.'

'Is that right? Do you know where I live? Do you? And do I have a fancy car and a fancy house bought with the Club's money after I nicked a whole fucking shipment off them? Do I?'

'The Club don't exist no more.'

Hussein chuckled, his chins and cheeks catching on late to the joke. He struggled with his jacket pockets until he pulled out a tiny phone, ridiculous in his fat hands.

'You are out of touch, my man. The Club just went quiet for a bit. And I don't think they'll be as interested in me as they will be in you. Did you seriously think you could swan up here and leave it all behind you? It doesn't work that way, Murdoch; at least, not if I've got anything to do with it.' He wiggled the phone out of the car window. 'So you get me two hundred grand in a month or a certain Mr Henry Wallis is going to know where you live.'

'Who the fuck is Henry Wallis?'

Hussein bit his lip, annoyed with himself. 'Point is, I call him and you're a dead man. And don't try any funny business. Anything happens to me, there's a solicitor who's got an envelope to open. Same story: your name, your address and who to give it to.'

'You must think I'm as thick as your lips,' Murdoch spat at him. 'What's to stop you shopping me anyway?'

Hussein squeezed the phone back into his pocket. 'Well, like you said, Ironstein, I don't exactly want them to know I'm out either, do I? So we're both happy. I want two hundred grand. Don't pretend you can't afford it.'

'Mate, I give you two hundred grand, you'll spend it on hamburgers in a week. Look at you.'

'Fuck you, Murdoch, you think you deserve your money any more than I do? You think you've earned it and I'm just lazy? You got lucky, Murdoch, that's all, and I got stuck with a shoulder full of lead and an examply sentence. Well, it's my turn for the luck. Two hundred grand cash in a month or you can kiss your little lifestyle goodbye. Kiss your little life goodbye, come to that.'

Murdoch wanted to kick the car again. Wanted to pull the door off it, wrench Hussein out and kick him to death on the street.

'A hundred and fifty,' he said.

Hussein laughed, not scared now. 'Two hundred.' He leant forward to turn the ignition key and on the third attempt the car coughed into life. 'By the end of January, or you're a dead man.'

Watching him drive away, Murdoch found he was covered in sweat and trembling. He needed to shower, needed to eat and sleep and think what the hell he was going to do. Instead, he stared after the Suzuki. Then, as soon as it had rounded the first bend, he sprinted after it.

### 31.

That afternoon, Davie caught himself staring out of his bedroom window for the third time in as many minutes. The sun was nudging into the hills across the lagoon, the sky above them beginning to bruise. Just as in Bill's house, although less dramatically, at this time of year the ripples on the water reflected right into his room, silhouetting everything in there – him, his computer, his lamp and books – into shimmering shadows on the wall. Davie blinked and looked away, picked up a sheaf of Hoxton Harte accounts and carried them into the lounge room. It didn't help. The comforting smell of the sofa, the stories of the lamps he clicked on one by one, the four surfboards lined up against the wall: everything was more interesting than the document in his hand.

'Earnings before income tax, depreciation and amortisation,' he read aloud. He could take all his stuff with him. Wherever he ended up, he could take his boards and his lamps and his crappy sofa. 'Changes in holdings of company directors.'

An hour and a half later, the lamps now providing the only light, Davie looked up from his reading. The stilt house was old enough and unrepaired enough to change its creaks and sighs to match the weather, but Davie knew them well. What he'd just heard was not a noise made by the house alone. He frowned, restarted the paragraph he was annotating and, a minute later, heard the noise again; or a similar but different noise, it was hard to tell. This time he put down his pen. Maybe it was the house giving up; maybe the whole place was about to collapse around him – that would solve everything. He heard it again, louder and slower this time, stood quickly, crossed the room in two strides and yanked open the front door. Natalie was six steps below him, a brown paper bag in her hand.

'One day,' she said, 'I'm going to make it up to your front door without you hearing me and when I do that, Davie Simms, you're screwed. You still don't lock it, do you?'

'I don't need to. I've got those stairs.'

Natalie came up the rest of the way, each step complaining beneath her, and pushed past him into the lounge room.

'Jesus, Davie, do you ever tidy up? Look at this place!'

'Come in, why don't you? It's so lovely to see you too. Oh, I mean, actually it *is* good to see you, Nat.'

'Don't get your hopes up, Sherlock.' She collapsed into the sofa he'd just vacated. 'I'm still furious with you. Just thought you might fancy a beer. You busy?'

She produced a six pack of Coopers from the brown paper bag and dumped it on the document-strewn coffee table.

'I'm guessing you've had a drink already?' Davie closed the door and gave it the well-aimed kick it needed to stay shut.

'It's not a crime. Friday night, after all. Thought I might find you down at the surf club. Or in your office, now that you've become such a hard worker.'

Davie walked over, tore two of the bottles from the cardboard, handed her one and opened the other for himself. 'Yeah, well, like you said, it's Friday.'

'And yet here you are, working away at home. Find anything useful?'

'I wouldn't know.' He sat down beside her. 'I don't really understand it all. Listen, what you doing for Chrissy?'

'Oh no, Davie, I told you, never again.'

'Mum and Dad would love to see you.'

'Yeah, well, give them my best and tell them I'd rather stick pins in my eyes. I don't know why you go yourself; it's not like you enjoy it.'

Davie shrugged his shoulders and started gathering the papers into improvised piles.

'You should ask Bill,' she said. 'Or is he too busy with his fancy new friends?'

'Bill doesn't do Christmas. I think it reminds him of, you know, being in prison and stuff.'

'Oh yeah, that figures.' Natalie deepened her voice. 'The hard man runs alone. He's probably at some fancy-pants party with Melissa Munday.'

Davie smirked until Natalie couldn't pretend not to notice.

'What?'

'You jealous, Nat?'

'Of what?'

'Of what! Of Melissa Munday. Getting to hang out with Bill Murdoch when it didn't work out with you and him and – ow!'

The pain in his arm from her sudden punch surprised him. It was Natalie's turn to smirk.

'Don't pretend,' he said, pulling back to a safe distance. 'I know you better than you know yourself. You still like him. You're never that snappy with anyone unless you fancy them. And you never hit me unless I'm telling the truth. You're jealous.'

191

'Me, jealous? What's to be jealous of? The best house in Montauban, a fancy car, swans around all day while the rest of us are slogging our guts out. And don't start me on where all his money came from. Doesn't it piss you off, Davie? The man's got it all, not a care in the world, and now he's hobnobbing with all those big shots and their—'

'Big shots? Do me a favour, Nat. Those people aren't big shots, they're just self-promoting morons. You couldn't stand being near them for more than five minutes.'

Natalie took swig of beer as she thought about it.

'Maybe you're right,' she said. 'It's like the job. You don't get promoted because you're good at something, you get promoted because you … self-promote.'

'Oh. No news then?'

She found a space on the table for her bottle and ripped a new one from the carton. 'No news would be good news. More experience required, apparently. More cases under my belt. Which, of course, I could only get if I had a Sergeant who doesn't think I should still be in uniform.'

Davie pulled his sympathetic face and counted to ten. 'I'm really sorry about the picture in the magazine, Nat. I'm sure Bill didn't know about it either.'

'Yeah, well, don't worry about it. I might have exaggerated a bit, I was so pissed off. Tell the truth, my Inspector's not the kind of guy who generally reads *Starstrike!* Not to say he won't see it in a dentist's waiting room at some point in the next five years. And my sarge wouldn't know Bill Murdoch from Adam. What's the latest with buggerlugs anyway?'

'Dunno. He's been acting weird the last few days. I think he's got a new lead on the case, except, of course, I'd be the last one to hear about it. He rang me at work on Wednesday in some kind of panic to tell me he'd had to borrow my car. He was in a mad rush, didn't have time to come and get the keys from the office, so he'd hot-wired it.'

'He stole your car?'

'No, he borrowed it. Not that I've heard from him much since. I'm sure it's fine.'

Natalie raised her hands in a strangle of frustration. Davie wasn't sure if it was meant for him or Murdoch.

'Listen,' he said. 'If it helps us solve the case, I really don't mind.'

'No. You wouldn't.'

'Hey, if it means I get to keep this place.'

Natalie looked around as if she was only now remembering where she was. She sighed and slid further down into the sofa.

'Tell me what our expert witness said.'

Davie forced himself not to smile. He gave her gist of the conversation between Bill and Professor Barker, how Charlie Holland's injuries could have been caused by being hit by a car. Once finished, he shrugged his shoulders – oh well, none of it mattered now – stood with a sigh and picked up the empties to carry them across to the kitchen. *Come on, come on, come on.* Natalie said nothing. But, when he got back to the sofa, she was staring at the ceiling, holding out a piece of paper.

'What's that?'

'You know what it is,' she said. 'Hurry up and read it before I change my mind.'

He snatched it, all pretence at despondency gone, and had read the information on it three times before Natalie stood and snatched it back.

'Now listen, Davie—'

'I know, I know. I didn't hear it from you. Oh Nat, thanks so much.'

'I wasn't going to say that. I was going to say don't get your hopes up. He's a drunk, Davie, and, trust me, there's no evidence Charlie Holland ever made it back to Rose Bay that night. Every time there's a murder, some troppo turns up saying they saw the whole thing. And, believe me, this guy's more nuts than most of them – it doesn't mean a thing. Get off me!'

He'd leaned in to hug her, but she twisted quickly out of the way, punching him viciously on the other arm before lifting her forefinger. 'And, so help me Davie, if you ever, ever mention this to anyone ...'

## 32.

Murdoch was parked in a bad part of Canterbury, a suburb that had once been in the west of Sydney until the west of Sydney carried on sprawling so far. Nowadays, Canterbury was almost inner west. One day it would be inner city. The street he was on was quiet, as many gaps as cars in front of its broken gates and garden walls. But twenty metres ahead of where Murdoch sat, the street crossed a main road and, there, traffic rumbled unevenly in both directions. On the opposite corner, sat a squalid pub.

This, Murdoch knew, was what he deserved. Sitting in Davie's poxy car, staring through traffic at a horrible pub. It wasn't like the bastard gods hadn't warned him. First a woman was looking for him, then some bloke in a white Corolla was following him. But had that been enough to remind him he belonged in a cave, back against the wall with a club in one hand? Like fuck it had. He'd carried on swanning around, living the life of Riley and letting it dull his senses. He'd thought he'd got a bit stupid, had thought about it long and hard while he was waiting for Davie at the university. But he hadn't understood the half of it. Jesus, what had he been on? Thinking the fancy life could be for him; thinking he could escape his fate when this was where he belonged. In some shitty part of town, stinking of fear and working out how to save his skin.

And yet. Even now, there was something in him that refused to let that other life go. To believe he didn't deserve a little part of it. Friday afternoon, he was away from Davie's Hyundai Excel for three minutes longer than he had needed to be. At the café two streets back, where they let him use the toilet, he'd used the time to buy a cup of tea and an oversized biscuit. Now, back in the car, he struggled the lid off the tea, balanced the cup on the passenger seat, ripped open the paper bag holding the biscuit and wedged his phone into the dashboard. He hit speed dial and hands free and listened to ringtones fill the Excel like signals from a distant planet. He was staring at the pub, the biscuit halfway to his mouth, when Suzie Bourne answered at last.

'Suzie, it's Bill. Murdoch. I'm really sorry but I'm not going to make it round today.'

'Oh.'

Seventy plus years of training in that 'Oh'. Nothing he could accuse it of, while it was accusing him of everything.

'Yeah, but it's not all bad news. We can do it over the phone, like. I can't get away but I can talk.'

'Well, it's not ideal.'

Murdoch wondered if he'd ever learn to talk like that. Disagreeing without sounding like it.

194

'Here, go on,' he said. 'We'll be talking just like normal. I've got a cuppa and everything.'

'I'm not very fond of the phone. I can hardly hear you as it is. It sounds like you're at the bottom of a well. It would be better if you could come here like you normally do.'

He put the biscuit back in the packet, switched his tea to the other hand, wrenched the phone through the steering wheel and took it off loudspeaker.

'Is that any better?'

'Oh goodness, that was loud. Where on earth are you?'

'I'm on a case. Tell the truth, I'm watching someone. That's why I can't leave, see. Can't let them out of my sight.'

'Oh.' A friendlier 'Oh' this: somewhere on the way to friendly at least. 'How exciting. I'm not surprised you don't want to come and sit with silly old me.'

'I didn't say that, did I? I said I couldn't come. Trust me, Suzie, I'd be much happier sitting in your lovely flat having a cuppa rather than in this horrible little car.'

Horrible because he'd been in it for five days straight, little for the same reason. The Excel had shrunk around him, the steering wheel banging his knees whenever he moved, the door and the gearstick crowding his forearms. He kept telling himself it had been a good idea not to take the Merc and, at first, it had been easy to believe. But, after five days of watching the pub, his arse stung, his back ached and he could smell every piece of litter on the floor. Worse than any of that was the boredom. He could only make Davie's radio speak crackly Arabic, surprisingly loud Chinese or, worst of all: cricket. And, of course, there was nothing to read amongst the rubbish on the floor.

'Well,' said Suzie slowly, 'I'm not sure.'

'Why not?'

There was a pause, like she'd been lying and now she had to make up an excuse. 'It's just that if we start going from meetings to phone calls, the next thing will be emails and then nothing at all. I'm enjoying writing this book – you know I am – but only if you're committed to seeing it through to the end. Otherwise, it's just a lot of hard work for nothing.'

'I am committed.' Murdoch struggled to find the strength to make his words sound honest. He shouldn't have called. He didn't want to talk about his old life any more, not when he was here in the middle of it. He had worked hard for years to get away from where he was sitting right now and talking to Suzie about his past life suddenly felt like another backward step. 'Honestly, I've just got to watch someone, that's gospel that is. If I wasn't committed, I wouldn't be … phoning … you, would I?'

Hussein had appeared in the door of the pub. He stood there for a second, a gap in the traffic revealing him clearly, and seemed to look towards the car. But, no, he was just steadying himself before manoeuvring his huge body down the step to the pavement.

'What about tomorrow?' Suzie's voice was firm – stubbornness, that's another thing they had in common – and Murdoch wanted to say fine, he'd be around in the morning. It was weird to be listening to her and looking at Hussein: weird they existed on the same planet. Hussein turned, as Murdoch knew he would, and waddled ten metres to a terraced house with filthy net curtains. The traffic had started up again, Hussein lost to view as a bus stopped, but when the bus moved on, he was still at his front door, struggling with the key.

'Here,' said Murdoch. 'Please, Suzie, I really want to do this. It's just I can't leave here. What d'you reckon?'

'Hang on.'

He heard her footsteps echo as she carried the phone along her hallway, then silence as she reached the carpeted living room. Then, as she clicked him onto loudspeaker, he heard her searching amongst papers. He took a sip of tea, too hot, and looked sadly at the biscuit.

'I need The Impossible Choice,' she said. 'You want to do two things that are mutually exclusive. If you do one, it makes the other impossible, but both are equally important. Vital, in fact.'

Murdoch wanted to laugh with relief. She was going to let him talk to her rather than sit in silence for another few hours. Still, he couldn't pretend to understand.

'I thought I was supposed to want one thing all the way through?' he said. 'The "desire line" and all that. Something I'd always wanted and the whole book was about getting it?'

196

'Ah, yes. That's at the beginning of a story, but that's too easy. To keep the reader interested, you need to start wanting something else too. Something that conflicts with the original desire. That way, somewhere in the middle of a story you have to make The Impossible Choice. Now, you told me you wanted to find that missing girl.'

'Yeah, well, I did.'

'And that's all you wanted all the time you were looking for her?'

She had him there. It was like Hussein had brought the Club's shipment back to life just by mentioning it. Murdoch closed his eyes and sighed. He wanted to tell Suzie he'd call her back after all, but then he thought of the empty evening ahead, of watching the street grow dark, the main road quieter and quieter until there was nothing to look at for hours. He told Suzie what had happened as quickly and as vaguely as he could.

'Still don't know why I came back after I'd done it,' he said. 'All the bleeding trouble it caused me. I could of walked off into the sunset at that point.'

He thought he could hear her pencil drawing its strange lines on her pad.

'Mmm,' she said after a while. 'Well, that's the thing with The Impossible Choice. Whatever the character chooses to do, it will land him in The Worst Possible Scenario.'

'Sounds about right.'

Across the busy junction, other regulars stumbled out of the pub. Empty men, meaningless outside its walls, half of them still with the look of prison. This is what the system had prepared them for: stumbling home pissed through a world that didn't care. Maybe Hussein was right: maybe Murdoch didn't deserve anything more than them. He listened to Suzie asking about the night of the shipment, the weather and the moonlight, and made up answers to keep her happy. After they'd said goodbye, he stared through the thinning traffic at Hussein's squalid house, at the dirty net curtain flickering grey and blue. It would flicker all night. Murdoch could walk in there now and stab the fat man while he slept in front of the telly. No one else had entered or left the place in four days. He was thinking about it, then dreaming about it – the knife too heavy and huge in his hands – when his phone burst into life.

# The Impossible Choice

## 33

The Eastern Suburbs ferry pushed itself noisily away, churning the water around it violently and then, as its wake spread out, setting all the boats in Rose Bay tilting their masts like metronomes. The ferry's churn disturbed the floating Rose Bay Wharf too – the rest of the harbour too big to care – unsteadying three passengers who had climbed out onto it. Two of them – father and daughter Murdoch thought at first, then maybe a couple in love – held each other tight and laughed at themselves. Laughed too much: the wharf was heavy with steel and safety glass, it hadn't wobbled that much. All the same, Murdoch smiled at them briefly as they walked up the ramp to the safety of land. They looked quickly away, neither smiling in return.

'Crikey, Bill, look at the state of you.'

Davie had followed the couple and now stood brushing harbour spray off his trouser legs. Murdoch scratched himself.

'Yeah, I smell too.'

'Nice. Does my car still exist?'

'Unfortunately, it does, mate. And I'll be happy if I never see the little shit heap again in my life.'

'Oh, don't mention it, you're welcome. Anytime. You going to tell me why you needed it?'

'No.'

'Bloody hell, Bill. You know how much this case means to me. You know—'

Davie stopped and looked at the sky.

'You all right, Davie?'

'I'm good.'

'You don't look good.'

'I'm good, I really am. It's just I'm running out of time. If we don't get this thing sorted in four or five weeks, Bill, I'm homeless. And then you just disappear on me and don't tell me if it's good or bad news. I'm going to lose my home. Can you imagine what that's like?'

Murdoch nodded, getting it for the first time, if he was honest. He walked up close to Davie and looked past him at all the little boats in the bay, the wake from the ferry still bouncing them.

'Listen,' he said quietly. 'I promise you, whatever it takes to get that bloke out of prison, I'll do it. If that's what's gonna get you to keep your place, I'll do anything. You got that? But taking your shit heap of a motor had nothing to do with it. I just had to see a man about a dog and I didn't want to do it in my car.'

Davie said, 'OK, sorry, thanks,' and Murdoch gave him a few seconds, outstaring a curious jogger until he'd passed.

'Right then,' he said. 'So, how'd you find this bloke anyway?'

Davie ran his hands over his face and through his hair. He turned and blinked at the million masts bobbing in the bay, then at the little car park beside them, then across the bare field that ran between the car park and the traffic of New South Head Road. Murdoch could see him remembering where they were and why.

'I came down yesterday,' he said. 'Gave out my number to a few people; offered a hundred-dollar reward.'

'Oh Jesus. And let me guess, you got lots of calls?'

'Just one. I reckon this is her.'

Murdoch followed Davie's nod to an old green hut opposite the wharf, open front and back, and reckoned so too. She was too sad and thin in her tatty yellow cardigan to be a Rose Bay commuter. Leaning in the waterside doorway of the hut, under an ancient *'Ferry Shelter'* sign, she was sucking on a rollie like her life depended on it, the breeze off the water stealing the smoke and messing with her hair. She scowled as they approached.

'Emily?'

'You Davie?'

She had a smaccent: a nasal drawl furious with the world and what it was going to do to her next. Davie stopped and nodded, then turned to Murdoch like he was in charge.

'Who's this?' said the girl. 'You said no police.'

'Do I look like a bleeding copper?' Murdoch said. 'Where's Flash Harry then?'

'Where's my money?'

'Show her the money, Davie.'

Davie pulled out his wallet, searched through it and then his pockets and came up with thirty-three dollars and fifty cents. Murdoch swore, pulled out his own wallet and found two fiddies. He stepped forward with them, then pulled back again as the girl reached up.

'Where is he?'

She pointed away from the water towards New South Head Road. The traffic there was as thick as ever, banking up and stretching as the lights changed. Murdoch couldn't see what she meant but Davie said, 'Oh yeah, gotcha,' took the money from Murdoch's hand and handed it over.

'Davie, you muppet!'

But it was too late: the girl was gone. Not running, just walking fast with a determined back, off to inject some capital into the black economy. There was no point in Murdoch going after her, he'd have to wrestle her to the ground and squeeze the life from her before she let go of those yellow notes. He turned back to find Davie had walked into the old ferry shelter and out the other side. Now he was striding across the bare field beyond, hands in his pockets and the wind in his stupid hair, like he was off to play cricket or inspect a farm. Murdoch swore again and ran to catch him up.

'Mind telling me what the fuck I'm missing?'

But then he saw it too. It was a bundle of brown rags lumped along a bench facing the water behind them. Nothing obviously human about it, apart from two feet sticking out one end. Another five metres and they both could smell him. That took the wind out of Davie's sails. He stopped like he'd come up against one of Professor Barker's photographs and turned to Murdoch with a nervous smile.

'Right. What's the plan?'

Murdoch rolled his eyes, pushed Davie out the way and yelled at the lump of rags on the bench. Nothing. Just the braking and rumbling of the traffic. Davie said something about waiting, but Murdoch ignored him, turned to the water, took a deep breath, turned back and walked up to the bench. He kicked the form lying there hard on the shins until it jerked to life and became a man pushing himself upright, bellowing obscenities with his eyes closed. He was older than Murdoch had expected. You didn't think someone could survive that long when they were out in all weathers. The man's face was swollen, like someone had filled it with something toxic and left it in the sun to see what would happen. His skin was stretched taut and shiny in places, broken in others, cheeks covered in webs of veins that reminded Murdoch of Professor Barker. The feet were difficult to look at: purple from the heels to the toes, yellow toenails beyond description.

'You Flash Harry?' said Murdoch.

'And who are you?'

The old man sat wobbling with his eyes still closed, the weight of his coat wanting him to lie down again. He lifted a leg to rub his shin and revealed dried vomit on his trousers. Murdoch reached into his jacket pocket and pulled out something he'd picked up on the way over.

'Know what this is, Harry?'

'Bill,' said Davie, 'I'm not sure that's appropriate.'

'Shut it. Here, Harry, know what this is?'

Murdoch unscrewed the lid, stepped forward into the stench and held the bottle under the old man's nose. Flash Harry's eyes opened, the whites rusty and flecked, and he reached out his hand in a surprisingly fluid movement. Murdoch pulled back fast, careful this time to keep out of Davie's reach too, spilling some of the whisky on the concrete beneath the bench. Flash Harry stared at the tiny drops.

'You can have all of this,' said Murdoch. 'The whole bottle, just for you.'

'Er, Bill ...'

'Or, Harry ... or it could all be for the grass.'

He tilted the bottle, the gold liquid catching the evening light as it fell to the ground. The old man roared and, after two attempts, managed to stand. He swayed from side to side, jaundiced eyes wide like he'd forgotten why he was on his feet. Behind him, a huge semi-trailer accelerated to beat the lights and, for a while, the three men stood there, two of them waiting for the noise to pass.

'... want exactly?' said the old man.

'What's your name?' said Murdoch, stepping back slowly out of the stench.

The man in front of him snapped to attention.

'Henry Arnold James Umpton, sir! "Flash" to my friends. Too flash for my enemies, aha.'

'OK, Flash, we just got a few questions for you. You give us a few answers and you can have this. No fucking about; it's all yours.'

'I will not tolerate foul language,' said the old man, sitting again with a bump that threatened to unbolt the bench from the concrete. The wind changed, or maybe Harry belched, and Murdoch and Davie each took a step backwards.

'About a year back, you saw a girl get run down over there near the wharf,' said Murdoch, pointing towards the water with the bottle. 'You told the police about it.'

'Don't worry,' said Davie. 'We're glad you did. We want to know about the car.'

Flash Harry looked at Davie, looked back at Murdoch, looked at Johnny Walker.

'*Nemo saltat sobrius*,' he said.

'You what?'

'A little drink might help refresh my memory.'

Murdoch shook his head and poured a little more whisky into the grass until the old man started talking.

'The authorities didn't believe me! I told them what I saw and they said, "Yes mate, no mate," and sent me away. "Mate" indeed! I was sober and they didn't believe me. *Salva veritate.*'

'Come again?'

'You'll give me the whisky?'

'Where was you sitting when it happened?'

'*In medio tutissimus ibis. Domus.*'

Murdoch was about to pour more liquid away, but Davie stopped him. 'It means something about his home. Something about ... being in the middle?'

Harry pulled himself upright, a swollen hand in his foul hair. 'I always talk more easily with an educated man.'

'Did you see the girl from here?' said Davie. 'Is this your home? Did you see her get run over from here? Over there?'

Davie turned and squinted across the field towards the harbour. Murdoch knew what he was thinking.

'Street lights,' he said. 'The field would of been dark, but look at them street lights around the car park and on the road near the water. It'd of been lit up like a stage, even through the rain.'

'But then anyone on New South Head Road would have seen it too.'

'Lovely blonde girl, she was,' said Harry. 'Blonde hair lifted in the wind. *Boni pastoris est tondere pecus non deglubere*, but he knocked her down, didn't he? Knocked her, pulled her, christened her in the briny deep.'

'Who?' said Davie. 'The man from the boat?'

Harry frowned and struggled to his feet again. He staggered towards Davie and grabbed him by the forearm. 'Boat?' he said. 'They're all boats!'

Murdoch waved the whisky until Davie could pull himself free.

'Who knocked her down, Harry?'

'The car!' The old man's nostrils flared towards the bottle. 'The Olympic car!'

'How could you see from here?'

'Not here. It was the beginning of the great flood, the return of Noah, the cleansing of the city of all it sins. *Horas non numero nisi serenas*. I was in there, home, wrapped up warm and lovely.'

He pointed towards the green hut where they'd met Emily, and which they'd walked through to get to the field.

*This is bullshit,* thought Murdoch. He and Davie were cajoling Flash Harry slowly across the grass, waving the whisky whenever he forgot where they were going. As they got closer to the old ferry shelter, he could see there was a makeshift bed inside, plastic bread trays and a pile of ancient blankets. He imagined being in the hut on a rainy night, hidden under blankets: the perfect spot for observing the patch of wharf the hut hid from the road.

'I was in there,' said Flash Harry proudly. 'In my own bed, watching a murder.'

'What happened? Tell us what happened, Harry, and you can have all the whisky.' Davie was doing a bad job of keeping the excitement from his voice.

'It was raining. Hard rain! Her big umbrella was like a rainbow without any sun to light it. He hit her with an Olympic car and then he pulled her in the water. She must have been heavier than she looked because he struggled.'

'Olympic?'

Harry scowled, started something in Latin and then let it go. Turning away from the hut, he stared back across the field at the traffic. Davie looked at Murdoch, who shrugged his shoulders.

'There,' said Harry, his body turning like a scarecrow in the wind as his hand followed an SUV through the lights.

'The Audi?' said Davie. 'Why's that— Oh, I get it. The rings, like the Olympics.'

He waited until another one passed.

'Like that one, Harry?'

'Olympics, but not that one. It had curves. Like the blonde. Like a black insect. Like a cockroach crawling through the night to spread death and betrayal. *Mors certa, hora incerta.*'

'You see the driver?' said Murdoch.

Harry turned with a hateful look and spat on the ground between them.

'Small, weak,' he said. 'Leant over the girl, pulled at her. Had to pull hard and hard and hard before he could get her in the water. And so, death returns into life. We christen the dead, we mourn the newborn child.'

'Look, Harry, there. Is that what you mean by a "cockroach" car?'

Davie had been staring into the traffic. Now it was his turn to point, and keep pointing until Harry, then Murdoch, turned and followed his gaze. The whisky slipped from Murdoch's grasp and thudded onto the grass beside him.

'That,' said Harry, 'is a silver car.'

'But the type, yeah? The same shape as the car that knocked down the blonde girl?'

'In black,' said Harry.

'Did you see the number plate?'

Harry shook his head angrily, filling the air around him.

'Shame,' said Davie. 'Still. A black Audi TT. All we need to do is find someone close to Harte who drives one of those. That's progress, isn't it?'

Murdoch shrugged his shoulders, leant down and picked up the whisky. He grabbed Flash Harry by a torn shoulder and shoved the bottle hard into his hands.

'Drink it,' he said. 'Drink the whole bleeding thing.'

## 34.

This time Murdoch was better prepared. He packed a bag of clothes, a sleeping bag and a dozen bottles of water. Took a long book he'd been meaning to read and, more realistically, magazines Anne Lincoln had kept back for him. But, as he parked and sat for hours on the Canterbury street, he found this time he was able stare into space and do nothing at all. Like he was fascinated by the drizzle settling on the littered asphalt; like he wanted to concentrate on that rather than on what he'd learned about Amanda and her fancy car. He'd thought when Hussein had turned up that he'd realised at last how swanning about with the Hoxton Harte crowd had blunted his intelligence. Jesus, the bastard gods must have laughed at that one. He hadn't realised a thing.

The street was even quieter than on his previous visit. The world was away for Christmas, up or down the coast, and Murdoch's Merc was one of only a dozen cars leaning in the gutters. He knew he was conspicuous. Not that it was the kind of neighbourhood where anyone would call the police about a man in a car, nor the kind where the police would respond. Still, he moved the Merc every so often out of self-discipline. Like that wasn't weeks too late.

From certain angles, as close to the junction as he dared to park, Murdoch could look through the holiday traffic straight into the pub's VIP room. Once or twice, he even saw Hussein's ankle as the fat man fed the poker machines, but mostly there was nothing new. Nothing to see but the dreary red-brick façade, the bar room doors that hardly ever opened and never to a face he hadn't seen before. The only change since his previous visit was that someone had graffitied 'shitcunts' across the wired windows. Which, thought Murdoch, just about summed things up.

On day three he turned his phone back on. Davie had been calling four times a day, the buzzing of the handset driving Murdoch mental until at last it clicked through to voicemail. Then Amanda had tried to call and he'd switched the thing off. But now he was bored enough to find out what was going on in the world.

'If you don't call me to let me know you're OK, I'll call the police to come and look for you and your car' read the most recent of Davie's twelve texts. Murdoch swore, buzzed down the window and dialled Davie's number.

'Bill? Are you OK? Oh my God, I thought something had happened. I imagined you'd been run down by a black Audi TT or something. Don't laugh, I'm not joking.'

'I'm fine,' said Murdoch. 'Did you call the police?'

'No, why? What's happened?'

'About me, you muppet. Listen, I'm fine, don't worry about it. I'm still seeing that man about that dog.'

'Oh. So not on the case, then?'

'Jesus Christ, Davie, it's Christmas. Give me a break.'

'No, no, it's fine. It's just, well … you know … like I said the other day, time's running out and Hannah's getting iffy.'

'She phoned again, did she?'

'No. But you know her, she'll be getting iffy. Every time the phone rings I'm terrified.'

Murdoch smiled. It was good to be talking again, even if it was only to Davie. He found a cigarette and pushed in the button for the lighter.

'So, Happy Christmas,' said Davie.

Murdoch coughed a small laugh. 'Happy Christmas, mate. Not today, is it?'

'Wow, you really do manage to avoid it. No, it's tomorrow. Hey, are you going to ask about my news or what?'

'What news?'

'Didn't you read my texts? I've found something out. Well, two things, really. I knew if I read enough of those stupid documents I'd find something. Imagine doing that for a job though. I mean, imagine you were a forensic accountant or—'

'What did you find out, Davie?'

The button popped out of the dashboard and Murdoch lit his cigarette. His ear was hurting from where he was pushing the phone hard against it. He took a deep breath and told himself to relax. Even if Davie did find anything, there were thousands of black Audi TT's in the world: it didn't mean a thing.

'Well, nine months ago when James Harte was arrested, Angus Hoxton owned twenty-four per cent of the company, right? Same as he had done since it was set up. But since then his ownership has been going steadily down, about three per cent a month. So now he's only got three per cent left.'

'So?'

'So why would he do that? For ten years he's had a quarter share in a company that was struggling to get by, hardly making any money at all. Did you know, in the early days after they floated, Hoxton Harte nearly went bankrupt? I reckon, for a while, that money Oscar Druitt's dad leant them was the only thing keeping them going. The agency was taking on new people while they could hardly pay the people they already had. Bills coming

206

out of their ears and still they took on these big jobs that made them next to nothing. So there they are, ten years struggling, and now Angus is selling out, just when they're chalking up serious profits for the first time? It doesn't make sense.'

'Makes sense to me. Didn't you tell me ages ago you were surprised by how low his salary was? Sounds like this explains how he affords to live the way he does. So he's not sensible about it; that's hardly news.'

'But why now? When never before? Anyway, listen to this. Guess who's been sending invoices to Hoxton Harte two or three times a year for the last two years?'

'Hookers R Us?

'Ha! No. Parramatta Road German. It's a mechanics, specialising in German cars. So I pulled up the invoices and guess what they're for? Bill? You still there?'

'I'm here.'

'They're for "Audi TT Repair and Maintenance" or "Audi Parts Replacement" or "TT Bodywork". They're on the Parramatta Road – go figure. I've phoned and checked out their website but they're closed until the new year. I'm heading down there as soon as.'

'No, don't do that.'

'Sorry?'

'I mean, don't rush into it, Davie. They might be involved, you know. In a position to destroy evidence or something. I should go.'

'Aw, thanks, mate. Yeah, let's both go. They don't open until the twelfth, so, hopefully, your man–dog situation will have freed you up by then. Here, you sure you don't want to come with me to my parents tomorrow? Or even just for dinner tonight?'

'Mate, I can't leave here, seriously.'

Davie made more Christmas noises, Murdoch's mind on the black Audi, and how quickly Davie might find out who owned it. He said he should go again, said 'Happy Christmas' again, and hung up. His phone was still in his hand when it started ringing again.

'Yes, Davie?'

'Oh, you are alive, then?'

It was like falling into a comfortable bed when you were determined not to sleep.

'Hello, Amanda.'

'Lord, don't sound so pleased to hear me. Where the hell have you been? Are you still working on this case or what?'

Murdoch knew he should hang up. Should claim bad reception or pretend he couldn't hear. But five days in Canterbury in a car by himself and then the opportunity to share space with her? He didn't care what she'd done, he was allowed to listen to her beautiful voice.

'I am,' he said. 'I'm on it now, in fact. There's been significant progress, but I can't tell you about it over the phone.'

'Really?' She didn't sound convinced. 'I wonder if you only answered because you thought it was your partner in crime. Or partner in law, I should say, although that makes it sound like one of you married the other one's sister. Go on, Bill, tell me what the progress is.'

'Really, I can't. Not now. Trust me.'

His voice creaked around the words with the effort of hiding his … what? Not anger, not disbelief. Just sadness at the whole situation. Maybe Amanda heard it. When she spoke again, her voice was softer, like she was trying to get them back on track.

'Well, could you at least pretend you're not unhappy it's me on the phone?'

'I am. I mean, I'm not … you know, unhappy.'

'Oh. Are you actually happy about it?'

He laughed despite himself. Answered in a voice that wasn't his own: the voice of a man who didn't know what she'd done. 'I am happy, Amanda. It's nice to hear your voice, love, really it is. I just didn't check the number and I was surprised. I was in the middle of something.'

'With a woman?'

'With my mate, Davie, what's halfway to the same thing. But not like you mean, no. Like I told you, I'm working. How are you?'

She told him how she was. Hating Christmas, dreading New Year, exhausted by the year she'd had and a potentially worse one to come. As he listened, Murdoch stared at the traffic on the main road – buses, cars, bicycles, taxis – trying to focus on it rather than picturing her. Where she was right now; what she might be wearing. He waited for her to nag him about his progress again and why he hadn't been in touch but, even that, when it came, was gentle.

'Could you really not have returned my calls? Did you lose your phone or something?'

'It broke,' he said, wishing it was true, wishing he hadn't answered Davie's call earlier in the week. 'Just got it back this morning, didn't I? I was going to call you.'

'Well, I beat you to it. Listen, did you get my messages about tonight? Everyone's going to be there; it'll be completely hideous. I think it would be good if you came. You'll meet a few of James's business contacts you've not met before and, almost as importantly, I'll have an escort. Please? I've got a new dress and I want to try and enjoy myself for once.'

He put up a good fight, but his mistake was thinking he could ever win: not against her arguments but against his own. He should confront her and see if she could explain her way out of things. Didn't he owe it to Davie to get to the truth? Did he seriously think Hussein was going anywhere?

It was one in the afternoon by the time she'd made him promise to be there. It took him three hours to get home in the holiday traffic, one hour to shower and change, then another three hours to get back to the city again. Seven hours to change his mind and he didn't consider it once, not even when the grey bled from the sky and tail lights and headlights began to blur. Instead, he made a call: no idea if the hotel would laugh at him or if his request was normal. The receptionist said she'd be surprised and put him on hold. But then, yes, sir, the Hilton had had a cancellation and, yes, sir, they would happily sell him the room. And, yes, sir, for an additional fee there was parking available. And he was supposed to change his mind?

Amanda, he had decided by then, would have an explanation. All he had to do was ask her and she'd give him the name of someone who could have taken her car. Or proof she herself couldn't have run down Charlie Holland, proof she hadn't used her second passport to get back into the country. The trouble was, Murdoch realised, deep down he knew he'd discovered the truth. Then, as he arrived in Sydney and the traffic got even worse, he realised that wasn't the trouble at all. The trouble was he didn't care.

George Street was mayhem. The few workers who'd stayed in their offices all day were at war with the last-minute shoppers, both crowds dodging the early revellers. Murdoch sat and watched it all: life on a distant screen. He was in a queue of vehicles turning off Pitt Street into the Hilton's forecourt, looking past the cars in front of him to where the forecourt opened onto George Street: a square-framed view of the passing hordes. The air was still humid, but the heavy sky was dry for now and he'd dropped the roof of the Mercedes for a slow roll past the city shopfronts, hoping the view of himself in a tuxedo would make him feel better. It didn't.

The Hilton's forecourt was more plate glass, more reflections of himself in the life he'd always wanted – what a fucking joke – and it was only at the very last minute that Murdoch noticed the reflection of his own car rolling into the reflection of the car in front. The scream from his brakes turned heads out on George Street, a gaggle of half-drunk girls stopping to laugh and shout something he couldn't hear. They were gone again in a second, but the two dark-haired staff greeting each car continued to stare until one of them rolled his eyes and dropped a comment to his colleague. The colleague wandered over.

'We all right there, sir?'

Murdoch forced a smile. 'Sorry about that, mate. Too many pretty girls on George Street. I was watching them instead of paying attention.'

The young valet – from Greece or Italy or Spain, somewhere they handed out thick black curls – smiled and told him not to worry about it. Sir. He asked Murdoch for his name and went to check it against a little screen, bright in the lectern that was his office. He was writing something onto a ticket when a grey-haired man, also in hotel uniform, came out and, nodding at Murdoch or his car, whispered something to him. The valet nodded, approached Murdoch and gave him his ticket.

'Have a good evening, sir, and a pleasurable stay at the Hilton.'

Once out of his car and through the hotel's rotating door, Murdoch turned to look through the glass as the valet parked his car, not following the others underground but reversing and pulling in to one side, opposite the foyer.

'Here,' he said to Angus, the first familiar face he found in the half-empty ballroom. 'They left my car outside instead of down in the car park. What's that all about, then?'

He knew the answer but he wanted to hear it, wanted Angus to be impressed. But Angus, sleek in this season's black tie, couldn't have cared less. He was scanning the room in a way that reminded Murdoch of Oscar Druitt at the races.

'It doesn't mean a thing,' he said. 'It just means you have a nice car. Wait ten minutes and a nicer one will come along, then they'll park you out of sight with everyone else.' He turned and smiled. 'Wouldn't have thought you cared about that kind of thing. Jesus, what happened to your face?'

Murdoch ignored the question and commented on three girls who'd braved the wooden dance floor, the first people to leave the clusters of guests at the bars. Angus snickered and started telling a story but, after a few sentences, he saw what he'd been looking for earlier, excused himself hurriedly and walked away. Murdoch caught himself standing like an abandoned puppy, turned and wandered over to the tall windows to look down on George Street. If anything, the chaos outside had increased and he was happy to stand and watch, calmer than everyone in sight. He looked at his reflection and forced a smile, noticed a reflection approaching from behind him and knew before the girl arrived that she'd come to ask him what he wanted to drink.

Half an hour later, the wooden dance floor still had only three girls dancing, but the carpet around it was struggling. The crowd had arrived and was arriving still. Murdoch inspected the guests slowly: the men in tuxedos and the women in smart dresses, all of them showing their teeth and shouting 'Ya, ya, ya!' over the music. In all the events he'd been to recently, even when he'd seen anyone he'd dealt to in the old days, he'd noticed they hadn't recognised him. Or maybe they had, but they didn't care. Because he was one of them now: someone who belonged at their fancy events, with a thick cardboard invitation to prove it. That's all it took, after all.

He remembered what Amanda had said about these people. 'They're vipers.' But where did you meet people who weren't? Someone slapped him hard on the back and he turned to find Benny Robbins. The solid little man was standing too close, one of his pudgy hands around a glass of red wine. He smelled of cigars.

'Mr Murdoch, what a pleasure. What you doing here by yourself?'

Murdoch stuck out a hand. 'Benny.'

'Answer the question, mate. What you doing here by yourself?'

The music had suddenly stopped and Robbins' voice was loud in the chatter it left behind.

'I could ask you the same thing,' said Murdoch, equally loudly.

Benny gestured with his wine glass, the red liquid swishing dangerously, towards the back of a full-length dress at the nearest edge of the crowd. The dress was white silk or satin or something: smooth fabric that told the world the woman in it wasn't wearing any underwear. She turned like she could feel their attention and Murdoch saw it was Phoebe Robbins. She gave him an inviting smile before returning slowly to her conversation. Murdoch wondered where Amanda was.

'And you?' said Robbins.

'Waiting for friends. Angus was here a second ago.'

There was applause at the other side of the room and they saw the heads of a band: five people stepping onto a little stage. The crowd swelled, backs closing in towards Murdoch and Robbins, forcing them closer together as the music started up, blurred and imperfect compared to the recorded tunes played a minute before.

'Waiting for Amanda, you mean,' said Robbins, curling his lip. It wasn't a question.

'Whatever.'

Robbins took a jerky swig of wine and raised his voice above the noise from the band.

'I've seen the way you look at her. You must think we're all as thick as pig shit. A friend of James Harte? Oh yeah, what kind of friend is that? You can't wait to—'

Murdoch turned his face close to Robbins. 'Say it, you turd. Just say one word about her and see what happens.'

Robbins stepped closer still, one foot pinning one of Murdoch's own to the ground.

'Benny, darling!' Phoebe Robbins had floated at speed towards them. 'Do come and talk to the Hazias; you promised you would.'

She pulled Robbins away, his furious red stare the last part of him to leave. Murdoch stared back until the man was turned by his wife towards a couple in the crowd. Looking down, Murdoch saw he was holding his beer bottle by its neck. He snorted and shook his head, turned the bottle and emptied it down his throat. Oscar Druitt was standing beside him.

'Jesus, Bill, I saw that. Benny Robbins was threatening you.'

'Yeah, well, thanks for stepping in.'

'You don't have to take that nonsense from him, you know. He thinks he's a hard man just because he spent time in prison. Oh, nothing personal. I mean, are you all right?'

Murdoch smiled and said he reckoned he'd survive. He shook Oscar's hand, looked him in the eye and wished him 'Happy Christmas'. Asked why Robbins had been in prison.

'Trading while insolvent, the bastard. Then contempt of court. This was years ago.'

'Trading while what? What's that then?'

'Insolvent. Basically, it means doing business when you've got no money to pay your bills. Robbins left two dozen creditors struggling to survive and paid no redundancy to the staff who lost their jobs. Not to mention owing me a couple of thou'. And did he do right by me, I mean, them, when he made big money at last? Of course not. The man is shameless.'

Oscar's face changed and he said, 'Back in a sec,' as a single word. Then, like Angus before him, he rushed away, pushing into the crowd that now filled every part of the room. But unlike Angus, Oscar was taller than most people there and, by standing on tiptoes, Murdoch could follow his tan as it edged politely between dark suits and colourful dresses. Eventually, it reached an even taller, heavily-built man in thick-framed glasses. The man in the glasses gave a joke smile, an ironic roll of the eyes, a tiny nod of the head.

'Have you seen Oscar?'

It was a re-run of the day at the races, Emma Druitt beside him with her imperfect timing. She was tiny in grey, a sparkling brooch like a Christmas decoration lopsided on her dress. She looked helpless in the crowded room.

'He was here a second ago.'

'Yes, well, I know that. I saw him from over there, but by the time I got here—' She was like a barrister, every question an accusation, every answer he gave wrong before he'd said it.

'You never seem to know where he is,' Murdoch snapped back at her. He couldn't help being rude to the woman, couldn't help regretting it immediately afterwards. She blinked at him heavily, at a loss for what to say.

'Oscar and me was talking about trading when you're insolvent,' Murdoch said gently, trying to make amends. 'It's illegal, you can go to prison for it. I didn't know that. I guess you'd know all about that, though, being an accountant?'

213

She went pale, bit her lip and blinked at him again. 'I was looking for Oscar,' she said, stumbling over the words. Like it was his fault she was always two minutes behind her husband. Murdoch shrugged his shoulders and said he was probably off with Angus somewhere, in the bathroom, maybe. Emma clearly knew what he was implying.

'Bloody hell,' she said with a sigh. 'Life would be so much easier if everyone could just behave.'

She started to say something else, but seemed to catch sight of someone behind him and waved a little hand. Murdoch turned and there was Amanda, waving back with a smile he could tell was costing her effort. She was in a full-length red dress, cleavage and jewels. Hair floating, long legs flashing as she approached.

'You're staring,' she said, reaching in to kiss him on the cheek.

'Can you blame me?'

'Amanda, you look amazing,' said Emma Druitt. 'But why are you so dressed up?' This from a woman in a dress as flat as her shoes.

Amanda laughed and said it was Christmas, she deserved a change, a break from the worrying. To stop her from disappearing into the crowd, Murdoch asked her how she was, joked with her about her answers, ignored Emma Druitt at his elbow until she mumbled an excuse and left them alone.

'I don't think she likes you,' said Amanda.

'She bleeding well hates me, no idea why. But it's not just her, ever since I got here people keep running off to the bathroom and leaving me by myself.'

He put on his innocent face – like he'd never heard of cocaine – and Amanda smiled and promised not to do the same. Then she remembered too late to tell him he didn't look so bad himself. *Now*, he thought, *do it now. 'Amanda, there's something I need to talk to you about.'* What, and ruin this perfect moment? They had the whole evening ahead of them. When she asked him about the progress he'd mentioned on the phone, he deflected by saying he'd tell her when they were alone. Amanda rolled her eyes at that, but soon followed his new line of conversation. Who was who, who was new. She confessed, teeth on her bottom lip, to being a little nervous, dressed up like this in front of this crowd. Then Angus found them and, a while after that, Emma and Oscar returned to make a circle.

Drinks flowed, conversation relaxed, they broke into small groups and shouted at each other over the music.

'Look,' Amanda whispered in Murdoch's ear, that hand pressing all the right buttons on his forearm again. 'Oscar must have come down off his last line.'

She turned him slightly so he could see. Angus was telling one of his stories, Emma frowning to hear every word. Oscar was nodding too and making intermittent eye contact, smiling at the right times, but every other second standing straight to look around the room. Murdoch knew who he was looking for. He watched Oscar spot the tall man with the thick-framed glasses standing a few metres behind Angus. Amanda was nudging her arm against Murdoch's and he whispered, yes, he'd seen it too; he'd been watching it all bloody evening. Angus was reaching the punchline of his story, gesticulating mid-sentence, but Oscar couldn't wait.

'Haw, haw, haw,' he said. 'Sorry, mate, just need to pop to the loo.'

Angus's reaction was immediate. He spun around and spotted the man with the glasses. Turning back, he caught hold of Oscar's arm and said something sharp to him at which Oscar frowned and tried to shake himself free. Angus hissed more words Murdoch couldn't make out until Oscar said, loud enough for them all to hear, 'And, anyway, you still owe me for last time.' He pulled at his arm again until Angus let him go with a curse, then stepped away through the heaving crowd. When Angus turned back, Murdoch looked away, pretending he hadn't seen. But even if that had worked, Angus had Emma's and Amanda's faces to cope with. He repeated his curse at them, pushed between them and disappeared towards the bar.

'See what I mean?' said Emma. 'If only everyone could just behave.'

The crowd in the room moved as one: every movement at one end rippling across to the other, no distinction between dancers and onlookers, waiting staff and drinkers, those on the way somewhere and those trying to hold their ground. But no matter where Murdoch stood, no matter who he was talking to, every time he looked up he saw Amanda. No excuse not to approach her, to guide her to the side of the room and tell her what he knew. What his progress had been. More than once he found himself staring: at her skin, her legs, her breasts pressing against the red dress. He drank more than normal. Ate strange foods, spoke to strangers, went outside twenty times to smoke twenty cigarettes. But even there Amanda found him, taking drags like a naughty schoolgirl. *Now,* he thought again and again. *She wants to know about progress, so tell her now. Let her explain.* Later, at her insistence, he danced. Shuffling at first, then moving around as she took his hands and encouraged him, listening to the music like she said. The Druitts – together for once – then Angus and a brunette who promised to look after him said goodbye and drifted away. Midnight came and went in an explosion of corks and string, the crowd thinned, the band stopped, slower music came over the speakers and still Amanda was there. She asked for a proper dance then and showed him how to do that too, one hand in hers held high, the other around her waist. 'Now you can shuffle,' she said and they did that, shuffling around like an old couple on a cruise ship until the lights came up and too soon they were back on dry land. There was only a dozen or so people left in the huge littered room. They blinked disappointedly in the brightness, retrieved handbags and jackets from chair backs, patted themselves down for keys and wallets and whatever they'd brought to the party. Murdoch walked Amanda down the quiet stairs to the foyer – terrified she'd ask again what his progress on the case had been – and waited while her car was brought around. When the valet drove the black Audi TT onto the shiny forecourt, he found himself staring at it. The car stared back, shameless, winking reflections of the lights overhead.

'Bill, are you all right?'

He shook himself back to reality, or at least to the blurred and beery world around him. He heard himself asking Amanda to confirm she was OK to drive, that she'd really had nothing to drink. What happened next was never clear to him. Was she only reaching up to politely kiss him goodnight? He was pretty sure her mouth didn't resist when he first kissed her lips, one hand on each of her shoulders.

'Bill, please!'

She definitely said this: his memories were clear from that point on. He opened his eyes, let her go and stood back unsteadily.

'Oh shit, Amanda, I'm sorry. Really. I'm pissed. Here, let me—'

'No, Bill. Please. You should go. Now.'

The lift was empty and he swore at himself aloud for twenty-two storeys. It wasn't enough and, in the darkness of his room, he stood banging his head slowly against the window between him and the falsely-lit world until the pain in his forehead grew stronger than the alcohol in his blood. He crossed the room and started kicking the wall instead – no idea which of several things was worse – until, after ten minutes, there was a knock at the door. Sober, he wouldn't have answered. The world was safest with him under the covers, locked in his cage, breathing himself down. He ripped the door open, ready to kill whoever was complaining and instead found Amanda, uncertain in the bright corridor.

'I don't know what I'm doing here,' she said. 'Oh my God, Bill, is that a new bruise on your forehead?'

She put her hand up to touch him where it hurt, but he pushed it harshly away. She smiled like she was trying not to cry and took a step towards him.

'Don't, Amanda.'

But her lips took the words from his mouth and swallowed them down into her.


35.


The offices of Deutsch & Bowler shut for a fortnight over Christmas with all sales staff forced to take annual leave. Davie had always thought of this as a bonus, another reason to grin and bear life as an estate agent. Despite parental visits and the on-again off-again Christmas weather, it wasn't a bad time of year to be in Montauban. The population doubled, the cafés filled, people were rehumanised by the holidays. Blow-ins he'd seen every summer since childhood reappeared and told him how lucky he was; how they wished they could live here all year.

But this year he found other beaches to surf. Or, when the waves there let him down, he filled the empty hours with bushwalks, sofa time, even outstanding tasks in the office. There was nothing to do on the case. He had read every document Amanda Hoxton had sent him and his recent calls and emails asking for more had gone unanswered. What did arrive, heavy with irony, was a thick envelope from his friend, Guy Hawthorne. As requested, Hawthorne had wrangled with James Harte's lawyers to produce a contract signed by them and by Harte. It was described in the handwritten note clipped to its front as: *'Tighter than I'd normally do, but this bastard's got a reputation.*' Hawthorne had picked up a different pen before he'd thought to add: '*Get him out and you'll get your money, so be sure to sign and return.*'

Weeks earlier it would have been a boost, something to wave under Murdoch's nose and get even him excited for once. But with the kitchen calendar about to expire and everyone in the world too busy to help, it felt like one cruel promise too many. Davie was tempted to leave the contract among the detritus on his coffee table. But like a man gasping for air even as he decides to drown, he found a pen and signed in the three places his friend had indicated. Half an hour later, when he dropped the signed and sealed document into the postbox outside the general store, it hit the bottom with a stubborn thud, as if it was determined to stay there forever.

New Year's Eve dragged itself around: never his favourite night of the year. There was too much pressure to review what he'd achieved, too many questions about plans and resolutions, too many people celebrating. Davie went to the cinema and watched two movies back to back, both worse than he'd expected, both a better option than anything he'd been invited to. He managed to stay out of Montauban until after dark, eating his last meal of the year in Bell Fair to the sound of competitively drunk teenagers, and cleaners squabbling in a strange language. He found himself jealous even of them.

Back in Montie, the streets were dark but busy, holidaymakers determined to have a summer's evening after an overcast day. Families strolled along the breezy front, kids dared each other down to the darkness of the beach, groups of shadows sat deciding what to do for dinner. Davie heard familiar voices and, turning, saw a seasonal family he knew, waiting for their order outside the bright fish and chip shop. Darting away from them across the road, he slunk past a shrug of teens drinking around a car and set off down one of the paths that ran dark between the dunes.

The sand was cooler than he'd thought; the water, when he reached it and let it surge around his ankles, less than tempting. Not swimming, how sensible. Further south, halfway down the beach, some kids had lit a fire, their gangly legs silhouetted and flitting against it. They'd be comparing fireworks and wondering what to do until it was time to light them. Passing bottles, forming couples or watching forlornly as others did. Davie sighed and walked in the opposite direction, looking up at the lights on the cliffs that towered away from the beach. He'd read too many reports lately, the line of houselights against the black sky looked like a sales forecast. Every one of the twelve houses was lit; the town was full: everyone else in the world having fun. Even Murdoch, holed up alone escaping Christmas, would be happy in his own way. Davie turned back for home then stopped and turned back, studying the houses on the cliffs again. Each one was lit up. He counted them to be sure – an unlit house would be invisible, a black gap between the others – but all twelve of them were there. This was Montauban's prime property: huge plots with multimillion-dollar views. It was his job to know how many there were, who owned each one. If any should be empty.

Across the sand, past the shops, over the roundabout and struggling in his thongs up the hill, Davie told himself he must have miscounted. There would be a mundane explanation. Whenever he thought something important or exciting was about to happen, there was always a mundane explanation. But when he reached the driveway up to James Harte's holiday home, there really was a light. It shone a dim yellow, then flickered as the thick bushes between the house and the road moved in the breeze. Davie pulled out his phone to call Murdoch, caught himself doing it and shoved it resolutely back into his pocket.

'You're being brave,' he told himself. 'You're being very brave.'

Montagne Road ran around the full perimeter of Montauban: south around the lagoon where Murdoch and Davie lived; east between the shops and the beach and then up then up the cliffs; north and west hugging the ridge that held the suburb against the coast. Like all the streets in town, it was poorly lit, the yellow pools from its street lights barely reaching each other. But it was a Christmas tree compared to the blackness of Harte's long driveway. Davie forced himself slowly forward, each step a leap of faith, the light in the house lost to view as the steep driveway leant into its curve. He felt twigs and stones through the plastic of his thongs and walked with both hands held in front of him, ready any minute to trip. One end of the house blacked out a square in the dark sky, and then, as he climbed towards it, became a broad double garage, its metallic doors vaguely reflective. Davie continued on past until he could see the front door shining like a beacon, a duff-duff of music discernible behind it, a figure rushing past on the other side of the glass. Davie froze, his skin shrinking and squeezing the breath from him. He forced himself to stay where he was, to calculate the distance to the road and whether he could have been seen. For long minutes nothing happened and, again, he told himself how brave he was. He looked back towards the garage. The views that gave these houses their value were at the back: full ocean vistas over gardens that ended in sudden cliffs. To see anyone in the living room, or one of the main bedrooms, or sitting on the deck, he'd have to creep along the side of the garage and into the clifftop garden. He turned his back on the front door and closed his eyes. To find the path – if there was a path – he'd need his eyes accustomed to the dark. Opening them again, he was surprised by how well this had worked. The darkness in front of the house was clearer, he could distinguish plants and the far corner of the garage. It was only later, when he thought the whole thing through, that he realised the reason he could see more clearly now was because all the lights in the house had suddenly been turned off.

# The Worst Possible Scenario

## 36

Earlier that same evening, Murdoch had taken his phone down to the bottom of his garden, leaving his house, for what felt like, the first time in weeks. Leaving Amanda's side for longer than he ever wanted to again. She kept calling what they were doing their *affair,* like she was proving she wasn't afraid of the word. Their affair, in her mind, had started the day she saw him at the races, shone up like an old penny made bright again. Their affair was the best Christmas and New Year she'd had in years. Their affair was nothing to feel guilty about. Murdoch wanted to give it a longer title, but was afraid of the extra word required. That kind of talk had always been a conversation overheard, a language he didn't speak. He had no idea if the deep and troubling happiness he felt now was the same thing at all.

They had spent Christmas Day and Boxing Day in the Hilton, waiting to get cabin fever or bored of each other, or for one of them to find an excuse and politely leave. In the end the room began to smell, even to them, and they had driven up the coast to Montauban. Murdoch had insisted they take his car, insisting again when they stopped off at her place in Vaucluse so she could change and pick up a bag.

'Are you sure, Bill?' He was learning the language of her frowns. 'James's car is sitting idle in the garage, it probably could do with a spin.'

Murdoch had smiled and shaken his head, frightened she'd find in it an excuse to change her mind. Waiting outside in the Merc, he had prepared himself for disappointment, the reasons she would just have remembered in the house. But then she arrived with a tiny case and a beautifully wicked smile. At his place, they continued like they were still in the hotel. Food went cold, envelopes piled up on the doormat, phones were left turned off. When they weren't making love – Amanda's words – they talked. His progress, he told her, was about a witness who might have seen a car hit Charlie Holland. No more than that. They'd attempt to find the man in the new year. Murdoch tried hating himself for the deceit, tried telling himself he was a coward, that he was breaking every promise he'd made to Davie and to himself. None of it worked. The spell of this perfect Christmas was stronger than he could break. Amanda looked pleased, then obeyed his instructions not to get her hopes up. Later she asked him about himself and he told her more of his life than he'd ever told anyone. When he asked about her life, she smiled sadly and said it couldn't have been more different. Easy, boring, dull. When he begged her for details, she grimaced and changed the subject. It was New Year's Eve before the topic of her husband joined them, hovering over the bed like a ghost in their cigarette smoke. It was early evening and they were both hungry, but talk of James Harte was too powerful to resist.

'He can't blame you,' Murdoch said to the ceiling. 'Not that he'll ever know, not from me. But, I mean, you shouldn't feel bad, not about this.'

Amanda laughed. 'Don't worry, I won't. I don't feel like guilty at all. In actual fact, I think I'm a paragon of virtue.'

He loved the way she spoke, the phrases he'd only read in books before. He felt her hand on his shoulder and rolled his head towards her to share her smile. Watched her take a drag on her fancy cigarette so its end glowed, crackled and dulled again.

'I told you,' she said, 'it was over between us years ago. We kept meaning to get a divorce, but never got round to it. James spent most of his time up here in Montauban with one girl or another, I always preferred it down in in the city. Trust me, no one knows better than me that I have every right to let him languish in jail.'

'So that's what you're going to do?'

She frowned and blew smoke in his face. 'Do you need to ask that, Bill? No, of course not. A marriage takes what a marriage takes. I'll get him out of prison, but then that's it. End of marriage.'

Murdoch looked back at the ceiling again. Then, frowning, away to the window.

Shortly after dark – while Davie was on the second of his two movies – Murdoch took his phone down to the bottom of his garden, to where his lawn ran into the black lagoon. He called Hannah Simms. They made pleasantries for as long as they could bear, Murdoch reassuring her he wasn't phoning her as Davie's next-of-kin ('What's he done this time?'), Hannah once again grateful for everything he'd done the previous year. Then there was a stumble, Murdoch starting to explain just as Hannah asked why he was calling. Neither were the type to laugh it off. Murdoch sighed and started again.

'You told Davie you want to sell his house.'

'My house.'

'Right, you want to sell your house. Hannah?'

'Sorry, was there a question?'

'You told Davie you want to sell the house and I know the rest, about the deadline and everything. Listen, if he doesn't make it, do you want me to buy it instead?'

'I don't see why not.'

'Five hundred grand, wasn't it?'

'Six hundred and fifty. At least to Davie it was. If I was selling it on the open market, I think I might get more than that.'

'With them stairs?'

'Well, I'm sure the market could decide the state of the house and its true value.'

Murdoch sighed again and looked up at the patio. Amanda's silhouette was up there, she'd come outside to look for him. He knew how well sound travelled up from the garden and turned away, hunched over the phone. The last thing he wanted was for Amanda to understand what he was about to do for her: close down a case that she didn't want solved.

'What if I was buying the house for Davie?' he whispered to Hannah. 'Then it wouldn't be on the open market, would it?'

'Well, not if you gave him the money and he bought it from me. There are tax implications either way, but if that's what you're suggesting, then it's fine by me.'

'I'm not suggesting that. I'm suggesting I give you the money and you give the house to Davie. Tell him you've changed your mind. Tell him you want him to have it.'

'Why would I do that?'

'Because you're so grateful to me for everything I did last year, remember? Will you think about it, Hannah? If there's a tax thingy, maybe I can make that up to you. What do you reckon?'

She told him she'd think about it and Murdoch scowled in the dark. Nobody ever said that and came back with an unqualified yes. He turned to glance up towards the house again, but Amanda was gone, the patio empty but for insect-filled light streaming through the French doors. He discussed some more details with Hannah, hung up and stayed at the bottom of the

223

garden, looking out across the lagoon for a while and wondering what the hell he was doing. Looking at his phone again, he was distracted by a reminder for a meeting the next day with Suzie Bourne. Once, in a different life, it had been a good idea to arrange it for New Year's Day, both of them confessing they'd have nothing better to do. He dialled her number.

'It's fine,' she said, in a way that told him it wasn't. 'We were silly to think we could ignore the new year rolling in. Not great, though, is it, starting it with a cancelled appointment?'

He remembered she was alone and remembered what that was like at this time of year. Christmas only just survived, New Year kicking you while you're down.

'Listen,' he said. 'Why don't you tell me now what you need next for the story? What would you want to hear about next?'

'Instead of you coming around?'

'So that when I come round, I'm nice and prepared. What's next?'

He heard her sigh, tired of tussling with him. 'I mentioned it to you once before. It's called the Worst Possible Scenario. You have to get into your absolute nightmare situation.'

'Ain't we already done that? The Impossible Choice and stuff?'

'Oh no, that first bit of trouble's only the beginning. And, don't worry, after Worst Possible Scenario things are going to get even worse. We'll have Hopeless and Alone to cope with. But we'll come to them in good time. For now, try and think about when things went really, horribly, awfully wrong last year.'

That was easy enough and Murdoch started telling her, but she interrupted and reminded him they were still going to meet. He said fine, he'd see her at her place in a couple of days, wished her 'Happy New Year' and hung up. Even if he found the strength to see this book thing through, he was going to have to break it to her that they could never publish it, not now.

Back on the patio, he hesitated, staring into the living room at Amanda as she sipped coffee and flicked through one of his magazines, then frowned at her phone and a text that had come in. The cool night followed him into the room.

'You all right, love?'

'What? Yes, I think so. I just got a text from our housekeeper saying someone left a note saying they'd borrowed James's car. I'm trying to remember who had the keys.' She remembered the magazine in her lap and smiled up at him. 'Why do you read this rubbish?'

'I like to see how the other half lives,' he said. 'What they wear, their houses, who they go out with even.'

'God, you won't find any of that in here. Their lives are normal, like ours, trust me.'

'Like yours, maybe; not like mine, least not till recently. All they ever do is go to swanky dos and wear fancy clothes. I reckon that's why they only ever get off with each other.'

Amanda smiled at him. 'Bill, any time you see these people wearing a recognisable brand or dating someone else famous, it's because someone's trying to sell something.' She turned the magazine and held it up for him to see, pointing at a picture of Melissa Munday. 'See her, she's a client of Hoxton Harte. She was a two-bit actress with a small part in a Wednesday evening drama. Angus got chatting to her at a party, brought her in to see James, she signed a contract; now you can't pick up one of these rags without reading about her so-called life. That marriage of hers was James's idea, and the pretend affair with the brother too. Melissa prefers the girls. That role on *Society*, you think she'd have got it without being an identity already?'

She laughed at his disappointment and his disbelief about Melissa Munday being gay, then showed him other stories, teaching him how to see through them. 'A friend' meant it was made up, a 'breaking story' had been written by someone's PR department, often a staffer at Hoxton Harte. Even the adverts she pulled apart: the images they used to persuade people how their lives were supposed to be. Nuclear families, strong-jawed men, photoshopped women. Murdoch was relieved when the early fireworks for children started and they could run upstairs to watch.

That night they played cards. Amanda taught him a complicated game, laughing at how quickly he learnt it, not only the rules but the strategies too, most of all, which questions to ask. She asked him where he'd got so good at cards and he told her 'in prison', so they talked about that for a while. Murdoch watched her carefully this time, reading her true reactions. But she seemed more sorry for him than anything else and he tried that on for size, not sure if he liked it or not. He was saved by the bell from deciding: his phone shrill between them. Davie's number was flashing up.

'Take it,' she said. 'You keep saying you should call him.'

Davie was breathless. 'Dude, you'll never guess what just happened to me.'

'Fine thanks, mate, how was your Christmas?'

'What? Oh yeah, fine. No, listen, Bill, you're never going to guess what just happened. I was just down on the beach and, guess what I saw? There was a light on in James Harte's house! So I went up there and snooped around a bit and there were people in there!'

Murdoch stood slowly and carried the phone to the kitchen. Flicked on the kettle like he wanted a cup of tea. 'When was this?'

'Just now. Guess what I saw? Go on, guess.'

Even with the kettle on, Amanda would hear every word.

'Tell me.'

'So anyway, I go up the driveway, right, up to this huge double garage at the top. And there's definitely people in there. And next thing I know, all the lights in the house have suddenly gone off. Well, I didn't think about it, but then suddenly the garage doors are opening. And I'm standing right outside them! So I basically had to throw myself into the bushes beside the driveway; there could have been a snake or a funnel-web or anything in there.'

'I'm guessing there wasn't.'

'No, thank goodness. You know, if there had been … anyway, so I'm standing there, or really crouching actually, as low as I can, and then this car comes out of the garage and guess what kind it is? Go on, guess.'

'Just tell me.'

'It was an Audi TT! Black, as far as I could tell.'

'Rego?'

'What?'

'Did you get the rego?'

'Well, the thing is, see, it was dark and it all happened really quickly. I barely had time to get out of the way and hide myself. I did think about the rego afterwards but, well, that was afterwards and the car was gone and everything. But it's good news, isn't it?'

The kettle reached its screaming crescendo and flicked itself off. In the sudden kitchen silence Murdoch found himself smiling. He turned and carried the conversation back into the living room. Amanda toying with a game of patience on the sofa.

'It is,' he said. 'It's bloody brilliant news.'

'So, listen, we need to ask Amanda Hoxton who has access to Harte's house and who drives a black Audi TT. Do you reckon you could get in touch with her? She's not answering my calls, she's probably away somewhere for Christmas.'

'I reckon I could do that.'

'Bill, I know you'll not like this, but do you reckon you could try and contact her tomorrow? First thing? I know it's New Year and everything—'

'Davie, calm down, I'll ask Amanda as soon as I can.' She looked up at the mention of her name and Murdoch gave her a wink. 'Then I'll get back to you, all right? Davie?'

'Yeah.'

'What else?'

'Nothing.'

'Davie, tell me what else you saw.'

'It sounds stupid and I'm not really sure. It's just, well, when I was halfway down the hill, I heard another car and looked back up and I thought I saw it go in there.'

'In where?'

'Into Harte's place. I didn't see it clearly, but I thought it went into his driveway. I ran back up, of course, but there was nothing. No lights on, no car in sight, although it could've been in the garage, of course.'

'And? What else, Davie? Tell me.'

'Well, it sounds silly, but *it* looked like an Audi TT too. I thought for a second it was the same car I'd just seen drive out of town. But it couldn't have been.'

Davie rabbited on, asking if there was anything else he should be doing, if he should watch Harte's house, how he was trying not to get his hopes up. Murdoch allowed him thirty seconds of this, said he was sure it would work out fine, yes really, and hung up. Amanda raised her eyebrows he sat on the arm of the sofa beside her.

'What did Davie want?'

'Nothing.'

She smiled at him impatiently, gathering up the cards and knocking them together until they were neat in her hand. 'Yes, he did. He wanted you to ask me something. What was it?'

'Who has access to your and James's house up here? Now that he's inside?'

'Why do you want to know that?'

Murdoch sighed, hesitated, then told her about Flash Harry in Rose Bay, what the old man had seen. About the significance of a black Audi TT, about what Davie had seen tonight. She stared away from him as she listened.

'So,' he said at last. 'Any ideas?'

'About what?'

'About who has access to your house up here.'

'You found this out when? About the car?'

'Just now, you heard. Davie just told me.'

'No, I mean about Charlie Holland being run down by a black TT.'

He thought back, trying to get it right. 'Tuesday before Christmas.'

'Over a week ago. And you're only telling me this now. Why would that be then?'

There was a look on her face he'd not seen before. He wanted to believe she was joking and gave her half a grin to convince her she was. She held his eye, bent the cards hard and let them spray across the coffee table.

'Why didn't you tell me about this before?' she said.

'I ... we didn't ...'

'Why didn't you ask me a week ago who drives a black Audi TT; who might have had reason to kill Charlie Holland? Bill? Why didn't you ask *me?*'

His phone started ringing again: *'Unidentified Caller'* and he picked it up.

'Don't you dare answer that!' Amanda's face was twisted and red. 'Why didn't you ask me about a bloody Audi?!'

She stood, picked up her phone and left the room. Murdoch silenced his own phone and went after her.

'Amanda.'

She was in the hallway, struggling with her handbag and jacket.

'What did you think I was doing here?' Her voice was deepened by the struggle against tears. 'Did you think I was just seducing my way out of murder? And that was OK? OK, that I'd killed a woman and put my husband in jail?'

'Amanda, it's not like that—'

She gave him a look of hatred, turned and opened the front door and stomped out into the night. He ran after her, swearing as the rough ground bit at his bare feet. He caught up with her at the top of his driveway where it flattened out to meet the road, dark beneath a low bottlebrush that hung over his and Mr Minter's bins. He grabbed her handbag, then her arm and turned her towards him.

'Tell me it wasn't like that!' she demanded. 'Tell me you didn't think it was me.'

The air around her lit up white, the edges of her hair and one shoulder illuminated, the rest of her in his shadow.

'Tell me you didn't think it was me!'

He was concentrating on his answer, working out how not to lie. He barely noticed the noise behind him, the sudden revving of a motor. Amanda was trying to free her arm from his grip, pulling hard, scowling at him to let her go. Tired of pulling, she pushed him instead, the change so sudden he lost his balance and started toppling back down his driveway, forced to let her go to avoid pulling her down after him. He fell badly, grazing the heel of a palm and a full forearm as he stopped himself rolling further. Swearing violently, he turned and looked up to her and only now noticed the noise of the car – tyres spinning and then shrieking as they found their grip. He looked towards it, a blackness of curves darker than the street-lit night, and struggled to his feet. Before he was fully up, Amanda screamed and then was suddenly silent. He clearly heard her head crack against the car's windscreen, then nothing but the car's engine revving stronger and the hollow plastic bins bouncing down the driveway around him. And then – what seemed like seconds later – the moist, one-sided smack of Amanda landing limp on the tarmac above him. As he scrambled to his feet and ran yelling up to the street, bangs and whistles sounded from every direction, and above him midnight fireworks lit the sky in crass and unnatural colours.

229

# Hopeless

## 37.

They made him drink hot sweet tea. Then others came and prodded him, shone lights in his eyes, cleaned and dressed his hand and arm, bothering him when they should have been looking after her.

'No,' said a burly bearded doctor, one hand heavy on Murdoch's forearm where Amanda's hand should have been. Amanda was dead. Like Murdoch didn't know that. Like he hadn't sat saying her name, whispering in her ear so she could hear his voice rather than the sky-cracking fireworks, holding her tight until the ambulance arrived too soon. Pulling the hem of her skirt back below her knees, arranging her hair across the mashed side of her face, failing to find her shoes. Dead or alive, she deserved their attention. They should be with her; he should be with her; they should leave him alone. The doctor with the beard said they could sedate him, and when he didn't like that, said they could have him restrained or removed from the hospital if he didn't calm down.

Then Natalie Conquest was there, face close in front of his and saying how sorry she was, saying, 'Come with me, we'll get out of here.'

He had no idea how long they sat in silence. They were in a quiet room with coloured glass in the walls, overly bright bulbs badly hidden by wooden frames. There were rows of chairs with an aisle down the middle, cheap red carpet hiding the tiles. Murdoch sat looking at a used tissue, left where it had fallen, stared at it for minutes thinking everything and nothing before remembering it was him who had dropped it. How long before? An hour, a minute? He bent and picked it up.

'Where are we?'

'It's called a "non-denominational prayer room".' Natalie was in a chair across the aisle. 'It's the only quiet room in the building.'

He registered the noises beyond the door behind them and remembered they were still in the hospital. Voices, trolleys and feet, indecipherable announcements: a normal world just metres away.

'Sounds busy,' he said.

'Busiest night of the year.'

230

He was cold and, remembering the blanket around his shoulders, pulled it tighter and closed his eyes.

'Thanks for coming, Nat. How'd you know?'

'I was on duty. I heard it called in and recognised your address. I came straight over and ... Bill, I'm so sorry, I really am, but I have to ask you some questions.'

He told her it was OK and answered them as if by rote. Client–detective relationship at first and then more since Christmas Eve. A hit-and-run. Nothing to do with his previous life; nothing to do with the case; no idea who it could have been. He pulled a face, like he was going to lose it and couldn't talk any more. Natalie started another question all the same but was interrupted by a loud creak behind them. Murdoch turned and saw Davie silhouetted against the white tiles and rushing white coats of the hospital.

'I've been looking for you everywhere!' he said.

Then, remembering himself, he let the door close behind him – the prayer room a prayer room again – walked up the aisle, shuffled past Murdoch, sat in the next seat and wrapped his long arms around him. Murdoch pushed him off eventually, turned away and wiped his nose on his blanket.

'What are you doing here?' he said.

'I came as soon as I heard.'

'Nah, I mean what are any of us doing here? Why do you bring a dead person to a hospital? What's the bleeding point of that?'

'Bill ...'

'I'm all right.'

Murdoch sat suddenly upright, pulled the blanket around him again and gave Davie and Natalie a fierce red-eyed smile, ignoring the glance that passed between them. Then Natalie apologised again and asked Murdoch if he'd seen the car.

'No. Black. No idea.'

'Your neighbour, a John Minter? He heard shouting, looked out and says he saw the whole thing. You falling down the drive, the car. He's really shaken up about it, but it means ... it means my colleagues have eliminated you from any suspicion for now. Anyway, about the car. This John Minter seems to have identified it as an Audi TT—'

Davie gasped. 'A TT!'

Murdoch swung round at him with narrowed eyes, but Davie ignored him.

'No way!' said Davie. 'No way, I don't—'

At last he saw Murdoch's expression and looked back at Natalie, wide-eyed: the new kid in the playground working out which bully will hurt him most.

'You know what,' said Murdoch quietly. 'I bet you a million dollars I know what you're thinking. A million dollars. You get it, Davie?'

'What's going on?' said Natalie.

Murdoch kept his back to her, staring at Davie, daring him to speak.

'Nothing. It's a coincidence.'

'A black Audi TT!' said Davie. 'But—'

Murdoch heard Natalie's chair move, then she appeared in the row of seats in front of them.

'What? What's going on? What's a coincidence?'

'It's the same car as Amanda owns,' said Murdoch. 'Owned. She drove a black Audi TT.'

'What?!'

Davie and Natalie said it together, both starting on another question, so Murdoch let himself go. Let the pain reach his eyes and weaken his mouth, let it reach down his throat and pull up sobs that threatened to choke him. Lying wasn't this easy; lying was resisting the truth. This was letting the truth beat him and pull him apart until they agreed Davie should take him home.

The Crown Road had never seemed so short. Murdoch wanted it to go on forever, the world black but for their headlights on the tarmac and the trees, curves swaying them gently to the sound of the engine. For once Davie knew not to talk and Murdoch was tempted to ask him to turn back – anywhere it didn't matter, just so long as they could drive on and on in silence, like they were travelling through space or something and nothing else was real. But he said nothing and soon the road ran into Montauban, drunks stumbling like zombies along the quiet streets.

Natalie had radioed ahead so the uniforms would let them bypass the crime scene and enter Murdoch's house. All the same, when Davie pulled up a hundred metres away, he and Murdoch sat in silence as they watched the blue flashing lights and half a dozen torches scouring the tarmac, shadowy figures straining at the police tape to enjoy the show.

'Come back to my place,' said Davie.

'You're all right. And you don't need to come in, I'm fine.'

'You're not fine, Bill. You're not supposed to be fine. I'm not stupid, you know. You don't have to tell me what she was doing at your house. What I don't understand is why you didn't want to tell Natalie about the Audi. It's got to be the same person—'

'Yeah, which is why I don't want Natalie knowing about it. I don't want the cops finding them before we do.'

'Bill, if this is about the reward, it doesn't matter—'

'It's not about the fucking reward!'

His voice was hoarse and not that loud, but the car seemed to rock at the noise. Murdoch sighed and spoke again, the restraint trembling his voice.

'Davie, you muppet, it's not about the reward. It's about getting the job done. You put the filth on something like this, anything can go wrong. Inadmissible evidence, prejudicial interrogation, I've used them all, trust me. And I'm not letting that get in the way of this, you hear me? I'm going to find out who done it and I'm going to make them pay. This is my case, got it?'

'Our case.'

'Yeah, our case, whatever.'

He heard Davie shuffling around in his seat again, the tiny car rocking, then felt something light land in his lap.

'What's this?'

'Twenty Lucky Strike. I got them at the petrol station.'

Which made the tremors come back to Murdoch's mouth for some reason. He wiped them away, forgetting the dressing on his hand and grazing his lip. He unwrapped the cigarettes and rolled down his window, the cool night air meeting his face.

'Got a light?'

Davie made a strange noise, shuffled again and opened his door, the whole car bouncing as he got out. He was back in two minutes, a lighter borrowed from one of the gawking shadows. Then the process was repeated in reverse until his tall shadow was next to Murdoch's again, the car low on its haunches.

They stayed there for another half an hour, Murdoch lighting each new cigarette off the previous one. When he'd made up his mind what he wanted to do, he got out of the car and leant in through the open window.

'I'll be going then. Thanks for the lift.'

He felt the car shift again as Davie started struggling out of his seat. 'I'm coming with you. I'll sleep on the sofa.'

'No, Davie, I don't want you to. I mean it. Come round in the morning.'

'I don't think you should be alone.'

'I've been alone all my life, I should be used to it by now. Do me a favour, mate, leave me be. Come round in the morning and we'll work out what to do.'

He walked off before Davie could protest further, ducking under the police tape and giving his name to the uniform who hurried over in protest.

'No visitors,' he told the constable they allowed him down his own driveway at last. 'I don't want to see no one, understand?'


38.


Before he went out again Murdoch made a small pile of Amanda's things in the living room. Her cigarettes from the coffee table, her lipsticked stubs from the ashtray. The plate she'd eaten her dinner off, her book, a light silk scarf. From the bedroom he fetched the bag of clothes she'd brought from Sydney, a book she'd not looked at since she'd arrived, a pillowcase full of underwear. Then he cleared up the cards from across the coffee table and found an earring. Went through every room three times to be sure nothing could surprise him in the weeks to come. Fuck the police and his promises to them not to remove anything. Fuck their need for clues, they had her handbag and her phone, that would have to do. Evidence was the last thing he wanted. He stuffed everything of Amanda's he'd found into her little case and carried it into the garden. Down on the lawn he splashed paraffin across it and set it alight, a whoomph of flame and a thousand sparks released into the night. Then he forced himself to turn and look up at the house, to remember she'd never be there again. Forced himself up the jagged steps to the empty living room as the fire cracked and slowed behind him, forced himself to look at the French doors framing an empty sofa. Then he took a torch, checked the fire had burnt everything beyond recognition and set off through the scrub that edged his garden.

The she-oaks beside the lagoon – the overgrown ground he'd walked through the first time he'd seen her – met Montagne Road after two hundred metres. Sometimes Murdoch walked to the shops this way when he wanted to avoid his neighbours, but, tonight, when the scrub ran out, he continued straight on, along the edge of the lagoon until it met the beach. It was past three o'clock by then, but he knew half the houses in Montagne Road would still be casting light: he could hear them before he left the scrub. Dance beats pumping into the night, shouts and laughter competing with the bass: a thousand people having fun. He knew he couldn't trust himself to behave if some drunk stumbled out and told him to cheer up, it might never happen. He took the long way around, along the beach. Here too, he met people celebrating or coupled, dancing or popping corks, but to them he was just another reveller, attracting no more attention than a slurred 'Happy New Year' or two. He counted his steps through the unresisting sand to stop himself thinking of anything else: twelve hundred and fifty along the beach, another five hundred back on the road, forty across the roundabout, two hundred and twelve up the steep hill to James Harte's house. None of it was any use – the image of Amanda loomed in the darkness again and again. Not dead on the tarmac or in the ambulance but lit white from the car that hit her. It was like the very first time he'd spoken to her, not so much fear in her face at what was happening as anger and shock that he was the cause of it.

The house at the top of the driveway was just as Davie had described: a squarish shape blacker than the dirty cloud cover, a huge double garage between the glazed front door and the darkness of the trees, the rest running back towards the cliffs. Murdoch tried the doors, then, with the help of his torch, found a crunchy pathway beside the garage. It went on for too long and soon he realised the rough brick beneath his left hand was part of the main house itself. He found a low window: sealed fast, no use. Further on was a bathroom – you could tell by the stippled glass – beyond that more featureless framed windows, modern and strong. He pushed on, following the pool of light from his little torch until at last the bricks ran out and a sudden strong breeze frisked him and told him he was near the cliff tops. Turning off the torch, he carried on walking until, as his eyes grew used to the darkness, a lawn slowly distinguished itself from the quivering plants. Soon he could hear the sea crashing onto the rocks below and felt the lawn beneath his feet run out, replaced with thicker growth: something with thorns that caught at his trousers. He gave up and turned back, studying the dark house squatting between him and the sky. Closest to the garden it was single storey, the black-faced room that gave onto the lawn holding a huge deck on its roof. Above that, a bare pergola framed the clouds in straight black lines. Murdoch remembered what Davie had told him he'd seen from the beach and searched for ten minutes, taking his time, until he found a firm drainpipe. He pocketed the torch and started on up.

Heavy wooden furniture stripped of its cushions sat in unexpected places across the deck, tripping and pulling at him like a warning not to go on. He kicked back at it, swearing in the dark, not willing to risk a torch that could be seen from the beach. He swore again when he reached the glass of the house: double doors and floor-to-ceiling windows, all so firmly locked that the handles wouldn't even turn in his hand. Something like defeat weighed on his shoulders, almost as heavy as sadness, and he shook it angrily away. He forced himself to check the windows to the sides of the door, then to take a step backwards and look up. To run his hands over every surface until, above the first door he'd tried, he hit the sharp edge of a transom window. It was sticking out by half an inch – you couldn't tell if you were winding it closed from inside. Murdoch found the heavy table that had bruised his thigh a quarter of an hour before, dragged it into place, then climbed carefully up.

There is an odour to a house that has been empty for too long. A fustiness of air unchanged, a suspicion of damp no matter how dry the building, a dusty cold and settled smell. James Harte's beach house didn't have it. Whoever had been there had sprayed something before they'd left: not furniture polish or cleaning fluid, it was too sickly sweet for that. Air freshener perhaps? Which meant not cleaning but hiding something. Murdoch started in the bedrooms, turning on lights as he progressed. A torch on a terrace might be noticed from the beach, a light in a house wouldn't be – not by anyone but Davie. Then he remembered he didn't care anyway. Let someone spot him, let the police come. The worst thing in the world had already happened: there was a freedom in that.

He could see from the carpets which bedroom they'd used. All the others still had broad strokes of hoovering on them, the air on the way to the smell of emptiness, even if it wasn't there yet. But in the bedroom above the front door was more air freshener. On the mattress, something else. Nothing so obvious as a stain, but the feel of warm bodies, or was he imagining that? Difficult not to think of a couple removing the bedspread and then carefully smoothing it out again. Difficult not to think of himself and— He used a fist to knock the idea out of his head.

The wardrobes and sleek bedside cabinets were empty; under the bed, there was nothing. Downstairs, the room that looked onto the lawn had been used too. The cushions on one sofa were more plumped than the other; the coffee table had been wiped, but not in the corners: white streaks and finger prints still smudging the glass. Murdoch ran his index finger roughly over each streak until his was showing white, sniffed it and put it on the end of his tongue. He lifted the glass out of the table and found more white powder in the metal frame, gathered that and tasted it too until his tongue tingled and numbed and he was sure of what he'd found. Nothing under the sofas, but down the back of the cushions was a torn green corner of metallic paper, the 'rex' of Durex clearly readable.

There was nothing in the bathrooms: the cabinets empty, only one shower damp and recently wiped. In the kitchen, nothing other than a tiny wet pool around a sponge in the cupboard under the sink. But in a black bin liner in the cupboard under the stairs – a space of chemical smells and buckets and mops – he found a pink polo shirt, creased and balled and stained with red wine, still damp. He checked its size, smelled it again, rolled it up and stuffed it into his jacket pocket. In the small toilet by the front door – nothing, and nothing anywhere else in the house either. He opened the front door, walked down the driveway to the plastic bins by the street and pulled out the single white bag he found there. Back in the house, he went through its contents. The rest of the condom packet and the condom too, complete with filling. Tissues, takeaway foils, half of the previous day's *Herald*, empty beer bottles, a broken glass wrapped in the rest of the paper, an empty whisky miniature, a cracked coffee cup. He took pictures with his phone, put everything back into the bin liner and washed his hands.

It was easy enough to find the door to the garage – less easy to talk himself through it, but seeing the car wasn't as bad as he'd thought. He'd have been more upset if he hadn't found it there. If it had truly disappeared; if whoever had taken Amanda from him had left no breadcrumbs to follow. He saw her face lit white in the night, rubbed his eyes and hit himself in the head again, counted to ten and carried on. The car had been wiped: no traces of flesh or fabric in the radiator or in the broken glass of the left-hand headlight. No blood on the dented bonnet, no hair caught in the cracks that ran across the windscreen, stretching in awkward lines from a central web that bent to the touch. He heard voices outside echoing up from street outside: drunks on the way home singing 'Auld Lang Syne' like they could make the party last. He waited until they had faded up the hill, lost in his thoughts, then blinked himself back to life, looking for the rag that had been used to clean the car. But there was nothing else in the garage. No cupboards, no benches, no toolboxes, wheelbarrows, children's toys – nothing. Just the car that had killed Amanda. He sat down in front of it, rubbing his hands along the radiator, then using them to wipe his cheeks. He curled up tight and lay down on the cold concrete floor, staring at the rego. HH1.

Half an hour later, he left the house by the front door, carrying the white bin liner by its tightly knotted neck, counting his steps all the way home.

39.

The days and nights blurred into each other, dull and out of focus. Murdoch found himself sitting in his living room in the middle of the day with all the lights on, or in the garden wondering when it had got dark. For hours at a time he would suddenly feel fine, start thinking rationally about what had happened; what he and Davie should do next. Then it would be like a wall had fallen on him and he was happy to stay buried, lying on his side on the floor or in bed, closing his eyes and waiting for sleep again. Someone started leaving food on his doorstep. It was well packaged in Tupperware, always a complete and cooked meal with a note of how long it needed in the microwave. The first time he found it, there was another note too: *It's important you eat even if you don't feel like it.* Schnitzel and chips, steak and aubergine, lamb casserole with rice. For days on end it was all he did eat, picking at it through the day, reheating it four or five times until the meat was inedible. The next morning, there'd be another meal.

Davie came every day; it was easier to let him in than argue through the letterbox. Often, he sat there saying nothing; sometimes they spoke about the weather, occasionally they talked about what to do next. The case was back on: Murdoch was clear about that. On Tuesday, Davie persuaded him out of the house – just a short walk, he had to get out sometime – but it was a mistake. Everyone had heard that a friend of his had died: the fancy woman who'd been looking for him a few weeks before. He could just imagine them making up the rest. The barman from the surf club, whose name he could never remember, crossed the street to touch him on the arm and say how sorry he was. In the general store, Anne Lincoln came around her counter and wrapped her beefy arms around him. Even Ruby from the bakery – they barely knew each other – came out onto the pavement to give him a sad smile. Murdoch wanted to be grateful; to let them know, yes, Amanda had meant a lot to him. But he despised every minute of it, hating the local grapevine more than ever. He scurried home with his head down, Davie apologising after him.

But Murdoch knew Davie was right. He had to get out more if he was going to find who killed Amanda. 'There's someone we haven't spoken to yet,' he told Davie on the phone that night. 'Someone who needs a visit.'

The temperature rose throughout the next day, patches of blue sky turning into sunshine by mid-afternoon. Murdoch got up early and, for the first time that year, showered and shaved before dressing. At lunchtime, he forced himself to eat all of the meal left on his doorstep that morning and, at two o'clock, he pulled up outside Davie's house, tugging at his tie and rolling his shoulders like that might make him more comfortable. At five past, he gave up, pulled the tie off and undid his top button. At ten past, he found his phone and punched the buttons until he found Davie's number. Wound down his window and listened to Davie's phone ringing through the thin wooden walls of the stilt house above him. Davie answered after five rings, shouted, 'Coming, coming!' and hung up. It was another ten minutes before he appeared in his best suit at the top of the creaking stairs. Murdoch watched him take them two at a time, remember something halfway down, turn and run back up into the house again. It was twenty past before he finally climbed into the car.

'Sorry, Bill. I've got all these cufflinks, but none of them match. And then these papers—'

He gestured with the manila folder in his hand: densely typed sheets he'd borrowed from the office. Murdoch told him not to worry about it. He'd scheduled for Davie being half an hour late: as far as he was concerned, they were ten minutes early.

'Weird seeing you in a suit,' Davie told him, once they'd climbed out of Montauban and were heading for the freeway.

'Likewise.'

'You look older.'

'You don't.'

Murdoch turned and gave Davie a grin, like he was a normal bloke and they were out having fun.

'Are you sure this is a good idea, Bill?'

'You asked me that last night. And again this morning. I think you might have texted it to me too.'

'Yeah, with good reason. I'm pretty sure impersonating a lawyer is a crime; we could get into real trouble.'

'Mate, if impersonating a lawyer was a crime, half the blokes what ever represented me should of been banged up when I was. Trust me, it'll be fine.'

'How can you be so sure? What are you looking at, by the way? Is someone behind us?'

Murdoch forced his eyes from the rear-view mirror and focused on the road ahead, listening as Davie continued his questions.

'And why do I have to come? You're much better at asking questions than me; you can see when people are lying.'

'Trust me, mate, I need you. You open your gob, you sound like a lawyer. I just sound like I need one. Wasn't it you what said you'd do whatever it took to help me? And didn't I say I'd do whatever it took to help you keep your house? Well, this is it, mate. This is what it takes.'

That shut him up. Davie was always a sucker for the BFF act. Murdoch turned on the radio and let Davie find a station he liked. Let him talk all the way to Stanmore. Like he, Murdoch, really was feeling OK and every kilometre, every minute, he didn't want to crawl under a rock and die.

Parramatta Road was clogged and sweating, the pollution between the car yards and the bathroom shops so thick you could almost see it. Utrecht Street – two neat rows of Victorian terraces a couple of blocks to the south – felt like a different suburb. The urban hum was still there, but it was mellowed by trees and bird song, a distant dog barking on the breeze.

Murdoch pulled up a safe distance from number twenty-two and reached behind him for his tie.

'I'm not sure about this, Bill.'

'Yeah, you've kind of made that clear. Now listen, what do we do when she tells us to get lost?'

'We walk away.'

'Because?'

'It's not the first time it's happened. The office keep stuffing up. We're happy to knock off for the day.'

'See, mate, nothing to worry about. We'll be in and out and gone before anyone's the wiser.'

Out of the car, Murdoch reached deep and found the energy to stride up to the house, jog up the steps to the front door and lean confidently on the bell. Then he retreated to the pavement and pushed Davie up the steps ahead of him. The woman who answered the door had straight brown hair tidied behind a brown Alice band, a white blouse tucked firmly into a belted tweed skirt. Only the skin behind her glasses gave away her youth.

'Jennifer Bailey?' said Davie, glancing at the file in his hand. 'John Yardley, Department of Public Prosecution. This is my colleague, Colin Andrews. We're here to talk to you about the James Harte case. We have an appointment?'

Jennifer Bailey looked Davie up and down, got the upper hand with the eye contact, and told him politely but firmly that he didn't have an appointment. At least, not with her.

'You didn't receive a letter?' said Davie. 'Should have been within the last three weeks?'

He looked at his file again, like he was checking the address.

'Absolutely not,' said Jennifer Bailey. 'I've not heard a thing.'

Murdoch watched, impressed, as Davie achieved a pitch-perfect sigh: his shoulders falling and the exasperation clear.

'This is very frustrating,' he said, backing down the steps. 'It's the, what, third time it's happened this month?'

'Fourth,' said Murdoch.

'We'll have to arrange for another time. The trial's not far away, so it may be short notice, I'm afraid. There are a few loose ends we need to tie up to be sure of a conviction. We'll be in touch, Ms Bailey.'

He looked at Murdoch shaking his head, then turned to walk away. Murdoch smiled apologetically up the steps. Jennifer Bailey smiled back.

'Listen, now that you're here you may as well come in. Will it take long?'

She led them into her chilly lounge room and offered them a seat on the sofa. Insisted on making coffee and plying them with crumbly biscuits. Like she was a school teacher and they deserved a nice treat for being nice children and sitting nicely in class. Davie started making small talk, until Murdoch coughed and scratched his temple. A good burn, he'd explained on the journey down, was a fast burn.

'Yes, well,' said Davie. 'Apologies, but we ought to get down to business.'

Jennifer checked her tiny watch. 'Yes, we should. My boyfriend's on earlies and I want to have his dinner ready for when he gets home.' She looked at their blank faces. 'He's a police officer. He's just finished his probation. You might know some of the same people?'

She checked the business cards they'd handed over to see if she recognised their names.

'At this stage in the proceedings, we like to run a case review,' said Davie quickly. 'We want to go through everything ... well, some things, with a fresh pair of ear—eyes. In case there's anything the others didn't pick up ... on.'

'Why? Don't you trust the police?'

Jennifer Bailey smirked, like it was a little joke middle-class white people were allowed to make with each other. Davie frowned.

'We don't trust anyone; that way we get a stronger case. Generally, after a death there's a lot of emotion, people can forget important details.' He looked at Murdoch, blushed and hurried on. 'So, if we could just start again, ask you some basic questions? Feel free to go into any details that you think might be relevant. Time permitting, of course.'

But time had lost its meaning for her. She told them in detail how the night of the murder had been her first date with the man she now lived with. Then about what she'd done since the murder – she couldn't bear to go back to Hoxton Harte, not after what had happened – how, after a slight stumble, her career had progressed all the same until now she led a team of people and still managed, on days like this, to work from home. They were lucky to have caught her on a Wednesday. *Luck,* thought Murdoch, who'd phoned her office to make an appointment, *was generally overrated.* He said nothing, just scratched his temple again and again, Davie driving the questions forward. It was thirty minutes before they got to anything interesting. First, they had to listen to Jennifer trying to remember the exact words Charlie had used to imply she was blackmailing James Harte. Something about secrets, something what ASIC would like to know. It seemed pretty clear for such a distant memory and Murdoch bet himself fifty bucks someone had coached her. Any good lawyer would do so before she got to court. He watched the young woman jealously as she talked. Death was so easy when it was someone you didn't care about; when it was years later and you were over it all.

It was when Jennifer mentioned her phone that he saw something. Nothing he could explain, just something not right. He rubbed his hands together.

'Sorry, why didn't you have your phone with you?' asked Davie.

'I told you, I left it at home that day. Then I went straight out to meet Michael. It was our first date.'

She turned to look at Murdoch, his hands rubbing silkily in the otherwise silent room.

'Er ... the phone?' said Davie. 'You left it at home?'

'Yes.' Jennifer put up a hand to check her flawless hair. 'So annoying.'

'Nah, you didn't.'

It was the first time Murdoch had spoken in the house and his voice surprised them. Jennifer Bailey composed a pleasantly confused face and put her head on one side.

'Excuse me?'

'You didn't leave your phone at home that day. Why would you say that?'

'I ... What do you ...' Jennifer noticed her hands were fluttering. She clasped them tightly together and stared down at them. 'I did. I left it here.'

'You wasn't even living here in them days.'

'Now, Jennifer,' said Davie – good cop – 'you are allowed to remember things differently. That does happen over time. If there's anything you want to tell us, something perhaps you forgot to mention before, you're allowed to do that.'

'I left my phone at home.'

She whispered it, trying to squeeze truth from the words.

'No,' said Murdoch. 'You didn't forget your phone. You're a sensible girl, a girl who likes things nice and tidy. Look at this lovely room, not a thing out of place. You're not the kind of girl who forgets her phone, not on the first day in a new job, not when you're going on a first date with a boy you like. What happened to it?'

She was Alice after she'd drunk the potion: shrinking in her chair as they watched. The woman who'd stood above them on the steps to the street was a little girl after all, quaking in her grown-up clothes. Davie took a breath to say something, but Murdoch held up a hand, so they sat waiting silently, Davie with his mouth half-open, Jennifer Bailey trembling. When she spoke at last, it was still to her hands, her voice so quiet Murdoch and Davie both leant in to hear.

'I didn't want her asking me for a lift.'

'Who's that, then? Charlie?'

She nodded without looking up, her pretence at adulthood unravelling further by the minute.

'Why would she ask you for a lift? She hardly knew you.'

'She was crazy!' Now she looked up, her wide eyes dry but red, her mouth uncertain. 'She was, well … you have no idea. We had lunch like once and she expected me to drop everything to go and pick her up off the boat. I didn't want to—'

'So you turned your phone off?'

'Ha! She wouldn't have let me get away with that. You didn't know her, she'd accused me of lying as it was. She'd implied she was blackmailing James Harte, I didn't know what she was capable of. So I … I didn't take it out with me. I admit it, I did it on purpose. I left it on my desk at work, that way other people would see it too and Charlie couldn't accuse me of lying.' The truth seemed to empower Jennifer again. She sighed deeply, sat up straight and once more patted her hair. 'Look, it's not my fault that awful man killed her. James Harte is obviously an animal and he deserves to be hanged if you ask me. He obviously got her off the boat, into the tender as if he was taking her to the wharf and, then, at some point later that, he killed her. It's obvious. Oh, look at the time. Michael will be home soon.'

Davie started pulling his papers together, but Murdoch didn't move. He was staring at Jennifer Bailey.

'What d'you mean he got her in a tender? What's a tender?'

'It's a little boat,' said Davie. 'Like a dinghy, for getting between larger boats and the shore.'

'Right. And why'd you say that then, Jennifer? That Harte got Charlie into the tender?'

'Well, that's what happened isn't it? As your colleague said, that's how people get between their yachts and the shore.'

'Yeah, but Charlie's body was found in the water. Her last known whereabouts were on Harte's yacht. What makes you think she made it back into this tender thing?'

Jennifer Bailey turned to Davie, appealing for reason, mouth open like she could breathe herself back in charge.

'How *do* you know she got off the yacht?' said Davie. 'How could you know that, unless ...'

'She did ask you for a lift!' Murdoch's voice was loud in the cold room. 'She phoned you. Except, nah, that would have shown up on her bill. Davie, I mean, John, didn't you say Charlie's phone records showed nothing unusual? Anyway, the police would've asked you about it, wouldn't they, Jennifer?' He was watching her closely. 'Text messages would show up too. So how could— Hang on, what's that internet messagy thing called?'

'Facebook Messenger?' said Davie. 'Snapchat? WhatsApp?'

Murdoch caught the look on Jennifer Bailey's face. 'Where's your phone, love?'

'No.' Jennifer Bailey stood quickly and started gathering their half-finished mugs of coffee. 'You need to leave now. You need to go away and leave me alone and make an appointment next time.'

'Don't you—'

'Jennifer!' said Davie. 'If you've been withholding police evidence but you tell us now, we can help you, it's fine. Really. But if you are called as a witness and you lie in court, that's perjury. And that's—'

'Two years,' said Murdoch. 'Two years in jail. And what d'you reckon your police fella would reckon to that? What was it Jennifer? Was it a WhatsApp?'

The mugs dropped to the table in an explosion of crockery and coffee, two of them breaking apart, all of them spilling brown liquid across the glass surface.

'It wasn't my fault!' She was crying, hands to her hair, refusing to look at them. 'He killed her, it's nothing to do with me. I couldn't have ... it wouldn't have made a difference.'

She started saying it again, willing it to be true, then sank back into her seat, one hand shielding her eyes like she couldn't stand the sight of their formal suits. There was another a minute of silence, Murdoch signalling to Davie not to break it.

'I deleted the app,' she said huskily. 'The next day I found all these WhatsApp messages. She was on her way; it was pouring with rain, she'd be there in half an hour; why hadn't I confirmed; she was losing Wi-Fi as they moved away from the yacht. Message after message after message, as if I'd agreed to pick her up; as if we'd arranged it, as if we were best friends or something. It's not my fault, don't you see? She was crazy. I told her—' She looked up and they could see her tears rolling down her nose and spreading over her top lip. 'It's not my fault! It's not, don't you understand? It's James Harte's fault. He killed her, not me!'

Back in the car, Murdoch closed his eyes and leant his head against the headrest. The sun had cooked the air in the Mercedes until now it was thick and heavy. He heard Davie get in beside him, the car shifting under his weight, but the idea of opening his eyes, starting the motor and driving home was beyond him.

'You all right, Bill?'

He managed a nod, leaving his chin on his chest.

'It's just we ought to get going. That boyfriend will be home soon. Do you want me to drive?'

Murdoch made himself nod again, forced his eyes open and got out of the car. Then, as soon as he was in the passenger seat and had talked himself into the seatbelt, he closed them again and listened to Davie work out the air conditioning, stall the car twice and mutter under his breath until a screech of tyres got them moving. He made himself breathe and think about nothing, searching for sleep. But his thoughts remained stubbornly logical and separate, tearing at facts, trying to find a way through to the truth. He sighed, gave up and opened his eyes again, watching the traffic on the Parramatta Road as Davie waited for a gap. But that was no good either and he had to close them a third time to avoid the onslaught of questions bubbling up beside him. He felt the car turn left, then, a minute later, thought he felt it turn left again. He told himself to ignore it; told himself he was asleep and no one could expect anything of him. But his weight shifted right again, and, a little while later, once more in the same direction, like Davie was driving them around in circles. Fantastic. Let Davie drive in circles all day if he wanted so long as he, Murdoch, could sit with his eyes closed and didn't have to talk. The car seemed to turn left once more, slowed and stopped. Davie was halfway out before Murdoch gave up.

'What you doing? Where are we?'

They were on the forecourt of a car dealership, tall orange banners snapping in the dirty breeze, three rows of cars with prices in their windows. Davie hesitated, unsure of whether to get back into the car or finish getting out. He chose to get out and, turning too soon, banged his head on the roof above the door as he leant back in to explain.

'This is Parramatta Road German,' he said, rubbing his forehead. 'It's where the Audi repair invoices to Hoxton Harte came from. They're not supposed to be open for another week, but we were driving past and I saw someone in the office. Stay here if you want, I'm just going to see what I can find out.'

'I'll come with you.'

'Really, you sure? Why don't you sleep?'

'I said I'll come with you. You might be good at the fancy lawyer stuff, mate, but this is a car dealership.'

They were parked at the bottom of an oil-stained ramp that ran up to a workshop. The huge roller door of the workshop was pulled down and padlocked, 'PRG' sprayed in a logo that didn't work on the bumpy aluminium. To the right of the ramp, a metre or so away from it, stood a glass-sided prefab office. Inside it was a man with a mobile phone in one hand and a desk phone in the other, bending down to look at something on his computer screen.

'You got any money on you?' said Murdoch.

'Why?'

'Do you?'

Murdoch watched Davie pull out his wallet and go through it slowly – like he'd ever had cash on him since the day he was born. He sighed and, turning his back on the glass office, went through his own wallet, counting out the fiddies until he had enough.

'You'll owe me half of this,' he said.

Davie shrugged and gave a smile that made Murdoch swear before he turned and walked over to the office, rubbing his eyes awake. At the sound of the door opening, the man on the phones looked up startled.

'Hang on,' he said to one of the phones. Then to Murdoch, 'Sorry, mate, we're closed until the twelfth.'

'It's important,' said Murdoch, letting the door close against Davie who pushed back and followed him in. 'I'll wait.'

'No, mate,' said the man on the phones. 'Seriously, we're closed.'

'Yeah, mate. Seriously. I'll wait.'

The man gave Murdoch a sour stare, found it equally matched and looked away. He was in his late thirties or early forties, grey eyes younger than his thinning hair and tired skin. Tall and once well-built, he was carrying too much weight: an athlete gone to seed.

'Listen,' he said to the mobile phone, 'I'm going to have to call you back. Yeah, I know. I said I'll call you back. Bye.' The desk phone he simply replaced in its cradle. 'So then, what's this all about?'

Murdoch put his hand in his pocket, but before he could bring out the notes, Davie had pushed past him, one hand out for a shake, the other holding a business card.

'John Yardley, Department of Public Prosecution. This is my colleague, Colin Andrews.'

The man behind the desk went paler still and smiled stiffly, pushing some papers on the desk together so only the top page was visible.

'Yeah?'

'You the boss here?'

'Yeah.' A tiny pause before he remembered to say, 'How can I help you?'

Davie explained about James Harte's approaching trial, the invoices the police had discovered, the need to understand them. The colour returned to car dealer's face. Whatever he was doing here with no one watching, it had nothing to do with Hoxton Harte.

'Yeah, I can tell you all about that,' he said. 'Did the deal myself, thank God, didn't have to pay any of my lazy bastards commission on it. Four TT's, paid in cash. I gave them a discount in return for all the maintenance and servicing. One of my better ideas.'

'Four?' said Davie. 'Four Audi TT's?'

'Yeah, one for each of the Directors or something like that. All in black. Jesus, I thought I was doing well, but them lot aren't short of a dollar. More money than sense, if you ask me. Within a year one of them had written his car off. Moron had it towed here like I'm a bloody origami expert or something. Lucky I didn't charge him the cost of removing the scrap.'

'Young guy,' said Murdoch. 'Curly black hair, probably in a nice suit, bit of a dickhead?'

'Not that young. Rich-looking, nice tan. He told me – I've no idea if it's true – the Director who owned the car was so pissed when he totalled it, the next day he didn't even remember doing it. It was only by luck he stumbled away from the thing before the police turned up.'

'When was this?'

The car dealer found a chair, sat down and tapped at his keyboard. After a second or two, he read a date from the screen. Davie gasped.

'That's four days after Charlie—' He left the sentence unfinished.

'Druitt,' said the dealer, still reading. 'That's it. That's the name of the fella who brought the car in. Oscar Druitt. Oh, hang on.'

He tapped at the keyboard and the information disappeared, replaced by an email inbox.

'Yeah,' he said. 'One of my million things to do. Request here from the same guy to book HH1 in for a repair job.'

'What's HH1?'

'That's the rego. They were all like that. HH1, HH2, HH3, HH4.'

'And whose was HH1?'

'Says here a Mr James Harte. HH2 was an Angus Hoxton – that's the one that got written off. HH3, Emma Druitt. HH4, Amanda Hoxton.'

Davie made the dealer promise not to touch the car, under threat of prosecution. Not to talk about this to anyone either. He should let Druitt bring the Audi in, but then keep it under lock and key until he and Mr Murdoch—I mean, Mr Andrews could get back there to examine it. Murdoch remembered Amanda laughing off his admiration of her car. 'It's a tax dodge,' she'd said. He should have asked her what she meant; maybe she'd have explained they all had one. Maybe then she'd still be alive.

## 40

He slept fitfully that night, dreams of loss and violence shaking him in the heat: a torture of sweat and tears that left him dazed and furious, staring at dirty light outside his window. He found his phone but he'd forgotten to charge it, the screen resistant to all his presses, so he threw it across the room, no way of knowing the time. But slowly the sky outside grew paler until it convinced him it was morning not evening, close to five o'clock and another day ahead of him.

In the kitchen he stood watching the phone come back to life, buzzy with messages, and tried to remember the previous evening. He'd dropped Davie off presumably; got into his pyjamas apparently. He yanked open the fridge and swore at the empty shelves but, out on his doorstep, whoever was bringing him meals had already been. He ate the food cold as he read through Davie's five texts – a mounting drama of concern. He thought about Jennifer Bailey and what she'd told them. No, it wasn't her fault Charlie Holland had died, in the same way it wasn't his fault Amanda was dead. He swore out loud and dialled Davie's number.

'Bill, where have you been, I've been so worried! Oh my God, what time is it?'

'I've been at home, asleep. But it's OK, I survived and now I'm awake again. What's up?'

'But I rang your doorbell for like hours yesterday.'

'Yeah, I unplugged it a few days ago, thank fuck. What's up?'

'Are you OK?'

'I'm fine, Davie. What's up?'

'I had a question.'

'Yeah, so you said in your texts and voicemails. It would have been more useful if you'd said what the question was. Still, it was pretty clear to me you had a question.'

'Can I come round later?'

Murdoch looked at the dishes in the sink – maybe he'd eaten the night before? – the bottles on the floor by the back door, the state of his pyjamas.

'No. What's the question?'

'Dude, it's really early.'

'Now or never, Davie. Out with it.'

'It's just I'm going to see Harte again today. I forgot to tell you. I wanted to know if there's anything specific I should ask him?'

'Apart from who has the keys to his car?'

'Oh yeah, of course. Anything else?'

'No.'

'You sure? Nothing?'

'Said so, didn't I? Right, I'm off now Davie. I'll call you later. If you can't get hold of me, it doesn't mean I'm in trouble, all right? It just means I'm not answering.'

He hung up, turned the phone off again and slid it across the kitchen table. Watched it meet the opposite edge and teeter there, unsure whether to throw itself off.

On the front of Murdoch's fridge was a magnet from the boxing gym in Kildare. He hadn't noticed it in years but, when he opened the fridge door to put away the remains of his meal, the magnet fell off and looked up at him from the dirty floor, its timetable a blur of tiny font. Not the worst idea in the world. He made himself a protein shake, stuffed some clothes into a gym bag and dragged himself out into the warm air. Apart from the cockatoos moaning in the gum tree over the road, no one else was awake. No one but a thick-set man smoking in a white Toyota two hundred yards down the road. Murdoch pretended not to notice, followed his bag into the Merc and drove off in a spray of gravel.

Around the first bend and half way to the shops he slowed and lowered his window. He thought he heard another car's engine somewhere behind him, but to be completely sure he hesitated at the general store, like he couldn't decide whether to climb the steep road out of town or go straight over the roundabout and up towards Harte's weekender. As soon as he saw movement, two hundred yards behind him where the tarmac was still shadowed by trees, he turned left and revved up the hill.

He'd never driven so fast along the Crown Road. He remembered Ed Springer asking him to do just that, remembered his promise to himself that he'd never be just another photograph, fading on a lamp post under a sad bunch of flowers. But that was a hundred years ago. Now he pushed the car to dangerous speeds, leant into blind corners so fast he crossed to the opposite lane, twice felt dirt and twigs with less than a full grip on his tyres. Halfway along, where the road straightened for a kilometre, he accelerated so fast the engine made a noise he'd not heard it make before. Then, at the next set of curves, he slowed as quickly as he could without the tyres singeing, decelerating fast on a downhill stretch and then, as he turned the tight bend at its bottom, stopping completely. He turned off the engine, took the keys from the ignition and left the car in the middle of the lane, jogging to the steep grass bank that pressed in on the left-hand side of the road. There he scrambled quickly up, hidden thorns scratching his hands and the grass staining his trousers, then forced himself to slow for the last few metres until he could turn and press himself into the angle, hovering over the road. Across the tarmac, thick woodland chippy with bellbirds continued the descent of the hillside, so steep that the tops of eucalypts no more than ten metres away were already below him. It was less than thirty seconds before he heard the white car. He guessed it was on the straight stretch of road, its engine revving in the warming air, the driver nervous Murdoch had got away.

He waited for empty seconds, leaning into the bank behind him, not allowing himself to think he might have made a mistake. He could hear the other car more clearly now, louder and louder until suddenly it was there: a white Toyota Camry, doing at least sixty as it came around the bend. It was the same guy all right: the big lump with a shaven head, that tattoo on his neck. The low easterly sun must have been reflected in his rear-view mirror because his face was lit clearly enough for Murdoch to see the split second when he saw the empty Mercedes in the road ahead of him. To see fear light up his features more brightly than the rising sun had done, his hands blurring as they flailed at the wheel. The Merc was Murdoch's sacrifice, his proof to himself he'd do whatever it took, but somehow the driver of the Camry avoided it, veering around it in a squealing curve and then – a miracle of driving – righting himself and returning to the left-hand lane. But here he over compensated. The tail of his car slammed into the green embankment ten metres down the road from Murdoch, the entire back of the Camry compressing – the left-hand tail light exploding in clattering plastic – then expanding again as the tyres screamed and left skid marks across the tarmac. The right-hand brake light flashed as the driver tried pumping the brakes, but the untouched Merc had used up all the morning's luck. The Camry continued diagonally across the road and out into the trees, flying for a metre or more before it began to drop. The noise of crushed and scattering plastic, of rubber tearing hysterically across the road, was replaced by a heavy cracking of wood and the metallic bouncing and crushing of the Camry as it rolled through the trees. Murdoch scrambled down to the tarmac and drove his car fifty metres forward to a flat area beside the next curve in the road: a dirty space of dried truck tracks and litter, crisp packets caught in the grass. Out of the car again, he followed the trail of skid marks, found a strong stick and made his way carefully down the broken slope.

# Alone

## 41

The guard behind the glass was new. A big lad – muscles, not fat, a round face under a thin veil of sweat. Nervous eyes and a smile that still came easily, a badge that read *'Trainee'* and a well-tied tie with the prison service insignia. Davie gave his name at the same time as the trainee asked for it and they both smiled awkwardly, the trainee throwing a nervous glance at the older bearded guard on the phone beside him: the man Davie had spoken to on previous visits.

'Identification please.'

Davie walked to the end of the counter and waited for the metal chute to open, threw in his driving licence and walked back. A minute later, he was still waiting, the young guard having difficulty with his computer.

'I'm here to see James Harte.'

'Er … yes, one second.'

Davie's phone buzzed in his hand and Murdoch's number flashed on its screen.

'You sure it's for today?' said the young guard. 'Mr—the prisoner had a visit only a few days ago.'

Davie killed the incoming call, fished out the letter confirming the date and time of his visit and held it up to the glass. The heat of the day had chased him down the freeway. Driving with his windows open had been an attempt at air conditioning that had succeeded only in delivering him to Longreach dirty and dry-lipped.

'Sorry,' said the trainee, smiling before he remembered not to. 'One second.'

He signalled for help to the man on the phone beside him who rolled his eyes and turned away. Davie pretended not to have seen it. How long before the young smile and neat tie turned into the older guard's attitude? Months? Weeks? He heard two women walk into the waiting room behind him, chewing gum loud in their accents.

'He factor.'

'Na!'

'Yeah, he factor and then he lefter!'

Davie's phone rang again just as the beard finished his call and graciously decided to review the trainee's computer screen. Davie didn't risk answering.

'My visit's for three p.m.,' he said.

Maybe if he was super helpful, nicer to everyone than they deserved, the universe would give him a break. Something good had to come of this visit: some new nugget of information.

'Don't worry, mate,' said the older guard. 'None of yous is going in till we've processed all of yous. Young Daniel here will get there in the end, won't you, Daniel? What's that say?'

He pointed at the screen only he and young Daniel could see, the trainee's top lip quivering in concentration.

'G&C?'

'Right. But this guy here ... show us your letter again, mate?'

Davie held it up to the glass.

'What's that say?'

'SS,' said Daniel. 'Standard scheduled.'

Davie looked back at his letter. He'd not noticed the reference code. Murdoch was calling his phone again.

'What's G&C?' he said.

'Grief and consolation,' said Daniel, keen to know the answer to something.

'Who came for that visit?'

'Er ... let's see ...'

'Direct family only,' said the bearded guard, reminding them who was in charge. 'We're not here to answer questions. And you, turn your phone off. So, Daniel, you put the name in there. No, not there, that's it. Then the code and ...' – mock surprise – '... there you go!'

'Thanks,' said the younger guard uncertainly.

He sat back relieved, looked through the glass at Davie – no smile this time – and said, 'Next.'

Harte's pilot light had gone out. That little flame behind his eyes that, on previous visits, had flickered away despite the jumpsuit and the greasy hair – the spark waiting for fuel – had finally disappeared. He shuffled in dull-eyed, barely nodding an acknowledgement to Davie and looking away immediately after as if he were ashamed. He sat slowly, then slouched back in his seat, staying there even after Davie had leaned in to confer across the table.

'I'm so sorry,' said Davie. 'I really am.'

'Great, thanks. Except sorry's not going to bring her back, is it?'

'We'll find them, whoever it is. There are new leads opening up all the time—'

'Oh really?' Now Harte sat forward, his hands landing heavily on the table between them. The noise created a bristle of attention in the nearest warden: an overweight pink man in a uniform two sizes too small for him. 'Like what?'

'Well, like, who has access to your house in Montauban? Do you let anyone use it?'

Harte looked at him strangely. 'What's that got to do with any of this? I just want to know who killed Amanda; why she's dead.' He leant further forward, as if the word had weakened him, and put his head in his hands. At last, he looked like the other men in there.

'We went to see Jennifer Bailey.'

Harte gave another tiny nod, his face still in his hands. 'Who?'

'The one who told the police Charlie was blackmailing you.'

Harte nodded again.

'She seems pretty convinced about the blackmail.'

Harte opened his fingers and looked out at Davie. 'And?'

'Is it true?'

'Is what true?'

'Was Charlie Holland blackmailing you?'

The light wasn't out after all. It flared from nowhere, firing Harte's words across the table.

'What do you think? You think I'd hire a couple of detectives to find out everything they could about who framed me and forget to tell them, oops, I was being blackmailed after all?'

The pink-faced warden waddled over and told Harte to keep his voice down. Harte ignored him.

'You think I hired a washed-up pop star and his thug of a friend to look after me when they couldn't even keep my wife alive? You think I don't know the little thug was banging her? My wife! You think I'm going to sit here and let you join the rest of the world in accusing me of things I haven't done?'

'I'm warning you, Harte,' said the guard, taller now he was beside them. 'You'll keep it down.'

Davie looked around self-consciously and saw everyone else in the room was watching them.

'Dude, keep it together,' he said, turning back to the table.

'Go fuck yourself,' said Harte, standing so quickly his chair fell over behind him. 'What's the point? What's the fucking point of all of this anyway?'

The pink warden made a signal and Davie turned again at the sound of footsteps running towards them. What happened next wasn't clear to him at first. He opened his eyes to find he was lying on his back, his chair still underneath him, his nose stinging and the lights strangely high above him. Before he'd managed to stand, the guards had started clearing the room.

'You too,' said the pink one, grabbing Davie upright and shoving him towards the exit. 'Out!'

Davie looked around and put a hand up to the pain in his face, not wanting to believe he'd actually been punched. Harte was face down on the floor beside the table, two guards heavy on top of him, another at his feet, none of them able to stop him from yelling.

'You're fired!' His voice gargled with effort and raw emotion. 'You and your hard-man friend, you're both bloody fired!'


42.


Murdoch had never got how business worked: not legally. Buying drugs cheap and selling them expensive, he could get that. But how a legal company got to the point where it could put millions into a building, hire people and pay them, spend money on adverts for the telly – that he didn't get. He fidgeted in his seat and looked for the hundredth time at the huge white foyer around him, at the lurid art on the wall behind the reception desk. It was late lunch time, a mini rush hour for those who'd made the mistake of going out into the heat of the day. Murdoch watched them coming back in through the arched doorway, individually or in pairs, standing in the sudden cool with their arms away from their sides, the men pulling at the back of their shirts, everyone complaining about the heat as they passed on their way to the lifts.

He'd forgotten what it was like to be in a busy office building, the harried hurried look of people, the snatches of overheard complaints: 'It used to be great here, fun and noise and expense account parties. Now it's all data and analysis and proven results.' He picked up one of the HHA annual reports from the table beside him, recognising it from copies he'd seen lying around at Davie's, and flipped through it like he cared. The photograph of Amanda surprised him and he flipped back to look again. It was part of a double page layout – one of four portraits, none of the Directors looking like themselves. They were too polished, too bland in corporate black and white, except for Emma Druitt who always looked like that.

'Bill! What are you doing here?'

Angus was washed out: a more fragile version of himself. Dark patches framed his eyes, his lips were dry and cracked, his hair up at strange angles. Murdoch stood and put out a hand that Angus used to pull him into a hug.

'You all right, Angus?'

'No. Jesus, Bill, this is totally fucked up. I'm a mess. I came in because I couldn't stand being at home but I'm useless.' He rubbed at his eyes with the heels of his palms, then looked at Murdoch blinking. 'God, you must be a mess too. I knew you and Amanda liked each other, although I didn't know you'd done anything about it. I'm glad though, mate. She deserved a bit of happiness after— I mean, I don't mind. Oh Christ, listen to me. I'm all over the place. I'm supposed to be organising the funeral but I haven't done a thing. I don't know where to start. Emma's going to have to do it.'

'Is Emma here?'

'Just saw her upstairs, she's on level four. What are you doing here?'

Murdoch shrugged. 'Personal stuff, I'm helping her out with something. Least I would be, if I could get past your receptionist.'

He nodded at the middle-aged woman behind the counter who was pretending not to watch them. Murdoch had been turning down her increasingly insistent offers of help for over an hour.

'Oh, don't worry about her,' said Angus. 'Pam, I'm taking my friend up to level four. All right?'

'Fine!' said the receptionist, trying to be sunny about it. 'But my name's still Patty.'

Angus ignored her and she, in turn, ignored Murdoch's apologetic smile. At the lift they met three men waiting in open-necked shirts. As Angus and

Murdoch approached, one of them told Angus how sorry he was, how sorry they all were, how upset. Then the others said the same thing in four different ways while Murdoch watched Angus struggle to find the right response. The lift arrived, but the shirts, still gathered around Angus telling him how much they, etcetera, were happy to let it go.

'Listen,' said Murdoch, sidestepping them. 'I'll see myself up. Catch you later, Angus, I'll call you.'

Angus looked up past the other men and smiled gratefully. He started to say something, but the lift doors closed before he had a chance.

On level four, a hurrying young woman, arms full of paper, pointed Murdoch in the right direction. At the far end of the floor, past countless messy workstations and young people on phones, two large desks faced each other. They were separated from the rest of the floor by a glass partition – abstract reflections wobbling slightly – in the middle of which was a glass door. A sign on the door read *'Finance – Confidential'*. Murdoch could see Emma Druitt in there: tiny behind her desk, typing relentlessly, her dark bob hiding all but the end of her nose. At the desk opposite her, sat a young man with a moustache and long hair tied in a ponytail, similarly bent over his keyboard. Like the two of them were seeing who could type the fastest.

Emma Druitt's face, when she looked up at last and saw him standing at the glass, was surprised for less than a second. She managed a smile no more or less convincing than ever, then stood and said something to the man opposite her which made him glance at Murdoch briefly before returning to his keyboard.

'This is a surprise,' she said, coming through the glass door and shaking Murdoch's hand. 'Let's go and find a meeting-room.'

'I'd of thought you had your own office.'

'No one has their own office any more. They went the same way as secretaries and tea ladies. Unpleasant and unproductive as it is, in a building as expensive as this one, we all have to share. I'm lucky to have that glass to keep me from everyone else's noise. In here.'

She had led him to a small meeting room halfway back to the lifts. It too was all glass, venetians down to keep out the glare from the outside windows but still two degrees warmer than the rest of the floor.

'How are you bearing up?' she asked him.

'I'm all right. You?'

'I'll survive.'

She looked as washed out as Angus, and Murdoch wondered if that was how he looked too. Like all the happiness had been sucked out of him, taking some eye colour and skin tone with it. He had thought he was angry with Emma Druitt but, now, all feeling abandoned him. Maybe he'd used it up on the broken man in the broken car at the bottom of the broken embankment. Either way, he suddenly cared less than he wanted to. He sat heavily in one of the metal-framed seats and ran his hand over his scalp.

'Can you guess why I'm here?'

'No.'

She was a bad liar, he thought. Too confident, too quick to reply.

'I was wondering, Emma, why you had me followed?'

'I don't know what you're talking about.'

She smiled again, an attempt at playing dumb, and twisted her wedding ring slowly with the thumb and forefinger of her other hand.

'Oh, come on, Emma, you bleeding well do. You hired a private detective by the name of Chris Jones to follow me every day for the last two months. You chose well, I'll give you that; I only noticed him a few times. And, from what he tells me, you've only given him two nights off in the last two months. He was lucky to spend Christmas and New Year with his family.'

She looked at him blankly, then shrugged her shoulders like she was giving up on a bad idea. 'He's not very good at respecting confidentiality, though, by the sounds of it.'

'Jesus, darling, give the guy a break. He was in a lot of pain when he told me and trying to avoid a whole lot more.'

'I suppose you beat him up. That's how you people behave, isn't it?'

'You people? Who's that then?'

'Criminals.'

He took that. Looked away first and sighed, asked again why she'd had him followed.

'Why shouldn't I, Bill? You appear in our lives, so keen to get to know us and find out all about us. A friend of James's from prison, no less! Well, he might think you're a friend, and you might have convinced Angus and Oscar and— Anyway, unlike everyone else around here, I prefer to know what I'm dealing with. So I had you followed and found out about you.'

'And what did you find out?'

260

She hesitated, unsure if she could trust herself. 'It's what I didn't find out which annoys me. It's what the police told me instead, that Amanda was killed coming out of your house, where she'd spent the previous few nights.'

'Right. And why she shouldn't she of?'

Emma Druitt pressed her lips together and stared at him with her mousey little eyes. 'Maybe you're right,' she said, after a while, her voice droning in the stale air. 'God knows, Amanda was free to do what she wanted, James certainly felt he was. Especially with that piece of trash who ended up dead. But tell me this, Bill, do you honestly believe that, if Amanda hadn't got mixed up with you, she'd be dead right now? I was right to have you followed. The only thing I did wrong was not finding a reason to get you away from us before you did any damage. It's your fault she's dead.'

He thought he could take that too. Thought he could ignore it and ask what was wrong with James's car, why Oscar had booked it in at the garage. But whatever it was he'd meant to say was out of reach. He felt like he hadn't slept or eaten in days. There was a tap on the glass door of the meeting room and they both turned. The ponytailed man who had been sitting at the desk opposite Emma's was holding up a phone with a pained expression on his face.

'I have to go,' Emma told Murdoch. 'Sorry.'

Out on the street, he walked one from end of Surry Hills to the other, trying to remember where he'd parked the Merc, forgetting what he was looking for and starting the search again. He'd found it – outside the doors of Hoxton Harte with a ticket on its windscreen – before he remembered to call Davie. No answer. Which made sense really: Davie being the kind of guy you couldn't get rid of until the one time you needed him urgently. Murdoch tried him again as he crossed the Harbour Bridge, punching the redial button every ten minutes as he drove north out of the city. Maybe he was imagining things, maybe it didn't matter that Emma Druitt knew that he and Amanda had been – what? 'Having an affair,' Amanda would have said. But it wasn't Amanda's words that were ringing in his ears. It was Emma Druitt's. *Do you honestly believe that if Amanda hadn't got mixed up with you that she'd be dead right now?* He swore out loud and hit the redial button again. Turned the radio on and forced himself to listen to it, anything but answer the question. *Do you honestly believe…?*

261

It was an hour and half – he was almost back in Montauban – before Davie at last picked up his phone. He sounded sulky and nasal.

'Davie, where the hell of you been? I've been trying to call you.'

'Yeah, I couldn't answer.'

'Where are you?'

'Accident and emergency.'

Murdoch was on the Crown Road by now, progress slow, half the road taped off after an earlier accident. He pulled the phone from its holder and took it off hands-free.

'What happened Davie? You all right?'

'No, I don't think I am. I think my nose might be broken. Or my cheek or something?'

'You been to see Harte yet?'

'It was Harte who hit me.'

'What? Jesus, Davie, what'd he hit you with?'

'His fist, I imagine, I wasn't really looking.'

'He hit you with his fist and you think your cheek might be broken? What you made of – glass?'

'Oh, well thank you for your typically moving sympathy.'

There was a silence on the other end of the line, but Murdoch was in no mood for making amends. All the same, when Davie asked him why he was calling, he decided not to admit he'd been trying to warn Davie that Harte might know about himself and Amanda. He ran his hand over his scalp.

'I wanted to make sure you asked Harte about who might be using his house.'

'Crikey, Bill, I'm not stupid. That's when he hit me.'

'You what? Really? You asked about the house and he hit you?'

'Well, I told him about Jennifer Bailey too. About her saying that Charlie was blackmailing him. I asked him if it was true and he hit me.'

Murdoch sighed. 'So not when you asked him about the house?'

'I don't know, Bill, I don't really remember. I've been assaulted, I'm in hospital where no one seems very interested in helping me and, above all, I've lost my home. It's all over. Harte's fired us both from the case.'

'You what?! You muppet, Davie, what d'you have to press him on the blackmail for? He'd already told you—'

'Don't, Bill.' Davie's voice was squeaky with indignation. 'Don't you dare blame this on me. I wasn't the one who, to quote James Harte, was "banging his wife".'

'Say that again!' Murdoch's mood erupted in the quiet of the car, he didn't care if he was shouting. 'Just you use those words about her again!'

'I'll say it whatever nice way you want me to say it, Bill, but thanks to you I've lost all chance of keeping my home.'

'Fuck your home! And fuck you. I've lost someone who I—someone who meant a lot to me.'

This time the silence on the other end of the line was so long that it was Murdoch who eventually gave in. But when he spoke, and then yelled, into his phone he found Davie was long gone.

### 43.

Murdoch was at a loss. There was no one else he needed to talk to, no questions he hadn't already asked, no leads to follow up. Without Davie calling, his phone lay dead and the days dragged, long and empty. He refused to allow himself to feel any guilt, to think again about the question Emma Druitt had asked. In prison, he'd seen too many men sink into self-hatred and he knew there weren't many that made it out again. The trick was to keep busy. So he tidied and cleaned every room in the house, emptied the place of alcohol, spent hours at the gym in Kildare. He ate well – the food deliveries to his door continued – and every afternoon he ran the streets of Montauban. He thought he might bump into Davie, told himself he didn't care either way, but he never did see him. He called Hannah to repeat his offer, but she was suddenly too busy with work, she said, she'd have to get back to him later. Evenings he cooked for himself, went to bed early and stared at the ceiling. None of it helped and he found himself crying at nothing. But then his alarm would ring and bang, he'd be up again, changing into his running clothes, another day and night out of the way.

Years before, he'd gone weeks at a time without talking to anyone, not properly. Where's this? Give me that. Shut your mouth. But he'd been a different person then. Now, he was so desperate for company he let Anne Lincoln talk to him for minutes on end. Days after he'd argued with Davie, it was half an hour on why he should learn to swim: the ocean was so refreshing, so liberating, everyone around here does it. He let her insist he take down the number from the postcard in her window that offered lessons, nodded and smiled at everything she said and walked away shaking his head slowly, wondering what he'd become. Halfway home he saw the ugliest man in the world, hands dragged down by his heavy shopping. The man crossed towards Murdoch.

'How have you been?'

'Fine thanks.' It was someone to talk to, a few less minutes to fill.

'Those meals OK? You get to them before the bush turkeys do?'

It took Murdoch a while to get it. When he did he swore, then apologised for it before thanking the man four times, one hand on his shoulder, like he needed something physical to prove how grateful he was. The man gave him his unfortunate smile.

'I left them because I heard that that lady who died was your girlfriend,' he said. 'But maybe that was just Montauban gossip. You know how people put two and two together.'

Murdoch shook his head. 'No, worst luck. Well, I mean, yeah, I s'pose she was in a way. We was only properly together a few days, though.'

The other man shook his head. 'That doesn't matter. It's the depth of a relationship, not the length of time, that counts. Anyway, if you were fond of her, then you owe it to her to stay healthy. One of you has to survive because otherwise even the memory of what you had together is gone.'

Murdoch rubbed his hand over his scalp. He wasn't about to cry here on the street.

'No one in the world knows what you're going through,' the man went on, ignoring the creasing of Murdoch's face, 'especially if you two weren't an item for too long. People will never understand, so don't expect them to. I'll keep bringing you food for another week or so. You look after yourself.'

Murdoch nodded again, examining the tarmac between his feet, and heard the man shuffle on past. He was ten yards away before Murdoch thought to look up and run after him.

'Listen,' he said when he caught up. He was touching the man's shoulder again, he couldn't help it. 'You've no idea what a beautiful thing you've done. There's been days when them meals was the only good thing in the world.'

The man smiled at him again and nodded, saying nothing.

'I don't know your name,' said Murdoch. 'I'm sorry, I never asked.'

'Will.'

'Will. Nice one.'

'Will Stevens. And you're Bill Murdoch. And you're going to be all right.'

Later that morning, he was at the bottom of his garden, examining the red robin, when his phone rang. Peter Christensen. *Who the hell's Peter Christensen?*

'Is that Bill Murdoch?'

'Who's asking?'

'This is Peter, Oscar Druitt introduced us at Huntingdon's. In the car-park? Listen, this might be a long shot, but I had a game set up for this morning and my opponent has just pulled out. I wondered if you were free and wanted a game?'

It was the last thing in the world he wanted: smiles and handshakes and nice conversation. But it was exercise and, more importantly, it was company. They arranged to meet as soon as Murdoch could get there. Fifteen minutes later he was throwing his sports bag into the car when the phone rang again. Silent for over a week and now it was ringing twice in an hour. Murdoch was tempted not to answer.

'What d'you want?'

'You got a calendar?' Hussein's voice was wheezy, like he was struggling with the effort of lifting the phone.

'You said the end of the month, Hussein. So I've got two weeks.'

'Nice to see you's paying attention. I've got to hire a car to get up there, wanted to make sure you're not wasting my money. Wanted to remind you not to try any funny business. I've been to see my solicitor friend and told him to keep checking in with me a few times a week, making sure I'm still alive. Day he comes round my house and I'm not there, off goes a letter all about little old you. You remember that?'

'The twenty-eighth,' said Murdoch. 'Be here before ten and gone by half past. Then that's it, you got it? Never again.'

He hung up before Hussein could think of anything cute to say, leant against the car and asked himself what he was waiting for. He should have dealt with this weeks ago, what had he been doing? Then he remembered and wiped his hand across his face. Did it again, harder the second time; then once even harder still.

'Twelve days,' he said to himself. 'Twelve days max.'

There was a traffic jam on the driveway up to Huntingdon's – Fords, Holdens and Mazdas amongst the luxury brands. Murdoch felt conspicuous surrounded by 4x4's and people movers – a childless man at a parents' evening – and wondered if the traffic was standard for a weekend. But at the car park in front of the clubhouse he found its explanation: a skip beside a patch of glistening tarmac, tape hanging low between orange traffic cones. A doddery old man wearing fluoros like fancy-dress smiled at the cars as he waved them on to the relief car park behind the service building. Murdoch asked him what was going on.

'We're taking away the gravel,' said the old man, too well-spoken for his outfit. 'The stuff costs a fortune in maintenance and some members have started complaining about the way it flicks up and scratches their cars. Not to mention what all the little animals like using it for. Oh look, aren't you lucky, this lady's just leaving.'

The small hallway of the club house was quiet after the chaos outside. Three men in shorts and polo shirts stood by the doorway to the drawing room but, otherwise, the space was just as he'd remembered it. The flowers on the table in the middle of the room, the narrow staircase running up one wall, Irene and her tight smile. He saw her a second before she saw him and had time to register her reaction. Nervous, he thought. She turned away to a pile of towels pretending she hadn't seen him.

'Can I help you?'

Mr Hughes was shorter than Murdoch had remembered him. He looked nervous too, like it was him who'd been asked to leave in the past.

'I'm here for a game of tennis with Peter Christensen,' said Murdoch. 'He's a member. I was supposed to meet him in the car park.'

'He's not here.'

'Yeah, I can see that. Is he in the drawing-room, d'you reckon?'

He turned to look in, but the three men at its entrance were five men now, two of them looking at Murdoch strangely, all of them blocking his view.

'He was looking for someone to play tennis with,' said Irene from behind the desk, one hand up to her neck. 'I know he called you. But then I saw him chatting with Oscar Druitt and I've not seen him since. He's probably outside – you should wait for him out there.'

He thanked her and she turned away without meeting his eye, the pile of towels still too interesting. He'd just passed the table with the flowers, halfway to the front door, when the men at the entrance to the drawing room stood apart to let someone through. Murdoch heard a voice say, 'That's him,' and, turning, saw it was Oscar Druitt.

'Hello, Oscar, mate.'

'You've got a bloody nerve coming here.'

'Scuse me?'

'No, I won't excuse you. How dare you, you grub.'

'Now then,' said Mr Hughes, scurrying forward and lifting the vase of flowers from the table. 'We don't want a scene. Mr ... this man was just leaving.'

'Yes,' said Druitt. 'He's leaving all right. And he's not coming back.'

He turned to the men around him, a small crowd now both sides of the narrow doorway. 'This is the bastard I was telling you about. Hired as a private detective to spy on us. Pretended to be a friend. Let us welcome him into our lives and all the time he's just after money. Well, you chose the wrong crowd, Murdoch. Bugger off.'

There was something less than genuine about Oscar's anger. Something sharper, something like fear. Whatever it was, it had inspired the men around him. They looked like a lynch mob.

'I was hired by your brother-in-law to prove his innocence,' Murdoch said slowly. Then to everyone at large, 'I was hired by James Harte.'

'Ha! And then what did you do? You started sleeping with his wife until one of your associates murdered her in cold blood.'

'You what? What associates?'

But there was no point. Murdoch could tell the jury had been prejudiced against him. Someone started pushing through from the back and the men in the doorway were forced to step forwards to let him through. Hughes had disappeared with his precious flowers, leaving Irene alone whispering into the phone. Suddenly Oscar was pushed to one side and Angus Hoxton stepped into the hallway.

'Bill, I thought you were a friend.' He looked uncertainly at Oscar. 'We thought you were a friend. We let you in, we took you places and ...

You were investigating us?! How dare you? How could you do that to poor Amanda?!'

Angus wasn't pretending to be angry. Or maybe he was, maybe he needed to prove something to himself. As Murdoch started to correct him about Amanda, Angus crossed the hallway in three short steps and slapped him across the face. It was such an effeminate gesture, Murdoch was tempted to laugh, but Angus was raising his hand again so, instead, he pushed him back with a firm hand on his chest.

'Listen, Angus ...'

'Get your hands off him,' one of the men in the doorway shouted, although none of them moved. Whatever Oscar had told them, it had also frightened them. Murdoch knew their hesitation wouldn't last.

'Oh, go fuck yourselves,' he spat at them all. 'All of you, take your fancy club and shove it up your arses.'

He turned to leave and the small crowd, realising they were safe from violence, started shouting back at him. A dozen angry men, most of them didn't even know him, telling him what a bogan he was and how he should go back to where he came from. They didn't want his type in here. As he crossed the condemned gravel, the men spilled out of the front door behind him, cursing him in the open air so that everyone in view – uniformed staff, mothers dragging children, drivers queuing and trying to park – all turned to stare. Murdoch had left the Merc facing the right way and pulled away easily enough, the spray of gravel keeping the men at bay, but he was a hundred metres down the driveway before he was away from their voices and the horribly true names they were calling him.

44.

The next day the heat really kicked in: thirty-four degrees at ten in the morning, the breeze an opened oven door. Murdoch woke late and naked, sweating through a hangover. The scene at Huntingdon's had broken his resolve and, on the way home, he'd picked up a case of Cooper's, drinking his way through it while flicking between action movies, old episodes of *Society* and porn. Now, in the stifling silence of the morning after, he tried to remember what had been on television and what had been in his dreams, wincing as he remembered the scene at the country club. Of all the people in the world, he'd hoped Angus would be the one to understand his pain. But he'd been around hurt often enough to know how, once a man has found someone to blame, he doesn't give it up easily. As for Oscar, Murdoch's senses might have been dulled in recent months, but he knew true hatred when he saw it. As he lay blinking on top of his damp sheet, he tried to find something positive in the situation and settled on the fact that everyone in the world who could tell him to get lost had already done it. That had to count for something.

He stood carefully, testing the impact on his head, and crossed the room to throw open the windows to the lagoon. It was hotter outside than in – some kind of hell – and he stumbled backwards to the bed, kicking over a glass of water on the way. Swearing sadly, he crouched down, trying to stop the water with his hands before it dwindled between the floorboards. He was scooping at it like a man in a desert when there was a sudden sharp noise from downstairs. In his still-drunk state, he thought the water had reached the wiring and set the doorbell off. He was halfway down the stairs, looking for the wires, when he realised there was someone at the door.

It wasn't Davie. If Davie was going to get over losing his house – or if he'd found out from Hannah that Murdoch had stopped it from happening – he'd have done so before now. And he'd have leant on the bell non-stop for five minutes, yelling Murdoch's name through the glass for good measure. Whoever was at the door today was less persistent. By the time Murdoch had got up to the front bedroom to peer down through the window, they had gone. He looked along the road but, apart from some kids flip-flopping back from the beach with hair and swimmers already dry, the baking tarmac was empty. Murdoch checked the other way, his head throbbing and his throat suddenly on fire, and noticed someone ringing Mr Minter's bell. A small woman in a khaki suit, like she was on safari, hunting for souls on a Sunday morning. Murdoch swore again and was about to drop the curtain when he saw his neighbour answer his door. As he watched, Mr Minter stepped outside and pointed over at Murdoch's house. Then Minter started, pointed up at the bedroom window, and, smiling, waved at Murdoch. The woman in the khaki suit turned also: it was Suzie Bourne in sunglasses, tiny out in the real world. Waving too but not smiling.

Murdoch was a tidy drunk. At some point the night before, he'd gathered together the bottles he'd emptied and lined them up on the kitchen counter. Beside them sat two ashtrays, rinsed and upended on the draining-board. The living room was spotless apart from his clothes (soaking for some reason) sitting in a pile in the middle of the rug. Before the doorbell rang again, he had managed to pull on some clothes, put the ceiling fans on full blast, push open the French doors and throw his clothes into the kitchen.

'Were you pretending not to be home?' Suzie said, blinking in from the harsh light. It really was a safari suit: strange beige material from another time. 'You needn't have bothered hiding from me. I just wanted to give you this.'

She held out a long white envelope with his name on it in her old-fashioned handwriting.

'Looks like a summons,' he said, not taking it.

'Quite the opposite. You obviously don't want to continue with our project so I'm giving you an out. This is a receipt for the money you've paid me so far and an invoice for the outstanding amount. Once you pay, we needn't bother each other again.'

'Here, no Suzie, don't do that. It's just it's been, I mean, I've been … I want to carry on, really.'

'You've not returned my calls for two weeks, you haven't turned up for our last two meetings and the one before that you insisted on holding over the phone. Don't be embarrassed, people change their minds all the time.' She was something more than furious. It reminded Murdoch of Oscar at Huntingdon's, except Suzie's anger wasn't driven by fear but, he thought, by hurt. He realised for the first time how much their book had meant to her. Remembered she was as bored and as lonely as him. 'Please take this from me,' she said. 'I'm too old to bend down to the ground and I don't want to throw it at your feet.'

'Come in, Suzie, it's hot out there. I'll make us some tea. Or something cooler.'

She smiled irritably, adjusted her old-fashioned sunglasses, and threw the envelope onto the doormat. Then she turned and started to struggle up the driveway to the road. Even now, it was difficult to believe it was her, existing outside the peaceful flat in Crosley. He couldn't believe he wasn't going to see her in it again.

'My girlfriend died,' he shouted after her, the word strange on his lips. It made him want to cry, the idea that he one day could have felt justified calling Amanda his 'girlfriend'. Still, he shouted the word again, not caring who else heard him. 'Just up there, on New Year's Eve. We was fighting and then a car came and hit her and she died. I've been ...' What? A mess? Focused on the case? More miserable than ever in his life? '... not answering my calls.'

He could smell the sweat on himself, last night's beer evaporating through his pores, dehydrating him further by the second. He should go inside and drink some water, sit under one of the fans. Suzie Bourne had turned and was looking down at him, standing not two metres from where Amanda had died. He walked out onto the harsh ground, hobbled up to her and took one of her hands.

'Please,' he said. 'I've not got no one else.'

# The Revelation About One's Self

## 45

Murdoch sat Suzie in the living room and they took turns apologising until she waved him off to the kitchen to make them both some tea. His best mugs looked worse than ever and he couldn't find anything like a biscuit, but he did find some Nurofen, three of which he knocked back with a quietly opened beer from the fridge. Suzie forbade him from apologising any more – the mugs, the state of him, the smell of smoking – and said how beautiful the living room was. How lucky he was to have such a mild room: her place was like an oven and would be till May.

'It's because it's built into the hill,' he said. 'Keeps it cool.'

The comment floated off in the breeze from the ceiling fans: small talk neither of them wanted to continue.

'I read about a hit-and-run in Montauban,' Suzie said after a while. 'I had no idea it was in any way connected to you. I'm so ... I'm allowed to say "sorry" because it's not an apology. I'm so sorry, I really am. I spend half my life going to funerals these days, but it's not so sad when someone's old. Half the time, it's a relief. At least your friend won't have to worry about losing her dignity and ... well ...'

He nodded and ran his hand over his scalp. 'We gonna finish this book, then?'

'Yes.' He saw her stop another apology. 'Let's. By the way, are you impressed I found your house?'

'Jesus, I didn't even think. How'd you manage it?'

'You described it so well, the lagoon, the road winding away from the beach and the shops. I knew it was either this one or the one next door. And there's the patio, I see, and, I presume, the red robin hedge is down there. Would you mind?'

Whether he minded or not, she was up on her feet, hands pulling her jacket back into shape and popping her sunglasses onto her nose. Ready for safari.

He had to walk backwards down the jagged steps to the lawn, one of her hands in each of his, terrified she was going to fall. It was slow work in the heat, and by the time they got to the spindly little hedge he was sweating again.

'We'll go back up through next door,' he told her. 'Mr Minter's got a path, he won't mind.'

Suzie turned from the red robin and looked up at him. 'One thing I'm struggling to get down is your accent. "Parf" and all that. I don't know how to get it across.'

He didn't know what to say to that, so pointed at the hedge instead. 'Can't get this bleeding thing to grow. Dunno what's wrong with it.'

'It's just slow,' she said. 'But everything's always growing, even when it doesn't seem to be, even in winter when it looks dead. As long as it's alive, it's still growing.' She sighed and walked into the shade of the huge turpentine, turning to study the view from there. 'So this is where you had The Battle last year?'

'I wouldn't call it a battle exactly. More like a scuffle. Then I got knocked on the back of the head with a spade.'

She put her head on one side and looked up at him. Even through her sunglasses he could see the blue in her eyes.

'Maybe I should drop your h's? No, it doesn't matter how violent The Battle is. It just has to be ... Actually, let's come back to The Battle in a minute. I can't wait to hear all the gory details! But first of all, we should talk about The Revelation About One's Self. The Revelation About One's Self is always the first step the main character must take to pull himself back from despair. It leads to The Surrender, and that leads to—'

To their right, a pair of kayaks drifted past on the lagoon, one of the paddlers raising a hand in greeting. Murdoch tutted and turned away, walking towards Minter's land. Suzie raised a tiny hand and called a vague 'hello' before turning and following him. When she spoke again, she seemed to have forgotten they weren't supposed to talk about The Battle just yet, unable to resist the gory details.

'So after you got hit on the head with the spade, what happened then? Was it very bloody?'

Murdoch shrugged. 'Dunno. I blacked out, Davie turned up with the cops and next thing I know I'm the local hero.'

'So he saved you again?'

'Who?'

'Davie. It seems like he's always saving you. Or helping you do things you can't do by yourself. The perfect sidekick, really.'

'Davie? That bollocks, he's useless.'

'Why on earth would you say that? Have you two fallen out?'

They'd reached Minter's tall back gate, Murdoch reaching over to find the bolt. If he didn't drink something soon he was going to faint.

'What makes you think we've fallen out?' he said.

'You said this morning you had no one else to talk to. I nearly asked you "What about Davie?" From what you've told me, he always been a good friend to you.'

Murdoch thought about it, then swore as the bolt slipped and pinched the skin on his finger. 'This bleeding gate,' he said. 'Just coming up your path, Mr Minter!'

Minter appeared on his deck above them, absurd in washing-up gloves.

'G'day, there. No problem, always happy to help you out, Mr Young!'

So Murdoch had to explain that to Suzie too.

# The Surrender

*Suzie Bourne talked on relentlessly. 'In The Revelation About One's Self,' she said, her eyes on Murdoch to be sure he was listening, 'the main character merely understands the mistakes they've made. But that's just the first step towards redemption. To really effect change, he or she has to be willing to adjust their way of thinking. And, of course, their way of behaving. If not, they won't survive.'*

### 46.

The heat made the news, forty-six degrees at one point, the hottest day on record. Loads of fuss about nothing, thought Murdoch, seeing as the records only went back a couple of hundred years. He stayed indoors and watched the Classics channel: an education in the stuff he'd heard about half his life. Sherlock Holmes and Doctor Watson, the Lone Ranger and Tonto, Batman and Robin, Crocket and Tubbs, Mulder and Scully. He thought he was safe with something called Nancy Drew, until she was helped out by the Hardy Boys. He gave up in the end and went to find his phone, lay on the sofa with it dead in his hand, wondering what he was supposed to say. Outside the day softened slowly, heavy silence giving way to birds and then a blackness full of insects. Eventually he got up, flicked on a few lights and rooted through drawers until he found a pad and pen. Leaning forwards from the sofa, he rested on the coffee table and wrote down a list of things to say and in what order. Phrases he could bear to use but would, he thought, still get the message across. He was on a version he didn't feel too embarrassed about when the phone – forgotten on the table beside the pad – vibrated and then rang at full volume, jarring in the half-lit room. Like Murdoch had thought about the call so much that the phone had rung Davie by itself. He stared at it for a second, then picked it up quickly before he could change his mind.

'Hello, Davie.'

'Bill, you won't believe this, listen—'

'No, Davie, you listen. I've been thinking and I want to say some stuff.'

'Can't it wait?' Davie was breathless, walking fast or just after a run.

'What? No, not really. It's important and I should of said it before now.' Murdoch picked up the list and leant back on the sofa. 'Listen, I've been a bit of a dickhead, haven't I? Got caught up in all that fancy stuff with that crowd; not Amanda, she was different, but the rest of them. I thought they was class and I'd be class hanging out with them. See, thing is, Davie, I grew up not having nothing like that and, well, it was like being on telly the whole time. I couldn't help it. It was like—'

'Oh Bill, you've not been drinking, have you?'

'No Davie, I haven't been bleeding well drinking. Listen will you, I want to say this.' Murdoch checked the paper in his hand. 'Them people, I thought they was my friends when really it's you what's been my friend ever since I moved up here and I've never told you it.'

'Told me what?'

'You're a good mate.'

'And?'

'And nothing. Just you're a good mate. And ...' Murdoch used his free hand to cover his eyes, then leant over sideways, the words contorting him until he was horizontal on the sofa. '... I'm sorry I wasn't always a good mate back. And, maybe it wasn't your fault. Any of what happened. I ... Maybe it was my fault.'

'And?'

'And I'm sorry. Really, I am, Davie.'

'That's all right, I forgive you. Now, listen, can I tell you what I phoned you about? I was working late tonight, trying to catch up on work stuff at last and, if I'm honest, not wanting to go home and start packing. Or just be at home at all because, well, you can imagine, and also, just the thought of where I'm going to put all that stuff! So not so much working late as house hunting online in the office really. Anyway, I came out about twenty minutes ago and I went down the beach, just for a walk, you know, because I've been inside all day and guess what I saw? There's a light on in James Harte's house! I'm walking up there now. Do you want to come and check it out?'

## 47

The night was utterly still, darkness smothered by heat, branches only moving under the claws of possums or between squabbling bats. Cicada sawmills worked in shifts, murmuring for minutes then revving up in waves, walls of sound washing across the car and irregularly softening away again. James Harte's house was silent and unlit.

'You said there was a bulb on,' said Murdoch.

He'd picked Davie up at the roundabout at the bottom of the hill and now they were whispering in the driveway opposite number thirty-four. They were being polite to each other, discussing recent events without talking about the awkward one. Davie didn't point out Murdoch was chain-smoking – either a cigarette or the lighter constantly orange between them – and Murdoch didn't comment on Davie's swollen nose. But after an hour of lengthening silences, Murdoch had to mention the obvious. The house they were watching appeared to be empty.

'There is a light on,' said Davie. 'It's at the back. I saw it from the beach. I double counted to be sure. We've just got to wait.'

'Right.'

Another silence, broken only Davie's restlessness. He was hatching an egg, not sure how to tell Murdoch about it.

'I went in there last week,' he said suddenly, excitement squeaking his voice.

'In where?'

'Harte's house.'

Murdoch took a deep drag on his Lucky, the heat from the tobacco competing with the air through the window. 'Oh yeah? How d'you manage that, then?'

'I found the keys in the office. We sold it for the previous owners. We always keep the keys in case the new owners want to rent it out, makes things easier as long as they come with us. Not that that was the case for Harte, of course, but, well, so few people ever think to change the locks. Crazy really.'

'You telling me you've got the keys to half the houses in Montauban?'

He saw Davie's silhouette wafting his smoke away, doing it gently so Murdoch wouldn't notice.

'I never thought of it that way before, but I suppose so, yeah. Anyway, I only remembered the other day and I thought what the hell. So I went in.'

'What d'you find?'

'Nothing. Not a bean.'

'Should of looked in the garage.'

'I did look in the garage. Nothing there either.'

Murdoch adjusted himself heavily in the leather seat and swore under his breath.

'What?' said Davie. 'Did I do something wrong?'

'No, I did. I'm an idiot. I'm sitting watching this place a week too late. Should of been up here every night since Amanda died.'

'Don't worry, I haven't noticed a light on here any other night.'

'Doesn't mean there's not been no one up here, though.'

Across the road, at the bottom of Harte's driveway, an anorexic fox appeared. It crossed the road, ribs and shoulder-blades clear through its skin, eyes huge and fearful, then dwindled into the dark again. Twenty minutes, thought Murdoch. No, thirty. Thirty minutes and it would be ten o'clock and he could politely tell Davie he'd made a mistake. It was almost that before either of them said another word, the car so quiet and dark that, when Davie suddenly spoke, Murdoch flinched.

'How've you been, Bill? About Amanda, I mean. You must have really liked her if you were willing to cover up about her driving a TT.'

'Listen, Davie, I wasn't going to let you lose your house to keep Amanda out of things. It wasn't like that. Still doesn't need to be.'

'That's not what I'm saying. I know you'd never do that. Hannah told me about your call, by the way.' Murdoch turned to look at him, but Davie's silhouette, shadow on shadow, was staring through the windscreen at the house over the road. 'I phoned her the other day to tell her I couldn't buy the house. I admit, I might have got a bit emotional. Anyway, she told me to calm down and stop packing, said you'd offered to buy it and pretend it was a gift from her.'

'She shouldn't of done that.'

'Crikey, Bill, you don't know her. She's so straight up and down. Just to let you know, though, I wouldn't have let you do that. I do have some pride.'

Murdoch couldn't think of anything polite to say to that, so they sat in darkness again for a while until Davie spoke again.

'I heard the funeral's on Monday. Do you want me to come?'

On the telly, when people were told they'd got cancer, everyone else's voices got muffled and the character could only hear what was in their heads. Or they developed tunnel vision, the screen blacking out around a tiny circle with the doctor's mouth talking in it. It was those things Murdoch thought about now, not the shock that he hadn't even thought about a funeral. The idea of what would happen if he went.

'Bill?'

'Yes, mate. I mean, no, you're all right. I didn't know it was on Monday, bit of a shock that's all. You don't need to come.'

'No, Bill, I mean look.'

Davie's hand appeared above the dashboard, a ghoulish shadow pointing across the road. A dull glow was pushing through the trees at the bottom of Harte's driveway. Murdoch crushed his cigarette into the ashtray and listened hard through the open window beside him. There was something less than silence beyond the cicadas, deep thuds and maybe a voice, all of it so dull and distant it could have come from anywhere. He rubbed his eyes and stared across the road, but there was nothing there, just darkness beyond the vaguely lamplit tarmac.

'There was something, wasn't there?' he said.

A whining garage door answered him, then the revving of an engine and the piercing white of headlights surprisingly high above them. Murdoch ducked sideways beside the gearstick, cracking heads with Davie who'd had the same idea. Neither of them complained or reeled away. They lay still, forcing their bodies into the small space below the level of the dashboard. Above them the interior of the Mercedes was swept with white light, not from one side to the other, but from bottom to top as the headlights descended the steep driveway and reached the road. As soon as all was dark again, Murdoch pushed against Davie and sat up. The car that had come out of James Harte's garage was almost at the bottom of the hill, at the small roundabout that led on to the shops and, right, to the steep road out of town. There were street lights down there, the junction a well-lit stage after the darkness they'd focused on for the last few hours. No way they could mistake the familiar make, model or colour of the car.

Even with his recent experience, Murdoch struggled to drive the Crown Road slowly enough. He kept telling himself he didn't need to see the Audi's gnts when he came around each corner, he could let it get a good kilometre ahead and still he couldn't lose it. But that wasn't strictly true. There was always the possibility the Audi would turn onto one of the dirt tracks that led down into the steep land either side of the road. Still, he resisted Davie beside him, having a period about why he wasn't going any faster, fidgeting silently or sighing loudly when they turned onto the straight stretch and saw how far ahead the red lights were. Murdoch decided on the speed limit: that's what a normal car would do, a car that wasn't following to find out who'd murdered Amanda. The Crown Road had never seemed so long, sixty kilometres an hour never so slow, but at last they rounded the curve outside the cemetery and the main Kildare Road came into view. This was where street lights started again and there sat the black Audi, waiting on its haunches for a gap in the traffic.

Now they had to keep closer, there were major junctions every few hundred metres. But there were more cars to shield them too, not to mention the night. Unless the driver of the Audi had already noticed them, they were just another pair of headlights.

'Two heads,' said Davie. 'There's two people in there. And in case you hadn't noticed, that's HH3, Emma Druitt's car.'

Murdoch hadn't noticed, but the next time they got close enough he saw. He had no idea what it meant. The roads grew brighter as they approached the outskirts of Crosley and then brighter still as they arrived in the city centre. Davie leant across and peered into the dashboard through the steering wheel.

'How far can you get on less than a quarter of a tank?'

Murdoch swore in answer and they had a stupid conversation about the pros and cons of filling up now and catching up with the Audi on the freeway or hoping the Audi would have to fill up too. Back and forth, repeating each other's arguments, both of them knowing the answer: as soon as they got past Crosley, they'd have to stop. But at Crosley football stadium, the Audi signalled right and surprised them both. Murdoch had no choice but to wait in the filter lane directly behind the car they were following. Neither of them spoke.

Now things were more difficult. Crosley after midnight on the hottest night of the year – even the zombies were indoors – and the driver of the Audi had nothing to look at but a pair of headlights in his or her rear-view mirror. So Murdoch turned left, left, and left again: only forty seconds before they were back on their original road, but long enough for the Audi to have disappeared. Davie had his phone out, scrolling through maps, tapping at the screen like he was sending Morse code.

'Try the train station,' he said.

'Why?'

'I don't know. There's nothing—'

He was cut short by the sudden brakes and violent reversing of the Mercedes. Murdoch had crossed a junction and spotted the Audi down to the left.

'Got it,' he said.

Davie's guess had been good. The black car was at a side entrance to the train station and a man was climbing out.

## 48.

The train was bored and playing a game, swaying its passengers towards sleep and then, from nowhere, juddering hard to keep them awake. It was the last train of the night: the train of the lucky or the desperate, no one in the freezing carriages complaining about their overblown response to the heat outside. No one but Murdoch. He sat rubbing at his arms and legs, changing seats twice in a vain attempt to escape the air conditioning, not caring what the other passengers thought. There were six of them in the carriage. Two old blokes, cheerily merry, discussing a football game in a conversation that dwindled as the late hour and their late age caught up with them. Further away, at the back of the carriage where Murdoch couldn't hear, was a wiry and wired couple, skin too bad for the harsh lights, scowls etched into their mouths. They were arguing, only the swear words audible: 'facking this' and 'facking that' interrupted by the clatter of the tracks. Closer, two rows away from Murdoch and facing him, was the guy he'd followed onto the train. Eighteen or nineteen, hair short at the sides and long on top, lively eyes and strangely dark lips, like he'd been drinking red wine or kissing too hard. He sat between headphones staring at the screen in his hands, the reflected colours of a pop video lighting his face as he nodded slightly and mouthed

281

to the tune. He looked up, caught Murdoch looking at him, held his gaze a second too long, then went back to his phone.

Murdoch rubbed his arms again and swore to himself. He should have let Davie follow the kid. It wasn't like Davie hadn't wanted to, whining it had been his idea about the train station and him who'd spotted the light in the house in the first place. Like this was a game and it was his turn to go first. Murdoch, knowing Davie wouldn't even have the money for a ticket, had just walked away, even then barely making the train in time. So now it was him freezing his bollocks off. He stood, ignoring the kid's soft glance, and walked unsteadily up and down the carriage, past the game talk and the argument and back, until he found an abandoned newspaper. Back in his seat, he spread it over his bare legs, rubbed the back of his neck and tried to remember how long it would be before they got to Sydney. He was sure the kid would drag him that far: he was the kind they got down there. Hanging around the train stations or probably just online these days.

At Koolewong, the arguing couple got off. Murdoch opened the closest door and stood there until the last minute, trying to breathe in warmth from the night. At Woy Woy, he did the same thing as one of the old blokes said goodbye to his mate, all handshakes and repeated jokes, squeezing the last fun from their evening. There were people waiting on the platform at Woy Woy, but noticing Murdoch's scars and stares, they chose other carriages to freeze in. Three down, one to go. The doors beeped and hissed and the train moved on, the air conditioning ramping up in excitement. Murdoch thought about jumping the dark-lipped kid there and then, pummelling him in public, getting his answer and leaving. What could one old man do about it? Nothing, apart from call the police on his mobile, pull the cord and stop the train, film it and get Murdoch done for GBH. So he waited – another two stops, opening the doors at Hawkesbury River and Cowan to breathe in the warmth. The rest of the time he just stared at the angular graffiti etched into the plastic seats or at a can of Mother that was rolling back and forth across the aisle. Anywhere but at his reflection.

They were at Hornsby before the old bloke left them alone. Murdoch forced himself to wait another two minutes, looking down through the shifting carriages to make sure no one was walking up the train. Once sure, he crossed the aisle quickly and pushed the kid's arm behind his back.

He was even younger than Murdoch had thought: young and light, no resistance in him at all. It was like forcing yourself on a girl and Murdoch recoiled from what he had to do. Even then the kid didn't take advantage, didn't shout out or elbow back with his free arm, didn't give a well-aimed kick and leg it. He was a boy used to not resisting, to giving up easily and escaping with minimum damage.

'Back pocket,' he said, his mouth struggling against plastic. 'It's all I've got apart from some coins.'

A fold of yellow notes was sticking out of the denim stretched across his arse, a price on what it covered.

'I don't want your money.'

The kid looked surprised and caught Murdoch's eye.

'Well, at least put a condom on,' he said.

Murdoch let go of him quickly and gave him a hard smack across the back of the head. Then train jerked suddenly and he had to reach to the seat across the aisle to stay upright. Any kind of fighter would have used that, kicking him hard in the stomach or the groin. The kid just cowered in his seat, tiny in its corner so Murdoch had to struggle again not to see his reflection towering over him.

'Where have you been tonight?'

'Out. With a mate. Nowhere.'

Murdoch slapped him hard across the face and the kid put his thin arms up too late and started crying. Murdoch pushed him down into the seat again and bent down so his mouth was next to the kid's ear.

'I'm going to cut you up if you don't start talking soon.'

'Montauban,' sniffled the boy. 'It's near Crosley.'

'Who with?'

'I don't know his full name. No, please! I really don't, Oscar something. We call him Clockwork.'

'We?'

'Me and a friend, the other boys. He likes to ...'

'How often?'

'Every week. Once a week, every Thursday. He never misses one, not even Christmas or New Year or Easter or anything. That's why we call him Clockwork. That, and the way he ...'

'Spare me the details. How long has this been going on?'

Three years at least.'

'You what?! How old are you?'

The kid looked up at Murdoch with huge eyes, the calculation clear in his face. How much could he get away with?

'Seventeen,' he said. 'I was fourteen when we started ... it was in ...'

He was so frightened he couldn't remember, stuttering backwards as he worked out the year. The train jerked again and started slowing. Murdoch got off him and went and stood by the door.

'I know where you live,' he shouted across the empty carriage. 'You get off the game or I'll tell your parents what you're up to.'

He thought he'd frightened him before, but now the kid went pale. His dark lips started quivering and tears welled in his eyes again.

'I will,' he said. 'Promise.'

'I mean it. I'll tell your parents. But only once I've cut your pretty lips off.'

The train jolted to a stop at a brutally lit platform, but the doors didn't open. Instead, Murdoch had to stand looking at his feet, listening to the kid sniffle and tidy himself up for two whole minutes until there was another jolt and at last the door button lit up. Murdoch jabbed at it and stepped into the heat, scowling into the train until it pulled the kid away into the night. Which left him alone, no idea where he was and, for the first hour or so, thinking he'd found out nothing more than Oscar Druitt was a bender. But at three in the morning, a freight train rumbled into his dreams and woke him up, stiff on a platform bench. Truck after truck after truck: millions of tonnes of something on the way to somewhere else. And accompanying it, until it was louder than the passing train, the sound of pennies beginning to drop.

# The Battle

*'Like I said,' Murdoch explained again. 'It wasn't a full-on battle. It was mostly just the two of us, scrapping down there in the garden.'*

*'Yes, and like I said, in a story The Battle isn't always a big fight. It doesn't have to be a physical fight at all. It just has to be the vital conflict. It's the penultimate scene normally, the thing everything else has been leading to. The main character – that's you, in this case – gets to face his opponent. Gloves off and everyone spills the beans, if you'll excuse the mixed metaphor.' She turned to look out at his garden, then looked back excitedly. He could tell she'd been picturing the violence. 'What was I saying? Oh yes, The Battle is the culmination of everything that's happened so far, the point the whole plot has been leading to. In a detective novel, it's the big revelation, where we find out "whodunit". Traditionally, you gather everyone in a room so all the characters can be present, although I don't suspect anyone does that any more.'*

### 49.

The temperature didn't fall below thirty degrees all night and the coast woke late and groggy, ill-equipped to take in the morning news. Bush fires had killed people across three states; there were blackouts and brownouts, pensioners dropping by the dozen. Davie, whistling a half-remembered tune, started waving at Natalie as soon as she was around the corner, as if she could miss him in the doorway of the police station.

'I looked for you all along the Crown Road,' he shouted out to her. 'I thought you rode in from Montie?'

She stared at him in silence until she was a metre away.

'Thanks, Davie,' she said. 'Now the whole of Crosley knows where I live. By the way, I don't know if anyone's told you, but it's going to be forty-three degrees today. Not exactly cycling weather.' She spotted his misshapen nose. 'Jesus, what happened to you?'

'How about I tell you over coffee?'

She checked her watch, told him she had to go into work, took her sunglasses off and looked at him more carefully.

'Nasty that. What do you want?'

285

' to talk to you. It's about the case; good news. Let's go and grab
..ee.'

'You do realise it's eight in the morning, don't you? You sure you've got
the right end of the day? I've never seen you out of bed before ten.'

But today Davie could resist anything. 'There's a place round the corner
that doesn't look too bad. You could go into the station, tell them where you
are and then there won't be a problem, will there? Come on, I'll buy you a
full fry-up.'

It was a Chinese-run place called The Flying Pan; funny if you thought
about it. Black and white tiles and fifties-style counters, cleaned to within an
inch of its life. The girl behind the counter greeted Natalie by name,
commented on the heat and found them a table at the back. Davie,
instructed by Murdoch to make sure he had some cash on him for once,
winced at the prices.

'Licence to print money this place,' said Natalie, squeezing into a booth.
'Only nice café in the centre of town. It won't last. Someone'll put a brick
through that window and they'll get sick of replacing it. Then they'll go up
the mall like everyone else.'

Davie let her complain about the local council and their lack of planning,
waiting until she'd drained her first flat white before he let her bring him to
the point.

'The thing is, Nat, we need your help.'

'Ha! Well, that figures. The answer's no, of course, but go on, make
me laugh.'

The waitress brought their food and Davie fell silent long enough for
Natalie to roll her eyes. When he started talking again he was hunched
forward in a whisper.

'We've solved the case. Well, Bill did. We both did. Anyway, we know
who killed Charlie Holland and why. And Amanda Hoxton. It's so
obvious really ...'

He told her everything. About the party at the Hilton, Oscar Druitt and
the rent boys, Harte punching him and firing them. Then, despite
Murdoch's strict instructions to the contrary, he told her about the visit to
Jennifer Bailey, how they'd each entered James Harte's house, about the
Audi garage on the Parramatta Road. Davie had known Natalie all his life,
she'd need more than a coffee and a free fried brekkie. It had to be a

confession, information only she was privy to. He let her interrupt with details of the laws they'd broken and the sentences they might get – he'd known in advance this would be the price – let her tell him when to go on and when to stop so she could think, for God's sake. He let her draw her conclusions aloud and explain them to him, as if Murdoch hadn't explained them down the phone already and again outside Epping station. He let her explain how little things now made sense, but how it was all circumstantial evidence, nothing solid enough for a conviction. He was telling her about trading while insolvent when she interrupted him, knife and fork upright in her hands, half her food still untouched.

'Where *is* Bill, Davie? Why isn't he telling me this himself?'

'I don't know. Down in Sydney somewhere, matter of life and death apparently. Nothing to do with the case.'

'And yet again you believe that.'

The waitress came back, wanting to know if they needed more coffee. Davie smiled 'yes', but it was too late: she had already caught Natalie's expression and was backing away.

'Yes, I do believe that,' he sighed. 'I trust Bill completely.'

Natalie spotted the remains of a sausage, speared it and tore it off her fork with her teeth. 'You should choose your friends more wisely.'

'Crikey, Nat, I don't know what you've got against Bill, but you've really got to get over it. He's not a bad person. What does he have to do to prove that to you?'

'Nothing. He can't. You can't just do away all the bad things you've done in your life by doing some good ones later on. It doesn't work that way.' She didn't sound convinced at her own argument, so Davie let her chew on it and swallow it, leaving her in silence until she said, 'So what's the plan?'

He told her the plan.

'Oh Davie, are you serious? Even if I could convince the Sydney murder squad not to throw you two inside for impersonating public prosecutors, the first thing they're going to do is drag everyone in and question them on your theories. It's not Hercule bloody Poirot.'

'We need a confession.'

'Too right, we need a bloody confession.'

'Which is only possible if Bill's there. Without him there, I don't think—'

287

'I'm not disagreeing with that,' Natalie snapped. 'I'm just saying the force aren't going to send out a load of officers to make an arrest just in case someone ends up confessing to a double murder. Even if they believe you, they'll have to follow procedure. Arrests, lawyers, the works.'

'That's what Bill said you'd say.'

She gave him a sour look, ripped off a corner of toast and used it to chase egg yolk around her plate. 'And what did he tell you to say when I said it?'

'He said to tell you about Plan B.'


## 50.


Murdoch too ate a full fried breakfast. He forced it down with coffee, knowing from experience he had to eat no matter what his stomach said. He'd called Davie too soon. He should have waited an hour for the first train to Crosley, then taken a taxi from there to Montauban. He could have showered and changed into clean clothes, sauntered over to Davie's and broken the news to him there. He'd still have had time to get to Canterbury before the pubs opened. The only thing was, he was worried he'd lose his nerve. So he'd made Davie drive his Merc down to Epping, leave it there with him and catch the train back to Crosley. Then, itchy with grubbiness, he'd driven himself the rest of the way south. Now he sat in a café that reminded him of England – cold, dirty, stinking of fat – and stared at three hours waiting ahead of him. Three hours to not think about what he had to do. He bought a paper and read it cover to cover, changing cafés three times, checking his watch every time he turned the page. Done with the paper, he bought a magazine, flipping through it fast and scowling at the pictures. The images were ridiculous to him now. He found a story about Melissa Munday and whether she was pregnant opposite an advert for the new series of *Society*. He couldn't believe he'd ever fallen for it. The watches, the cars, the brands and identities competing for his money. It was nothing but a con. He got to the end of the magazine, turned it over and started again.

Later, he sat and stared through another café's windows as the rush hour grew and grew, everyone impatient to get somewhere they didn't want to be. He watched cars cut each other up, buses leave late runners behind, people on the pavement pass too close without even seeing each other. He'd forgotten what the city did to people, how too many humans in one place made humans less human to each other. It reminded him of the animals and suddenly he realised what was bothering him. It wasn't the idea of what he was planning for Hussein – fuck that lard-arse, he had it coming – it was the idea of who he had to deal with to make it happen. The Bill Murdoch he'd become had escaped that world and, even at this distance, it smelled disgusting to him now.

He was almost back at his car when he saw Hussein on the other side of the crossroads, leaning against the pub. Murdoch had seen him do this before, but it was a shock all the same. Like somehow the fat man had worked out what he was up to and was waiting for him, phone in hand, ready to call the man he'd threatened him with. Henry Wallis, whoever that was. But Hussein was just playing a game or sending a text or doing whatever it was he did that took up his attention each morning until magically – no hands, no greeting, just a slowly opening door – the pub opened for business. Murdoch made a note of the time, leant against his car and forced himself to wait a full ten minutes. It was already too hot to be standing out of the shade, he could feel the sweat forming on his forehead and across the back of his shoulders. but he waited until the hands on his watch told him he could move. Then he spat into the gutter and walked slowly to the busy intersection. He waited for a gap – why did they call it rush hour when it went on half the day? – crossed and stepped into the pub.

From the entrance to the badly lit VIP room, Hussein looked like a cheap toy you'd win at a fair. He was at the last pokie machine in a row of four, perched on a stool, his huge folds covering the seat so only the thick metal rod was visible. Murdoch thought of Andy Arthur at the races, shocked at how recently he'd lived in that world: parties and invitations and thinking those people liked him. Prison felt more recent than that. Hussein was eating peanuts, dipping one hand repeatedly into a large bowl with *'Free for patrons'* printed on the side then sliding them lazily into his mouth. With his other hand, he was feeding coins into the machine, reflections of cherries and numbers swirling across his brow and cheeks. A ray of sunshine had broken into the room, hitting the wall behind Hussein and lighting up half of a gambling helpline poster, reflecting *'bling help'* and blurring everything else.

'Hello, Ibrahim.'

Hussein pulled his attention away from the spinning wheels, dusted some crumbs off his dirty shirt and pushed himself straighter on the stool.

'Mr Murdoch, how nice to see you.' It was still strange to match the menacing voice to this wreck of a body. In the old days, Hussein had had some form about him.

'You better be here with my money,' he said.

Murdoch crossed the garish carpet in two steps and gave Hussein a few left jabs to the head, his right hand all over him. The fat man was taken by surprise, any fighting instincts too deeply buried, and by the time he pushed Murdoch off – stumbling him backwards into the next pokie machine to set it rocking gently in the dim light – his ear and nose were darker than the rest of his face.

'What the fuck you doing, Murdoch?'

'Just reminding you of what it feels like to get punched. Wanted to lay my hands on you before I lost the chance. Didn't you used to box? What weight category would you be in now? Super-fat bastard?'

'What the fuck? Do I have to remind you about my friend with the letter?'

'You don't have a friend with a letter. You don't have a friend, except maybe your mate at the races. You don't even have a life. You just walk between your house, four doors up there, and here. When you're not there, you're here. When you're not here, you're there. No one ever visits you, no one talks to you, no one even sees you, what, given your size, is a fucking miracle. You're just a big black hole, Hussein. The chances of you knowing a lawyer are less than you knowing what muesli is.'

Hussein told him to fuck off, but that's all he said. He sat dusting himself down, unable to hold Murdoch's eye, pulling his shirt straight until Murdoch got nervous and started walking away before it was too late. When he looked back Hussein was touching his nose carefully with one hand, the next already poised to put another coin in the machine.

Outside, the day was blinding and loud. It felt five degrees warmer than when Murdoch had entered the pub and he could feel the night spent on the platform: the tight tug of his T-shirt, the stench from his armpits, a layer of dirt all over. The mate at the races was the risk he could do nothing about. If Hussein knew him, who knew who else he might really know? He blinked and forced himself to focus. This might not be a fail-safe plan, but it was the only one he had. He hurried around the corner into the street that ran off

290

the crossroads opposite the one he'd parked in: a hill running down between thickly parked cars. There was no doorway to hide in, so he squatted between a grey Fiat and a dirty old Suzuki, the traffic noise from the main road suddenly dulled. He pulled out the phone he'd lifted from Hussein's breast pocket and started working it out, his fingers awkward on the tiny buttons as he looked for the stored number. It wasn't easy. Hussein had spelled Henry as *'Hemry'*, Wallis with a 'V'. But Murdoch found it at last; no need to panic, stay calm, concentrate. He coughed and practised his voice, ignored the sound of feet on the pavement beside him, coughed again and dialled the number. Across the road, a mother was dragging a small girl up towards the crossroads. The girl, pausing between a car and a van, spotted Murdoch and pulled at her mother's hand. The mother shouted and pulled her on. The phone was answered on the first ring.

'Yes?'

'Mr Wallis?'

'Who is this?'

'Mr Henry Wallis? My name's Ibrahim Hussein. You don't know me.'

'What do you want?'

'The question is what do *you* want? Do you want to stay out of jail? Do you want me to keep my mouth shut even though I know how your operation runs, where it comes in and where it goes out? How much you turn over every month?'

Silence. Murdoch forced himself to wait. No matter what happened now, even if Hussein found him squatting there between the cars on his phone, he just had to wait. He knew what Wallis would be doing; he'd seen it done. He'd be signalling someone, or maybe turning on the software himself. When Wallis spoke again, his voice trembled with something. Anger or concentration maybe. Not fear.

'Well, Mr Hussein, if you want to do business we should meet.'

'Forget it. I want two hundred thou' in cash in two days' time or you're going down. I'll call you back to tell you where.'

Murdoch hung up, deleted the most recently dialled number, and stood shakily. There was the traffic noise, the sun hot on the back of his neck, the world going along normally like nothing had happened. He rubbed his hand across his scalp, wiped his face with his T-shirt, and headed back to the pub. This time Hussein saw him coming. He couldn't get off his seat quickly enough but he did deflect the approach with a defensive left across his own face and strong right hook towards Murdoch's. Murdoch ducked but couldn't avoid it entirely. An ugly signet ring on Hussein's little finger caught him beside his left eye and jarred him with pain. Still, he stayed in close, right elbow above his head as he slipped Hussein's phone back into the breast pocket of the shirt. Like he was trying to get in close and work the fat man's ribs; like anyone would bother looking for them. The ribs that got punished were Murdoch's – Hussein still had strength under there somewhere – until the fat man took him by the shoulders and pushed him away.

'Get off me!' he shouted, a weakness in his voice Murdoch hadn't heard before. 'Fuck off and leave me alone.'

'I know where you live too, you fat bastard. You've got nothing on me I haven't got on you.'

'Leave me alone.'

Hussein was sulking, no argument left in him. Murdoch didn't want to see it. He wanted Hussein greedy and dangerous: vermin needing removal. He opened his mouth but said nothing. Turned instead and, as requested, left the fat man alone. He didn't want to be there when the call came in.

Back at the Merc he checked his reflection. The cut beside his eye was pumping steadily, a thick line of red down his cheek and neck, attacking the collar of his T-shirt. He rifled through the boot looking for a towel or some tissues trying not to think of that last image of Hussein. The beaten-up loser who nobody loved. He'd be happy enough in a minute or two, but it wouldn't last. It would be a woman who called. Lucky Hussein would have won a competition or inherited some money or, better if they knew their man, he'd be due some benefits he hadn't been paid. Anything to keep him on the phone.

In the boot of the Mercedes Murdoch found a tennis sock. He pressed it against his head and climbed into his baking car, buzzing down the windows and forcing himself to wait and watch without the comfort of air conditioning. The whole thing took less than an hour. A tall bloke in a suit too nice for the neighbourhood wandered into view along the main road, looking up at each house before spotting the pub on the corner. He was in and out again in under a minute. Big bloke, part Aboriginal, kind of bloke who could move fast and stop you moving even faster. He looked around and across the road, down the street where Murdoch was parked. But Murdoch had done the same: he knew he was invisible if he didn't move. Off the bloke walked again, lost from view, but in a minute, he was back, taking instructions down the phone by the look of it. He hung up, dialled a number and then was back into the pub again. Murdoch, staring hard at the open pub door, saw him cross from the bar towards the VIP room, like he was trying to find the source of a noise. A second later, there he was on the pavement again, waiting like a man on a date, checking his watch and looking casual. Within ten minutes a big black van had blocked Murdoch's view.

Murdoch had looked forward to this bit. He'd thought he might get close so he could listen to Hussein's screams of protest. *'No, no, a dead man stole my phone and pretended to be me!'* Now he was happy to stay put, pushing the dirty sock against his wound, suffering in the direct sun. It was difficult enough to see the van wobble as something heavy was forced into it, the doors slammed shut, the big man in the nice suit joining the others in the front before it sped away. It was like watching the telly on with the sound down, not wanting to look, but not being able to turn away. He waited two minutes, then forced himself back across the road. The VIP room was empty but for a trail of coins and peanuts across the sticky carpet.


51.


St Mark's Church was a sharp, stone building: a little piece of England on a corner of prime real estate. Murdoch arrived there showered, shaven and in an outfit bought head to toe less than an hour before. The wound on his head was less well-dressed: a botch job by a chemist who'd made him promise to get some stitches as soon as his wedding was over. She was young and Indian and enthusiastic, so excited about the wedding story he soon wished he'd chosen another lie. What was the bride's name? What did she look like? She was sure they'd be very happy together. He should have told her he was going to a funeral.

The hearse was a shock he wasn't ready for. It sat empty ahead of the limousines parked in front of the church. Despite all the chemist's questions, he'd forgotten Amanda would be there too. He'd parked in the church's shadow, but now, at the reminder of Amanda's dead body, he

293

leant forward to turn the key in the ignition again. Davie could look after things for once. But there Davie was, tapping at his window, with Natalie crossing the road behind him. She was in uniform, never her best look, especially not on a day as hot as today: a tomboy in a polyester skirt. She signalled he should stay in the car, then walked round and climbed into the passenger seat, while Davie got in the back, the warm air piling in with them.

'Bloody hell, Bill.' Natalie was looking at his bandage. 'What happened to you this time?'

'Accident.'

'Well, I'm sure you deserved it. You ready?'

When he didn't answer, Davie leant forward and put a hand on his shoulder. 'You all right, Bill?'

'I'm fine. What we waiting for?'

As if in response, a Black Maria appeared in his wing mirror, filling it slowly until it crept past, turned left and parked beside the church. First out was a uniform, standing to one side almost as respectfully as James Harte, no handcuffs, climbed down and stood beside him. Murdoch was surprised. In all his conversations with Davie (now lying flat in the back of the car), Murdoch had imagined the man from the magazines. Tanned, fit, so good-looking, you had to admit it. This was a man with the air taken out: a skinhead with skin hanging like sadness. Murdoch thought about what prison had done to Hussein and wondered if all the weight evened out somehow; what he himself would have looked like if he'd had a life before he went inside.

'Wow, he's had all his hair cut off!' Davie was peeking between the front seats. 'Do you think he's gone religious or something?'

'Only two haircuts in prison,' said Murdoch. 'Razor cut or no cut.'

'Can't trust anyone with scissors,' said Natalie.

Murdoch looked at her. He hadn't thought she'd know that. A plain-clothes something – copper or screw, it wasn't clear – followed Harte out of the van. He said something, Harte nodded and they all walked into the church, passing two men at the door.

'Who's that?'

'Big one's private security,' said Natalie. 'Davie, for goodness sake, you can sit up now. The family were worried about press, apparently. Or rubberneckers. It's an invitation-only event. That's why I'm in uniform; we don't want anyone asking who I am.'

'And the other one.'

He was a short bald man, fit in a suit that had seen too many funerals. He might as well have been in a uniform himself.

'Mate of mine from Sydney detectives. Unofficially, though, OK? He's staying outside. This doesn't work and neither of us were here. But if it does, I thought we could use an extra pair of hands.'

'All of the credit, none of the blame. Sounds about right.'

'Natalie didn't have to come,' said Davie from the back seat. 'Did you, Nat?'

'No, I didn't, this isn't even my patch. And I don't have to stay either. Maybe me and DC Cohen should go home right now?'

'No.' Murdoch found his fingers were on Natalie's sleeve. 'Please, I need you here. Both of you.'

She stared at him open-mouthed before her face softened in something like sympathy.

'Say that again.'

He snorted, told her to dream on and got out of the car.

The church was smaller inside than he'd thought, not much more than a dozen pairs of pews between tall stone pillars. Only the first few rows were occupied. Murdoch thought he spotted Angus's curly hair down near the front. He'd be there somewhere; they all would: it was a social event after all. Murdoch sat next to Davie in the empty pew nearest the church door and found himself staring down the aisle at the coffin, clear and dark against the altar. He tried not to think about Amanda being in there but, for the second time that morning, found he couldn't look away from the thing he didn't want to see. He tried to focus on the flowers on its top: a simple bunch of lilies, the kind of thing Amanda would have chosen herself. Who would have organised that? Surely not Emma Druitt? His view was interrupted by Natalie walking slowly down the aisle and then bending to speak to someone in the front pew. When she walked back up, the plain-clothes man from the Black Maria was beside her. The two of them stood in the light from the door, whispering back and forth, Murdoch turning to watch them so his back was to anyone else doing the same. The man from the van was frowning, looking doubtful, shaking his head. Murdoch turned towards the altar again, leaning forward with his hands over his face like a man deep in prayer.

'I don't think I can do this.'

'What?' Davie had never been the best of whisperers. 'What do you mean?'

'I didn't think she'd be lying there. I thought, I dunno. She's in there, Davie. She's right there. She'd think this was … inappropriate.'

He felt Davie wrap one of his long arms around him. It was claustrophobic and stuck his damp shirt against his shoulders, but he let the arm stay there for a minute or two before shrugging it off and wiping his palms on his trousers.

'You'll have to do it, Davie. Sorry, mate.'

'What?!'

The man from the Black Maria strode past them, shoes echoing on the hard tiles, and took his place in the distant front pew again. He didn't look happy. Then Natalie took a pew across the aisle and it was the hospital waiting room all over again, the last memory he needed.

'Now,' she said.

'You what?'

'You've got to do it now, Bill. Before the service. They won't keep him back for a second afterwards.'

'But I can't.'

'Get up there!'

It was all in whispers, but so furious that some of the closer mourners turned to look. No one Murdoch recognised.

'I can't do it. Not with her there.'

Natalie stood, maybe about to leave, but before she could Davie pushed past Murdoch into the aisle. He strode to the front, arriving at the coffin just as a vicar in billowing robes appeared in a doorway to one side.

'I'm sorry to disturb you, ladies and gentlemen,' said Davie, his voice light and echoing amongst the high-ceilinged stone. 'But I need to make an announcement. My name is Davie Simms and, I … er … I'm in a position to say who killed Amanda Hoxton. As you are her closest family, I thought you should know first. And … well, I'm going to tell you who killed Charlie Holland too, so James here can get out of prison.'

The effect on the congregation was immediate. Either side of the aisle, mourners who had been bent and hushed started talking and turning and adjusting themselves. Murdoch wouldn't have been surprised if they'd started throwing things or rushing forward as one to grab Davie and throw him out of the church. He was reminded of the scene at Huntingdon's: a crowd about to get ugly.

'This is outrageous!' Oscar Druitt, in the front row across the aisle from Harte and his minders, was on his feet. 'This is completely outrageous.'

'Shut up, Oscar, and sit down.'

James Harte had stood too and, although he was speaking calmly, his voice was more powerful than his brother-in-law's. Oscar sat immediately and everyone else fell quiet too, waiting to hear what else Harte had to say. It was like he had something over them. Like, even sad and shorn, he was a man you had to obey. Then Harte turned and looked to the back of the church, looked at Murdoch sitting there and Murdoch felt it too. The man was so confident you'd have to be an idiot not to agree with him. At a single tug on his sleeve from the uniform beside him, Harte sat down again.

'Yes,' said Davie, hands twisting at each other: a five-year-old confessing a crime. 'You see, unfortunately, the killer is here in the church with us and … Oh, first I should tell you how we found out. I mean, how we know who it was …'

Murdoch swore under his breath, apologised to Amanda or God or maybe Hussein and – an act from nowhere – crossed himself before standing and walking down the aisle. Angus was the first to see him. He was sitting directly behind James Harte, next to the brunette from Christmas Eve. He stood and tried squeezing past her.

'You bastard!' he shouted. 'You killed her, I knew it.'

Before Angus could get any further, the heavy from the van, the one who'd consulted with Natalie, turned and pushed him heavily into his seat.

'Shut it, you muppet,' said Murdoch. 'I didn't kill her and you know it. Why would the police come in here now with me, if it was me what done it?' On cue, half the mourners turned and looked behind them. Natalie was staring furiously at Murdoch. 'They've brought me in cos I'm the only one what can prove it.'

Angus continued to stare poisonously, but Murdoch could see he was curious. Everyone else was curious too, all of them staring and waiting to hear. The Hoxtons and the Hartes, a red-eyed Benny Robbins and his wife, Phoebe, beside him, Henderson and Smith from the cricket, even Peter Christensen from Huntingdon's. Murdoch blinked and looked up to the distant curves of stone above him, no idea what to say next. He knew he had less than a minute before they turned against him too. Then the vicar stepped forward and said something soft in a vicary tone, a gentle hand at Murdoch's elbow. Murdoch shrugged him off.

'Davie's right,' he said. 'The killer's here now. Confident, you see; convinced they've got away with it; thinking they're too clever and too careful to get caught. Trouble is, they're *too* clever, *too* careful.'

He looked around, finding the right faces in the crowd, forcing himself to focus.

'So I'd like to start with asking Emma Druitt a few questions.'

Half the congregation shuffled again, looking around to see where she was, whispering back and forth. Then Emma herself looked up, like she'd missed everything till now, surprised to see people looking at her.

'Me?' she said, eyes wide. 'What do you want from me?'

'You had a private detective put on me, didn't you?' Murdoch said it louder than he'd meant to, competing with the mutterings from the pews. 'You got someone to follow me and work out who I was. Why would you do that?'

As he stepped backwards, turning so he could talk to Emma Druitt but face the others, the corner of Amanda's coffin prodded him in his lower back. His mind went blank again. What was he doing here, in this old church talking to people who'd never believe? Harte was staring at him, eyes bright but narrowed.

'Why shouldn't she?' Oscar barked. 'We all wondered who the hell you were, turning up out of nowhere and pretending to be a friend of James. As if James would have anyone like you for a friend! Emma suggested the idea of a private detective to me and I agreed it was a good idea.'

The joke of this woke Murdoch up. 'Yeah, nice one, Oscar. Very loyal of you, mate. But I don't think anyone who's ever met the two of you is gonna believe Emma's ever asked your opinion in her life.'

Murdoch felt Davie shift nervously beside him, a man who knew when he was losing an audience. 'Get on with it, Bill.'

'And anyway, Oscar, what you don't realise is Emma knew who I was all the time. I wasn't supposed to know that. I was supposed to think it was just Amanda and James who knew about me being a detective. But Amanda let it slip the first time I met her. She said, "My sister-in-law and I had difficulty finding you." And then all the boxes of financial data arrived and Amanda was supposed to have got us all that info without Emma knowing about it? You must have been so tempted to hide the info about the early years, Emma, but you're too smart for that, aren't you? You knew it would look dodgy if anything was missing, so you sent too much info instead. But you know your trouble, Emma? You like people to know you're smart. So, the first time you met me, on the terrace at Benny Robbins's place, you slipped up. You asked me if I was looking for Montauban, showing off how clever you are. But why would you ask me about Montie, if you didn't know who I was and where I lived? And let me guess, James, you didn't know about the second detective neither. Did you, James?'

Harte hesitated a second too long. 'Why shouldn't she hire someone else?'

'What for? What would make her so nervous?'

'The fact that you were sleeping with his wife.' Emma Druitt said it slowly and clearly, unashamed of her surroundings. One or two of the mourners murmured to each other, the few who hadn't known.

'Which someone went and told James,' said Murdoch, 'to get us fired off the case as soon as they could. But without your detective, you wouldn't have known about it neither, so that can't be why you hired him. No, what made you nervous was the idea that we might find something else out. And then we did start finding stuff out, didn't we? Like the way you was buying Angus out of the company. You can thank Davie here for that. He might not look much but he's a whizz on the old facts and figures, he is. See, I reckon James here didn't know about that neither. Did you, James?'

Harte sat motionless and Murdoch could see him thinking, that flame in his eyes Davie had always gone on about.

'Nah, I didn't think so. Cos you knew Angus couldn't be trusted with money. You knew he'd drink it or snort it or gamble it away in weeks. Isn't that right?'

'How dare you.'

This from Angus himself, but said to his hands like he didn't want to look up and see everyone agreeing it was true. Murdoch ignored him.

'That's why you never bought him out, isn't it, James? Because he's your mate and you wanted to protect him from himself. Give him the smallest salary you could. But Emma here doesn't care about that. All she cares about is the business, isn't that right, Emma?'

She rolled her eyes at Murdoch's stare. 'Are we here for a business meeting? A discussion of the merits of our various directors? I think we've all had enough of this nonsense. This is a funeral, for goodness sake. James?'

But Harte wouldn't look at her. He pulled at his shirt cuffs, caught himself doing it and gripped his knees instead. Murdoch saw there were tiny flecks of hair stuck to his neck, he must have had his hair shorn that morning. Angus, behind him, was sobbing quietly, the brunette rubbing his back as she glowered at Murdoch.

'Enough!' Oscar Druitt was on his feet again, hands on hips, the only sensible chap in the room. 'None of this is relevant to how Amanda died. It doesn't make sense. You're deranged, Murdoch.'

'Bang on, Oscar. It doesn't explain who killed Amanda, but it does show how much your wife cares about that agency, don't it? She'll do anything to keep it alive, won't you, Emma? You've got no loyalty to nothing but the business. And anyone what gets in the way, well, it's just rubbish disposal, innit? "Trash." That's what you called Charlie Holland. Trash what was blackmailing you, unfortunately. Trash what told Jennifer Bailey about it. Except Jennifer misunderstood, she thought Charlie was blackmailing James here.'

Silence. Davie shifted his weight from one foot to the other and, for a second, Murdoch thought it was all over. No one was going to confess.

'Blackmailing me about what?' said Harte.

His voice was loud and clear amongst the echoes of the church, impossible to say who it was questioning. The rest of the congregation had held its breath. Emma Druitt shrugged her shoulders, concentrating on the tissue in her hands, so it was up to Murdoch to answer.

'Blackmailing you about the fact that, just after you floated the company, you was trading while insolvent.'

He hadn't admitted to either Natalie or Davie how much of this was a guess. He couldn't remember the evening at the Hilton too well, but he remembered Emma Druitt's reaction to his words that night. The way the blood had drained from her face. Now, he watched James Harte turn in his seat, adjusting himself to look at his sister. But Emma Druitt raised her eyebrows and shook her head, no idea what this madman was talking about.

'Trouble is,' said Murdoch, 'Jennifer Bailey's phone.'

Again, the awkward silence, the pressure to prove he wasn't crazy. He saw Natalie stand up slowly at the back of the church. Had she given up on him so soon?

'She left it at work on the night of the murder.' Murdoch was speaking slowly, determined to sound more confident. 'On her desk. In that little bit of the floor behind the glass where just the two of you worked, Emma. You couldn't pretend not to hear it, could you? All night long, messages coming in from Charlie Holland. "I'm on the way to Rose Bay", "I'll be there in half an hour", "Come and get me." Everyone knows you hate noise at work, that's why you had that glass put up in the first place. And you're supposed to have ignored all them pingy little messages coming in? From a woman what was blackmailing you, threatening to report the agency to … to the …'

'ASIC,' said Davie.

Oscar Druitt was on his feet again, exploding in a fury of spittle. 'Emma was with me on the night of Charlie Holland's murder!!'

'Charlie Holland was killed on a Thursday,' said Murdoch calmly. 'And Emma's never with you on a Thursday, is she now, Oscar? Shall we talk about that instead? About what you do at James's beach house every Thursday night, regular as clockwork?'

It hit Oscar on the beauty spot. The colour drained from his tan, the whole church echoing to the thud as he sank back into the pew. Murdoch could have kissed him. Now the fuse was alight. All he had to do was blow the spark gently along.

'You spend half your life in the office, Emma. So why lie about where you were that night?'

'This is ridiculous.'

She said it like she was barely listening, but Murdoch knew he was getting close. He just needed to keep the spark moving along the wire.

'And then I mentioned "trading while insolvent" – me and my big mouth. I didn't mean nothing by it, but you thought I knew everything.

I'll regret saying them words till the day I die. Because that meant I was your next target, didn't it, Emma? You pulled off your detective, telling him he could have New Year's off, and I bet that was you calling me on the mobile, wanting me out on the street when Amanda ran out instead. It was manslaughter, not murder. Because you were aiming the car at me, you bitch, when you hit Amanda and killed her.'

He felt Davie's arm on his shoulder. He'd lost the crowd again, fury and foul language turning them. A couple in the second row stood up to leave, but found Natalie in their way, ushering them gently back to their seats. James Harte was listening intently.

'The only thing what I don't understand,' said Murdoch – careful now, this was all he had – 'is why you couldn't say killing Charlie was an accident? You didn't need to lie about being at work and seeing all them WhatsApps come in. You could of said you went to pick her up and hit her by mistake. I mean, you couldn't of guessed the tide was going to drag her up to Vaucluse Bay. So why'd you let your own brother sit in prison for a crime you committed? Why would you let the world think James was being blackmailed by Charlie Holland, when really it was you? And then I realised,' – puff, puff, puff – 'you needed James out of the way too, didn't you, Emma? Him and Angus, they spend money even faster than they can make it. James isn't fit to run the agency proper. No one is, apart from you. No one's got the balls. All you needed was to get rid of James and Angus, bring on the big corporate jobs, take over the whole shop—'

'No.'

'And Amanda was being unfaithful anyway, so she didn't deserve to live.'

'No. I mean—'

'You used Angus's car to kill Charlie, didn't you, Emma? Then you wrote it off and got Oscar to take it to the repair shop. Easy enough to convince everyone it was Angus what done it, and Angus himself wouldn't have a clue that he hadn't. You must have been so disappointed when no one worked out Charlie had been knocked down.'

In the corner of his eye Murdoch saw Angus flinch at this, sitting straight and staring at Emma who was now silently shaking her head.

'Except that gave you an even better opportunity, didn't it? James is in prison, so let him rot, and now you can buy Angus out. Buy his shares off him as quickly as he'll take the cash.'

'No!' Emma's voice was less certain now. 'No, I ...'

'But the car was a good idea, wasn't it, Emma? So you thought you'd try again and frame Oscar for the second murder. That'll stop him mucking you around. So you left his pink polo shirt stained with red wine up at the house in Montie on a Thursday night, even though him and his boys only ever drink white. You never did tell her, did you, Oscar? You can't stand red wine. But no one's going to believe that, are they? All you had to do, Emma, was get Oscar's prints onto James's car once you'd killed me with it. Which is why, when you were planning to knock me off, you got Oscar to book it in at the mechanics for a repair the following Monday. You knew this time everyone would put two and two together.'

Oscar woke up at that.

'You bitch,' he said. 'You bloody bitch. You said—'

'No!!!'

Emma Druitt screamed it: a huge and ugly scream for such a small woman. Like all the emotions she should have ever shown before now had been waiting for this moment. She climbed over Oscar, smacking his hands out of the way, and ran towards Murdoch and Davie, her flat shoes clattering on the tiles, turning at the last second to grab onto the pew in front of her brother.

'I knew we'd get you out, Jamie,' she said. 'I knew it. I would never have let you stay in there ...'

She was reaching over the front of the seat, trying to put her arms around him. But Harte was looking at his hands again, shaking his head.

'Em, Em, Em,' Murdoch heard him say. 'You and your ambition.'

'Jamie, don't listen to him. I had to save us, that little tart would have taken away everything we've worked for. And I didn't mean to kill Amanda; I'm so sorry, it was an accident. I would never have harmed her, you know it. And she was being unfaithful anyway, she was sleeping with ... *him!*'

The hatred and fury of her life were in the last word as she took one hand from her brother's shoulders to point at Murdoch. James Harte stood suddenly, Emma letting go of him too late and stumbling slightly backwards. Before she could right herself, and before either of the men at his sides could stop him, Harte leant forwards and hit his sister's face with an open-handed slap that resonated around the church. It unleashed the energy that had been bubbling under the congregation since Davie had

303

started speaking. Everyone but Oscar Druitt seemed to stand, running and pushing and shouting at each other. Natalie pushing down the crowded aisle, Angus climbing over the front pew and into Murdoch's fist, Harte struggling with the heavies from the prison van. And in the middle of it all, Emma Druitt, lying curled like a foetus in her black dress, screaming into the floor.

# The Resolution

## 52.

Murdoch thought he'd never see any of the Hoxton Harte crowd again and he was almost right. He avoided any news of Emma's trial – he'd had enough of viewing misery he'd caused – and Angus, Oscar, all the people they'd introduced him to, disappeared from his life as suddenly as Amanda had done. He did hear – through Davie – of James Harte's release from prison and then, over the following weeks, of the wrangles between H___ ___yers and Davie's friend, Guy Hawthorne. Murdoch was remind___ ___ little he understood the world. He'd thought a contract was a contract, but Harte and his lawyers thought differently. He gave up listening in the end, just nodded or shook his head when Davie came around and ranted. There were confidentiality agreements, clauses determining interest upon non-payment, and no end of things in Latin. On top of that was the drama of managing Hannah to wait until the funds came through. But then, one day, there was Davie with a bottle of Bollinger and a smile that threatened to eat his face. After that, if Murdoch ever wanted to talk to him, he had to go round and shout over hammering or drilling or sanding as Davie tarted up his overpriced shack.

Murdoch made sure to keep himself busy. Telly and gossip mags had lost their appeal and he told himself it was because he could see through them now. In reality, they reminded him of Amanda. Angus, Oscar and Emma barely occupied his thoughts but, left to his own devices, Murdoch spent too much time thinking about Amanda Hoxton and what life might have been like with her. He joined Taradale Tennis Club and formed ambitions to climb up through the divisions. He ran every day and trained at Punch in Kildare twice a week. He started to learn to swim in secret, determined to have something in his life the population of Montauban didn't know about. And every Thursday afternoon he sat in Suzie Bourne's living room and drank tea.

He'd worried her visit on that baking-hot day would be the last time he saw her. He couldn't explain why, but there was something final about it. Like the old lady really was determined to deliver that white envelope and then say goodbye. But less than a week after the scene at Amanda's funeral, she phoned and asked if he wouldn't mind coming to her next time, as per their original agreement. So they started up again, like anything that happened outside of her flat really didn't matter. Four Thursdays after that – once she'd dragged him in detail through what she needed for The Battle – he arrived with flowers, thinking she'd present him in turn with a thick manuscript to take away. But it turned out they weren't finished with the story.

'We need The Resolution,' Suzie said, passing him a tea with her papery hands, steadying the cup against the saucer. Tiny ancient spoons had joined the setting and Murdoch wondered if it had taken her that long to decide he wouldn't run off with the silver.

'What, like we need to see the baddy in prison?' he said. 'Sorry for all the stuff they've done?'

'God no, not at all. No, we need something that shows an end to the bigger story, some kind of finality outside of the facts of the plot.'

He liked the way he didn't have to pretend any more. Didn't have to nod and meet her eye and pretend he had a clue what she was on about.

'Nah, try again.'

'Well, think about a film. Even the most ridiculous action-based smash-'em-up movie doesn't end with the baddy dying in a big explosion. There's always a brief little scene at the end: the hero reunited with his wife or the two friends setting off on the trip back home, the parents hugging the missing children. It's The Resolution. It's like a full stop, or like writing *"The End"*. Without a little scene to close things down, you'd put the book down and not be satisfied. It's like the coffee at the end of a meal.'

She was struggling and he wondered if even she knew what she meant.

'Like a happy ending?' he tried.

'Well … yes. If it *is* a happy ending, then you need a little scene to show the happiness. But it doesn't have to be. Sometimes it's better if there's a sadness to it, to stop it being too sentimental.'

'An unhappy ending?'

'A bittersweet ending. Life's more like that, don't you think? Not a hundred per cent one way or the other? Or maybe something unclear, something that leaves the reader wondering what the truth really is?'

He told her he'd think about it. Said the Georgie Walker case had ended up with him moving to Montie and that had been a good thing. It was strange, he realised, how recently he hadn't known that. Suzie said she'd see what she could do with that and offered him more cake. A sign they were allowed to talk about something else.

It was another two months before she gave him something to read. Autumn had shaken the green from the view outside her living room window and bare branches scratched the horizon, the sky an emptier, paler blue. For weeks they'd barely spoken about the book. If she wanted to know a detail she'd phone or email and there was no excuse for most of his Thursday visits except for sharing tea and biscuits. Neither of them ever mentioned this. It was like they were both afraid to break the spell of whatever their relationship had become. But then, one day, there the manuscript was: three hundred pages on the table next to the tray.

'I've called it *Headland*,' she said. 'What do you think? Do you get it?'

He didn't at first, but the question made him think about it and then he did. He smiled, picked up the pages and flipped through them.

'Not now!'

She pulled them gently from his hands and put them into a small carrier bag ready beside her seat.

'Now, if you don't like it …'

'I'm sure it's fine.'

'Fine! God, it might be many things but let's hope it's not "fine". Oh, don't look at me like that. Let's talk about something else. I was thinking of a pseudonym. Something to rhyme with "dead". Something to rhyme with "kill more"?'

If it was a joke, Murdoch didn't get it.

'Would you do another one?' he asked, surprising himself as much as her. He'd had no idea there was another book to write. 'About what happened this summer. I know you've wanted to ask about it and, I have to admit, it might do me some good to tell it to you.'

She smiled in a way he didn't understand.

'We could call it *Class Act*,' he said. 'That's how it works, innit? You pick a detail what means something bigger?'

'Really, Bill, one thing at a time. Let's see if you like this one first.'

She put the paper-heavy bag on the table and slid it towards him straight-faced. Like either of them might not want to do this again.

## 53

On the drive home he remembered how long he'd been away from England. Twenty-two degrees and he wasn't sure if wanted the top down. He pulled over, stowed the manuscript safely in the boot and drove the rest of the way with autumn whipping around him. He was almost back in Montauban – the last few curves of the Crown Road before the turning down to the roundabout – when a red Lamborghini came up hugging the road in the opposite direction. He didn't hear it stop and turn, but he did hear its engine growing louder again, the red car soon in his rear-view mirror. By the time he'd reached the roundabout at the bottom of the hill, it was right behind him, and as he turned right onto the road between the shops and the beach, the other car flashed, a hand out of the window for a wave.

Murdoch parked in front of the general store and the Lamborghini followed suit. Then, before he even had his seatbelt off, James Harte was leaning on his door. He wasn't yet the man from the magazines but he wasn't that far off. Tanned again, he looked well-fed and well-exercised, an intimidating brightness in his eyes. His hair had grown back to its normal length and as he leant and looked in at Murdoch, it fluttered in the wind.

'Bill, we've never properly met.'

Harte stuck out his hand and cracked a smile. Not a sad smile, not the embarrassed, awkward, uncomfortable smile you might give to the man your wife had preferred.

'I hear you're selling your house,' said Murdoch.

'Yep, it's time. Too many memories here for me. I think I might head overseas for a few years.'

'What about the agency?'

'Sold that too! Like the house, too many memories. I suppose, I owe you some thanks.'

'You're all right, you paid your bill. Davie's too.'

Harte smiled again, a bit too hard, and ran a hand through his hair.

'You're probably the only person in the world who can understand my grief,' he said. 'I know you were very fond of Amanda.'

Murdoch looked away.

'Anyway,' Harte went on. 'I'm sorry we were so deceptive with you. I know she'd never have meant to hurt you.'

He felt the car bounce and turned to find Harte was halfway back to the Lamborghini. But only halfway, not all the way. Dawdling, just in front of the open door to the general store, right where Anne Lincoln could hear.

'What you talking about?'

Harte turned. 'Oh, come on now, Bill. Surely, you've worked it out by now. About Amanda?'

Later, Murdoch knew he should have driven off. Or maybe should have got out and punched Harte in the face, seen what that did to the light in his eyes.

'What?' he said. 'What about Amanda?'

'Nothing. Don't worry about it.'

'What about Amanda?!'

Harte sighed sadly and opened the door to his Lamborghini. Just in case.

'She was just doing her job,' he said. 'We consulted carefully after she first met you. Davie was easy – desperate for money, we knew that would work. But with you ... well, it was difficult to think what would motivate you. It was Amanda who came up with the solution. She said the way you looked at her, it was obvious really.'

Now Murdoch undid his seatbelt.

'Yeah, right,' he said, getting out of the car. 'Except that's how you think; Amanda was different. She'd never even say something like that.'

'She said she'd do whatever it took. "A marriage takes what a marriage takes," she always said. Maybe she went a little further than I'd have hoped, but I thought it unfair to leave you thinking she'd done anything other than motivate you. Sorry.'

Harte smiled again and climbed down into his car, reversing loudly and then roaring up the hill and out of town. Murdoch leant back heavily against the Merc.

'Never.'

He said the word aloud, then said it again and again as he drove the last hundred metres home. He would never allow himself to believe it.

# Epilogue: The Very Last Line

'Don't get so hung up on the details,' Suzie told him one Thursday, as they grappled over what she'd written and how. Murdoch wasn't convinced.

'But I want whoever reads this thing to really get it. Davie's not that blond and Natalie's better-looking than what you said. I want people to see things exactly.'

'They can't,' she said. 'They never will. At least, not the way you do. They'll see it in their own way and that's what will make it real for them. The trick is, you see, to give the reader just enough information so they can picture things, but not so much information that they can't use their own imagination. After all, no matter how much information you put in, it's the reader who writes the book in the end.'

He laughed at that. What the bleeding hell was that supposed to mean?

'Listen,' she said. 'Think about when I describe you. I'll say you've got short red hair, yes? But what's "short"? A number one, a number two, a soldier's cut, anything above the ears? What's "red"? Ginger, orange, strawberry blond? If ten people read this book, they'll have ten different images of you.'

'Yeah, so put more details in. Or make me handsomer; I promise I won't mind.'

Suzie sighed, but he could see she was enjoying the fight. 'Bill, no matter what words I put into this book, whoever reads it will always imagine things in their own way. Through their own history, their own experience, their own view of the world. That's what I mean when I say the reader writes the book. Even the fact you want me to write your story is due to the reader. You only want me to write it because you think it might get read. But – and this is important – that depends on me writing it the way the reader wants. There's a clearly understood contract that's agreed at the very start of a book. Readers don't want to hear about you going to the bathroom or sleeping at night or driving for hours on end.

They expect me to miss those bits out, just as they expect things to happen in a certain way, and I have to give them what they want. They want a beginning, a middle and an end, and all the other normal parts of the structure. They want suspects and clues and, eventually, clear answers. And, before any of that happens, they want a murder.' She laughed, a little joke between her and the readers, Murdoch abandoned on the sofa with his biscuit. 'In fact, if anyone ever asks you whodunit, there's only ever one answer for the reader: "You did. And you know you did."'

# The End

# BASE NATURE

Murdoch returns for his darkest case yet.

How far can you push a man before he reveals his base nature?
Reluctant detective, Bill Murdoch, is about to find out.

Murdoch takes on two cases in as many days. First he is hired to find local man, Scott Patterson, the victim of a mysterious abduction. Then an impressive stranger arrives in town with a tempting offer.

But has Patterson really been abducted? And is the stranger all he appears to be?

As Murdoch gives in to temptation and risks everything by returning to his old criminal ways, the hunt for Scott Patterson takes an unexpected turn. Soon Murdoch and his partner, Davie Simms, are dragged into a depraved underworld of human trafficking, prostitution and torture, where they will find evil on their doorstep and face a desperate fight for their lives.

*Base Nature* ('A Bill Murdoch Mystery' series, Book #3) is the sensational new mystery from Ged Gillmore. Prepare yourself for a breathless journey to the darkest corners of human nature.

For news on upcoming books, please visit www.gedgillmore.com